LAWRENCE BLOCK
"A SUPERIOR STORYTELLER"

San Antonio Express-News

**"IF THERE'S ONE CRIME WRITER
CURRENTLY CAPABLE OF MATCHING
THE NOIRISH LEGACIES
OF RAYMOND CHANDLER AND
DASHIELL HAMMETT,
IT'S LAWRENCE BLOCK."**

San Francisco Chronicle

**"SIMPLY THE BEST WRITER
WORKING AT HIS TRADE TODAY"**

Mystery News

**"BLOCK'S WRITING IS AS GRITTY
AS A NEW YORK STREET—
AND AS PULSATING WITH LIFE
AND RELENTLESS ENERGY"**

Orange County Register

**"FOR CLEAN, CLOSE-TO-THE-BONE PROSE,
THE LINE GOES FROM DASHIELL HAMMETT
TO JAMES M. CAIN TO LAWRENCE BLOCK.
HE'S *THAT* GOOD."**

Martin Cruz Smith, author of *Gorky Park*

LAWRENCE BLOCK

SOME DAYS YOU

GET THE BEAR

AVON BOOKS ▰ NEW YORK

AVON BOOKS
A division of
The Hearst Corporation
1350 Avenue of the Americas
New York, New York 10019

Copyright © 1963, 1966, 1967, 1982, 1984, 1985, 1986, 1989, 1990, 1991, 1992, and 1993 by Lawrence Block
Inside cover author photo by Athena Gassoumis
Published by arrangement with the author
Library of Congress Catalog Card Number: 92-16708
ISBN: 0-380-71568-6

Published in hardcover by William Morrow and Company, Inc.; for information address Permissions Department, William Morrow and Company, Inc., 1350 Avenue of the Americas, New York, New York 10019.

First Avon Books Printing: October 1994

AVON TRADEMARK REG. U.S. PAT. OFF. AND IN OTHER COUNTRIES. MARCA REGISTRADA, HECHO EN U.S.A.

Printed in the U.S.A.

RA 10 9 8 7 6 5 4 3 2

ACKNOWLEDGMENTS

The author would like to acknowledge the magazines that first published some of these stories. "Answers to Soldier," "A Blow for Freedom," "By the Dawn's Early Light," and "The Burglar Who Dropped In on Elvis" first appeared in *Playboy*. "As Good As a Rest," "Cleveland in My Dreams," "The Ehrengraf Alternative," "The Ehrengraf Nostrum," and "Like a Bug on a Windshield" made their initial appearance in *Ellery Queen's Mystery Magazine*, "Death Wish," "Good for the Soul," "Passport in Order," and "Some Things a Man Must Do" in *Alfred Hitchcock's Mystery Magazine*. "Some Days You Get the Bear" was first published in *Penthouse*, "Something to Remember You By" in *New Mystery*, and "Hilliard's Ceremony" in *The Armchair Detective*. Three stories first appeared in original anthologies: "How Would You Like It?" in *Psycho-Path II*, "Batman's Helpers" in the Private Eye Writers of America's *Justice for Hire*, and "The Merciful Angel of Death" in the International Association of Crime Writers' *New Mystery Anthology*. "Someday I'll Plant More Walnut Trees" and "The Tulsa Experience" are published here for the first time.

CONTENTS

Introduction   11
By the Dawn's Early Light   15
Cleveland in My Dreams   34
Some Things a Man Must Do   45
Answers to Soldier   58
Good for the Soul   74
The Ehrengraf Alternative   89
Someday I'll Plant More Walnut Trees   105
The Burglar Who Dropped In on Elvis   122
As Good As a Rest   137
Death Wish   147
The Merciful Angel of Death   157
The Tulsa Experience   171
Some Days You Get the Bear   183
Passport in Order   201
Something to Remember You By   209
Hilliard's Ceremony   218
The Ehrengraf Nostrum   240
Like a Bug on a Windshield   254
A Blow for Freedom   271
How Would You Like It?   283
Batman's Helpers   288

9

INTRODUCTION

Short stories should speak for themselves. Writers, on the other hand, probably shouldn't.

Nevertheless, certain observations spring to mind as I ready this collection for publication. I seem compelled to write them down.

Most of these stories were written after 1984, when the latter of my two previous collections was published. Four stories, however, date from the sixties. They were written twenty to thirty years before the rest, and first published in *Alfred Hitchcock's Mystery Magazine*. They didn't make it into *Sometimes They Bite* or *Like a Lamb to Slaughter* as a result of space limitations or, in one instance, because I had lost track of the story over the years.

I was unsure at first whether or not to include them in the present collection. They are early efforts, and strike me as less finely wrought than later work. But what the hell do I know? I decided at length that I'm embarrassed not so much by the stories as by the recollection of the impossibly young fellow who wrote them. I like them enough to want them preserved, and so I've included them, for you to like or not.

* * *

I was similarly hesitant about including the story I've placed first, "By the Dawn's Early Light." But not because I was embarrassed by it or for it.

I wrote the story to keep a promise. Some years previously Bob Randisi had told me of a proposal he was circulating for an anthology of original private eye stories. If he found a publisher, would I furnish a story about my detective, Matthew Scudder? I said I would, fairly sure I would never be called upon to perform.

By the time Otto Penzler contracted to publish Bob's anthology, I had written and published *Eight Million Ways to Die*, the fifth Scudder novel and, it seemed to me, the last. Scudder was sober now, he'd had a catharsis, his fictional *d'être* had lost its *raison*—and how was I supposed to write anything further about him? Attempts at a sixth novel had fallen horribly flat, and the last thing I wanted to do was try a short story.

But I had given my word—always a mistake—and I felt honor-bound to keep it, especially after all the whining that Bob and Otto did. And what a stroke of luck for me, because I not only managed to write the story but a year later found a way to expand it into a novel, *When the Sacred Ginmill Closes*. By keeping a promise I had restored a series to life. Now, having just completed the eleventh novel about Scudder, I am profoundly grateful to this short story, and to the two fellows who guilt-tripped me into writing it.

Why, then, wouldn't I want the story anthologized? Not because I don't like it, but because I prefer it in its expanded version. As a short story it runs around 8,700 words; as a novel it stretches to 90,000, incorporating a couple of plot lines and several major characters not to be found in the short story. I'm uncommonly fond of the novel, and wouldn't want anyone to miss it, or to like it less, for having read the short story first.

Still, how can I be so ungrateful to the story as to exclude it? Besides giving new life to my most successful character, it did very nicely on its own. It constituted my first appearance in *Playboy*, and it won an Edgar award from the Mystery Writers of America as well as a Shamus award from the Private Eye Writers of America.

So here it is. I hope you like it, and I hope you run right out and buy the novel, too.

There are two other stories about Scudder. "Batman's Helpers" started out as the opening chapter of my first stab at a novel that ultimately became *A Dance at the Slaughterhouse*. When I aborted that version, it struck me that the opening was complete in itself, although it lacked a resolution. Rather than try to graft one onto it, I chose to publish it as a sort of vignette, a day in the life.

"The Merciful Angel of Death" was written specifically for the anthology Jerome Charyn edited for the International Association of Crime Writers. The mood and theme would put it out of bounds for most magazines.

Besides Scudder, a couple of other series characters of mine are represented here. Bernie Rhodenbarr has appeared in five novels, Martin H. Ehrengraf in five short stories besides the two in the present volume. And I find I have more to say about Keller, the protagonist of "Answers to Soldier." I suspect, too, that I may someday write again about Atuele, the shamanic healer who presides over "Hilliard's Ceremony."

Most of my writing over the years has come under the broad heading of crime fiction, a house in which there are indeed many mansions. And most of the stories here are crime stories.

A few are not. The title character in "Hilliard's Ceremony" is an agent in place, but that doesn't make it a spy story—although it helped furnish *The Armchair Detective* with an excuse to publish it. "Cleveland in My Dreams" ran in *EQMM* because Eleanor Sullivan liked it, but it's certainly not crime fiction. Neither is "Some Days You Get the Bear."

Why do I mention this?

Many years ago a guest of mine asked for a beer. I found a can of ale in the refrigerator and poured it into a glass for him. He took a sip and recoiled in shock. "This is ale!" he sputtered.

"I know," I said. "It's all I've got. Is it all right? Don't you like ale?"

"I like ale just fine," he said. "But when you have your

mouth set for beer, and you get ale, it's very damned disconcerting."

So there you have it. Some of these stories are beer and some are ale, and I leave it to you to sort them out. I only hope none of them have gone flat.

BY THE DAWN'S
EARLY LIGHT

All this happened a long time ago.

Abe Beame was living in Gracie Mansion, though even he seemed to have trouble believing he was really the mayor of the city of New York. Ali was in his prime, and the Knicks still had a year or so left in Bradley and DeBusschere. I was still drinking in those days, of course, and at the time it seemed to be doing more for me than it was doing to me.

I had already left my wife and kids, my home in Syosset and the NYPD. I was living in the hotel on West Fifty-seventh Street where I still live, and I was doing most of my drinking around the corner in Jimmy Armstrong's saloon. Billie was the nighttime bartender. A Filipino youth named Dennis was behind the stick most days.

And Tommy Tillary was one of the regulars.

He was big, probably 6′2″, full in the chest, big in the belly, too. He rarely showed up in a suit but always wore a jacket and tie, usually a navy or burgundy blazer with gray-flannel slacks or white duck pants in warmer weather. He had a loud voice that boomed from his barrel chest and a big, clean-shaven face that was innocent around the pouting mouth and knowing around the eyes. He was somewhere in his late forties and he drank a lot of top-shelf scotch. Chivas,

as I remember it, but it could have been Johnnie Black. Whatever it was, his face was beginning to show it, with patches of
permanent flush at the cheekbones and a tracery of broken
capillaries across the bridge of the nose.

We were saloon friends. We didn't speak every time we
ran into each other, but at the least we always acknowledged
each other with a nod or a wave. He told a lot of dialect jokes
and told them reasonably well, and I laughed at my share of
them. Sometimes I was in a mood to reminisce about my days
on the force, and when my stories were funny, his laugh was
as loud as anyone's.

Sometimes he showed up alone, sometimes with male
friends. About a third of the time, he was in the company of
a short and curvy blonde named Carolyn. "Carolyn from the
Caro-line" was the way he occasionally introduced her, and
she did have a faint Southern accent that became more pronounced as the drink got to her.

Then, one morning, I picked up the *Daily News* and read
that burglars had broken into a house on Colonial Road, in
the Bay Ridge section of Brooklyn. They had stabbed to death
the only occupant present, one Margaret Tillary. Her husband,
Thomas J. Tillary, a salesman, was not at home at the time.

I hadn't known Tommy was a salesman or that he'd had a
wife. He did wear a wide yellow-gold band on the appropriate
finger, and it was clear that he wasn't married to Carolyn from
the Caroline, and it now looked as though he was a widower.
I felt vaguely sorry for him, vaguely sorry for the wife I'd never
even known of, but that was the extent of it. I drank enough
back then to avoid feeling any emotion very strongly.

And then, two or three nights later, I walked into Armstrong's and there was Carolyn. She didn't appear to be waiting for him or anyone else, nor did she look as though she'd
just breezed in a few minutes ago. She had a stool by herself
at the bar and she was drinking something dark from a lowball
glass.

I took a seat a few stools down from her. I ordered two
double shots of bourbon, drank one and poured the other into
the black coffee Billie brought me. I was sipping the coffee
when a voice with a Piedmont softness said, "I forget your
name."

I looked up.

"I believe we were introduced," she said, "but I don't recall your name."

"It's Matt," I said, "and you're right, Tommy introduced us. You're Carolyn."

"Carolyn Cheatham. Have you seen him?"

"Tommy? Not since it happened."

"Neither have I. Were you-all at the funeral?"

"No. When was it?"

"This afternoon. Neither was I. There. Whyn't you come sit next to me so's I don't have to shout. Please?"

She was drinking a sweet almond liqueur that she took on the rocks. It tastes like dessert, but it's as strong as whiskey.

"He told me not to come," she said. "To the funeral. He said it was a matter of respect for the dead." She picked up her glass and stared into it. I've never known what people hope to see there, though it's a gesture I've performed often enough myself.

"Respect," she said. "What's he care about respect? I would have just been part of the office crowd; we both work at Tannahill; far as anyone there knows, we're just friends. And all we ever were is friends, you know."

"Whatever you say."

"Oh, *shit*," she said. "I don't mean I wasn't fucking him, for the Lord's sake. I mean it was just laughs and good times. He was married and he went home to Mama every night and that was jes' fine, because who in her right mind'd want Tommy Tillary around by the dawn's early light? Christ in the foothills, did I spill this or drink it?"

We agreed she was drinking them a little too fast. It was this fancy New York sweet-drink shit, she maintained, not like the bourbon she'd grown up on. You knew where you stood with bourbon.

I told her I was a bourbon drinker myself, and it pleased her to learn this. Alliances have been forged on thinner bonds than that, and ours served to propel us out of Armstrong's, with a stop down the block for a fifth of Maker's Mark—her choice—and a four-block walk to her apartment. There were exposed brick walls, I remember, and candles stuck in straw-wrapped bottles, and several travel posters from Sabena, the Belgian airline.

We did what grown-ups do when they find themselves

alone together. We drank our fair share of the Maker's Mark and went to bed. She made a lot of enthusiastic noises and more than a few skillful moves, and afterward she cried some.

A little later, she dropped off to sleep. I was tired myself, but I put on my clothes and sent myself home. Because who in her right mind'd want Matt Scudder around by the dawn's early light?

Over the next couple of days, I wondered every time I entered Armstrong's if I'd run into her, and each time I was more relieved than disappointed when I didn't. I didn't encounter Tommy, either, and that, too, was a relief and in no sense disappointing.

Then, one morning, I picked up the *News* and read that they'd arrested a pair of young Hispanics from Sunset Park for the Tillary burglary and homicide. The paper ran the usual photo—two skinny kids, their hair unruly, one of them trying to hide his face from the camera, the other smirking defiantly, and each of them handcuffed to a broad-shouldered, grim-faced Irishman in a suit. You didn't need the careful caption to tell the good guys from the bad guys.

Sometime in the middle of the afternoon, I went over to Armstrong's for a hamburger and drank a beer with it. The phone behind the bar rang and Dennis put down the glass he was wiping and answered it. "He was here a minute ago," he said. "I'll see if he stepped out." He covered the mouthpiece with his hand and looked quizzically at me. "Are you still here?" he asked. "Or did you slip away while my attention was diverted?"

"Who wants to know?"

"Tommy Tillary."

You never know what a woman will decide to tell a man or how a man will react to it. I didn't want to find out, but I was better off learning over the phone than face-to-face. I nodded and took the phone from Dennis.

I said, "Matt Scudder, Tommy. I was sorry to hear about your wife."

"Thanks, Matt. Jesus, it feels like it happened a year ago. It was what, a week?"

"At least they got the bastards."

There was a pause. Then he said, "Jesus. You haven't seen a paper, huh?"

"That's where I read about it. Two Spanish kids."

"You didn't happen to see this afternoon's *Post*."

"No. Why, what happened? They turn out to be clean?"

"The two spics. Clean? Shit, they're about as clean as the men's room in the Times Square subway station. The cops hit their place and found stuff from my house everywhere they looked. Jewelry they had descriptions of, a stereo that I gave them the serial number, everything. Monogrammed shit. I mean, that's how clean they were, for Christ's sake."

"So?"

"They admitted the burglary but not the murder."

"That's common, Tommy."

"Lemme finish, huh? They admitted the burglary, but according to them it was a put-up job. According to them, I hired them to hit my place. They could keep whatever they got and I'd have everything out and arranged for them, and in return I got to clean up on the insurance by overreporting the loss."

"What did the loss amount to?"

"Shit, *I* don't know. There were twice as many things turned up in their apartment as I ever listed when I made out a report. There's things I missed a few days after I filed the report and others I didn't know were gone until the cops found them. You don't notice everything right away, at least I didn't, and on top of it, how could I think straight with Peg dead? You know?"

"It hardly sounds like an insurance setup."

"No, of course it wasn't. How the hell could it be? All I had was a standard homeowner's policy. It covered maybe a third of what I lost. According to them, the place was empty when they hit it. Peg was out."

"And?"

"And I set them up. They hit the place, they carted everything away, and I came home with Peg and stabbed her six, eight times, whatever it was, and left her there so it'd look like it happened in a burglary."

"How could the burglars testify that you stabbed your wife?"

"They couldn't. All they said was they didn't and she

wasn't home when they were there, and that I hired them to do the burglary. The cops pieced the rest of it together."

"What did they do, take you downtown?"

"No. They came over to the house, it was early, I don't know what time. It was the first I knew that the spics were arrested, let alone that they were trying to do a job on me. They just wanted to talk, the cops, and at first I talked to them, and then I started to get the drift of what they were trying to put on to me. So I said I wasn't saying anything more without my lawyer present, and I called him, and he left half his breakfast on the table and came over in a hurry, and he wouldn't let me say a word."

"And the cops didn't take you in or book you?"

"No."

"Did they buy your story?"

"No way. I didn't really tell 'em a story, because Kaplan wouldn't let me say anything. They didn't drag me in, because they don't have a case yet, but Kaplan says they're gonna be building one if they can. They told me not to leave town. You believe it? My wife's dead, the *Post* headline says, 'Quiz Husband in Burglary Murder,' and what the hell do they think I'm gonna do? Am I going fishing for fucking trout in Montana? 'Don't leave town.' You see this shit on television, you think nobody in real life talks this way. Maybe television's where they get it from."

I waited for him to tell me what he wanted from me. I didn't have long to wait.

"Why I called," he said, "is Kaplan wants to hire a detective. He figured maybe these guys talked around the neighborhood, maybe they bragged to their friends, maybe there's a way to prove they did the killing. He says the cops won't concentrate on that end if they're too busy nailing the lid shut on me."

I explained that I didn't have any official standing, that I had no license and filed no reports.

"That's okay," he insisted. "I told Kaplan what I want is somebody I can trust, somebody who'll do the job for me. I don't think they're gonna have any kind of a case at all, Matt, but the longer this drags on, the worse it is for me. I want it cleared up, I want it in the papers that these Spanish assholes did it all and I had nothing to do with anything. You name a fair fee and I'll pay it, me to you, and it can be cash in your hand if you don't like checks. What do you say?"

He wanted somebody he could trust. Had Carolyn from the Caroline told him how trustworthy I was?

What did I say? I said yes.

I met Tommy Tillary and his lawyer in Drew Kaplan's office on Court Street, a few blocks from Brooklyn's Borough Hall. There was a Syrian restaurant next door and, at the corner, a grocery store specializing in Middle Eastern imports stood next to an antique shop overflowing with stripped-oak furniture and brass lamps and bedsteads. Kaplan's office ran to wood paneling and leather chairs and oak file cabinets. His name and the names of two partners were painted on the frosted-glass door in old-fashioned gold-and-black lettering. Kaplan himself looked conservatively up to date, with a three-piece striped suit that was better cut than mine. Tommy wore his burgundy blazer and gray-flannel trousers and loafers. Strain showed at the corners of his blue eyes and around his mouth. His complexion was off, too.

"All we want you to do," Kaplan said, "is find a key in one of their pants pockets, Herrera's or Cruz's, and trace it to a locker in Penn Station, and in the locker there's a footlong knife with their prints and her blood on it."

"Is that what it's going to take?"

He smiled. "It wouldn't hurt. No, actually, we're not in such bad shape. They got some shaky testimony from a pair of Latins who've been in and out of trouble since they got weaned to Tropicana. They got what looks to them like a good motive on Tommy's part."

"Which is?"

I was looking at Tommy when I asked. His eyes slipped away from mine. Kaplan said, "A marital triangle, a case of the shorts and a strong money motive. Margaret Tillary inherited a little over a quarter of a million dollars six or eight months ago. An aunt left a million two and it got cut up four ways. What they don't bother to notice is he loved his wife, and how many husbands cheat? What is it they say—ninety percent cheat and ten percent lie?"

"That's good odds."

"One of the killers, Angel Herrera, did some odd jobs at

the Tillary house last March or April. Spring cleaning; he hauled stuff out of the basement and attic, a little donkeywork. According to Herrera, that's how Tommy knew him to contact him about the burglary. According to common sense, that's how Herrera and his buddy Cruz knew the house and what was in it and how to gain access."

"The case against Tommy sounds pretty thin."

"It is," Kaplan said. "The thing is, you go to court with something like this and you lose even if you win. For the rest of your life, everybody remembers you stood trial for murdering your wife, never mind that you won an acquittal.

"Besides," he said, "you never know which way a jury's going to jump. Tommy's alibi is he was with another lady at the time of the burglary. The woman's a colleague; they could see it as completely aboveboard, but who says they're going to? What they sometimes do, they decide they don't believe the alibi because it's his girlfriend lying for him, and at the same time they label him a scumbag for screwing around while his wife's getting killed."

"You keep it up," Tommy said, "I'll find myself guilty, the way you make it sound."

"Plus he's hard to get a sympathetic jury for. He's a big handsome guy, a sharp dresser, and you'd love him in a gin joint, but how much do you love him in a courtroom? He's a securities salesman, he's beautiful on the phone, and that means every clown who ever lost a hundred dollars on a stock tip or bought magazines over the phone is going to walk into the courtroom with a hard-on for him. I'm telling you, I want to stay the hell *out* of court. I'll *win* in court, I know that, or the worst that'll happen is I'll win on appeal, but who needs it? This is a case that shouldn't be in the first place, and I'd love to clear it up before they even go so far as presenting a bill to the grand jury."

"So from me you want—"

"Whatever you can find, Matt. Whatever discredits Cruz and Herrera. I don't know what's there to be found, but you were a cop and now you're private, and you can get down in the streets and nose around."

I nodded. I could do that. "One thing," I said. "Wouldn't you be better off with a Spanish-speaking detective? I know enough to buy a beer in a bodega, but I'm a long way from fluent."

Kaplan shook his head. "A personal relationship's worth more than a dime's worth of '*Me llamo Matteo y ¿como está usted?*' "

"That's the truth," Tommy Tillary said. "Matt, I know I can count on you."

I wanted to tell him all he could count on was his fingers. I didn't really see what I could expect to uncover that wouldn't turn up in a regular police investigation. But I'd spent enough time carrying a shield to know not to push away money when somebody wants to give it to you. I felt comfortable taking a fee. The man was inheriting a quarter of a million, plus whatever insurance his wife had carried. If he was willing to spread some of it around, I was willing to take it.

So I went to Sunset Park and spent some time in the streets and some more time in the bars. Sunset Park is in Brooklyn, of course, on the borough's western edge, above Bay Ridge and south and west of Green-Wood Cemetery. These days, there's a lot of brownstoning going on there, with young urban professionals renovating the old houses and gentrifying the neighborhood. Back then, the upwardly mobile young had not yet discovered Sunset Park, and the area was a mix of Latins and Scandinavians, most of the former Puerto Ricans, most of the latter Norwegians. The balance was gradually shifting from Europe to the islands, from light to dark, but this was a process that had been going on for ages and there was nothing hurried about it.

I talked to Herrera's landlord and Cruz's former employer and one of his recent girlfriends. I drank beer in bars and the back rooms of bodegas. I went to the local station house, I read the sheets on both of the burglars and drank coffee with the cops and picked up some of the stuff that doesn't get on the yellow sheets.

I found out that Miguelito Cruz had once killed a man in a tavern brawl over a woman. There were no charges pressed; a dozen witnesses reported that the dead man had gone after Cruz first with a broken bottle. Cruz had most likely been carrying the knife, but several witnesses insisted it had been tossed to him by an anonymous benefactor, and there hadn't been enough evidence to make a case of weapons possession, let alone homicide.

I learned that Herrera had three children living with their mother in Puerto Rico. He was divorced but wouldn't marry his current girlfriend because he regarded himself as still married to his ex-wife in the eyes of God. He sent money to his children when he had any to send.

I learned other things. They didn't seem terribly consequential then and they've faded from memory altogether by now, but I wrote them down in my pocket notebook as I learned them, and every day or so I duly reported my findings to Drew Kaplan. He always seemed pleased with what I told him.

I invariably managed a stop at Armstrong's before I called it a night. One night she was there, Carolyn Cheatham, drinking bourbon this time, her face frozen with stubborn old pain. It took her a blink or two to recognize me. Then tears started to form in the corners of her eyes, and she used the back of one hand to wipe them away.

I didn't approach her until she beckoned. She patted the stool beside hers and I eased myself onto it. I had coffee with bourbon in it and bought a refill for her. She was pretty drunk already, but that's never been enough reason to turn down a drink.

She talked about Tommy. He was being nice to her, she said. Calling up, sending flowers. But he wouldn't see her, because it wouldn't look right, not for a new widower, not for a man who'd been publicly accused of murder.

"He sends flowers with no card enclosed," she said. "He calls me from pay phones. The son of a bitch."

Billie called me aside. "I didn't want to put her out," he said, "a nice woman like that, shit-faced as she is. But I thought I was gonna have to. You'll see she gets home?"

I said I would.

I got her out of there and a cab came along and saved us the walk. At her place, I took the keys from her and unlocked the door. She half sat, half sprawled on the couch. I had to use the bathroom, and when I came back, her eyes were closed and she was snoring lightly.

I got her coat and shoes off, put her to bed, loosened her clothing, and covered her with a blanket. I was tired from all that and sat down on the couch for a minute, and I almost dozed off myself. Then I snapped awake and let myself out.

I went back to Sunset Park the next day. I learned that Cruz had been in trouble as a youth. With a gang of neighborhood kids, he used to go into the city and cruise Greenwich Village, looking for homosexuals to beat up. He'd had a dread of homosexuality, probably flowing as it generally does out of a fear of a part of himself, and he stifled that dread by fagbashing.

"He still doan' like them," a woman told me. She had glossy black hair and opaque eyes, and she was letting me pay for her rum and orange juice. "He's pretty, you know, an' they come on to him, an' he doan' like it."

I called that item in, along with a few others equally earthshaking. I bought myself a steak dinner at the Slate over on Tenth Avenue, then finished up at Armstrong's, not drinking very hard, just coasting along on bourbon and coffee.

Twice, the phone rang for me. Once, it was Tommy Tillary, telling me how much he appreciated what I was doing for him. It seemed to me that all I was doing was taking his money, but he had me believing that my loyalty and invaluable assistance were all he had to cling to.

The second call was from Carolyn. More praise. I was a gentleman, she assured me, and a hell of a fellow all around. And I should forget that she'd been bad-mouthing Tommy. Everything was going to be fine with them.

I took the next day off. I think I went to a movie, and it may have been *The Sting*, with Newman and Redford achieving vengeance through swindling.

The day after that, I did another tour of duty over in Brooklyn. And the day after that, I picked up the *News* first thing in the morning. The headline was nonspecific, something like KILL SUSPECT HANGS SELF IN CELL, but I knew it was my case before I turned to the story on page three.

Miguelito Cruz had torn his clothing into strips, knotted the strips together, stood his iron bedstead on its side, climbed onto it, looped his homemade rope around an overhead pipe, and jumped off the up-ended bedstead and into the next world.

That evening's six o'clock TV news had the rest of the story. Informed of his friend's death, Angel Herrera had recanted his original story and admitted that he and Cruz had conceived and executed the Tillary burglary on their own. It had been Miguelito who had stabbed the Tillary woman when she walked in on them. He'd picked up a kitchen knife while Herrera watched in horror. Miguelito always had a short temper, Herrera said, but they were friends, even cousins, and they had hatched their story to protect Miguelito. But now that he was dead, Herrera could admit what had really happened.

I was in Armstrong's that night, which was not remarkable. I had it in mind to get drunk, though I could not have told you why, and that *was* remarkable, if not unheard of. I got drunk a lot those days, but I rarely set out with that intention. I just wanted to feel a little better, a little more mellow, and somewhere along the way I'd wind up waxed.

I wasn't drinking particularly hard or fast, but I was working at it, and then somewhere around ten or eleven the door opened and I knew who it was before I turned around. Tommy Tillary, well dressed and freshly barbered, making his first appearance in Jimmy's place since his wife was killed.

"Hey, look who's here!" he called out and grinned that big grin. People rushed over to shake his hand. Billie was behind the stick, and he'd no sooner set one up on the house for our hero than Tommy insisted on buying a round for the bar. It was an expensive gesture—there must have been thirty or forty people in there—but I don't think he cared if there were three hundred or four hundred.

I stayed where I was, letting the others mob him, but he worked his way over to me and got an arm around my shoulders. "This is the man," he announced. "Best fucking detective ever wore out a pair of shoes. This man's money," he told Billie, "is no good at all tonight. He can't buy a drink; he can't buy a cup of coffee; if you went and put in pay toilets since I was last here, he can't use his own dime."

"The john's still free," Billie said, "but don't give the boss any ideas."

"Oh, don't tell me he didn't already think of it," Tommy

said. "Matt, my boy, I love you. I was in a tight spot, I didn't want to walk out of my house, and you came through for me."

What the hell had I done? I hadn't hanged Miguelito Cruz or coaxed a confession out of Angel Herrera. I hadn't even set eyes on either man. But he was buying the drinks, and I had a thirst, so who was I to argue?

I don't know how long we stayed there. Curiously, my drinking slowed down even as Tommy's picked up speed. Carolyn, I noticed, was not present, nor did her name find its way into the conversation. I wondered if she would walk in—it was, after all, her neighborhood bar, and she was apt to drop in on her own. I wondered what would happen if she did.

I guess there were a lot of things I wondered about, and perhaps that's what put the brakes on my own drinking. I didn't want any gaps in my memory, any gray patches in my awareness.

After a while, Tommy was hustling me out of Armstrong's. "This is celebration time," he told me. "We don't want to sit in one place till we grow roots. We want to bop a little."

He had a car, and I just went along with him without paying too much attention to exactly where we were. We went to a noisy Greek club on the East Side, I think, where the waiters looked like Mob hit men. We went to a couple of trendy singles joints. We wound up somewhere in the Village, in a dark, beery cave.

It was quiet there, and conversation was possible, and I found myself asking him what I'd done that was so praiseworthy. One man had killed himself and another had confessed, and where was my role in either incident?

"The stuff you came up with," he said.

"What stuff? I should have brought back fingernail parings, you could have had someone work voodoo on them."

"About Cruz and the fairies."

"He was up for murder. He didn't kill himself because he was afraid they'd get him for fag-bashing when he was a juvenile offender."

Tommy took a sip of scotch. He said, "Couple days ago, huge black guy comes up to Cruz in the chow line. 'Wait'll you get up to Green Haven,' he tells him. 'Every blood there's gonna have you for a girlfriend. Doctor gonna have to cut you a brand-new asshole, time you get outa there.' "

I didn't say anything.

"Kaplan," he said. "Drew talked to somebody who talked to somebody, and that did it. Cruz took a good look at the idea of playin' drop the soap for half the jigs in captivity, and the next thing you know, the murderous little bastard was dancing on air. And good riddance to him."

I couldn't seem to catch my breath. I worked on it while Tommy went to the bar for another round. I hadn't touched the drink in front of me, but I let him buy for both of us.

When he got back, I said, "Herrera."

"Changed his story. Made a full confession."

"And pinned the killing on Cruz."

"Why not? Cruz wasn't around to complain. Who knows which one of 'em did it, and for that matter, who cares? The thing is, you gave us the lever."

"For Cruz," I said. "To get him to kill himself."

"And for Herrera. Those kids of his in Santurce. Drew spoke to Herrera's lawyer and Herrera's lawyer spoke to Herrera, and the message was, 'Look, you're going up for burglary whatever you do, and probably for murder; but if you tell the right story, you'll draw shorter time, and on top of that, that nice Mr. Tillary's gonna let bygones be bygones and every month there's a nice check for your wife and kiddies back home in Puerto Rico.' "

At the bar, a couple of old men were reliving the Louis-Schmeling fight, the second one, where Louis punished the German champion. One of the old fellows was throwing roundhouse punches in the air, demonstrating.

I said, "Who killed your wife?"

"One or the other of them. If I had to bet, I'd say Cruz. He had those little beady eyes; you looked at him up close and you got that he was a killer."

"When did you look at him up close?"

"When they came and cleaned the house, the basement, and the attic. Not when they came and cleaned me out; that was the second time."

He smiled, but I kept looking at him until the smile lost its certainty. "That was Herrera who helped around the house," I said. "You never met Cruz."

"Cruz came along, gave him a hand."

"You never mentioned that before."

"Oh, sure I did, Matt. What difference does it make, anyway?"

"Who killed her, Tommy?"

"Hey, let it alone, huh?"

"Answer the question."

"I already answered it."

"You killed her, didn't you?"

"What are you, crazy? Cruz killed her and Herrera swore to it, isn't that enough for you?"

"Tell me you didn't kill her."

"I didn't kill her."

"Tell me again."

"I didn't fucking kill her. What's the matter with you?"

"I don't believe you."

"Oh, Jesus," he said. He closed his eyes, put his head in his hands. He sighed and looked up and said, "You know, it's a funny thing with me. Over the telephone, I'm the best salesman you could ever imagine. I swear I could sell sand to the Arabs, I could sell ice in the winter, but face-to-face I'm no good at all. Why do you figure that is?"

"You tell me."

"I don't know. I used to think it was my face, the eyes and the mouth; I don't know. It's easy over the phone. I'm talking to a stranger, I don't know who he is or what he looks like, and he's not lookin' at me, and it's a cinch. Face-to-face, especially with someone I know, it's a different story." He looked at me. "If we were doin' this over the phone, you'd buy the whole thing."

"It's possible."

"It's fucking certain. Word for word, you'd buy the package. Suppose I was to tell you I did kill her, Matt. You couldn't prove anything. Look, the both of us walked in there, the place was a mess from the burglary, we got in an argument, tempers flared, something happened."

"You set up the burglary. You planned the whole thing, just the way Cruz and Herrera accused you of doing. And now you wriggled out of it."

"And you helped me—don't forget that part of it."

"I won't."

"And I wouldn't have gone away for it anyway, Matt. Not a chance. I'da beat it in court, only this way I don't have to go to court. Look, this is just the booze talkin', and we can forget it in the morning, right? I didn't kill her, you didn't accuse me, we're still buddies, everything's fine. Right?"

Blackouts are never there when you want them. I woke up the next day and remembered all of it, and I found myself wishing I didn't. He'd killed his wife and he was getting away with it. And I'd helped him. I'd taken his money, and in return I'd shown him how to set one man up for suicide and pressure another into making a false confession.

And what was I going to do about it?

I couldn't think of a thing. Any story I carried to the police would be speedily denied by Tommy and his lawyer, and all I had was the thinnest of hearsay evidence, my own client's own words when he and I both had a skinful of booze. I went over it for a few days, looking for ways to shake something loose, and there was nothing. I could maybe interest a news-paper reporter, maybe get Tommy some press coverage that wouldn't make him happy, but why? And to what purpose?

It rankled. But I would just have a couple of drinks, and then it wouldn't rankle so much.

Angel Herrera pleaded guilty to burglary, and in return, the Brooklyn D.A.'s Office dropped all homicide charges. He went Upstate to serve five to ten.

And then I got a call in the middle of the night. I'd been sleeping a couple of hours, but the phone woke me and I groped for it. It took me a minute to recognize the voice on the other end.

It was Carolyn Cheatham.

"I had to call you," she said, "on account of you're a bour-bon man and a gentleman. I owed it to you to call you."

"What's the matter?"

"He ditched me," she said, "and he got me fired out of Tannahill and Company so he won't have to look at me around the office. Once he didn't need me to back up his story, he let go of me, and do you know he did it over the phone?"

"Carolyn—"

"It's all in the note," she said. "I'm leaving a note."

"Look, don't do anything yet," I said. I was out of bed,

fumbling for my clothes. "I'll be right over. We'll talk about it."

"You can't stop me, Matt."

"I won't try to stop you. We'll talk first, and then you can do anything you want."

The phone clicked in my ear.

I threw my clothes on, rushed over there, hoping it would be pills, something that took its time. I broke a small pane of glass in the downstairs door and let myself in, then used an old credit card to slip the bolt of her spring lock.

The room smelled of cordite. She was on the couch she'd passed out on the last time I saw her. The gun was still in her hand, limp at her side, and there was a black-rimmed hole in her temple.

There was a note, too. An empty bottle of Maker's Mark stood on the coffee table, an empty glass beside it. The booze showed in her handwriting and in the sullen phrasing of the suicide note.

I read the note. I stood there for a few minutes, not for very long, and then I got a dish towel from the Pullman kitchen and wiped the bottle and the glass. I took another matching glass, rinsed it out and wiped it, and put it in the drainboard of the sink.

I stuffed the note in my pocket. I took the gun from her fingers, checked routinely for a pulse, then wrapped a sofa pillow around the gun to muffle its report. I fired one round into her chest, another into her open mouth.

I dropped the gun into a pocket and left.

They found the gun in Tommy Tillary's house, stuffed between the cushions of the living-room sofa, clean of prints inside and out. Ballistics got a perfect match. I'd aimed for soft tissue with the round shot into her chest, because bullets can fragment on impact with bone. That was one reason I'd fired the extra shots. The other was to rule out the possibility of suicide.

After the story made the papers, I picked up the phone and called Drew Kaplan. "I don't understand it," I said. "He was free and clear; why the hell did he kill the girl?"

"Ask him yourself," Kaplan said. He did not sound happy.

"You want my opinion, he's a lunatic. I honestly didn't think he was. I figured maybe he killed his wife, maybe he didn't. Not my job to try him. But I didn't figure he was a homicidal maniac."

"It's certain he killed the girl?"

"Not much question. The gun's pretty strong evidence. Talk about finding somebody with the smoking pistol in his hand, here it was in Tommy's couch. The idiot."

"Funny he kept it."

"Maybe he had other people he wanted to shoot. Go figure a crazy man. No, the gun's evidence, and there was a phone tip—a man called in the shooting, reported a man running out of there, and gave a description that fitted Tommy pretty well. Even had him wearing that red blazer he wears, tacky thing makes him look like an usher at the Paramount."

"It sounds tough to square."

"Well, somebody else'll have to try to do it," Kaplan said. "I told him I can't defend him this time. What it amounts to, I wash my hands of him."

I thought of that when I read that Angel Herrera got out just the other day. He served all ten years because he was as good at getting into trouble inside the walls as he'd been on the outside.

Somebody killed Tommy Tillary with a homemade knife after he'd served two years and three months of a manslaughter stretch. I wondered at the time if that was Herrera getting even, and I don't suppose I'll ever know. Maybe the checks stopped going to Santurce and Herrera took it the wrong way. Or maybe Tommy said the wrong thing to somebody else and said it face-to-face instead of over the phone.

I don't think I'd do it that way now. I don't drink anymore, and the impulse to play God seems to have evaporated with the booze.

But then, a lot of things have changed. Billie left Armstrong's not long after that, left New York, too; the last I heard, he was off drink himself, living in Sausalito and making candles. I ran into Dennis the other day in a bookstore on lower Fifth Avenue full of odd volumes on yoga and spiritualism and holistic healing. And Armstrong's is scheduled to close the end of next month. The lease is up for renewal, and I suppose the next you know, the old joint'll be another Korean fruit market.

I still light a candle now and then for Carolyn Cheatham and Miguelito Cruz. Not often. Just every once in a while.

CLEVELAND
IN MY DREAMS

"**S**o," Loebner said. "You continue to have the dream."
    "Every night."

"And it is always without variation yet? Perhaps you will tell me the dream again."

"Oh, God," said Hackett. "It's the same dream, all right? I get a phone call, I have to go to Cleveland, I drive there, I drive back. End of dream. What's the point of going through it every time we have a session? Unless you just can't remember the dream from one week to the next."

"That is interesting," Loebner said. "Why do you suppose I would forget your dream?"

Hackett groaned. You couldn't beat the bastards. If you landed a telling shot, they simply asked you what you meant by it. It was probably the first thing they taught them in shrink school, and possibly the only thing.

"Of course I remember your dream," Loebner went on smoothly. "But what is important is not my recollection of it but what it means to you, and if you recount it once more, in the fullest detail, perhaps you will find something new in it."

What was to be found in it? It was the ultimate boring dream, and it had been boring months ago when he dreamed it the first time. Nightly repetition had done nothing to enliven it. Still, it might give him the illusion that he was getting something out of the session. If he just sprawled on the couch for what was left of his fifty minutes, he ran the risk of falling asleep.

Perchance to dream.

"It's always the same dream," he said, "and it always starts the same way. I'm in bed and the phone rings. I answer it. A voice tells me I have to go to Cleveland right away."

"You recognize this voice?"

"I recognize it from other dreams. It's always the same voice. But it's not the voice of anyone I know, if that's what you mean."

"Interesting," Loebner said.

To you perhaps, thought Hackett, "I get up," he said. "I throw on some clothes. I don't bother to shave, I'm in too much of a hurry. It's very urgent that I go to Cleveland right away. I go down to the garage and unlock my car, and there's a briefcase on the front passenger seat. I have to deliver it to somebody in Cleveland.

"I get in the car and start driving. I take I-71 all the way. That's the best route, but even so it's just about two hundred fifty miles door to door. I push it a little and there's no traffic to speak of at that hour, but it's still close to four hours to get there."

"The voice on the phone has given you an address?"

"No, I just somehow know where I'm supposed to take the briefcase. Hell, I *ought* to know, I've been there every night for months. Maybe the first time I was given an address, it's hard to remember, but by now I know the route and I know the destination. I park in the driveway, I ring the bell, the door opens, a woman accepts the briefcase and thanks me—"

"A woman takes the briefcase from you?" Loebner said.

"Yes."

"What does this woman look like?"

"That's sort of vague. She just reaches out and takes the briefcase and thanks me. I'm not positive it's the same woman each time."

"But it is always a woman?"

"Yes."

"Why do you suppose that is?"

"I don't know. Maybe her husband's out, maybe he works nights."

"She is married, this woman?"

"I don't *know*," said Hackett. "I don't know anything about her. She opens the door, she takes the briefcase, she thanks me, and I get back in my car."

"You never enter the house? She does not offer you a cup of coffee?"

"I'm in too much of a hurry," Hackett said. "I have to get home. I get in the car, I backed out of the driveway, and I'm gone. It's another two hundred fifty miles to get home, and I'm dog-tired. I've already been driving four hours, but I push it, and I get home and go to bed."

"And then?"

"And then I barely get to sleep when the alarm rings and it's time to get up. I never get a decent night's sleep. I'm exhausted all the time, and my work's falling off and I'm losing weight, and sometimes I'm just about hallucinating at my desk, and I can't stand it, I just can't *stand* it."

"Yes," Loebner said. "Well, I see our hour is up."

"Now let us talk about this briefcase," Loebner said at their next meeting. "Have you ever tried to open it?"

"It's locked."

"Ah. And you do not have the key?"

"It has one of those three-number combination locks."

"And you do not know the combination?"

"Of course not. Anyway, I'm not supposed to open the briefcase. I'm just supposed to deliver it."

"What do you suppose is in the briefcase?"

"I don't know."

"But what do you suppose *might* be in it?"

"Beats me."

"State secrets, perhaps? Drugs? Cash?"

"For all I know it's dirty laundry," Hackett said. "I just have to deliver it to Cleveland."

"You always follow the same route?" Loebner said at their next session.

"Naturally," Hackett said. "There's really only one way to get to Cleveland. You take I-71 all the way."

"You are never tempted to vary the route?"

"I did once," Hackett remembered.

"Oh?"

"I took I-75 to Dayton, I-70 east to Columbus, and then I picked up I-71 and rode it the rest of the way. I wanted to do something different, but it was the same boring ride on the same boring kind of road, and what did I accomplish? It's thirty-five miles longer that way, so all I really did was add half an hour to the trip, and my head barely hit the pillow before it was time to get up for work."

"I see."

"So that was the end of that experiment," Hackett said. "Believe me, it's simpler if I just stick with I-71. I could drive that highway in my sleep."

Loebner was dead.

The call, from the psychiatrist's receptionist, shocked Hackett. For months he'd been seeing Loebner once a week, recounting his dream, waiting for some breakthrough that would relieve him of it. While he had just about given up anticipating that breakthrough, neither had he anticipated that Loebner would take himself abruptly out of the game.

He had to call back to ask how Loebner had died. "Oh, it was a heart attack," the woman told him. "He just passed away in his sleep. He went to sleep and never woke up."

Later, Hackett found himself entertaining a fantasy. Loebner, sleeping the big sleep, would take over the chore of dreaming Hackett's dream. The little psychiatrist could rise every night to convey the dreaded briefcase to Cleveland while Hackett slept dreamlessly.

It was such a seductive notion that he went to bed expecting it to happen. No sooner had he dozed off, though, than he was in the dream again, with the phone ringing and the voice at the other end telling him what he had to do.

"I wasn't going to continue with another psychiatrist," Hackett explained, "because I don't really think I was getting anywhere with Dr. Loebner. But I'm not getting anywhere on my own, either. Every night I dream this goddamned dream and it's ruining my health. I'm here because I don't know what else to do."

"Figures," said the new psychiatrist, whose name was Krull. "That's the only reason anybody goes to a shrink."

"I suppose you want to hear the dream."

"Not particularly," said Krull.

"You don't?"

"In my experience," Krull said, "there's nothing duller than somebody else's dream. But it's probably a good place to get started, so let's hear it."

While Hackett recounted the dream, sitting upright in a chair instead of lying on a couch, Krull fidgeted. This new shrink was a man about Hackett's age, and he was dressed casually in khakis and a polo shirt with a reptile on the pocket. He was clean-shaven and had a crew cut. Loebner had looked the way a psychiatrist was supposed to look.

"Well, what do you want to do now?" Hackett asked when he'd finished. "Should I try to figure out what the dream means or do you want to suggest what the dream might mean or what?"

"Who cares?"

Hackett stared at him.

"Really," Krull said, "do you honestly give a damn what your dream means?"

"Well, I—"

"I mean," said Krull, "what's the problem here? The problem's not that you're in love with your raincoat, the problem's not that they potty-trained you too early, the problem's not that you're repressing your secret desire to watch *My Little Margie* reruns. The problem is you're not getting any rest. Right?"

"Well, yes," Hackett said. "Right."

"You have this ditsy dream every night, huh?"

"Every night. Unless I take a sleeping pill, which I've done half a dozen times, but that's even worse in the long run. I don't really *feel* rested—I have a sort of hangover all day from the pill, and I find drugs a little worrisome, anyway."

"Mmmm," Krull said, clasping his hands behind his head and leaning back in his chair. "Let's see now. Is the dream scary? Filled with terror?"

"No."

"Painful? Harrowing?"

"No."

"So the only problem is exhaustion," Krull said.

"Yes."

"Exhaustion that's perfectly natural, because a man who drives five hundred miles every night when he's supposed to be resting is going to be beat to hell the next day. Does that pretty much say it?"

"Yes."

"Sure it does. You can't drive five hundred miles every night and feel good. But"—he leaned forward—"I'll bet you could drive half that distance, couldn't you?"

"What do you mean?"

"What I mean," said Krull, "is there's a simple way to solve your problem." He scribbled on a memo pad, tore off the top sheet, handed it to Hackett. "My home phone number," he said. "When the guy calls and tells you to go to Cleveland, what I want you to do is call me."

"Wait a minute," Hackett said. "I'm asleep while this is happening. How the hell can I call you?"

"In the *dream* you call me. I'll come over to your place, I'll get in the car with you, and we'll drive to Cleveland together. After you deliver the briefcase, you can just curl up in the backseat and I'll drive back. You ought to be able to get four hours' sleep on the way home, or close to it."

Hackett straightened up in his chair. "Let me see if I understand this," he said. "I get the call, and I turn around and call you, and the two of us drive to Cleveland together. I drive there, and you drive back, and I get to nap on the drive home."

"Right."

"You think that would work?"

"Why not?"

"It sounds crazy," Hackett said, "but I'll try it."

The following morning he called Krull. "I don't know how to thank you," he said.

"It worked?"

"Like a charm. I got the call, I called you, you came over, and off we went to Cleveland together. I drove there, you drove back, I got a solid three and a half hours in the backseat, and I feel like a new man. It's the craziest thing I ever heard of, but it worked."

"I thought it would," Krull said. "Just keep doing it every time you have the dream. Call me the end of the week and let me know if it's still working."

At the week's end, Hackett made the phone call. "It works better than ever," he said. "It's gotten so I'm not dreading that phone call either, because I know we'll have a good time on the road. The drive to Cleveland is a pleasure now that I've got you in the car to talk to, and the nap I get on the way home makes all the difference in the world. I can't thank you enough."

"That's terrific," Krull told him. "I wish all my patients were as easily satisfied."

And that was that. Every night Hackett had the dream, and every night he drove to Cleveland and let the psychiatrist take the wheel on the way home. They talked about all sorts of things on the way to Cleveland—girls, baseball, Kant's categorical imperative, and how to know when it was time to discard a disposable razor. Sometimes they talked about Hackett's personal life, and he felt he was getting a lot of insight from their conversations. He wondered if he ought to send Krull a check for services rendered and asked Krull the following night in the dream. The dream-Krull told him not to worry about it: "After all," he said, "you're paying for the gas."

Hackett's health improved. He was able to concentrate better, and the improvement showed in his work. His love life improved as well, after having virtually ceased to exist. He felt reborn, and he was beginning to love his life.

Then he ran into Feverell.

"My God," he said. "Mike Feverell."

"Hello, George."

"How've you been, Mike? Lord, it's been years, hasn't it? You look—"

"I look like hell," Feverell said. "Don't I?"

"I wasn't going to say that."

"You weren't? I don't know why not, because it's the truth. I look terrible and I know it."

"How's your health, Mike?"

"My health? That's what's ridiculous. My health is fine, perfectly fine. I don't know how much longer I can go on before I just plain drop dead, but in the meantime my health is a hundred percent."

"What's wrong?"

"Oh, it's too stupid to talk about."

"Oh?"

"It's this recurring dream," Feverell said. "I have the same dream every goddamned night, and it's driving me nuts."

The room seemed to fill up with light. Hackett took his friend's arm. "Let's get a couple of beers," he said, "and you can tell me all about your dream."

"It's stupid," Feverell said. "It's an adolescent sex fantasy. I'm almost ashamed to talk about it, but the thing is I can't seem to do anything about it."

"Tell me."

"Well, it's the same every night," Feverell said. "I go to sleep and the doorbell rings. I get up, put on a robe, answer the door, and there are three beautiful women there. They want to come in, and they want to have a party."

"A party?"

"What they want," said Feverell, "is for me to make love to them."

"And?"

"And I do."

"It sounds," said Hackett, "like a wonderful dream. It sounds like a dream people would pay money to have."

"You'd think that, wouldn't you?"

"What's the problem?"

"The problem," said Feverell, "is that it's too much. I make love to all three of them and I'm exhausted, drained, an empty shell, and no sooner do I drift off to sleep than the alarm clock's ringing and it's time to get up. I'm too old for three women in one night, and these aren't hasty encounters. It takes the whole night to satisfy them all, and I've got no strength left for the rest of my life."

"Interesting," said Hackett, in a manner not altogether unlike the late Dr. Loebner's. "Tell me, are they always the same women?"

Feverell shook his head. "If they were," he said, "it'd be a cinch, because I wouldn't keep getting turned on. But every night it's three brand-new ladies, and the only common denominator is that they're all gorgeous. Tall ones, short ones, light ones, dark ones. Blondes, brunettes, redheads. Even a bald one the other night."

"That must have been interesting."

"It was damned interesting," Feverell said, "but who needs it? Too much is still too much. I can't resist them, I can't turn them down, but I'll tell you, I shudder when the doorbell rings." He sighed. "I suppose it relates to being divorced a little over a year and some kind of performance anxiety, something like that. Or do you suppose there's a deeper cause?"

"Who cares?"

Feverell stared at him.

"Really," said Hackett. "What's the difference why you're having the dream? The *dream* is the problem, isn't it?"

"Well, yeah, I guess so. But—"

"As a matter of fact," Hackett went on, "the dream isn't the problem either. The problem is that there are too many women in it."

"Well—"

"If there were just one woman," Hackett said, "you'd do just fine, wouldn't you?"

"I suppose so—but there's always three, and no matter how much I want to I can't seem to tell two of them to go away. I don't want to hurt their feelings, see, and it'd be impossible to choose among them anyway—"

"Suppose you only had to make love to one of them," Hackett said. "Could you handle that?"

"Sure, but—"

"And then you could get plenty of sleep after she left."

"I guess so, but—"

"And you'd be rested in the morning. In fact, after a dream like that you'd probably feel like a million dollars, wouldn't you?"

"What are you getting at, George?"

"Simple," said Hackett. "Simplest thing in the world."

He got out a business card and scribbled on the back. "My home phone number," he said, thrusting the card at Feverell. "Go ahead, take it."

"What am I supposed to do with this?"

"Memorize it," Hackett said, "and when the doorbell rings tonight, call me."

"What do you mean, call you? I'm supposed to get up out of a sound sleep and call you? And then what happens? Is it like AA or something—you come over and we have coffee and you talk me out of dreaming?"

Hackett shook his head. "You don't get up," he said. "In the *dream* you call me. You call me, and then you go open the door and let the girls in."

"What's the point of that?"

"The point is that I've got a friend, a psychiatrist as it happens, a very nice clean-cut type of guy. You'll call me, and I'll call him, and the two of us'll come over to your place."

"You're going to schlepp some shrink to my house in the middle of the night?"

"This is in the dream," Hackett told him. "We'll come over, and you'll make love to one of the girls, whichever one you choose, and I'll take one, and my friend'll take one. And after you're done with your girl you can go to sleep, and you'll be perfectly well rested in the morning. And we can do this every night you have the dream. All you have to do is call me and we'll show up and help you out."

Feverell stared at him. "If only it would work."

"It will."

"There was a Chinese girl the other night who was just plain out of this world," Feverell said. "But I couldn't really relax and enjoy her, because the Jamaican and the Norwegian girls were in the other room and, well—"

Hackett clapped his friend on the shoulder. "Call me," he said. "Your troubles are over."

The following morning, on his way to work, Hackett gave himself up to a feeling of supreme well being. He had repaid Krull's kindness to him in the best way possible, by passing on the favor to another. At his desk that morning, he waited for the phone to ring with a report from Feverell.

But Feverell didn't call. Not that morning, not the next morning, not all week. And something kept Hackett from calling Feverell.

Until finally he ran into him on the street during the noon hour—and Feverell looked *terrible*! Bags under his eyes, deeper than ever. Sallow skin, trembling hands. "Mike!" he said. "Mike, are you all right?"

"Do I look all right?"

"No, you don't," Hackett said honestly. "You look awful."

"Well, I *feel* awful," Feverell said savagely. "And I don't feel a whole lot better for being told how terrible I look, but thanks all the same."

"Mike, what's wrong?"

"What's wrong? You know damned well what's wrong. It's this dream I've been having. I told you the whole story. Or did it slip your mind?"

Hackett sighed. "You're still having the dream?"

"Of course I'm still having the dream."

"Mike," Hackett said, "when the doorbell rings, before you do anything else, you were going to call me, remember?"

"Of course I remember."

"So?"

"So I've called you. Every night I call you, for all the good it does."

"You do?"

"Of course I do, every goddamned night."

"And then I come over? And I bring my friend?"

"Oh, right," said Feverell. "Your famous friend, the clean-cut psychiatrist. Whom I've yet to meet, because he doesn't come over and neither do you. Every night I call you, and every night you hang up on me."

"I hang up on you?" Hackett stared. "Why would I do a thing like that?"

"I don't know," said Feverell. "I don't have the slightest idea. But every night I call you and you don't even let me get a word in edgewise. 'I'm sorry,' you say, 'but I can't talk to you now, I'm on my way to Cleveland.' Cleveland yet! And you hang up on me!"

SOME THINGS
A MAN MUST DO

Just a few minutes before twelve on one of the best Sunday nights of the summer, a clear and fresh-aired and moonlit night, Thomas M. "Lucky Tom" Carroll collected his black snap-brim hat from the hat-check girl at Cleo's Club on Broderick Avenue. He tipped the girl a crisp dollar bill, winked briskly at her, and headed out the front door. He was fifty-two, looked forty-five, felt thirty-nine. He flipped his expensive cigar into the gutter and strolled to the Cleo's Club parking lot next door, where his very expensive, very large car waited in the parking space reserved for it.

When he had settled himself behind the wheel with the key fitted snugly in the ignition, he suddenly felt that he might not be alone.

Hearing a clicking sound directly behind him, Carroll stiffened, and then the little man in the backseat shot him six times in the back of the head. While the shots echoed deafeningly, the little man opened the car door, jammed his gun into the pocket of his suit jacket, and scurried off down the street as fast as he could, which was not terribly fast at all. He peeled his white gloves from his tiny hands, and managed to slow down a bit. Holding the white gloves in one hand, he looked rather like the White Rabbit rushing frenetically to keep his appointment with the Duchess.

Finney and Mattera caught the squeal. The scene was packed with onlookers, but Finney and Mattera didn't share their overwhelming interest in the spectacle. They came, they looked, they confirmed there were no eyewitnesses to question, and they went over to the White Tower for coffee. Let the lab boys sweat it out all night, searching through a coal mine for a black cat that wasn't there. Fingerprints? Evidence? Clues? A waste of time.

"Figure the touch man is on a plane by now," Finney said. "Be on the West Coast before the body's cold."

"Uh-huh."

"So Lucky Tom finally bought it. Nice of him to pick a decent night for it. You hate to leave the station house when it's raining. But a night like this, I don't mind it at all."

"It's a pleasure to get out."

"It is at that," said Finney. He stirred his coffee thoughtfully, wondering as he did so if there were a way of stirring your coffee without seeming thoughtful about it. "I wonder," he said, "why anyone would want to kill him."

"Good question. After all, what did he ever do? Strongarm robbery, assault, aggravated assault, assault with a deadly weapon, extortion, three murders we knew of and none we could prove—"

"Just trivial things," said Finney.

"Undercover owner of Cleo's Club, operator of three illegal gambling establishments—"

"Four."

"Four? I only knew three." Mattera finished his coffee. "Loan-shark setup, number-two man in Barry Beyer's organization, not too much else. We did have a rape complaint maybe eight years ago—"

"A solid citizen."

"The best."

"A civic leader."

"None other."

"It was sure one peach of a professional touch," Finney said. "Six shots fired point-blank. Revenge, huh?"

"Something like that."

"No bad blood coming up between Beyer and Archie Moscow?"

"Haven't heard a word. They've been all peace and quiet for years. Two mobs carve up the city instead of each other. No bad blood spilled in the streets of our fair city. Instead of killing each other they cool it, and rob the public."

"True public spirit," said Finney. "The reign of law and order. It makes one proud to serve the cause of law and order in this monument to American civic pride."

"Shut up," Mattera said.

Approximately two days and three hours later, three men walked out the front door at 815 Cameron Street. The establishment they left didn't have an official name, but every cab-driver in town knew it. Good taste precludes a precise description of the principal business activity conducted therein; suffice it to say that seven attractive young ladies lived there, and that it was neither a nurses' residence nor a college dormitory.

The three men headed for their car. They had parked it next to a fire hydrant, supremely confident that no police officer who noted its license number would have the temerity to hang a parking ticket on the windshield. The three men were trusted employees of Mr. Archer Moscow. They had come to collect the week's receipts, and, incidentally, to act as a sort of quality-control inspection team.

As they reached the street, a battered ten-year-old convertible drew up slowly alongside them. The driver, alone in the car, leaned across the front seat and shot the center man in the chest with a sawed-off shotgun. Then he quickly scooped an automatic pistol from the seat and used it to shoot the other two men, three times each. He did all of this very quickly, and all three men were very dead before they hit the sidewalk.

The man stomped on the accelerator pedal and the car leaped forward as if startled. The convertible took the corner on two wheels and as suddenly slowed its speed to twenty-five miles an hour. The little man drove four blocks, parked the car, and raised the convertible top. He disassembled the sawed-off shotgun and packed it away in his thin black attaché case with the automatic, removed the jumper wire from the ignition switch, and left the car. Once outside the car he removed his white gloves and put them, too, inside the attaché case. His own car was parked right around the corner. He put the attaché case into his trunk, got into his car, and went home.

Finney and Mattera got the squeal again, only this time it was a pain in the neck, good weather notwithstanding. This time there were eyewitnesses, and sometimes eyewitnesses can be a pain in the neck, and this was one of those times. One of the eyewitnesses reported that the killer had been on foot, but this was a minority opinion. All of the other witnesses agreed there had been a murder car. One said that it was a convertible, another that it was a sedan, and a third that it was a panel truck. There were two other minority opinions as well. One witness said there had been three killers. Another said one. The rest agreed on two, and Finney and Mattera figured three sounded reasonable, since two guns had been used, and someone had to drive the car, whatever kind of car it was. Then they asked the witnesses if they would be able to identify the killer or killers, and all of the witnesses suddenly remembered that this was a gangster murder, and what was apt to happen to eyewitnesses who remembered what killers looked like, and they all agreed, strange as it may seem, that they had not gotten a good look at the killers at all.

Finney had to ask the stupid questions, and Mattera had to write down the stupid answers, and it was an hour before they got over to the White Tower.

"Eyewitnesses," said Finney, "are notoriously unreliable."

"Eyewitnesses are a pain in the neck."

"True. Three more solid citizens—"

"Three of Archie Moscow's solid citizens this time—Joe Dant and Third-Time Charlie Weiss and Big Nose Murchison. How would you like to have a name like Big Nose Murchison?"

"He doesn't even have a nose now," said Finney. "And couldn't smell much if he did."

"How do you figure it?"

"Well, as they said on Pearl Harbor Day—"

"Uh-huh."

"This do look like war, sir."

"Mmmmm," said Mattera. "Doesn't make sense, does it? You would think we would have heard something. That's usually the nice thing about being a cop. You get to hear things, things the average citizen may not know about. You don't always get to do anything about what you hear, but you hear about it. We're only in this business because it gives us the feeling of being on the inside."

"I thought it was for the free coffee," said the counterman. They drank, pretending not to hear him.

"We're going to look real bad, you know," Finney said. "If Moscow and Beyer have a big hate going, they're going to spill a lot of blood, and the chance of solving any of those jobs isn't worth pondering." He broke off suddenly, pleased with himself. He was fairly certain he had never used "pondering" in conversation before.

"And," he went on, "with various killers flying in and out of town and leaving us with a file of unsolved homicides, the newspapers may start hinting that we are not the best police force in the world."

"Everybody knows we're the best money can buy," said Mattera.

"Isn't it the truth," said Finney.

"And what bothers me most," said Mattera, "is the innocent men who will die in a war like this. Men like Big Nose, for example."

"Pillars of the community."

"We'll miss them," said Mattera.

The following afternoon, Mr. Archer Moscow used his untapped private line to call the untapped private line of Mr. Barry Beyer. "You had no call to do that," he said.

"To do what?"

"Dant and Third-Time and Big Nose," said Moscow. "You know I didn't have a thing to do with Lucky Tom. You got no call for revenge."

"Who was it hit Lucky Tom?"

"How should I know?"

"Well," said Beyer, reasonably, "then how should I know who hit Dant and Third-Time and Big Nose?"

There was a long silent moment. "We've been friends a long time," Moscow said. "We have kept things cool, and we have all done very nicely that way—with no guns, and no blasting a bunch of guys out of revenge for something which we never did to Lucky Tom in the first place."

"If I thought you hit Lucky Tom—"

"The bum," said Moscow, "was not worth killing."

"If I thought you did it," Beyer went on, "I wouldn't go and shoot up a batch of punks like Dant and Third-Time and Big Nose. You know what I'd do?"

"What?"

"I'd go straight to the top," said Beyer. "I'd kill *you*, you bum!"

"That's no way to talk, Barry."

"You had no call to kill Lucky Tom. So maybe he was holding out a little in Ward Three, it don't make no difference."

"You had no call to kill those three boys."

"You don't know what killing is, bum."

"Yeah?" Moscow challenged.

"Yeah!"

That night, a gentleman named Mr. Roswell "Greasy" Spune turned his key in his ignition and was immediately blown from this world into the next. The little man with the small hands and the white gloves watched from a tavern across the street. Mr. Spune was a bagman for Barry Beyer's organization. Less than two hours after Mr. Spune's abrupt demise, six of Barry Beyer's boys hijacked an ambulance from the hospital garage. Five sat in back, and the sixth, garbed in white, drove the sporty vehicle through town with the pedal on the floor and the siren wide open. "This takes me back," one of them was heard to say. "This is the way it used to be before the world went soft in the belly. This is what you would call doing things with a little class."

The ambulance pulled up in front of a West Side tavern where the Moscow gang hung out. The ambulance tailgate burst open, and the five brave men and true emerged with submachine guns and commenced blasting away. Eight of Archie Moscow's staunchest associates died in the fray, and only one of the boys from the ambulance crew was killed in return.

Moscow retaliated the next day, shooting up two Beyer-operated card games, knocking off two small-time dope peddlers, and gunning down a Beyer lieutenant as he emerged from his bank at two-thirty in the afternoon. The gunman who accomplished this last feat then raced down an alleyway into the waiting arms of a rookie patrolman, who promptly shot him dead. The kid had been on the force only three months and was sure he would be up on departmental charges for forgetting to fire two warning shots into the air. Instead he got an on-the-spot promotion to detective junior grade.

By the second week of the war, the pace began to slow down. Pillars of both mobs were beginning to realize that a state of war demanded wartime security measures. One could not wander about without a second thought as in time of peace. One could not visit a meeting or a nightclub or a gaming house or a girlfriend without posting a guard, or even several guards. In short, one had to be very careful.

Even so, not everyone was careful enough. Muggsy Lopez turned up in the trunk of his car wearing a necktie of piano wire. Look-See Logan was found in his own kidney-shaped swimming pool with his hands and feet tied together and a few quarts of chlorinated water in his lungs. Benny Benedetto looked under the hood of his brand-new car, found a bomb wired to the ignition, removed it gingerly and dismantled it efficiently, and climbed behind the steering wheel clucking his tongue at the perfidy of his fellow man. But he completely missed the bomb wired to the gas pedal. It didn't miss him; they picked him up with a mop.

The newspapers screamed. The city fathers screamed. The police commissioner screamed. Finney and Mattera worked double-duty and tried to explain to their wives that this was war. Their wives screamed.

It was war for three solid months. It blew hot and cold, and there would be rumors of high-level conferences, of face-to-face meets between Archer Moscow and Barry Beyer, cautious summit meetings held on neutral ground. Then, for a week, the killings would cease, and the word would go out that a truce had been called. Then someone would be gunned down or stabbed or blown to bits, and the war would start all over again.

At the end of the third month there was supposed to be another truce in progress, but by now no one was taking truce talk too seriously. There had not been a known homicide in five days. The count now stood at eighty-three dead, several more wounded, five in jail, and two missing in action. The casualties were almost perfectly balanced between the two mobs. Forty of Beyer's men were dead, forty-three Moscow men were in their graves, and each gang had one man missing.

That night, as usual, Finney and Mattera prowled the uneasy streets in an unmarked squad car. Only this particular night was different. This night they caught the little man.

Mattera was the one who spotted him. He noticed someone sitting in a car on Pickering Road, with the lights out and the motor running. His first thought was that it was high school kids necking, but there was only one person there, and the person seemed to be doing something, so Mattera slowed to a stop and killed the lights.

The little man straightened up finally. He opened the car door, stepped out, and saw Finney and Mattera standing in front of him with drawn revolvers.

"Oh, my," said the little man.

Finney moved past him, checked the car. "Cute job," he said. "He's got this little gun lashed to the steering column, and there's a wire hooked around the trigger and connected to the gas pedal. You step on the gas and the gun goes off and gets you right in the chest. I read about a bit like that down in Texas. Very professional."

Mattera looked at the little man and shook his head. "Professional," he said. "A little old guy with glasses. Who belongs to the car, friend?"

"Ears Carradine," said the little man.

"One of Moscow's boys," Finney said. "You work for Barry Beyer, friend?"

The little man's jaw dropped. "Oh, goodness, no," he said. His voice was high-pitched, reedy. "Oh, certainly not."

"Who do you work for?"

"Aberdeen Pharmaceutical Supply," the little man said. "I'm a research chemist."

"You're a *what*?"

The little man took off his gloves and wrung them sadly in his hands. "Oh, this won't do at all," he said unhappily. "I suppose I'll have to tell you everything now, won't I?"

Finney allowed that this sounded like a good idea. The little man suggested they sit in the squad car. They did, one on either side of him.

"My name is Edward Fitch," the little man said. "Of

course, there's no reason on earth why you should have heard of me, but you may recall my son. His name was Richard Fitch. I called him Dick, of course, because Rich Fitch would not have done at all. I'm sure you can appreciate that readily enough."

"Get to the point," Mattera said.

"Well," said Mr. Fitch, "is his name familiar?"

It wasn't.

"He killed himself in August," Mr. Fitch said. "Hanged himself, you may recall, with the cord from his electric razor. I gave him that razor, actually. A birthday present, oh, several years ago."

"Now I remember," Finney said.

"I didn't know at the time just why he had killed himself," Mr. Fitch went on. "It seemed an odd thing to do. And then I learned that he had lost an inordinate amount of money gambling—"

"Inordinate," Finney said, choked with admiration.

"Indeed," said Mr. Fitch. "As much as five thousand dollars, if I'm not mistaken. He didn't have the money. He was trying to raise it, but evidently the sum increased day by day. Interest, so to speak."

"So to speak," echoed Finney.

"He felt the situation was hopeless, which was inaccurate, but understandable in one so young, so he took his own life." Mr. Fitch paused significantly. "The man to whom he owed the money," he said, "and who was charging him appalling interest, and who had won the money in an unfair gambling match, was Thomas M. Carroll."

Finney's jaw dropped. Mattera said, "You mean Lucky Tom—"

"Yes," said Mr. Fitch. For a moment he did not say anything more. Then, sheepishly, he raised his head and managed a tiny smile. "The more I learned about the man, the more I saw there were no legal means of bringing him to justice, and it became quite clear to me that I had to kill him. So I—"

"You killed Lucky Tom Carroll."

"Yes, I—"

"Six times. In the back of the head."

"I wanted to make it look like a professional killing," Mr. Fitch said. "I felt it wouldn't do to get caught."

"And then Beyer hit back the next night," Finney said, "and from there on it was war."

"Well, not exactly. There are some things a man must do," Mr. Fitch said. "They don't seem to fit into the law, I know. But—but they do seem right, you see. After I'd killed Mr. Carroll I realized everyone would assume it had been a revenge killing. A gangland slaying, the papers called it. I thought how very nice it would be if the two gangs really grew mad at one another. I couldn't kill them all myself, of course, but once things were set properly in motion—"

"You just went on killing," Mattera said.

"Like a one-man army," Finney said.

"Not exactly," said Mr. Fitch. "Of course I killed those three men on Cameron Street, and bombed that Mr. Spune's car, but then I just permitted nature to take its course. Now and then things would quiet down and I had to take an active hand, yet I didn't really do all that much of the killing."

"How much?"

Mr. Fitch sighed.

"How many did you kill, Mr. Fitch?"

"Fifteen. I don't really like killing, you know."

"If you liked it, you'd be pretty dangerous, Mr. Fitch. Fifteen?"

"Tonight would have been the sixteenth," Mr. Fitch said.

For a while no one said anything. Finney lit a cigarette, gave one to Mattera, and offered one to Mr. Fitch. Mr. Fitch explained that he didn't smoke. Finney started to say something and changed his mind.

Mattera said, "Not to be nasty, Mr. Fitch, but just what were you looking to accomplish?"

"I should think that's patently obvious," Mr. Fitch said gently. "I wanted to wipe out these criminal gangs, these mobs."

"Wipe them out," Finney said.

"You know, let them kill each other off."

"Kill each other off." He nodded.

"That's correct."

"And you thought that would work, Mr. Fitch?"

Mr. Fitch looked surprised. "But it *is* working, isn't it?"

"Uh—"

"I'm reminded of the anarchists around the turn of the century," said Mr. Fitch. "Of course, they were an unpleasant sort of men, but they had an interesting theory. They felt that if enough kings were assassinated, sooner or later no one would care to be king."

"That's an interesting theory," Finney said.

"So they went about killing kings. There aren't many kings these days," Mr. Fitch said quietly. "When you think about it, there are rather few of them about. Oh, I'm certain there are other explanations, but still—"

"I guess it's something to think about," Mattera said.

"It is," said Finney. "Mr. Fitch, what happens when you run through all the gangsters in town?"

"I suppose I would go on to another town."

"Another town?"

"I seem to have a calling for this sort of work," Mr. Fitch said. "But that's all over now, isn't it? You've arrested me, and there will have to be a trial, of course. What do you suppose they'll do to me?"

"They ought to give you a medal," said Mattera.

"Or put up a statue of you in front of City Hall," said Finney.

"I'm serious—"

"So are we, Mr. Fitch."

They fell silent again. Mattera thought about all the criminals who had been immune three months ago and who were now dead, and how much nicer a place it was without them. Finney tried to figure out how many kings there were. Not many, he decided, and the ones that were left didn't really do anything.

"I suppose you'll want to take me to jail now," said Mr. Fitch.

Mattera cleared his throat. "I'd better explain something to you, Mr. Fitch," he said. "A police officer is a very busy man. He can't waste his time with a lot of kooky stories that he might hear. Finney and I, uh, have crooks to catch. Things like that."

"What Mattera means, Mr. Fitch, is a nice old guy like you ought to run home to bed. We enjoy talking to you, and I really admire the way you speak, but Mattera and I, we're

busy, see. We've got an inordinate lot of crooks to catch . . ."
There! ". . . and you ought to go on home, so to speak."

"Oh," said Mr. Fitch. "Oh. Oh, bless you!"

They watched him scurry away, and they smoked more
cigarettes, and remained silent for a very long time. After a
while Mattera said, "A job like this, you got to do something
crazy once in a while."

"Sure."

"I never did anything this crazy before. You?"

"No."

"That nutty little guy. How long do you figure he'll get
away with it?"

"Who knows?"

"Fifteen so far. Fifteen—"

"Uh-huh. And close to seventy others that they did themselves."

A light went on across the street. A door opened, and a
man walked toward his car. The man had ears like an ele-
phant. "Ears Carradine," Mattera said. "Better get him before
he gets into the car."

"You tell him."

"Hell, you're closer."

Carradine stopped to light a cigarette. He shook out the
match and flung it aside.

"I had him nailed to the wall on an aggravated-assault
thing a few years back," Finney said. "I had three witnesses
that pinned him good—and not a breath of doubt."

"Witnesses."

"Two of them changed their minds and one disappeared.
Never turned up."

"You better tell him," Mattera said.

"Funny the way that little guy had that car gimmicked.
Read about it in the paper, you know, but I never saw anything
like it before. Cute, though."

"He's getting in the car," Mattera said.

"You would wonder if a thing like that would work,
wouldn't you?"

"You would at that. You should have told him, but it's
that kind of a crazy night, isn't it?"

"He might see it himself."

"He might."

He didn't. They heard the ignition, and then the single shot, and Ears Carradine slumped over the wheel.

Mattera started up the squad car and pulled away from the curb. "How about that," he said. "It worked like a charm."

"Sixteen," said Finney.

ANSWERS TO SOLDIER

Keller flew United to Portland. He read a magazine on the leg from JFK to O'Hare, ate lunch on the ground, and watched the movie on the nonstop flight from Chicago to Portland. It was a quarter to three local time when he carried his hand luggage off the plane, and then he had only an hour's wait before his connecting flight to Roseburg.

But when he got a look at the size of the plane he walked over to the Hertz desk and told them he wanted a car for a few days. He showed them a driver's license and a credit card and they let him have a Ford Taurus with thirty-two hundred miles on the clock. He didn't bother trying to refund his Portland-to-Roseburg ticket.

The Hertz clerk showed him how to get on I-5. He pointed the Taurus in the right direction and set the cruise control three miles over the posted speed limit. Everybody else was going a few miles an hour faster than that but he was in no hurry, and he didn't want to invite a close look at his driver's license. It was probably all right, but why ask for trouble?

It was still light out when he took the off-ramp for the second Roseburg exit. He had a reservation at the Douglas Inn, a Best Western on Stephens Street. He found it without any trouble. They had him in a ground-floor room in the front, and he had them change it to one in the rear, and a flight up.

He unpacked, showered. The phone book had a street map of downtown Roseburg and he studied it, getting his bearings, then tearing it out and taking it with him when he went out for a walk. The little print shop was only a few blocks away on Jackson, two doors in from the corner between a tobacconist and a photographer with his window full of wedding pictures. A sign in Quik-Print's window offered a special on wedding invitations, perhaps to catch the eye of bridal couples making arrangements with the photographer.

Quik-Print was closed, of course, as were the tobacconist and the photographer and the credit jeweler next door to the photographer and, as far as Keller could tell, everybody in the neighborhood. Keller didn't stick around long. Two blocks away he found a Mexican restaurant that looked dingy enough to be authentic. He bought a local paper from the coin box out front and read it while he ate his chicken enchiladas. The food was good, and ridiculously inexpensive. If the place were in New York, he thought, everything would be three and four times as much and there'd be a line in front.

The waitress was a slender blonde, not Mexican at all. She had short hair and granny glasses and an overbite, and she sported an engagement ring on the appropriate finger, a diamond solitaire with a tiny stone. Maybe she and her fiancé had picked it out at the credit jeweler's, Keller thought. Maybe the photographer next door would take their wedding pictures. Maybe they'd get Burt Engleman to print their wedding invitations. Quality printing, reasonable rates, service you can count on.

In the morning he returned to Quik-Print and looked in the window. A woman with brown hair was sitting at a gray metal desk, talking on the telephone. A man in shirtsleeves stood at a copying machine. He wore horn-rimmed glasses with round lenses, and his hair was cropped short on his egg-shaped head. He was balding, and this made him look older, but Keller knew he was only thirty-eight.

Keller stood in front of the jeweler's and pictured the waitress and her fiancé picking out rings. They'd have a double-ring ceremony, of course, and there would be something engraved on the inside of each of their wedding bands, something no one else would ever see. Would they live in an apartment? For a while, he decided, until they saved the down payment for a starter home. That was the phrase you saw in real estate ads and Keller liked it. A starter home, something to practice on until you got the hang of it.

At a drugstore on the next block he bought an unlined paper tablet and a black felt-tipped pen. He used four sheets of paper before he was pleased with the result. Back at Quik-Print, he showed his work to the brown-haired woman.

"My dog ran off," he explained. "I thought I'd get some flyers printed, post them around town."

LOST DOG, he'd printed. *Part Ger. Shepherd. Answers to Soldier. Call 765-1904.*

"I hope you get him back," the woman said. "Is it a him? Soldier sounds like a male dog, but it doesn't say."

"It's a male," Keller said. "Maybe I should have specified."

"It's probably not important. Did you want to offer a reward? People usually do, although I don't know if it makes any difference. If I found somebody's dog I wouldn't care about a reward, I'd just want to get him back with his owner."

"Everybody's not as decent as you are," Keller said. "Maybe I should say something about a reward. I didn't even think of that." He put his palms on the desk and leaned forward, looking down at the sheet of paper. "I don't know," he said. "It looks kind of homemade, doesn't it? Maybe I should have you set it in type, do it right. What do you think?"

"I don't know," she said. "Ed? Would you come and take a look at this, please?"

The man in the horn rims came over and said he thought a hand-lettered look was best for a lost-dog notice. "It makes it more personal," he said. "I could do it in type for you, but I think people would respond to it better as it is. Assuming somebody finds the dog, that is."

"I don't suppose it's a matter of national importance anyway," Keller said. "My wife's attached to the animal and I'd like to recover him if it's possible, but I've a feeling he's not to be found. My name's Gordon, by the way. Al Gordon."

"Ed Vandermeer," the man said. "And this is my wife, Betty."

"A pleasure," Keller said. "I guess fifty of these ought to be enough. More than enough, but I'll take fifty. Will it take you long to run them?"

"I'll do it right now. Take about three minutes, cost you three-fifty."

"Can't beat that," Keller said. He uncapped the felt-tipped pen. "Just let me put in something about a reward," he said.

Back in his motel room he put through a call to a number in White Plains. When a woman answered he said, "Dot, let me speak to him, will you?" It took a few minutes, and then he said, "Yeah, I got here. It's him, all right. He's calling himself Vandermeer now. His wife's still going by Betty."

The man in White Plains asked when he'd be back.

"What's today, Tuesday? I've got a flight booked Friday but I might take a little longer. No point rushing things. I found a good place to eat. Mexican joint, and the motel set gets HBO. I figure I'll take my time, do it right. Engleman's not going anywhere."

He had lunch at the Mexican café. This time he ordered the combination plate. The waitress asked if he wanted the red or the green chili.

"Whichever's hotter," he said.

Maybe a mobile home, he thought. You could buy one cheap, a nice doublewide, make a nice starter home for her and her fellow. Or maybe the best thing for them was to buy a duplex and rent out half, then rent out the other half when they were ready for something nicer for themselves. No time at all you're in real estate, making a nice return, watching your holdings appreciate. No more waiting on tables for her, and pretty soon her husband can quit slaving at the lumber mill, quit worrying about layoffs when the industry hits one of its slumps.

How you do go on, he thought.

He spent the afternoon walking around town. In a gun shop the proprietor, a man named McLarendon, took some rifles and shotguns off the wall and let him get the feel of them. A sign on the wall said, GUNS DON'T KILL PEOPLE UNLESS YOU AIM REAL GOOD. Keller talked politics with McLarendon, and socioeconomics. It wasn't that tricky to figure out McLarendon's position and to adopt it as one's own.

"What I really been meaning to buy," Keller said, "is a handgun."

"You want to protect yourself and your property," McLarendon said.

"That's the idea."

"And your loved ones."

"Sure."

He let the man sell him a gun. There was, locally, a cooling-off period. You picked out your gun, filled out a form, and four days later you could come back and pick it up.

"You a hothead?" McLarendon asked him. "You fixing to lean out the car window, shoot a state trooper on your way home?"

"It doesn't seem likely."

"Then I'll show you a trick. We just backdate this form and you've already had your cooling-off period. I'd say you look cool enough to me."

"You're a good judge of character."

The man grinned. "This business," he said, "a man's got to be."

It was nice, a town that size. You got in your car and drove for ten minutes and you were way out in the country.

Keller stopped the Taurus at the side of the road, cut the ignition, rolled down the window. He took the gun from one pocket and the box of shells from the other. The gun—McLarendon kept calling it a weapon—was a .38-caliber revolver with a two-inch barrel. McLarendon would have liked to sell him something heavier and more powerful. If Keller had wanted, McLarendon probably would have been thrilled to sell him a bazooka.

He loaded the gun and got out of the car. There was a beer can lying on its side perhaps twenty yards off. Keller aimed at it, holding the gun in one hand. A few years ago they started firing two-handed in cop shows on TV, and nowadays that was all you saw, television cops leaping through doorways and spinning around corners, gun gripped rigidly in both hands, held out in front of their bodies like a fire hose. Keller thought it looked silly. He'd feel self-conscious, holding a gun like that.

He squeezed the trigger. The gun bucked in his hand, and he missed the beer can by several feet. The report of the gunshot echoed for a long time.

He took aim at other things—at a tree, at a flower, at a white rock the size of a clenched fist. But he couldn't bring himself to fire the gun again, to break the stillness with another gunshot. What was the point, anyway? If he used the gun he'd be too close to miss. You got in close, you pointed, you fired. It wasn't rocket science, for God's sake. It wasn't neurosurgery. Anyone could do it.

He replaced the spent cartridge and put the loaded gun in the car's glove compartment. He spilled the rest of the shells into his hand and walked a few yards from the road's edge, then hurled them with a sweeping sidearm motion. He gave the empty box a toss and got back in the car.

Traveling light, he thought.

Back in town, he drove past Quik-Print to make sure they were still open. Then, following the route he'd traced on the map, he found his way to 1411 Cowslip, a Dutch colonial house on the north edge of town. The lawn was neatly trimmed and fiercely green, and there was a bed of rosebushes on either side of the path leading from the sidewalk to the front door.

One of the leaflets at the motel told how roses were a local specialty. But the town had been named not for the flower but for Aaron Rose, a local settler.

He wondered if Engleman knew that.

He circled the block, parked two doors away on the other side of the street from the Engleman residence. *Vandermeer, Edward*, the White Pages listing had read. It struck Keller as an unusual alias. He wondered if Engleman had picked it out himself, or if the feds had selected it for him. Probably the latter, he decided. "Here's your new name," they would tell you, "and here's where you're going to live, and who you're going to be." There was an arbitrariness about it that somehow appealed to Keller, as if they relieved you of the burden of decision. Here's your new name, and here's your new driver's license with your new name already on it. You like scalloped potatoes in your new life, and you're allergic to bee stings, and your favorite color is blue.

Betty Engleman was now Betty Vandermeer. Keller wondered why her first name hadn't changed. Didn't they trust Engleman to get it right? Did they figure him for a bumbler, apt to blurt out "Betty" at an inopportune moment? Or was it sheer coincidence, or sloppiness on their part?

Around six-thirty the Englemans came home from work. They rode in a Honda Civic hatchback with local plates. They had evidently stopped to shop for groceries on the way home. Engleman parked in the driveway while his wife got a bag of groceries from the back. Then he put the car in the garage and followed her into the house.

Keller watched lights go on inside the house. He stayed where he was. It was starting to get dark by the time he drove back to the Douglas Inn.

On HBO, Keller watched a movie about a gang of criminals who have come to a small town in Texas to rob the bank. One of the criminals was a woman, married to one of the other gang members and having an affair with another. Keller thought that was a pretty good recipe for disaster. There was a prolonged shoot-out at the end, with everybody dying in slow motion.

When the movie ended he went over to switch off the set. His eye was caught by the stack of flyers Engleman had run off for him. LOST DOG. *Part Ger. Shepherd. Answers to Soldier. Call 765-1904.* REWARD.

Excellent watchdog, he thought. Good with children.

A little later he turned the set back on again. He didn't get to sleep until late, didn't get up until almost noon. He went to the Mexican place and ordered *huevos rancheros* and put a lot of hot sauce on them.

He watched the waitress's hands as she served the food and again when she took his empty plate away. Light glinted off the little diamond. Maybe she and her husband would wind up on Cowslip Lane, he thought. Not right away, of course, they'd have to start out in the duplex, but that's what they could aspire to. A Dutch colonial with that odd kind of pitched roof. What did they call it, anyway? Was that a mansard roof or did that word describe something else? Was it a gambrel, maybe?

He thought he ought to learn these things sometime. You saw the words and didn't know what they meant, saw the houses and couldn't describe them properly.

He had bought a paper on his way into the café, and now he turned to the classified ads and read through the real estate listings. Houses seemed very inexpensive. You could actually buy a low-priced home here for twice what he would be paid for the week's work.

There was a safe-deposit box no one knew about rented under a name he'd never used for another purpose, and in it he had enough cash to buy a nice home here for cash. Assuming you could still do that. People were funny about cash these days, leery of letting themselves be used to launder drug money.

Anyway, what difference did it make? He wasn't going to live here. The waitress could live here, in a nice little house with mansards and gambrels.

Engleman was leaning over his wife's desk when Keller walked into Quik-Print. "Why, hello," he said. "Have you had any luck finding Soldier?"

He remembered the name, Keller noticed.

"As a matter of fact," he said, "the dog came back on his own. I guess he wanted the reward."

Betty Engleman laughed.

"You see how fast your flyers worked," he went on. "They brought the dog back even before I got the chance to post them. I'll get some use out of them eventually, though. Old Soldier's got itchy feet, he'll take off again one of these days."

"Just so he keeps coming back," she said.

"Reason I stopped by," Keller said, "I'm new in town, as you might have gathered, and I've got a business venture I'm getting ready to kick into gear. I'm going to need a printer, and I thought maybe we could sit down and talk. You got time for a cup of coffee?"

Engleman's eyes were hard to read behind the glasses. "Sure," he said. "Why not?"

* * *

They walked down to the corner, Keller talking about what a nice afternoon it was, Engleman saying little beyond agreeing with him. At the corner Keller said, "Well, Burt, where should we go for coffee?"

Engleman just froze. Then he said, "I knew."

"I know you did, I could tell the minute I walked in there. How?"

"The phone number on the flyer. I tried it last night. They never heard of a Mr. Gordon."

"So you knew last night. Of course, you could have made a mistake on the number."

Engleman shook his head. "I wasn't going on memory. I ran an extra flyer and dialed the number right off it. No Mr. Gordon and no lost dog. Anyway, I think I knew before then. I think I knew the minute you walked in the door."

"Let's get that coffee," Keller said.

They went into a place called the Rainbow Diner and had coffee at a table on the side. Engleman added artificial sweetener to his and stirred it long enough to dissolve marble chips. He had been an accountant back East, working for the man Keller had called in White Plains. When the feds were trying to make a RICO case against Engleman's boss, Engleman was a logical place to apply pressure. He wasn't really a criminal, he hadn't done much of anything, and they told him he was going to prison unless he rolled over and testified. If he did what they said, they'd give him a new name and move him someplace safe. If not, he could talk to his wife once a month through a wire screen, and have ten years to get used to it.

"How did you find me?" he wanted to know. "Somebody leaked it in Washington?"

Keller shook his head. "Freak thing," he said. "Somebody saw you on the street, recognized you, followed you home."

"Here in Roseburg?"

"I don't think so. Were you out of town a week or so ago?"

"Oh, God," Engleman said. "We went down to San Francisco for the weekend."

"That sounds right."

"I thought it was safe. I don't even know anybody in San Francisco, I was never there in my life. It was her birthday, we figured nothing could be safer. I don't know a soul there."

"Somebody knew you."

"And followed me back here?"

"I don't even know. Maybe they got your plate and had somebody run it. Maybe they checked your registration at the hotel. What's the difference?"

"No difference."

He picked up his coffee and stared into the cup. Keller said, "You knew last night. Did you call someone?"

"Who?"

"I don't know. You're in the witness-protection program. Isn't there somebody you can call when this happens?"

"There's somebody I can call," Engleman said. He put his cup back down again. "It's not that great a program," he said. "It's great when they're telling you about it, but the execution leaves a lot to be desired."

"I've heard that," Keller said.

"Anyway, I didn't call anybody. What are they going to do? Say they stake my place out, the house and the print shop, and they pick you up. Even if they make something stick against you, what good does it do me? We have to move again because the guy'll just send somebody else, right?"

"I suppose so."

"Well, I'm not moving anymore. They moved us three times and I don't even know why. I think it's automatic, part of the program, they move you a few times during the first year or two. This is the first place we really settled into since we left, and we're starting to make money at Quik-Print, and I like it. I like the town and I like the business. I don't want to move."

"The town seems nice."

"It is," Engleman said. "It's better than I thought it would be."

"And you didn't want to develop an accounting practice?"

"Never," Engleman said. "I had enough of that, believe me. Look what it got me."

"You wouldn't necessarily have to work for crooks."

"How do you know who's a crook and who isn't? Anyway, I don't want any kind of work where I'm always looking at the inside of somebody else's business. I'd rather have my own little business, work there side by side with my wife, we're right there on the street and you can look in the front window and see us. You need stationery, you need business cards, you need invoice forms, I'll print 'em for you."

"How did you learn the business?"

"It's a franchise kind of a thing, a turn-key operation. Anybody could learn it in twenty minutes."

"No kidding," Keller said.

"Oh, yeah. Anybody."

Keller drank some of his coffee. He asked if Engleman had said anything to his wife, learned that he hadn't. "That's good," he said. "Don't say anything. I'm this guy, weighing some business ventures, needs a printer, has to have, you know, arrangements so there's no cash-flow problem. And I'm shy talking business in front of women, so the two of us go off and have coffee from time to time."

"Whatever you say," Engleman said.

Poor scared bastard, Keller thought. He said, "See, I don't want to hurt you, Burt. I wanted to, we wouldn't be having this conversation. I'd put a gun to your head, do what I'm supposed to do. You see a gun?"

"No."

"The thing is, I don't do it, they send somebody else. I come back empty, they want to know why. What I have to do, I have to figure something out. You don't want to run."

"No. The hell with running."

"Well, I'll figure something out," Keller said. "I've got a few days. I'll think of something."

After breakfast the next morning Keller drove to the office of one of the realtors whose ads he'd been reading. A woman about the same age as Betty Engleman took him around and showed him three houses. They were modest homes but decent and comfortable, and they ranged between forty and sixty thousand dollars.

He could buy any of them out of his safe-deposit box.

"Here's your kitchen," the woman said. "Here's your half-bath. Here's your fenced yard."

"I'll be in touch," he told her, taking her card. "I have a business deal pending and a lot depends on the outcome."

He and Engleman had lunch the next day. They went to the Mexican place and Engleman wanted everything very mild. "Remember," he told Keller, "I used to be an accountant."

"You're a printer now," Keller said. "Printers can handle hot food."

"Not this printer. Not this printer's stomach."

They each drank a bottle of Carta Blanca with the meal. Keller had another bottle afterward. Engleman had a cup of coffee.

"If I had a house with a fenced yard," Keller said, "I could have a dog and not worry about him running off."

"I guess you could," Engleman said.

"I had a dog when I was a kid," Keller said. "Just the once, I had him for about two years when I was eleven, twelve years old. His name was Soldier."

"I was wondering about that."

"He wasn't part shepherd. He was a little thing, I suppose he was some kind of terrier cross."

"Did he run off?"

"No, he got hit by a car. He was stupid about cars, he just ran out in the street. The driver couldn't help it."

"How did you happen to call him Soldier?"

"I forget. Then when I did the flyer, I don't know, I had to put *answers to something*. All I could think of were names like Fido and Rover and Spot. Like signing John Smith on a hotel register, you know? Then it came to me, Soldier. Been years since I thought about that dog."

After lunch Engleman went back to the shop and Keller returned to the motel for his car. He drove out of town on the same road he'd taken the day he bought the gun. This time he rode a few miles farther before pulling over and cutting the engine.

He got the gun from the glove box and opened the cylinder, spilling the shells out into his palm. He tossed them underhand, then weighed the gun in his hand for a moment before hurling it into a patch of brush.

McLarendon would be horrified, he thought. Mistreating a weapon in that fashion. Showed what a judge of character the man was.

He got back in his car and drove back to town.

* * *

He called White Plains. When the woman answered he said, "You don't have to disturb him, Dot. Just tell him I didn't make my flight today. I changed the reservation, I moved it ahead to Tuesday. Tell him everything's okay, only it's taking a little longer, like I thought it might." She asked how the weather was. "It's real nice," he said. "Very pleasant. Listen, don't you think that's part of it? If it was raining I'd probably have it taken care of, I'd be home by now."

Quik-Print was closed Saturdays and Sundays. Saturday afternoon Keller called Engleman at home and asked him if he felt like going for a ride. "I'll pick you up," he offered.

When he got there Engleman was waiting out in front. He got in and fastened his seat belt. "Nice car," he said.

"It's a rental."

"I didn't figure you drove your own car all the way out here. You know, it gave me a turn. When you said how about going for a ride. You know, going for a ride. Like there's a connotation."

"Actually," Keller said, "we probably should have taken your car. I figured you could show me the area."

"You like it here, huh?"

"Very much," Keller said. "I've been thinking. Suppose I just stayed here."

"Wouldn't he send somebody?"

"You think he would? I don't know. He wasn't killing himself trying to find you. At first, sure, but then he forgot about it. Then some eager beaver in San Francisco happens to spot you and sure, he tells me to go out and handle it. But if I just don't come back—"

"Caught up in the lure of Roseburg," Engleman said.

"I don't know, Burt, it's not a bad place. You know, I'm going to stop that."

"What?"

"Calling you Burt. Your name's Ed now, so why don't I call you Ed? What do you think, Ed? That sound good to you, Ed, old buddy?"

"And what do I call you?"

"Al's fine. What should I do, take a left here?"

"No, go another block or two," Engleman said. "There's a nice road, leads through some very pretty scenery."

A while later Keller said, "You miss it much, Ed?"

"Working for him, you mean?"

"No, not that. The city."

"New York? I never lived in the city, not really. We were up in Westchester."

"Still, the whole area. You miss it?"

"No."

"I wonder if I would." They fell silent, and after perhaps five minutes he said, "My father was a soldier, he was killed in the war when I was just a baby. That's why I named the dog Soldier."

Engleman didn't say anything.

"Except I think my mother was lying," he went on. "I don't think she was married, and I have a feeling she didn't know who my father was. But I didn't know that when I named the dog. When you think about it, it's a stupid name anyway for a dog, Soldier. It's probably stupid to name a dog after your father, as far as that goes."

Sunday he stayed in the room and watched sports on television. The Mexican place was closed; he had lunch at Wendy's and dinner at a Pizza Hut. Monday at noon he was back at the Mexican café. He had the newspaper with him, and he ordered the same thing he'd ordered the first time, the chicken enchiladas.

When the waitress brought coffee afterward, he asked her, "When's the wedding?"

She looked utterly blank. "The wedding," he repeated, and pointed at the ring on her finger.

"Oh," she said. "Oh, I'm not engaged or anything. The ring was my mom's from her first marriage. She never wears it, so I asked could I wear it, and she said it was all right. I used to wear it on the other hand but it fits better there."

He felt curiously angry, as though she'd betrayed the fantasy he'd spun out about her. He left the same tip he always left and took a long walk around town, gazing in windows, wandering up one street and down the next.

He thought, Well, you could marry her. She's already got

the engagement ring. Ed'll print your wedding invitations, except who would you invite?

And the two of you could get a house with a fenced yard, and buy a dog.

Ridiculous, he thought. The whole thing was ridiculous.

At dinnertime he didn't know what to do. He didn't want to go back to the Mexican café but he felt perversely disinclined to go anywhere else. One more Mexican meal, he thought, and I'll wish I had that gun back so I could kill myself.

He called Engleman at home. "Look," he said, "this is important. Could you meet me at your shop?"

"When?"

"As soon as you can."

"We just sat down to dinner."

"Well, don't ruin your meal," Keller said. "What is it, seven-thirty? How about if you meet me in an hour."

He was waiting in the photographer's doorway when Engleman parked the Honda in front of his shop. "I didn't want to disturb you," he said, "but I had an idea. Can you open up? I want to see something inside."

Engleman unlocked the door and they went in. Keller kept talking to him, saying how he'd figured out a way he could stay in Roseburg and not worry about the man in White Plains. "This machine you've got," he said, pointing to one of the copiers. "How does this work?"

"How does it work?"

"What does that switch do?"

"This one?"

Engleman leaned forward, and Keller got the loop of wire out of his pocket and dropped it around the other man's neck. The garrote was fast, silent, deadly. Keller made sure Engleman's body was where it couldn't be seen from the street, made sure to wipe his prints off any surfaces he might have touched. He turned off the lights, closed the door behind him.

He had already checked out of the Douglas Inn, and now he drove straight to Portland, with the Ford's cruise control set just below the speed limit. He drove half an hour in silence, then turned on the radio and tried to find a station he could stand. Nothing pleased him and he gave up and switched it off.

Somewhere north of Eugene he said, "Jesus, Ed, what else was I going to do?"

He drove straight through to Portland and got a room at the ExecuLodge near the airport. In the morning he turned in the Hertz car and dawdled over coffee until his flight was called.

He called White Plains as soon as he was on the ground at JFK. "It's all taken care of," he said. "I'll come by sometime tomorrow. Right now I just want to get home, get some sleep."

The following afternoon in White Plains Dot asked him how he'd liked Roseburg.

"Really nice," he said. "Pretty town, nice people. I wanted to stay there."

"Oh, Keller," she said. "What did you do, look at houses?"

"Not exactly."

"Every place you go," she said, "you want to live there."

"It's nice," he insisted. "And living's cheap compared to here. A person could have a decent life."

"For a week," she said. "Then you'd go nuts."

"You really think so?"

"Come *on*," she said. "Roseburg, Oregon? Come on."

"I guess you're right," he said. "I guess a week's about as much as I could handle."

A few days later he was going through his pockets before taking some clothes to the cleaners. He found the Roseburg street map and went over it, remembering where everything was. Quik-Print, the Douglas Inn, the house on Cowslip. The Mexican café, the other places he'd eaten. The gun shop. The houses he'd looked at.

He folded the map and put it in his dresser drawer. A month later he came across it, and for a moment he couldn't place it. Then he laughed. And tore it in half, and in half again, and put it in the trash.

GOOD FOR
THE SOUL

In the morning, Warren Cuttleton left his furnished room on West Eighty-third Street and walked over to Broadway. It was a clear day, cool, but not cold, bright but not dazzling. At the corner, Mr. Cuttleton bought a copy of the *Daily Mirror* from the blind newsdealer who sold him a paper every morning and who, contrary to established stereotype, recognized him by neither voice nor step. He took his paper to the cafeteria where he always ate breakfast, kept it tucked tidily under his arm while he bought a sweet roll and a cup of coffee, and sat down alone at a small table to eat the roll, drink the coffee, and read the *Daily Mirror* cover to cover.

When he reached page three, he stopped eating the roll and set the coffee aside. He read a story about a woman who had been killed the evening before in Central Park. The woman, named Margaret Waldek, had worked as a nurse's aide at Flower Fifth Avenue Hospital. At midnight her shift had ended. On her way home through the park, someone had thrown her down, assaulted her, and stabbed her far too many times in the chest and abdomen. There was a long and rather colorful story to this effect, coupled with a moderately grisly picture of the late Margaret Waldek. Warren Cuttleton read the story and looked at the grisly picture.

And remembered.

The memory rushed upon him with the speed of a rumor. A walk through the park. The night air. A knife—long, cold—in one hand. The knife's handle moist with his own urgent perspiration. The waiting, alone in the cold. Footsteps, then coming closer, and his own movement off the path and into the shadows, and the woman in view. And the awful fury of his attack, the fear and pain in the woman's face, her screams in his ears. And the knife, going up and coming down, rising and descending. The screams peaking and abruptly ending. The blood.

He was dizzy. He looked at his hand, expecting to see a knife glistening there. He was holding two thirds of a sweet roll. His fingers opened. The roll dropped a few inches to the tabletop. He thought that he was going to be sick, but this did not happen.

"Oh, God," he said, very softly. No one seemed to hear him. He said it again, somewhat louder, and lit a cigarette with trembling hands. He tried to blow out the match and kept missing it. He dropped the match to the floor and stepped on it and took a very large breath.

He had killed a woman. No one he knew, no one he had ever seen before. He was a word in headlines—fiend, attacker, killer. He was a murderer, and the police would find him and make him confess, and there would be a trial and a conviction and an appeal and a denial and a cell and a long walk and an electrical jolt and then, mercifully, nothing at all.

He closed his eyes. His hands curled up into fists, and he pressed his fists against his temples and took furious breaths. Why had he done it? What was wrong with him? Why, why, why had he killed?

Why would *anyone* kill?

He sat at his table until he had smoked three cigarettes, lighting each new one from the butt of the one preceding it. When the last cigarette was quite finished he got up from the table and went to the phone booth. He dropped a dime and dialed a number and waited until someone answered the phone.

"Cuttleton," he said. "I won't be in today. Not feeling well."

One of the office girls had taken the call. She said that it was too bad and she hoped Mr. Cuttleton would be feeling better. He thanked her and rang off.

Not feeling well! He had never called in sick in the twenty-three years he had worked at the Bardell Company, except for two times when he had been running a fever. They would believe him, of course. He did not lie and did not cheat and his employers knew this. But it bothered him to lie to them.

But then it was no lie, he thought. He was not feeling well, not feeling well at all.

On the way back to his room he bought the *Daily News* and the *Herald Tribune* and the *Times*. The *News* gave him no trouble, as it too had the story of the Waldek murder on page three, and ran a similar picture and a similar text. It was harder to find the stories in the *Times* and the *Herald Tribune*; both of those papers buried the murder story deep in the second section, as if it were trivial. He could not understand that.

That evening he bought the *Journal American* and the *World Telegram* and the *Post*. The *Post* ran an interview with Margaret Waldek's half sister, a very sad interview indeed. Warren Cuttleton wept as he read it, shedding tears in equal measure for Margaret Waldek and for himself.

At seven o'clock, he told himself that he was surely doomed. He had killed and he would be killed in return.

At nine o'clock, he thought that he might get away with it. He gathered from the newspaper stories that the police had no substantial clues. Fingerprints were not mentioned, but he knew for a fact that his own fingerprints were not on file anywhere. He had never been fingerprinted. So, unless someone had seen him, the police would have no way to connect him with the murder. And he could not remember having been seen by anyone.

He went to bed at midnight. He slept fitfully, reliving every unpleasant detail of the night before—the footsteps, the attack, the knife, the blood, his flight from the park. He awoke for the last time at seven o'clock, woke at the peak of a nightmare with sweat streaming from every pore.

Surely there was no escape if he dreamed those dreams night after endless night. He was no psychopath; right and wrong had a great deal of personal meaning to him. Redemption in the embrace of an electrified chair seemed the least horrible of all possible punishments. He no longer wanted to get away with the murder. He wanted to get away *from* it.

He went outside and bought a paper. There had been no developments in the case. He read an interview in the *Mirror* with Margaret Waldek's little niece, and it made him cry.

He had never been to the police station before. It stood only a few blocks from his rooming house but he had never passed it, and he had to look up its address in the telephone directory. When he got there he stumbled around aimlessly looking for someone in a little authority. He finally located the desk sergeant and explained that he wanted to see someone about the Waldek killing.

"Waldek," the desk sergeant said.

"The woman in the park."

"Oh. Information?"

"Yes," Mr. Cuttleton said.

He waited on a wooden bench while the desk sergeant called upstairs to find out who had the Waldek thing. Then the desk sergeant told him to go upstairs where he would see a Sergeant Rooker. He did this.

Rooker was a young man with a thoughtful face. He said yes, he was in charge of the Waldek killing, and just to start things off, could he have name and address and some other details?

Warren Cuttleton gave him all the details he wanted. Rooker wrote them all down with a ballpoint pen on a sheet of yellow foolscap. Then he looked up thoughtfully.

"Well, that's out of the way," he said. "Now what have you got for us?"

"Myself," Mr. Cuttleton said. And when Sergeant Rooker frowned curiously he explained, "I did it. I killed that woman, that Margaret Waldek, I did it."

Sergeant Rooker and another policeman took him into a private room and asked him a great many questions. He explained everything exactly as he remembered it, from beginning to end. He told them the whole story, trying his best to avoid breaking down at the more horrible parts. He only broke down twice. He did not cry at those times, but his chest filled and his throat closed and he found it temporarily impossible to go on.

Questions—

"Where did you get the knife?"

"A store. A five-and-ten."

"Where?"

"On Columbus Avenue."

"Remember the store?"

He remembered the counter, a salesman, remembered paying for the knife and carrying it away. He did not remember which store it had been.

"Why did you do it?"

"I don't know."

"Why the Waldek woman?"

"She just . . . came along."

"Why did you attack her?"

"I wanted to. Something . . . came over me. Some need, I didn't understand it then, I don't understand it now. Compulsion. I just had to do it!"

"Why kill her?"

"It happened that way. I killed her, the knife, up, down. That was why I bought the knife. To kill her."

"You planned it?"

"Just . . . hazily."

"Where's the knife?"

"Gone. Away. Down a sewer."

"What sewer?"

"I don't remember. Somewhere."

"You got blood on your clothes. You must have, she bled like a flood. Your clothes at home?"

"I got rid of them."

"Where? Down a sewer?"

"Look, Ray, you don't third-degree a guy when he's trying to confess something."

"I'm sorry. Cuttleton, are the clothes around your building?"

He had vague memories, something about burning. "An incinerator," he said.

"The incinerator in your building?"

"No. Some other building, there isn't any incinerator where I live. I went home and changed, I remember it, and I bundled up the clothes and ran into another building and put everything in an incinerator and ran back to my room. I washed. There was blood under my fingernails, I remember it."

They had him take off his shirt. They looked at his arms and his chest and his face and his neck.

"No scratches," Sergeant Rooker said. "Not a mark, and she had stuff under her nails, from scratching."

"Ray, she could have scratched herself."

"Mmmm. Or he mends quick. Come on, Cuttleton."

They went to a room, fingerprinted him, took his picture, and booked him on suspicion of murder. Sergeant Rooker told him that he could call a lawyer if he wanted one. He did not know any lawyers. There had been a lawyer who had notarized a paper for him once, long ago, but he did not remember the man's name.

They took him to a cell. He went inside, and they closed the door and locked it. He sat down on a stool and smoked a cigarette. His hands did not shake now for the first time in almost twenty-seven hours.

Four hours later Sergeant Rooker and the other policeman came into his cell. Rooker said, "You didn't kill that woman, Mr. Cuttleton. Now why did you tell us you did?"

He stared at them.

"First, you had an alibi and you didn't mention it. You went to a double feature at Loew's Eighty-third, the cashier recognized you from a picture and remembered you bought a ticket at nine-thirty. An usher also recognized you and remembers you tripped on your way to the men's room and he had to give you a hand, and that was after midnight. You went straight to your room, one of the women lives downstairs remembers that. The fellow down the hall from you swears you were in your room by one and never left it and the lights were out fifteen minutes after you got here. Now why in the name of heaven did you tell us you killed that woman?"

This was incredible. He did not remember any movies. He did not remember buying a ticket, or tripping on the way to the men's room. Nothing like that. He remembered only the lurking and the footsteps and the attack, the knife and the screams, the knife down a sewer and the clothes in some incinerator and washing away the blood.

"More. We got what must be the killer. A man named Alex

Kanster, convicted on two counts of attempted assault. We picked him up on a routine check and found a bloody knife under his pillow and his face torn and scratched, and I'll give three-to-one he's confessed by now, and he killed the Waldek woman and you didn't, so why the confession? Why give us trouble? Why lie?"

"I don't lie," Mr. Cuttleton said.

Rooker opened his mouth and closed it. The other policeman said, "Ray, I've got an idea. Get someone who knows how to administer a polygraph thing."

He was very confused. They led him to another room and strapped him to an odd machine with a graph, and they asked him questions. What was his name? How old was he? Where did he work? Did he kill the Waldek woman? How much was four and four? Where did he buy the knife? What was his middle name? Where did he put his clothes?

"Nothing," the other policeman said. "No reaction. See? He *believes* it, Ray."

"Maybe he just doesn't react to this. It doesn't work on everybody."

"So ask him to lie."

"Mr. Cuttleton," Sergeant Rooker said, "I'm going to ask you how much four and three is. I want you to answer six. Just answer six."

"But it's seven."

"Say six anyway, Mr. Cuttleton."

"Oh."

"How much is four and three?"

"Six."

He reacted, and heavily. "What it is," the other cop explained, "is he believes this, Ray. He didn't mean to make trouble, he believes it, true or not. You know what an imagination does, how witnesses swear to lies because they remember things wrong. He read the story and he believed it all from the start."

They talked to him for a long time, Rooker and the other policeman, explaining every last bit of it. They told him he felt guilty, he had some repression deep down in his sad soul, and this made him believe that he had killed Mrs. Waldek when, in fact, he had not. For a long time he thought that they were crazy, but in time they proved to him that it was quite impossible for him to have done what he said he had done. It could not have happened that way, and they proved it, and there was no argument he could advance to tear down the proof they offered him. He had to believe it.

Well!

He believed them, he knew they were right and he—his memory—was wrong. This did not change the fact that he remembered the killing. Every detail was still quite clear in his mind. This meant, obviously, that he was insane.

"Right about now," Sergeant Rooker said, perceptively, "you probably think you're crazy. Don't worry about it, Mr. Cuttleton. This confession urge isn't as uncommon as you might think. Every publicized killing brings us a dozen confessions, with some of them dead sure they really did it. You have the urge to kill locked up inside somewhere, you feel guilty about it, so you confess to what you maybe wanted to do deep in your mind but would never really do. We get this all the time. Not many of them are as sure of it as you, as clear on everything. The lie detector is what got to me. But don't worry about being crazy, it's nothing you can't control. Just don't sweat it."

"Psychological," the other policeman said.

"You'll probably have this bit again," Rooker went on. "Don't let it get to you. Just ride it out and remember you couldn't possibly kill anybody and you'll get through all right. But no more confessions. Okay?"

For a time he felt like a stupid child. Then he felt relieved, tremendously relieved. There would be no electrified chair. There would be no perpetual burden of guilt.

That night he slept. No dreams.

That was March. Four months later, in July, it happened again. He awoke, he went downstairs, he walked to the corner, he bought the *Daily Mirror*, he sat down at a table with his sweet roll and his coffee, he opened the paper to page three, and he read about a schoolgirl, fourteen, who had walked home the night before in Astoria and who had not reached her home because some man had dragged her into an alley and had slashed her throat open with a straight razor. There was a grisly picture of the girl's body, her throat cut from ear to ear.

Memory, like a stroke of white lightning across a flat black sky. Memory, illuminating all.

He remembered the razor in his hand, the girl struggling in his grasp. He remembered the soft feel of her frightened young flesh, the moans she made, the incredible supply of blood that poured forth from her wounded throat.

The memory was so real that it was several moments before he remembered that his rush of awful memory was not a new phenomenon. He recalled that other memory, in March, and remembered it again. That had been false. This, obviously, was false as well.

But it could not be false. He *remembered* it. Every detail, so clear, so crystal clear.

He fought with himself, telling himself that Sergeant Rooker had told him to expect a repeat performance of this false-confession impulse. But logic can have little effect upon the certain mind. If one holds a rose in one's hand, and feels that rose, and smells the sweetness of it, and is hurt by the prick of its thorns, all the rational thought in creation will not serve to sway one's conviction that this rose is a reality. And a rose in memory is as unshakable as a rose in hand.

Warren Cuttleton went to work that day. It did him no good, and did his employers no good either, since he could not begin to concentrate on the papers on his desk. He could only think of the foul killing of Sandra Gitler. He knew that he could not possibly have killed the girl. He knew, too, that he had done so.

An office girl asked him if he was feeling well, he looked all concerned and unhappy and everything. A partner in the firm asked him if he had had a physical checkup recently. At five o'clock he went home. He had to fight with himself to stay away from the police station, but he stayed away.

The dreams were very vivid. He awoke again and again. Once he cried out. In the morning, when he gave up the attempt to sleep, his sheets were wet with his perspiration. It had soaked through to the mattress. He took a long shivering shower and dressed. He went downstairs, and he walked to the police station.

Last time, he had confessed. They had proved him innocent. It seemed impossible that they could have been wrong, just as it seemed impossible that he could have killed Sandra

Gitler, but perhaps Sergeant Rooker could lay the girl's ghost for him. The confession, the proof of his own real innocence—then he could sleep at night once again.

He did not stop to talk to the desk sergeant. He went directly upstairs and found Rooker, who blinked at him.

"Warren Cuttleton," Sergeant Rooker said. "A confession?"

"I tried not to come. Yesterday, I remembered killing the girl in Queens. I know I did it, and I know I couldn't have done it, but—"

"You're sure you did it."

"Yes."

Sergeant Rooker understood. He led Cuttleton to a room, not a cell, and told him to stay there for a moment. He came back a few moments later.

"I called Queens Homicide," he said. "Found out a few things about the murder, some things that didn't get into the paper. Do you remember carving something into the girl's belly?"

He remembered. The razor, slicing through her bare flesh, carving something.

"What did you carve, Mr. Cuttleton?"

"I . . . I can't remember, exactly."

"You carved *I love you*. Do you remember?"

Yes, he remembered. Carving *I love you*, carving those three words into that tender flesh, proving that his horrid act was an act of love as well as an act of destruction. Oh, he remembered. It was clear in his mind, like a well-washed window.

"Mr. Cuttleton. Mr. Cuttleton, that wasn't what was carved in the girl. Mr. Cuttleton, the words were unprintable, the first word was unprintable, the second word was *you*. Not *I love you*, something else. That was why they kept it out of the papers, that and to keep off false confessions which is, believe me, a good idea. Your memory picked up on that the minute I said it, like the power of suggestion. It didn't happen, just like you never touched that girl, but something got triggered in your head so you snapped it up and remembered it like you remembered everything you read in the paper, the same thing."

For several moments he sat looking at his fingernails

while Sergeant Rooker sat looking at him. Then he said, slowly, "I knew all along I couldn't have done it. But that didn't help."

"I see."

"I had to prove it. You can't remember something, every last bit of it, and then just tell yourself that you're crazy. That it simply did not happen. I couldn't sleep."

"Well."

"I had dreams. Reliving the whole thing in my dreams, like last time. I knew I shouldn't come here, that it's wasting your time. There's knowing and knowing, Sergeant."

"And you had to have it proved to you."

He nodded miserably. Sergeant Rooker told him it was nothing to sweat about, that it took some police time but that the police really had more time than some people thought, though they had less time than some other people thought, and that Mr. Cuttleton could come to him anytime he had something to confess.

"Straight to me," Sergeant Rooker said. "That makes it easier, because I understand you, what you go through, and some of the other boys who aren't familiar might not understand."

He thanked Sergeant Rooker and shook hands with him. He walked out of the station, striding along like an ancient mariner who had just had an albatross removed from his shoulders. He slept that night, dreamlessly.

It happened again in August. A woman strangled to death in her apartment on West Twenty-seventh Street, strangled with a piece of electrical wire. He remembered buying an extension cord the day before for just that purpose.

This time he went to Rooker immediately. It was no problem at all. The police had caught the killer just minutes after the late editions of the morning papers had been locked up and printed. The janitor did it, the janitor of the woman's building. They caught him and he confessed.

On a clear afternoon that followed on the heels of a rainy morning in late September, Warren Cuttleton came home from the Bardell office and stopped at a Chinese laundry to pick up his shirts. He carried his shirts around the corner to a drugstore on Amsterdam Avenue and bought a tin of aspirin tablets. On the way back to his rooming house he passed—or started to pass—a small hardware store.

Something happened.

He walked into the store in robotish fashion, as though some alien had taken over control of his body, borrowing it for the time being. He waited patiently while the clerk finished selling a can of putty to a flat-nosed man. Then he bought an ice pick.

He went back to his room. He unpacked his shirts—six of them, white, stiffly starched, each with the same conservative collar, each bought at the same small haberdashery—and he packed them away in his dresser. He took two of the aspirin tablets and put the tin in the top drawer of the dresser. He held the ice pick between his hands and rubbed his hands over it, feeling the smoothness of the wooden handle and stroking the cool steel of the blade. He touched the tip of his thumb with the point of the blade and felt how deliciously sharp it was.

He put the ice pick in his pocket. He sat down and smoked a cigarette, slowly, and then he went downstairs and walked over to Broadway. At Eighty-sixth Street he went downstairs into the IRT station, dropped a token, passed through the turnstile. He took a train uptown to Washington Heights. He left the train, walked to a small park. He stood in the park for fifteen minutes, waiting.

He left the park. The air was chillier now and the sky was quite dark. He went to a restaurant, a small diner on Dyckman Avenue. He ordered the chopped sirloin, very well done, with french-fried potatoes and a cup of coffee. He enjoyed his meal very much.

In the men's room at the diner he took the ice pick from his pocket and caressed it once again. So very sharp, so very strong. He smiled at the ice pick and kissed the tip of it with his lips parted so as to avoid pricking himself. So very sharp, so very cool.

He paid his check and tipped the counterman and left the diner. Night now, cold enough to freeze the edge of thought. He walked through lonely streets. He found an alleyway. He waited, silent and still.

Time.

His eyes stayed on the mouth of the alley. People passed—

boys, girls, men, women. He did not move from his position. He was waiting. In time the right person would come. In time the streets would be clear except for that one person, and the time would be right, and it would happen. He would act. He would act fast.

He heard high heels tapping in staccato rhythm, approaching him. He heard nothing else, no cars, no alien feet. Slowly, cautiously, he made his way toward the mouth of the alley. His eyes found the source of the tapping. A woman, a young woman, a pretty young woman with a curving body and a mass of jet-black hair and a raw red mouth. A pretty woman, his woman, the right woman, this one, yes, now!

She moved within reach, her high-heeled shoes never altering the rhythm of their tapping. He moved in liquid perfection. One arm reached out, and a hand fastened upon her face and covered her raw red mouth. The other arm snaked around her waist and tugged at her. She was off-balance, she stumbled after him, she disappeared with him into the mouth of the alley.

She might have screamed, but he banged her head on the cement floor of the alley and her eyes went glassy. She started to scream later, but he got a hand over her mouth and cut off the scream. She did not manage to bite him. He was careful.

Then, while she struggled, he drove the point of the ice pick precisely into her heart.

He left her there, dead and turning cold. He dropped the ice pick into a sewer. He found the subway arcade and rode the IRT back to where he had come from, went to his room, washed hands and face, got into bed and slept. He slept very well and did not dream, not at all.

When he woke up in the morning at his usual time he felt as he always felt, cool and fresh and ready for the day's work. He showered and he dressed and he went downstairs, and he bought a copy of the *Daily Mirror* from the blind newsdealer.

He read the item. A young exotic dancer named Mona More had been attacked in Washington Heights and had been stabbed to death with an ice pick.

He remembered. In an instant it all came back, the girl's body, the ice pick, murder—

He gritted his teeth together until they ached. The realism

of it all! He wondered if a psychiatrist could do anything about it. But psychiatrists were so painfully expensive, and he had his own psychiatrist, his personal and no-charge psychiatrist, his Sergeant Rooker.

But he remembered it! Everything, buying the ice pick, throwing the girl down, stabbing her—

He took a very deep breath. It was time to be methodical about this, he realized. He went to the telephone and called his office. "Cuttleton here," he said. "I'll be late today, an hour or so. A doctor's appointment. I'll be in as soon as I can."

"It's nothing serious?"

"Oh, no," he said. "Nothing serious." And, really, he wasn't lying. After all, Sergeant Rooker did function as his personal psychiatrist, and a psychiatrist was a doctor. And he did have an appointment, a standing appointment, for Sergeant Rooker had told him to come in whenever something like this happened. And it was nothing serious, that too was true, because he knew that he was really very innocent no matter how sure his memory made him of his guilt.

Rooker almost smiled at him. "Well, look who's here," he said. "I should have figured, Mr. Cuttleton. It's your kind of crime, isn't it? A woman assaulted and killed, that's your trademark, right?"

Warren Cuttleton could not quite smile. "I . . . the More girl. Mona More."

"Don't those strippers have wild names? Mona More. As in Mon Amour. That's French."

"It is?"

Sergeant Rooker nodded. "And you did it," he said. "That's the story?"

"I know I couldn't have, but—"

"You ought to quit reading the papers," Sergeant Rooker said. "Come on, let's get it out of your system."

They went to the room. Mr. Cuttleton sat in a straight-backed chair. Sergeant Rooker closed the door and stood at the desk. He said, "You killed the woman, didn't you? Where did you get the ice pick?"

"A hardware store."

"Any special one?"

"It was on Amsterdam Avenue."

"Why an ice pick?"

"It excited me, the handle was smooth and strong, and the blade was so sharp."

"Where's the ice pick now?"

"I threw it in a sewer."

"Well, that's no switch. There must have been a lot of blood, stabbing her with an ice pick. Loads of blood?"

"Yes."

"Your clothes get soaked with it?"

"Yes." He remembered how the blood had been all over his clothes, how he had had to hurry home and hope no one would see him.

"And the clothes?"

"In the incinerator."

"Not in your building, though."

"No. No, I changed in my building and ran to some other building, I don't remember where, and threw the clothes down the incinerator."

Sergeant Rooker slapped his hand down on the desk. "This is getting too easy," he said. "Or I'm getting too good at it. The stripper was stabbed in the heart with an ice pick. A tiny wound and it caused death just about instantly. Not a drop of blood. Dead bodies don't bleed, and wounds like that don't let go with much blood anyhow, so your story falls apart like wet tissue. Feel better?"

Warren Cuttleton nodded slowly. "But it seemed so horribly real," he said.

"It always does." Sergeant Rooker shook his head. "You poor son of a gun," he said. "I wonder how long this is going to keep up." He grinned wryly. "Much more of this and one of us is going to snap."

THE EHRENGRAF ALTERNATIVE

"**W**hat's most unfortunate," Ehrengraf said, "is that there seems to be a witness."

Evelyn Throop nodded in fervent agreement. "Mrs. Keppner," she said.

"Howard Bierstadt's housekeeper."

"She was devoted to him. She'd been with him for years."

"And she claims she saw you shoot him three times in the chest."

"I know," Evelyn Throop said. "I can't imagine why she would say something like that. It's completely untrue."

A thin smile turned up the corners of Martin Ehrengraf's mouth. Already he felt himself warming to his client, exhilarated by the prospect of acting in her defense. It was the little lawyer's great good fortune always to find himself representing innocent clients, but few of those clients were as single-minded as Miss Throop in proclaiming their innocence.

The woman sat on the edge of her iron cot with her shapely legs crossed at the ankle. She seemed so utterly in possession of herself that she might have been almost anywhere but in a jail cell, charged with the murder of her lover. Her age, according to the papers, was forty-six. Ehrengraf would have guessed her to be perhaps a dozen years younger.

She was not rich—Ehrengraf, like most lawyers, did have a special fondness for wealthy clients—but she had excellent breeding. It was evident not only in her exquisite facial bones but in her positively ducal self-assurance.

"I'm sure we'll uncover the explanation of Mrs. Keppner's calumny," he said gently. "For now, why don't we go over what actually happened."

"Certainly. I was at my home that evening when Howard called. He was in a mood and wanted to see me. I drove over to his house. He made drinks for both of us and paced around a great deal. He was extremely agitated."

"Over what?"

"Leona wanted him to marry her. Leona Weybright."

"The cookbook writer?"

"Yes. Howard was not the sort of man to get married, or even to limit himself to a single relationship. He believed in a double standard and was quite open about it. He expected his women to be faithful while reserving the option of infidelity to himself. If one was going to be involved with Howard Bierstadt, one had to accept this."

"As you accepted it."

"As I accepted it," Evelyn Throop agreed. "Leona evidently pretended to accept it but could not, and Howard didn't know what to do about her. He wanted to break up with her but was afraid of the possible consequences. He thought she might turn suicidal and he didn't want her death on his conscience."

"And he discussed all of this with you."

"Oh, yes. He often confided in me about his relationship with Leona." Evelyn Throop permitted herself a smile. "I played a very important role in his life, Mr. Ehrengraf. I suppose he would have married me if there'd been any reason to do so. I was his true confidante. Leona was just one of a long string of mistresses."

Ehrengraf nodded. "According to the prosecution," he said carefully, "you were pressuring him to marry you."

"That's quite untrue."

"No doubt." He smiled. "Continue."

The woman sighed. "There's not much more to say. He went into the other room to freshen our drinks. There was the report of a gunshot."

"I believe there were three shots."

"Perhaps there were. I can only remember the volume of the noise. It was so startling. I rushed in immediately and saw him on the floor, the gun by his outstretched hand. I guess I bent over and picked up the gun. I don't remember doing so, but I must have done because the next thing I knew I was standing there holding the gun." Evelyn Throop closed her eyes, evidently overwhelmed by the memory. "Then Mrs. Keppner was there—I believe she screamed, and then she went off to call the police. I just stood there for a while and then I guess I sat down in a chair and waited for the police to come and tell me what to do."

"And they brought you here and put you in a cell."

"Yes. I was quite astonished. I couldn't imagine why they would do such a thing, and then it developed that Mrs. Keppner had sworn she saw me shoot Howard."

Ehrengraf was respectfully silent for a moment. Then he said, "It seems they found some corroboration for Mrs. Keppner's story."

"What do you mean?"

"The gun," Ehrengraf said. "A .32-caliber revolver. I believe it was registered to you, was it not?"

"It was my gun."

"How did Mr. Bierstadt happen to have it?"

"I brought it to him."

"At his request?"

"Yes. When we spoke on the telephone, he specifically asked me to bring the gun. He said something about wanting to protect himself from burglars. I never thought he would shoot himself."

"But he did."

"He must have done. He was upset about Leona. Perhaps he felt guilty, or that there was no way to avoid hurting her."

"Wasn't there a paraffin test?" Ehrengraf mused. "As I recall, there were no nitrite particles found in Mr. Bierstadt's hand, which would seem to indicate he had not fired a gun recently."

"I don't really understand those tests," Evelyn Throop said. "But I'm told they're not absolutely conclusive."

"And the police gave you a test as well," Ehrengraf went on. "Didn't they?"

"Yes."

"And found nitrite particles in your right hand."

"Of course," Evelyn Throop said. "I'd fired the gun that evening before I took it along to Howard's house. I hadn't used it in the longest time, since I first practiced with it at a pistol range, so I cleaned it and to make sure it was in good operating condition I test-fired it before I went to Howard's."

"At a pistol range?"

"That wouldn't have been convenient. I just stopped at a deserted spot along a country road and fired a few shots."

"I see."

"I told the police all of this, of course."

"Of course. Before they gave you the paraffin test?"

"After the test, as it happens. The incident had quite slipped my mind in the excitement of the moment, but they gave me the test and said it was evident I'd fired a gun, and at that point I recalled having stopped the car and firing off a couple of rounds before continuing on to Howard's."

"Where you gave Mr. Bierstadt the gun."

"Yes."

"Whereupon he in due course took it off into another room and fired three shots into his heart," Ehrengraf murmured. "Your Mr. Bierstadt would look to be one of the most determined suicides in human memory."

"You don't believe me."

"But I do believe you," he said. "Which is to say that I believe you did not shoot Mr. Bierstadt. Whether or not he did in fact die by his own hand is not, of course, something to which either you or I can testify."

"How else could he have died?" The woman's gaze narrowed. "Unless he really was genuinely afraid of burglars, and unless he did surprise one in the other room. But wouldn't I have heard sounds of a struggle? Of course, I was in another room a fair distance away, and there was music playing, and I did have things on my mind."

"I'm sure you did."

"And perhaps Mrs. Keppner saw the burglar shoot Howard, and then she fainted or something. I suppose that's possible, isn't it?"

"Eminently possible," Ehrengraf assured her.

"She might have come to when I had already entered the room and picked up the gun, and the whole incident could

ave been compressed in her mind. She wouldn't remember
having fainted and so she might now actually believe she saw
me kill Howard, while all along she saw something entirely
different." Evelyn Throop had been looking off into the middle
distance as she formulated her theory and now she focused
her eyes upon the diminutive attorney. "It could have happened that way," she said, "couldn't it?"

"It could have happened precisely that way," Ehrengraf
said. "It could have happened in any of innumerable ways. Ah,
Miss Throop"—and now the lawyer rubbed his small hands
together—"that's the whole beauty of it. There are any number
of alternatives to the prosecution's argument, but of course
they don't see them. Give the police a supposedly ironclad
case and they look no further. It is not their task to examine
alternatives. But it is our task, Miss Throop, to find not merely
an alternative but the correct alternative, the ideal alternative.
And in just that fashion we will make a free woman of you."

"You seem very confident, Mr. Ehrengraf."

"I am."

"And prepared to believe in my innocence."

"Unequivocally. Without question."

"I find that refreshing," Evelyn Throop said. "I even believe you'll get me acquitted."

"I fully expect to," Ehrengraf said. "Now let me see, is
there anything else we have to discuss at present?"

"Yes."

"And what would that be?"

"Your fee," said Evelyn Throop.

Back in his office, seated behind a desk which he kept
as untidy as he kept his own person immaculate, Martin H.
Ehrengraf sat back and contemplated the many extraordinary
qualities of his latest client. In his considerable experience,
while clients were not invariably opposed to a discussion of
his fees, they were certainly loath to raise the matter. But
Evelyn Throop, possessor of dove-gray eyes and remarkable
facial bones, had proved an exception.

"My fees are high," Ehrengraf had told her, "but they are
payable only in the event that my clients are acquitted. If you
don't emerge from this ordeal scot-free, you owe me nothing.
Even my expenses will be at my expense."

"And if I get off?"

"Then you will owe me one hundred thousand dollars. And I must emphasize, Miss Throop, that the fee will be due me however you win your freedom. It is not inconceivable that neither of us will ever see the inside of a courtroom, that your release when it comes will appear not to have been the result of my efforts at all. I will, nevertheless, expect to be paid in full."

The gray eyes looked searchingly into the lawyer's own. "Yes," she said after a moment. "Yes, of course. Well, that seems fair. If I'm released I won't really care how the end was accomplished, will I?"

Ehrengraf said nothing. Clients often whistled a different tune at a later date, but one could burn that bridge when one came to it.

"One hundred thousand dollars seems reasonable," the woman continued. "I suppose any sum would seem reasonable when one's life and liberty hangs in the balance. Of course, you must know I have no money of my own."

"Perhaps your family—"

She shook her head. "I can trace my ancestors back to William the Conqueror," she said, "and there were Throops who made their fortune in whaling and the China trade, but I'm afraid the money's run out over the generations. However, I shouldn't have any problem paying your fee."

"Oh?"

"I'm Howard's chief beneficiary," she explained. "I've seen his will and it makes it unmistakably clear that I held first place in his affections. After a small cash bequest to Mrs. Keppner for her loyal years of service, and after leaving his art collection—which, I grant you, *is* substantial—to Leona, the remainder comes to me. There may be a couple of cash bequests to charities but nothing that amounts to much. So while I'll have to wait for the will to make its way through probate, I'm sure I can borrow on my expectations and pay you your fee within a matter of days of my release from jail, Mr. Ehrengraf."

"A day that should come in short order," Ehrengraf said.

"That's your department," Evelyn Throop said, and smiled serenely.

Ehrengraf smiled now, recalling her smile, and made a

little tent of his fingertips on the desktop. An exceptional woman, he told himself, and one on whose behalf it would be an honor to extend himself.

It was difficult, of course. Shot with the woman's own gun, and a witness to swear that she'd shot him. Difficult, certainly, but scarcely impossible.

The little lawyer leaned back, closed his eyes, and considered alternatives.

Some days later, Ehrengraf was seated at his desk reading the poems of William Ernest Henley, who had written so confidently of being the master of one's fate and the captain of one's soul. The telephone rang. Ehrengraf set his book down, located the instrument amid the desktop clutter, and answered it.

"Ehrengraf," said Ehrengraf.

He listened for a moment, spoke briefly in reply, and replaced the receiver. Smiling brightly, he started for the door, then paused to check his appearance in a mirror.

His tie was navy blue, with a demure below-the-knot pattern of embroidered rams' heads. For a moment Ehrengraf thought of stopping at his house and changing it for his Caedmon Society necktie, one he'd taken to wearing on triumphal occasions. He glanced at his watch and decided not to squander the time.

Later, recalling the decision, he wondered if it hinted at prescience.

"Quite remarkable," Evelyn Throop said. "Although I suppose I should have at least considered the possibility that Mrs. Keppner was lying. After all, I knew for a fact that she was testifying to something that didn't happen to be true. But for some reason I assumed it was an honest mistake on her part."

"One hesitates to believe the worst of people," Ehrengraf said.

"That's exactly it, of course. Besides, I rather took her for granted."

"So, it appears, did Mr. Bierstadt."

"And that was his mistake, wasn't it?" Evelyn Throop sighed. "Dora Keppner had been with him for years. Who would have guessed she'd been in love with him? Although I gather their relationship was physical at one point."

"There was a suggestion to that effect in the note she left."

"And I understand he wanted to get rid of her—to discharge her."

"The note seems to have indicated considerable mental disturbance," Ehrengraf said. "There were other jottings in a notebook found in Mrs. Keppner's attic bedroom. The impression seems to be that either she and her employer had been intimate in the past or that she entertained a fantasy to that effect. Her attitude in recent weeks apparently became less and less the sort proper to a servant, and either Mr. Bierstadt intended to let her go or she feared that he did and—well, we know what happened."

"She shot him." Evelyn Throop frowned. "She must have been in the room when he went to freshen the drinks. I thought he'd put the gun in his pocket but perhaps he still had it in his hand. He would have set it down when he made the drinks and she could have snatched it up and shot him and been out of the room before I got there." The gray eyes moved to encounter Ehrengraf's. "She didn't leave any fingerprints on the gun."

"She seems to have worn gloves. She was wearing a pair when she took her own life. A test indicated nitrite particles in the right glove."

"Couldn't they have gotten there when she committed suicide?"

"It's unlikely," Ehrengraf said. "She didn't shoot herself, you see. She took poison."

"How awful," Evelyn Throop said. "I hope it was quick."

"Mercifully so," said Ehrengraf. Clearly this woman was the captain of her soul, he thought, not to mention master of her fate. Or ought it to be mistress of her fate?

And yet, he realized abruptly, she was not entirely at ease.

"I've been released," she said, "as is of course quite obvious. All charges have been dropped. A man from the District Attorney's Office explained everything to me."

"That was considerate of him."

"He didn't seem altogether happy. I had the feeling he didn't really believe I was innocent after all."

"People believe what they wish to believe," Ehrengraf said smoothly. "The state's whole case collapses without their star witness, and after that witness has confessed to the crime herself and taken her life in the bargain, well, what does it matter what a stubborn district attorney chooses to believe?

"The important thing," Ehrengraf said, "is that you've been set free. You're innocent of all charges."

"Yes."

His eyes searched hers. "Is there a problem, Miss Throop?"

"There is, Mr. Ehrengraf."

"Dear lady," he began, "if you could just tell me—"

"The problem concerns your fee."

Ehrengraf's heart sank. Why did so many clients disappoint him in precisely this fashion? At the onset, with the sword of justice hanging over their throats, they agreed eagerly to whatever he proposed. Remove the sword and their agreeability went with it.

But that was not it at all.

"The most extraordinary thing," Evelyn Throop was saying. "I told you the terms of Howard's will. The paintings to Leona, a few thousand dollars here and there to various charities, a modest bequest to Mrs. Keppner—I suppose she won't get that now, will she?"

"Hardly."

"Well, that's something. Though it doesn't amount to much. At any rate, the balance is to go to me. The residue, after the bequests have been made and all debts settled and the state and federal taxes been paid, all that remains comes to me."

"So you explained."

"I intended to pay you out of what I received, Mr. Ehrengraf. Well, you're more than welcome to every cent I get. You can buy yourself a couple of hamburgers and a milkshake."

"I don't understand."

"It's the damned paintings," Evelyn Throop said. "They're worth an absolute fortune. I didn't realize how much he spent on them in the first place or how rapidly they appreciated in value. Nor did I have any idea how deeply mortgaged everything else he owned was. He had some investment reversals over the past few months and he'd taken out a second mortgage on his home and sold off stocks and other holdings. There's a little cash and a certain amount of equity in the real estate, but it'll take all of that to pay the estate taxes on the several million dollars' worth of paintings that go free and clear to that bitch Leona."

"You have to pay the taxes?"

"No question about it," she said bitterly. "The estate pays the taxes and settles the debts. Then all the paintings go straight to America's favorite cook. I hope she chokes on them." Evelyn Throop sighed heavily, collected herself. "Please forgive the dramatics, Mr. Ehrengraf."

"They're quite understandable, dear lady."

"I didn't intend to lose control of myself in that fashion. But I feel this deeply. I know Howard had no intention of disinheriting me and having that woman get everything. It was his unmistakable intention to leave me the greater portion, and a cruel trick of fate has thwarted him in that purpose. Mr. Ehrengraf, I owe you one hundred thousand dollars. That was our agreement and I consider myself bound by it."

Ehrengraf made no reply.

"But I don't know how I can possibly pay you. Oh, I'll pay what I can, as I can, but I'm a woman of modest means. I couldn't honestly expect to discharge the debt in full within my lifetime."

"My dear Miss Throop." Ehrengraf was moved, and his hand went involuntarily to the knot of his necktie. "My dear Miss Throop," he said again, "I beg you not to worry yourself. Do you know Henley, Miss Throop?"

"Henley?"

"The poet," said Ehrengraf, and quoted:

"In the fell clutch of circumstance,
I have not winced nor cried aloud:
Under the bludgeonings of chance
My head is bloody, but unbowed.

"William Ernest Henley, Miss Throop. Born 1849, died 1903. Bloody but unbowed, Miss Throop. 'I have not yet begun to fight.' That was John Paul Jones, Miss Throop, not a poet at all, a naval commander of the Revolutionary War, but the sentiment, dear lady, is worthy of a poet. 'Things are seldom what they seem, Skim milk masquerades as cream.' William Schwenk Gilbert, Miss Throop."

"I don't understand."

"Alternatives, Miss Throop. Alternatives!" The little lawyer was on his feet, pacing, gesticulating with precision. "I tell you only what I told you before. There are always alternatives available to us."

The gray eyes narrowed in thought. "I suppose you mean we could sue to overturn the will," she said. "That occurred to me, but I thought you only handled criminal cases."

"And so I do."

"I wonder if I could find another lawyer who would contest the will on a contingency basis. Perhaps you know someone—"

"Ah, Miss Throop," said Ehrengraf, sitting back down and placing his fingertips together. "Contest the will? Life is too short for litigation. An unlikely sentiment for an attorney to voice, I know, but nonetheless valid for it. Put lawsuits far from your mind. Let us first see if we cannot find"—a smile blossomed on his lips—"the Ehrengraf alternative."

Ehrengraf, a shine on his black wing-tip shoes and a white carnation on his lapel, strode briskly up the cinder path from his car to the center entrance of the Bierstadt house. In the crisp autumn air, the ivy-covered brick mansion in its spacious grounds took on an aura suggestive of a college campus. Ehrengraf noticed this and touched his tie, a distinctive specimen sporting a half-inch stripe of royal blue flanked by two narrower stripes, one of gold and the other of a particularly vivid green, all on a deep navy field. It was the tie he had very nearly worn to the meeting with his client some weeks earlier.

Now, he trusted, it would be rather more appropriate.

He eschewed the doorbell in favor of the heavy brass knocker, and in a matter of seconds the door swung inward. Evelyn Throop met him with a smile.

"Dear Mr. Ehrengraf," she said. "It's kind of you to meet me here. In poor Howard's home."

"Your home now," Ehrengraf murmured.

"Mine," she agreed. "Of course, there are legal processes to be gone through but I've been allowed to take possession. And I think I'm going to be able to keep the place. Now that the paintings are mine, I'll be able to sell some of them to pay the taxes and settle other claims against the estate. But let me show you around. This is the living room, of course, and here's the room where Howard and I were having drinks that night—"

"That fateful night," said Ehrengraf.

"And here's the room where Howard was killed. He was preparing drinks at the sideboard over there. He was lying here when I found him. And—"

Ehrengraf watched politely as his client pointed out where everything had taken place.

Then he followed her to another room where he accepted a small glass of Calvados.

For herself, Evelyn Throop poured a pony of Bénédictine.

"What shall we drink to?" she asked him.

To your spectacular eyes, he thought, but suggested instead that she propose a toast.

"To the Ehrengraf alternative," she said.

They drank.

"The Ehrengraf alternative," she said again. "I didn't know what to expect when we last saw each other. I thought you must have had some sort of complicated legal maneuver in mind, perhaps some way around the extortionate tax burden the government levies upon even the most modest inheritance. I had no idea the whole circumstances of poor Howard's murder would wind up turned utterly upside down."

"It was quite extraordinary," Ehrengraf allowed.

"I had been astonished enough to learn that Mrs. Keppner had murdered Howard and then taken her own life. Imagine how I felt to learn that she *wasn't* a murderer and that she *hadn't* committed suicide but that she'd actually *herself* been murdered."

"Life keeps surprising us," Ehrengraf said.

"And Leona Weybright winds up hoist on her own soufflé. The funny thing is that I was right in the first place. Howard *was* afraid of Leona, and evidently he had every reason to be. He'd apparently written her a note, insisting that they stop seeing each other."

Ehrengraf nodded. "The police found the note when they searched her quarters. Of course, she insisted she had never seen it before."

"What else could she say?" Evelyn Throop took another delicate sip of Bénédictine and Ehrengraf's heart thrilled at the sight of her pink tongue against the brim of the tiny glass.

"But I don't see how she can expect anyone to believe her. She murdered Howard, didn't she?"

"It would be hard to establish that beyond a reasonable doubt," Ehrengraf said. "The supposition exists. However, Miss Weybright does have an alibi, and it might not be easily shaken. And the only witness to the murder, Mrs. Keppner, is no longer available to give testimony."

"Because Leona killed her."

Ehrengraf nodded. "And that," he said, "very likely *can* be established."

"Because Mrs. Keppner's suicide note was a forgery."

"So it would appear," Ehrengraf said. "An artful forgery, but a forgery nevertheless. And the police seem to have found earlier drafts of that very note in Miss Weybright's desk. One was typed on the very machine at which she prepares her cookbook manuscripts. Others were written with a pen found in her desk, and the ink matched that on the note Mrs. Keppner purportedly left behind. Some of the drafts are in an imitation of the dead woman's handwriting, one in a sort of mongrel cross between the two women's penmanship, and one—evidently she was just trying to get the wording to her liking—was in Miss Weybright's own unmistakable hand. Circumstantial evidence, all of it, but highly suggestive."

"And there was other evidence, wasn't there?"

"Indeed there was. When Mrs. Keppner's body was found, there was a glass on a nearby table, a glass with a residue of water in it. An analysis of the water indicated the presence of a deadly poison, and an autopsy indicated that Mrs. Keppner's death had been caused by ingesting that very substance. The police, combining two and two, concluded not illogically that Mrs. Keppner had drunk a glass of water with the poison in it."

"But that's not how it happened?"

"Apparently not. Because the autopsy also indicated that the deceased had had a piece of cake not long before she died."

"And the cake was poisoned?"

"I should think it must have been," Ehrengraf said carefully, "because police investigators happened to find a cake with one wedge missing, wrapped securely in aluminum foil and tucked away in Miss Weybright's freezer. And that cake, when thawed and subjected to chemical analysis, proved to have been laced with the very poison which caused the death of poor Mrs. Keppner."

Miss Throop looked thoughtful. "How did Leona try to get out of that one?"

"She denied she ever saw the cake before and insisted she had never baked it."

"And?"

"And it seems to have been prepared precisely according to an original recipe in her present cookbook-in-progress."

"I suppose the book will never be published now."

"On the contrary, I believe the publisher has tripled the initial print order."

Ehrengraf sighed. "As I understand it, the presumption is that Miss Weybright was desperate at the prospect of losing the unfortunate Mr. Bierstadt. She wanted him, and if she couldn't have him alive she wanted him dead. But she didn't want to be punished for his murder, nor did she want to lose out on whatever she stood to gain from his will. By framing you for his murder, she thought she could increase the portion due her. Actually, the language of the will probably would not have facilitated this, but she evidently didn't realize it, any more than she realized that by receiving the paintings she would have the lion's share of the estate. In any event, she must have been obsessed with the idea of killing her lover and seeing her rival pay for the crime."

"How did Mrs. Keppner get into the act?"

"We may never know for certain. Was the housekeeper in on the plot all along? Did she actually fire the fatal shots and then turn into a false witness? Or did Miss Weybright commit the murder and leave Mrs. Keppner to testify against you? *Or* did Mrs. Keppner see what she oughtn't to have seen and then, after lying about you, try her hand at blackmailing Miss Weybright? Whatever the actual circumstances, Miss Weybright realized that Mrs. Keppner represented either an immediate or a potential hazard."

"And so Leona killed her."

"And had no trouble doing so." One might call it a piece of cake, Ehrengraf forbore to say. "At that point it became worth her while to let Mrs. Keppner play the role of murderess. Perhaps Miss Weybright became acquainted with the nature of the will and the estate itself and realized that she would already be in line to receive the greater portion of the estate, that it was not necessary to frame you. Furthermore, she saw that you were not about to plead guilty to a reduced charge or to attempt a Frankie-and-Johnny defense, as it were. By shunting the blame onto a dead Mrs. Keppner, she forestalled the possibility of a detailed investigation which might have pointed the finger of guilt in her own direction."

"My goodness," Evelyn Throop said. "It's quite extraordinary, isn't it?"

"It is," Ehrengraf agreed.

"And Leona will stand trial?"

"For Mrs. Keppner's murder."

"Will she be convicted?"

"One never knows what a jury will do," Ehrengraf said. "That's one reason I much prefer to spare my own clients the indignity of a trial."

He thought for a moment. "The district attorney might or might not have enough evidence to secure a conviction. Of course, more evidence might come to light between now and the trial. For that matter, evidence in Miss Weybright's favor might turn up."

"If she has the right lawyer."

"An attorney can often make a difference," Ehrengraf allowed. "But I'm afraid the man Miss Weybright has engaged won't do her much good. I suspect she'll wind up convicted of first-degree manslaughter or something of the sort. A few years in confined quarters and she'll have been rehabilitated. Perhaps she'll emerge from the experience with a slew of new recipes."

"Poor Leona," Evelyn Throop said, and shuddered delicately.

"Ah, well," Ehrengraf said. " 'Life is bitter,' as Henley reminds us in a poem. It goes on to say:

"Riches won but mock the old, unable years;
Fame's a pearl that hides beneath a sea of tears;
   Love must wither, or must live alone and weep.
In the sunshine, through the leaves, across the flowers,
While we slumber, death approaches through the
   hours . . .
                    Let me sleep.

"Riches, fame, love—and yet we seek them, do we not? That will be one hundred thousand dollars, Miss Throop, and— Ah, you have the check all drawn, have you?" He accepted it from her, folded it, and tucked it into a pocket.

"It is rare," he said, "to meet a woman so businesslike and yet so unequivocally feminine. And so attractive."

There was a small silence. Then: "Mr. Ehrengraf? Would you care to see the rest of the house?"

"I'd like that," said Ehrengraf, and smiled his little smile.

SOMEDAY I'LL PLANT MORE WALNUT TREES

There is a silence that is just stillness, just the absence of sound, and there is a deeper silence that is more than that. It is the antithesis, the aggressive opposite, of sound. It is to sound as antimatter is to matter, an auditory black hole that reaches out to swallow up and nullify the sounds of others.

My mother can give off such a silence. She is a master at it. That morning at breakfast she was thus silent, silent as she cooked eggs and made coffee, silent while I spooned baby oatmeal into Livia's little mouth, silent while Dan fed himself and while he smoked the day's first cigarette along with his coffee. He had his own silence, sitting there behind his newspaper, but all it did was insulate him. It couldn't reach out beyond that paper shield to snatch other sound out of the air.

He finished and put out his cigarette, folded his paper. He said it was supposed to be hot today, with rain forecast for late afternoon. He patted Livia's head, and with his forefinger drew aside a strand of hair that had fallen across her forehead.

I can see that now, his hand so gentle, and her beaming up at him, wide-eyed, gurgling.

Then he turned to me, and with the same finger and the same softness he reached to touch the side of my face. I did not draw away. His finger touched me, ever so lightly, and then he reached to draw me into the circle of his arms. I smelled his shirt, freshly washed and sun-dried, and under it the clean male scent of him.

We looked at each other, both of us silent, the whole room silent. And then Livia cooed and he smiled quickly and chucked me under the chin and left. I heard the screen door slam, and then the sounds of the car as he drove to town. When I could not hear it anymore I went over to the radio and switched it on. They were playing a Tammy Wynette song. "Stand by your man," Tammy urged, and my mother's silence swallowed up the words.

While the radio played unheard I changed Livia and put her in for her nap. I came back to the kitchen and cleared the table. My mother waved a hand at the air in front of her face.

"He smokes," I said.

"I didn't say anything," she said.

We did the dishes together. There is a dishwasher but we never use it for the breakfast dishes. She prefers to run it only once a day, after the evening meal. It could hold all the day's dishes, they would not amount to more than one load in the machine, but she does not like to let the breakfast and lunch dishes stand. It seems wasteful to me, of time and effort, and even of water, although our well furnishes more than we ever need. But it is her house, after all, and her dishwasher, and hers the decision as to when it is to be used.

Silently she washed the dishes, silently I wiped them. As I reached to stack plates in a cupboard I caught her looking at me. Her eyes were on my cheek, and I could feel her gaze right where I had felt Dan's finger. His touch had been light. Hers was firmer.

I said, "It's nothing."

"All right."

"Dammit, Mama!"

"I didn't say anything, Tildie."

I was named Matilda for my father's mother. I never knew her, she died before I was born, before my parents met. I was never called Matilda. It was the name on my college diploma, on my driver's license, on Livia's birth certificate, but no one ever used it.

"He can't help it," I said. "It's not his fault."

Her silence devoured my words. On the radio Tammy

Wynette sang a song about divorce, spelling out the word. Why were they playing all her records this morning? Was it her birthday? Or an anniversary of some failed romance?

"It's not," I said. I moved to her right so that I could talk to her good ear. "It's a pattern. His father was abusive to his mother. Dan grew up around that. His father drank and was free with his hands. Dan swore he would never be like that, but patterns like that are almost impossible to throw off. It's what he knows, can you understand that? On a deep level, deeper than intellect, bone deep, that's how he knows to behave as a man, as a husband."

"He marked your face. He hasn't done that before, Tildie."

My hand flew to the spot. "You knew that—"

"Sounds travel. Even with my door closed, even with my good ear on the pillow. I've heard things."

"You never said anything."

"I didn't say anything today," she reminded me.

"He can't help it," I said. "You have to understand that. Didn't you see him this morning?"

"I saw him."

"It hurts him more than it hurts me. And it's my fault as much as it's his."

"For allowing it?"

"For provoking him."

She looked at me. Her eyes are a pale blue, like mine, and at times there is accusation in them. My gaze must have the same quality. I have been told that it is penetrating. "Don't look at me like that," my husband has said, raising a hand as much to ward off my gaze as to threaten me. "Damn you, don't you look at me like that!"

Like what? I'd wondered. How was I looking at him? What was I doing wrong?

"I do provoke him," I told her. "I make him hit me."

"How?"

"By saying the wrong thing."

"What sort of thing?"

"Things that upset him."

"And then he has to hit you, Tildie? Because of what you say?"

"It's a *pattern*," I said. "It's the way he grew up. Men who drink have sons who drink. Men who beat their wives have 'sons who beat their wives. It's passed on over the generations like a genetic illness. Mama, Dan's a good man. You see how he is with Livia, how he loves her, how she loves him."

"Yes."

"And he loves me, Mama. Don't you think it tears him up when something like this happens? Don't you think it eats at him?"

"It must."

"It does!" I thought how he'd cried last night, how he'd held me and touched the mark on my cheek and cried. "And we're going to try to do something about it," I said. "To break the pattern. There's a clinic in Fulton City where you can go for counseling. It's not expensive, either."

"And you're going?"

"We've talked about it. We're considering it."

She looked at me and I made myself meet her eyes. After a moment she looked away. "Well, you would know more about this sort of thing than I do," she said. "You went to college, you studied, you learned things."

I studied art history. I can tell you about the Italian Renaissance, although I have already forgotten much of what I learned. I took one psychology course in my freshman year and we observed the behavior of white rats in mazes.

"Mama," I said, "I know you disapprove."

"Oh, no," she said. "Tildie, that's not so."

"It's not?"

She shook her head. "I just hurt for you," she said. "That's all."

We live on 220 acres, only a third of them level. The farm has been in our family since the land was cleared early in the last century. It has been years since we farmed it. The MacNaughtons run sheep in our north pastures, and Mr. Parkhill leases forty acres, planting alfalfa one year and field corn the next. Mama has some bank stock and some utilities, and the dividends plus what she's paid for the land rent are enough to keep her. There's no mortgage on the land and the taxes have stayed low. And she has a big kitchen garden. We eat out of it all summer long and put up enough in the fall to carry us through the winter.

Dan studied comparative lit while I studied art history.

He got a master's and did half the course work for a doctorate and then knew he couldn't do it anymore. He got a job driving a taxi and I worked waiting tables at Paddy Mac's, where we used to come for beer and hamburgers when we were students. When I got pregnant with Livia he didn't want me on my feet all day but we couldn't make ends meet on his earnings as a cabdriver. Rents were high in that city, and everything cost a fortune.

And we both loved country living, and knew the city was no place to bring up Livia. So we moved here, and Dan got work right away with a construction company in Caldwell. That's the nearest town, just six miles from us on county roads, and Fulton City is only twenty-two miles.

After that conversation with Mama I went outside and walked back beyond the garden and the pear and apple orchard. There's a stream runs diagonally across our land, and just beyond it is the spot I always liked the best, where the walnut trees are. We have a whole grove of black walnuts, twenty-six trees in all. I know because Dan counted them. He was trying to estimate what they'd bring.

Walnut is valuable. People will pay thousands of dollars for a mature tree. They make veneer from it, because it's too costly to use as solid wood.

"We ought to sell these off," Dan said. "Your mama's got an untapped resource here. Somebody could come in, cut 'em down, and steal 'em. Like poachers in Kenya, killing the elephants for their ivory."

"No one's going to come onto our land."

"You never know. Anyway, it's a waste. You can't even see this spot from the house. And nobody does anything with the nuts."

When I was a girl my mama and I used to gather the walnuts after they fell in early autumn. Thousands fell from the trees. We would just gather a basketful and crack them with a hammer and pick the meat out. My hands always got black from the husks and stayed that way for weeks.

We only did this a few times. It was after Daddy left, but while Grandma Yount was still alive. I don't remember Grandma bothering with the walnuts, but she did lots of other things. When the cherries came in we would all pick them and she would bake pies and put up jars of the rest, and she'd boil the pits to clean them and sew scraps of cloth to make beanbags. There are still beanbags in the attic that Grandma Yount made. I'd brought one down for Livia and fancied I could still smell cherries through the cloth.

"We could harvest the walnuts," I told Dan. "If you want."

"What for? You can't get anything for them. Too much trouble to open and hardly any meat in them. I'd sooner harvest the trees."

"Mama likes having them here."

"They're worth a fortune. And they're a renewable resource. You could cut them and plant more and someday they'd put your grandchildren through college."

"You don't need to cut them to plant more. There's other land we could use."

"No point planting more if you're not going to cut these, is there? What do we need them for?"

"What do our grandchildren need college for?"

"What's that supposed to mean?"

"Nothing," I'd said, backing away.

And hours later he'd taken it up again. "You meant I wasted my education," he said. "That's what you meant by that crack, isn't it?"

"No."

"Then what did you mean? What do I need a master's for to hammer a nail? That's what you meant."

"It's not, but evidently that's how you'd rather hear it."

He hit me for that. I guess I had it coming. I don't know if I deserved it, I don't know if a woman deserves to get hit, but I guess I provoked it. Something makes me say things I shouldn't, things he'll take amiss. I don't know why.

Except I do know why, and I'd walked out of the kitchen and across to the walnut grove to keep from talking about it to Mama. Because he had his pattern and I had mine.

His was what he'd learned from his daddy, which was to abuse a woman, to slap her, to strike her with his fists. And mine was a pattern I'd learned from my mama, which was to make a man leave you, to taunt him with your mouth until one day he put his clothes in a suitcase and walked out the door.

In the mornings it tore at me to hear the screen door slam.

Because I thought, Tildie, one day you'll hear that sound and it'll be for the last time. One day you'll do what your mother managed to do, and he'll do like your father did and you'll never see him again. And Livia will grow up as you did, in a house with her mother and her grandmother, and she'll have cherry-pit beanbags to play with and she'll pick the meat out of black walnuts, but what will she do for a daddy? And what will you do for a man?

All the rest of that week he never raised his hand to me. One night Mama stayed with Livia while Dan and I went to a movie in Fulton City. Afterward we went to a place that reminded us both of Paddy Mac's, and we drank beer and got silly. Driving home, we rolled down the car windows and sang songs at the top of our lungs. By the time we got home the beer had worn off but we were still happy and we hurried upstairs to our room.

Mama didn't say anything next morning but I caught her looking at me and knew she'd heard the old iron bedstead. I thought, *You hear a lot, even with your good ear pressed against the pillow*. Well, if she had to hear the fighting, let her hear the loving, too.

She could have heard the bed that night, too, although it was a quieter and gentler lovemaking than the night before. There were no knowing glances the next day, but after the screen door closed behind Dan and after Livia was in for her nap, there was a nice easiness between us as we stood side by side doing the breakfast dishes.

Afterward she said, "I'm so glad you're back home, Tildie."

"So you don't have to do the dishes all by yourself."

She smiled. "I knew you'd be back," she said.

"Did you? I wonder if I knew. I don't think so. I thought I wanted to live in a city, or in a college town. I thought I wanted to be a professor's wife and have earnest conversations about literature and politics and art. I guess I was just a country girl all along."

"You always loved it here," she said. "Of course it will be yours when I'm gone, and I had it in mind that you'd come back to it then. But I hoped you wouldn't wait that long."

She had never left. She and her mother lived here, and

when she married my father he just moved in. It's a big old house, with different wings added over the years. He moved in, and then he left, and she just stayed on.

I remembered something. "I don't know if I thought I'd live here again," I said, "but I always thought I would die here." She looked at me, and I said, "Not so much die here as be buried here. When we buried Grandma I thought, *Well, this is where they'll bury me someday*. And I always thought that."

Grandma Yount's grave is on our land, just to the east of the pear and apple orchard. There are graves there dating back to when our people first lived here. The two children Mama lost are laid to rest there, and Grandma Yount's mother, and a great many children. It wasn't that long ago that people would have four or five children to raise one. You can't read what's cut into most of the stones, it's worn away with time, and it wears faster now that we have the acid rain, but the stones are there, the graves are there, and I always knew I'd be there, too.

"Well, I'll be there, too," Mama said. "But not too soon, I hope."

"No, not soon at all," I said. "Let's live a long time. Let's be old ladies together."

I thought it was a sweet conversation, a beautiful conversation. But when I told Dan about it we wound up fighting.

"When she goes," he said, "that's when those walnuts go to market."

"That's all you can think about," I said. "Turning a beautiful grove into dollars."

"That timber's money in the bank," he said, "except it's not in the bank because anybody could come in and haul it out of there behind our backs."

"Nobody's going to do that."

"And other things could happen. It's no good for a tree to let it grow beyond its prime. Insects can get it, or disease. There's one tree already that was struck by lightning."

"It didn't hurt it much."

"When they're my trees," he said, "they're coming down."

"They won't be your trees."

"What's that supposed to mean?"

"Mama's not leaving the place to you, Dan."

"I thought what's mine is yours and what's yours is mine."

"I love those trees," I said. "I'm not going to see them cut." His face darkened, and a muscle worked in his jaw. This was a warning sign, and I knew it as such, but I was stuck in a pattern, God help me, and I couldn't leave it alone. "First you'd sell off the timber," I said, "and then you'd sell off the acreage."

"I wouldn't do that."

"Why? Your daddy did."

Dan grew up on a farm that came down through his father's father. Unable to make a living farming, first his grandfather and then his father had sold off parcels of land little by little, whittling away at their holdings and each time reducing the potential income of what remained. After Dan's mother died his father had stopped farming altogether and drank full time, and the farm was auctioned for back taxes while Dan was still in high school.

I knew what it would do to him and yet I threw that in his face all the same. I couldn't seem to help it, any more than he could help what followed.

At breakfast the next day the silence made me want to scream. Dan read the paper while he ate, then hurried out the door without a word. I couldn't hear the screen door when it banged shut or the car engine when it started up. Mama's silence—and his, and mine—drowned out everything else.

I thought I'd burst when we were doing the dishes. She didn't say a word and neither did I. Afterward she turned to me and said, "I didn't go to college so I don't know about patterns, or what you do and what it makes him do."

The *quattrocento* and rats in a maze, that's all I learned in college. What I know about patterns and family violence I learned watching Oprah and Phil Donahue, and she watched the same programs I did. ("He blacked your eye and broke your nose. He kicked you in the stomach while you were pregnant. How can you stay with a brute like this?" "But I love him, Geraldo. And I know he loves me.")

"I just know one thing," she said. "It won't get better. And it will get worse."

"No."

"Yes. And you know it, Tildie."

"No."

He hadn't blacked my eye or broken my nose, but he had hammered my face with his fists and it was swollen and discolored. He hadn't kicked me in the stomach but he had shoved me from him. I had been clinging to his arm. That was stupid, I knew better than to do that, it drove him crazy to have me hang on him like that. He had shoved me and I'd gone sprawling, wrenching my leg when I fell on it. My knee ached now, and the muscles in the front of that thigh were sore. And my rib cage was sore where he'd punched me.

But I love him, Geraldo, Oprah, Phil. And I know he loves me.

That night he didn't come home.

I couldn't sit still, couldn't catch my breath. Livia caught my anxiety and wouldn't sleep, couldn't sleep. I held her in my arms and paced the floor in front of the television set. Back and forth, back and forth.

At midnight finally I put her in her crib and she slept. Mama was playing solitaire at the pine table. Only the top is pine, the base is maple. An antique, Dan pronounced it when he first saw it, and better than the ones in the shops. I suppose he had it priced in his mind, along with the walnut trees.

I pointed out a move. Mama said, "I know about that. I just haven't decided whether I want to do it, that's all." But she always says that. I don't believe she saw it.

At one I heard our car turn off the road and onto the gravel. She heard it, too, and gathered up the cards and said she was tired now, she'd just turn in. She was out of the room and up the stairs before he came in the door.

He was drunk. He lurched into the room, his shirt open halfway to his waist, his eyes unfocused. He said, "Oh, Jesus, Tildie, what's happening to us?"

"Shhh," I said. "You'll wake the baby."

"I'm sorry, Tildie," he said. "I'm sorry, I'm so goddam sorry."

Going up the stairs, he spun away from me and staggered into the railing. It held. I got him upstairs and into our room, but he passed out the minute he lay down on our bed. I got his shoes off, and his shirt and pants, and let him sleep in his socks and underwear.

In the morning he was still sleeping when I got up to take

care of Livia. Mama had his breakfast on the table, his coffee poured, the newspaper at his place. He rushed through the kitchen without a word to anybody, tore out the door and was gone. I moved toward the door but Mama was in my path.

I cried, "Mama, he's leaving! He'll never be back!"

She glanced meaningfully at Livia. I stepped back, lowered my voice. "He's leaving," I said, helpless. He had started the car, he was driving away. "I'll never see him again."

"He'll be back."

"Just like my daddy," I said. "Livvy, your father's gone, we'll never see him again."

"Stop that," Mama said. "You don't know how much sticks in their minds. You mind what you say in front of her."

"But it's true."

"It's not," she said. "You won't lose him that easy. He'll be back."

In the afternoon I took Livia with me while I picked pole beans and summer squash. Then we went back to the pear and apple orchard and played in the shade. After a while I took her over to Grandma Yount's grave. We'll all be here someday, I wanted to say, your grandma and your daddy and your mama, too. And you'll be here when your time comes. This is our land, this is where we all end up.

I might have said this, it wouldn't hurt for her to hear it, but for what Mama said. I guess it's true you don't know what sticks in their minds, or what they'll make of it.

She liked it out there, Livia did. She crawled right up to Grandma Yount's stone and ran her hand over it. You'd have thought she was trying to read it that way, like a blind person with Braille.

He didn't come home for dinner. It was going on ten when I heard the car on the gravel. Mama and I were watching television. I got up and went into the kitchen to be there when he came in.

He was sober. He stood in the doorway and looked at me. Every emotion a man could have was there on his face.

"Look at you," he said. "I did that to you."

My face was worse than the day before. Bruises and swellings are like that, taking their time to ripen.

"You missed dinner," I said, "but I saved some for you. I'll heat up a plate for you."

"I already ate. Tildie, I don't know what to say."

"You don't have to say anything."

"No," he said. "That's not right. We have to talk."

We slipped up to our room, leaving Mama to the television set. With our door closed we talked about the patterns we were caught in and how we seemed to have no control, like actors in a play with all their lines written for them by someone else. We could improvise, we could invent movements and gestures, we could read our lines in any of a number of ways, but the script was all written down and we couldn't get away from it.

I mentioned counseling. He said, "I called that place in Fulton City. I wouldn't tell them my name. Can you feature that? I called them for help but I was too ashamed to tell them my name."

"What did they say?"

"They would want to see us once a week as a couple, and each of us individually once a week. Total price for the three sessions would be eighty dollars."

"For how long?"

"I asked. They couldn't say. They said it's not the sort of change you can expect to make overnight."

I said, "Eighty dollars a week. We can't afford that."

"I had the feeling they might reduce it some."

"Did you make an appointment?"

"No. I thought I'd call tomorrow."

"I don't want to cut the trees," I said. He looked at me. "To pay for it. I don't want to cut Mama's walnut trees."

"Tildie, who brought up the damn trees?"

"We could sell the table," I said.

"What are you talking about?"

"In the kitchen. The pine-top table, didn't you say it was an antique? We could sell that."

"Why would I want to sell the table?"

"You want to sell those trees bad enough. You as much as said that as soon as my mama dies you'll be out back with a chain saw."

"Don't start with me," he said. "Don't you start with me, Tildie."

"Or what? Or you'll hit me? Oh, God, Dan, what are we doing? Fighting over how to pay for the counseling to keep from fighting. Dan, what's the matter with us?"

I went to embrace him but he backed away from me. "Honey," he said, "we better be real careful with this. They were telling me about escalating patterns of violence. I'm afraid of what could happen. I'm going to do what they said to do."

"What's that?"

"I want to pack some things," he said. "That's what I came home to do. There's that Welcome Inn Motel outside of Caldwell, they say it's not so bad and I believe they have weekly rates."

"No," I said. "No."

"They said it's best. Especially if we're going to start counseling, because that brings everything up and out into the open, and it threatens the part of us that wants to be in this pattern. Tildie, from what they said it'd be dangerous for us to be together right now."

"You can't leave," I said.

"I wouldn't be five miles away. I'd be coming for dinner some nights, we'd be going to a movie now and then. It's not like—"

"We can't afford it," I said. "Dan, how can we afford it? Eighty dollars a week for the counseling and God knows how much for the motel, and you'd be having most of your meals out, and how can we afford it? You've got a decent job but you don't make that kind of money."

His eyes hardened but he breathed in and out, in and out, and said, "Tildie, just talking like this is a strain, don't you see that? We can afford it, we'll find a way to afford it. Tildie, don't grab on to my arm like that, you know what it does to me. Tildie, stop it, will you for God's sake stop it?"

I put my arms around my own self and hugged myself. I was shaking. My hands just wanted to take hold of his arm. What was so bad about holding on to your husband's arm? What was wrong with that?

"Don't go," I said.

"I have to."

"Not now. It's late, they won't have any rooms left anyhow. Wait until morning. Can't you wait until morning?"

"I was just going to get some of my things and go."

"Go in the morning. Don't you want to see Livvy before you go? She's your daughter, don't you want to say good-bye to her?"

"I'm not leaving, Tildie. I'm just staying a few miles from here so we'll have a chance to keep from destroying ourselves. My God, Tildie, I don't want to leave you. That's the whole point, don't you see that?"

"Stay until morning," I said. "Please?"

"And will we go through this again in the morning?"

"No," I said. "I promise."

We were both restless, but then we made love and that settled him, and soon he was sleeping. I couldn't sleep, though. I lay there for a time, and then I put a robe on and went down to the kitchen and sat there for a long time, thinking of patterns, thinking of ways to escape them. And then I went back up the stairs to the bedroom again.

I was in the kitchen the next morning before Livia woke up. I was there when Mama came down, and her eyes widened at the sight of me. She started to say something but then I guess she saw something in my eyes and she stayed silent.

I said, "Mama, we have to call the police. You'll mind the baby when they come for me. Will you do that?"

"Oh, Tildie," she said.

I led her up the stairs again and into our bedroom. Dan lay facedown, the way he always slept. I drew the sheet down and showed her where I'd stabbed him, slipping the kitchen knife between two ribs and into the heart. The knife lay on the table beside the bed. I had wiped the blood from it. There had not been very much blood to wipe.

"He was going to leave," I said, "and I couldn't bear it, Mama. And I thought, Now he won't leave, now he'll never leave me. I thought, This is a way to break the pattern. Isn't that crazy, Mama? It doesn't make any sense, does it?"

"My poor Tildie."

"Do you want to know something? I feel safe now, Mama. He won't hit me anymore and I never have to worry about him leaving me. He can't leave me, can he?" Something caught in my throat. "Oh, and he'll never hold me again, either. In the circle of his arms."

I broke then, and it was Mama who held me, stroking my forehead, soothing me. I was all right then, and I stood up straight and told her she had better call the police.

"Livia'll be up any minute now," she said. "I think she's awake, I think I heard her fussing a minute ago. Change her and bring her down and feed her her breakfast."

"And then?"

"And then put her in for her nap."

After I put Livia back in her crib for her nap Mama told me that we weren't going to call the police. "Now that you're back where you belong," she said, "I'm not about to see them take you away. Your baby needs her mama and I need you, too."

"But Dan—"

"Bring the big wheelbarrow around to the kitchen door. Between the two of us we can get him down the stairs. We'll dig his grave in the back, we'll bury him here on our land. People won't suspect anything. They'll just think he went off, the way men do."

"The way my daddy did," I said.

Somehow we got him down the stairs and out through the kitchen. The hardest part was getting him into the old wheelbarrow. I checked Livia and made sure she was sleeping soundly, and then we took turns with the barrow, wheeling it out beyond the kitchen garden.

"What I keep thinking," I said, "is at least I broke the pattern."

She didn't say anything, and what she didn't say became one of her famous silences, sucking up all the sound around us. The barrow's wheel squeaked, the birds sang in the trees, but now I couldn't hear any of that.

Suddenly she said, "Patterns." Then she didn't say anything more, and I tried to hear the squeak of the wheel.

Then she said, "He never would have left you. If he left he'd only come back again. And he never would have quit hitting you. And each time would be a little worse than the last."

"It's not always like it is on *Oprah*, Mama."

"There's things you don't know," she said.

"Like what?"

The squeaking of the wheel, the song of birds. She said, "You know how I lost the hearing in the one ear?"

"You had an infection."

"That's what I always told you. It's not true. Your daddy cupped his hands and boxed my ears. He deafened me on the one side. I was lucky, nothing happened to the other ear. I still hear as good as ever out of it."

"I don't believe it," I said.

"It's the truth, Tildie."

"Daddy never hit you."

"Your daddy hit me all the time," she said. "All the time. He used his hands, he used his feet. He used his belt."

I felt a tightening in my throat. "I don't remember," I said.

"You didn't know. You were little. What do you think Livia knows? What do you think she'll remember?"

We walked on a ways. I said, "I just remember the two of you hollering. I thought you hollered and finally he left. That's what I always thought."

"That's what I let you think. It's what I wanted you to think. I had a broken jaw, I had broken ribs, I had to keep telling the doctor I was clumsy, I kept falling down. He believed me, too. I guess he had lots of women told him the same thing." We switched, and I took over the wheelbarrow. She said, "Dan would have done the same to you, if you hadn't done what you did."

"He wanted to stop."

"They can't stop, Tildie. No, not that way. To your left."

"Aren't we going to bury him alongside Grandma Yount?"

"No," she said. "That's too near the house. We'll dig his grave across the stream, where the walnut grove is."

"It's beautiful there."

"You always liked it."

"So did Dan," I said. I felt so funny, so light-headed. My world was turned upside down and yet it felt safe, it felt solid. I thought how Dan had itched to cut down those walnut trees. Now he'd lie forever at their feet, and I could come back here whenever I wanted to feel close to him.

"But he'll be lonely here," I said. "Won't he? Mama, won't he?"

* * *

The walnut trees lose their leaves early in the fall, and they put on less of a color show than the other hardwoods. But I like to come to the grove even when the trees are bare. Sometimes I bring Livia. More often I come by myself.

I always liked it here. I love our whole 220 acres, every square foot of it, but this is my favorite place, among these trees. I like it even better than the graveyard over by the pear and apple orchard. Where the graves have stones, and where the women and children of our family are buried.

THE BURGLAR WHO DROPPED IN ON ELVIS

"I know who you are," she said. "Your name is Bernie Rhodenbarr. You're a burglar."

I glanced around, glad that the store was empty save for the two of us. It often is, but I'm not usually glad about it.

"Was," I said.

"Was?"

"Was. Past tense. I had a criminal past, and while I'd as soon keep it a secret I can't deny it. But I'm an antiquarian bookseller now, Miss Uh—"

"Danahy," she supplied. "Holly Danahy."

"Miss Danahy. A dealer in the wisdom of the ages. The errors of my youth are to be regretted, even deplored, but they're over and done with."

She gazed thoughtfully at me. She was a lovely creature, slender, pert, bright of eye and inquisitive of nose, and she wore a tailored suit and flowing bow tie that made her look at once yieldingly feminine and as coolly competent as a Luger.

"I think you're lying," she said. "I certainly hope so. Because an antiquarian bookseller is no good at all to me. What I need is a burglar."

"I wish I could help you."

"You can." She laid a cool-fingered hand on mine. "It's almost closing time. Why don't you lock up? I'll buy you a drink and tell you how you can qualify for an all-expense-paid trip to Memphis. And possibly a whole lot more."

"You're not trying to sell me a time-share in a thriving lakeside resort community, are you?"

"Not hardly."

"Then what have I got to lose? The thing is, I usually have a drink after work with—"

"Carolyn Kaiser," she cut in. "Your best friend, she washes dogs two doors down the street at the Poodle Factory. You can call her and cancel."

My turn to gaze thoughtfully. "You seem to know a lot about me," I said.

"Sweetie," she said, "that's my *job*."

"I'm a reporter," she said. "For the *Weekly Galaxy*. If you don't know the paper, you must never get to the supermarket."

"I know it," I said. "But I have to admit I'm not what you'd call one of your regular readers."

"Well, I should hope not, Bernie. Our readers move their lips when they think. Our readers write letters in crayon because they're not allowed to have anything sharp. Our readers make the *Enquirer*'s readers look like Rhodes scholars. Our readers, face it, are D-U-M."

"Then why would they want to know about me?"

"They wouldn't, unless an extraterrestrial made you pregnant. That happen to you?"

"No, but Bigfoot ate my car."

She shook her head. "We already did that story. Last August, I think it was. The car was an AMC Gremlin with a hundred and ninety-two thousand miles on it."

"I suppose its time had come."

"That's what the owner said. He's got a new BMW now, thanks to the *Galaxy*. He can't spell it, but he can drive it like crazy."

I looked at her over the brim of my glass. "If you don't want to write about me," I said, "what do you need me for?"

"Ah, Bernie," she said. "Bernie the burglar. Sweetie pie, you're my ticket to Elvis."

* * *

"The best possible picture," I told Carolyn, "would be a shot of Elvis in his coffin. The *Galaxy* loves shots like that but in this case it would be counterproductive in the long run, because it might kill their big story, the one they run month after month."

"Which is that he's still alive."

"Right. Now the second-best possible picture, and better for their purposes overall, would be a shot of him alive, singing 'Love Me Tender' to a visitor from another planet. They get a chance at that picture every couple of days, and it's always some Elvis impersonator. Do you know how many full-time professional Elvis Presley impersonators there are in America today?"

"No."

"Neither do I, but I have a feeling Holly Danahy could probably supply a figure, and that it would be an impressive one. Anyway, the third-best possible picture, and the one she seems to want almost more than life itself, is a shot of the King's bedroom."

"At Graceland?"

"That's the one. Six thousand people visit Graceland every day. Two million of them walked through it last year."

"And none of them brought a camera?"

"Don't ask me how many cameras they brought, or how many rolls of film they shot. Or how many souvenir ashtrays and paintings on black velvet they bought and took home with them. But how many of them got above the first floor?"

"How many?"

"None. Nobody gets to go upstairs at Graceland. The staff isn't allowed up there, and people who've worked there for years have never set foot above the ground floor. And you can't bribe your way up there, either, according to Holly, and she knows because she tried, and she had all the *Galaxy*'s resources to play with. Two million people a year go to Graceland, and they'd all love to know what it looks like upstairs, and the *Weekly Galaxy* would just love to show them."

"Enter a burglar."

"That's it. That's Holly's masterstroke, the one designed to win her a bonus and a promotion. Enter an expert at illegal entry, i.e., a burglar. *Le* burglar, *c'est moi*. Name your price, she told me."

"And what did you tell her?"

"Twenty-five thousand dollars. You know why? All I could think of was that it sounded like a job for Nick Velvet. You remember him, the thief in the Ed Hoch stories who'll only steal worthless objects." I sighed. "When I think of all the worthless objects I've stolen over the years, and never once has anyone offered to pay me a fee of twenty-five grand for my troubles. Anyway, that was the price that popped into my head, so I tried it out on her. And she didn't even try to haggle."

"I think Nick Velvet raised his rates," Carolyn said. "I think his price went up in the last story or two."

I shook my head. "You see what happens? You fall behind on your reading and it costs you money."

Holly and I flew first class from JFK to Memphis. The meal was still airline food, but the seats were so comfortable and the stewardess so attentive that I kept forgetting this.

"At the *Weekly Galaxy*," Holly said, sipping an after-dinner something-or-other, "everything's first class. Except the paper itself, of course."

We got our luggage, and a hotel courtesy car whisked us to the Howard Johnson's on Elvis Presley Boulevard, where we had adjoining rooms reserved. I was just about unpacked when Holly knocked on the door separating the two rooms. I unlocked it for her and she came in carrying a bottle of scotch and a full ice bucket.

"I wanted to stay at the Peabody," she said. "That's the great old downtown hotel and it's supposed to be wonderful, but here we're only a couple of blocks from Graceland, and I thought it would be more convenient."

"Makes sense," I agreed.

"But I wanted to see the ducks," she said. She explained that ducks were the symbol of the Peabody, or the mascot, or something. Every day the hotel's guests could watch the hotel's ducks waddle across the red carpet to the fountain in the middle of the lobby.

"Tell me something," she said. "How does a guy like you get into a business like this?"

"Bookselling?"

"Get real, honey. How'd you get to be a burglar? Not for

the edification of our readers, because they couldn't care less. But to satisfy my own curiosity."

I sipped a drink while I told her the story of my misspent life, or as much of it as I felt like telling. She heard me out and put away four stiff scotches in the process, but if they had any effect on her I couldn't see it.

"And how about you?" I said after a while. "How did a nice girl like you—"

"Oh, Gawd," she said. "We'll save that for another evening, okay?" And then she was in my arms, smelling and feeling better than a body had a right to, and just as quickly she was out of them again and on her way to the door.

"You don't have to go," I said.

"Ah, but I do, Bernie. We've got a big day tomorrow. We're going to see Elvis, remember?"

She took the scotch with her. I poured out what remained of my own drink, finished unpacking, took a shower. I got into bed, and after fifteen or twenty minutes I got up and tried the door between our two rooms, but she had locked it on her side. I went back to bed.

Our tour guide's name was Stacy. She wore the standard Graceland uniform, a blue-and-white-striped shirt over navy chinos, and she looked like someone who'd been unable to decide whether to become a stewardess or a cheerleader. Cleverly, she'd chosen a job that combined both professions.

"There were generally a dozen guests crowded around this dining table," she told us. "Dinner was served nightly between nine and ten P.M., and Elvis always sat right there at the head of the table. Not because he was head of the family but because it gave him the best view of the big color TV. Now that's one of fourteen TV sets here at Graceland, so you know how much Elvis liked to watch TV."

"Was that the regular china?" someone wanted to know.

"Yes, ma'am, and the name of the pattern is Buckingham. Isn't it pretty?"

I could run down the whole tour for you, but what's the point? Either you've been there yourself or you're planning to go or you don't care, and at the rate people are signing up for the tours, I don't think there are many of you in the last group. Elvis was a good pool player, and his favorite game was rotation. Elvis ate his breakfast in the Jungle Room, off a cypress coffee table. Elvis's own favorite singer was Dean Martin. Elvis liked peacocks, and at one time over a dozen of them roamed the grounds of Graceland. Then they started eating the paint off the cars, which Elvis liked even more than he liked peacocks, so he donated them to the Memphis Zoo. The peacocks, not the cars.

There was a gold rope across the mirrored staircase, and what looked like an electric eye a couple of stairs up. "We don't allow tourists into the upstairs," our guide chirped. "Remember, Graceland is a private home and Elvis's aunt Miss Delta Biggs still lives here. Now I can tell you what's upstairs. Elvis's bedroom is located directly above the living room and music room. His office is also upstairs, and there's Lisa Marie's bedroom, and dressing rooms and bathrooms as well."

"And does his aunt live up there?" someone asked.

"No, sir. She lives downstairs, through that door over to your left. None of us have ever been upstairs. Nobody goes there anymore."

"I bet he's up there now," Holly said. "In a La-Z-Boy with his feet up, eating one of his famous peanut-butter and banana sandwiches and watching three television sets at once."

"And listening to Dean Martin," I said. "What do you really think?"

"What do I really think? I think he's down in Paraguay playing three-handed pinochle with James Dean and Adolf Hitler. Did you know that Hitler masterminded Argentina's invasion of the Falkland Islands? We ran that story but it didn't do as well as we hoped."

"Your readers didn't remember Hitler?"

"Hitler was no problem for them. But they didn't know what the Falklands were. Seriously, where do I think Elvis is? I think he's in the grave we just looked at, surrounded by his nearest and dearest. Unfortunately, 'Elvis Still Dead' is not a headline that sells papers."

"I guess not."

We were back in my room at the HoJo, eating a lunch Holly had ordered from room service. It reminded me of our in-flight meal the day before, luxurious but not terribly good.

"Well," she said brightly, "have you figured out how we're going to get in?"

"You saw the place," I said. "They've got gates and guards and alarm systems everywhere. I don't know what's upstairs, but it's a more closely guarded secret than Zsa Zsa Gabor's true age."

"That'd be easy to find out," Holly said. "We could just hire somebody to marry her."

"Graceland is impregnable," I went on, hoping we could drop the analogy right there. "It's almost as bad as Fort Knox."

Her face fell. "I was sure you could find a way in."

"Maybe I can."

"But—"

"For one. Not for two. It'd be too risky for you, and you don't have the skills for it. Could you shinny down a gutterspout?"

"If I had to."

"Well, you won't have to, because you won't be going in." I paused for thought. "You'd have a lot of work to do," I said. "On the outside, coordinating things."

"I can handle it."

"And there would be expenses, plenty of them."

"No problem."

"I'd need a camera that can take pictures in full dark. I can't risk a flash."

"That's easy. We can handle that."

"I'll need to rent a helicopter, and I'll have to pay the pilot enough to guarantee his silence."

"A cinch."

"I'll need a diversion. Something fairly dramatic."

"I can create a diversion. With all the resources of the *Galaxy* at my disposal, I could divert a river."

"That shouldn't be necessary. But all of this is going to cost money."

"Money," she said, "is no object."

"So you're a friend of Carolyn's," Lucian Leeds said. "She's wonderful, isn't she? You know, she and I are the next-closest thing to blood kin."

"Oh?"

"A former lover of hers and a former lover of mine were

brother and sister. Well, sister and brother, actually. So that makes Carolyn my something-in-law, doesn't it?"

"I guess it must."

"Of course," he said, "by the same token, I must be related to half the known world. Still, I'm real fond of our Carolyn. And if I can help you—"

I told him what I needed. Lucian Leeds was an interior decorator and a dealer in art and antiques. "Of course I've been to Graceland," he said. "Probably a dozen times, because whenever a friend or relative visits that's where one has to take them. It's an experience that somehow never palls."

"I don't suppose you've ever been on the second floor."

"No, nor have I been presented at court. Of the two, I suppose I'd prefer the second floor at Graceland. One can't help wondering, can one?" He closed his eyes, concentrating. "My imagination is beginning to work," he announced.

"Give it free rein."

"I know just the house, too. It's off Route 51 across the state line, just this side of Hernando, Mississippi. Oh, and I know someone with an Egyptian piece that would be perfect. How soon would everything have to be ready?"

"Tomorrow night?"

"Impossible. The day after tomorrow is barely possible. Just barely. I really ought to have a week to do it right."

"Well, do it as right as you can."

"I'll need trucks and schleppers, of course. I'll have rental charges to pay, of course, and I'll have to give something to the old girl who owns the house. First I'll have to sweet-talk her, but there'll have to be something tangible in it for her as well, I'm afraid. But all of this is going to cost you money."

That had a familiar ring to it. I almost got caught up in the rhythm of it and told him money was no object, but I managed to restrain myself. If money wasn't the object, what was I doing in Memphis?

"Here's the camera," Holly said. "It's all loaded with infrared film. No flash, and you can take pictures with it at the bottom of a coal mine."

"That's good," I said, "because that's probably where I'll wind up if they catch me. We'll do it the day after tomorrow. Today's what, Wednesday? I'll go in Friday."

"I should be able to give you a terrific diversion."

"I hope so," I said. "I'll probably need it."

Thursday morning I found my helicopter pilot. "Yeah, I could do it," he said. "Cost you two hundred dollars, though."

"I'll give you five hundred."

He shook his head. "One thing I never do," he said, "is get to haggling over prices. I said two hundred, and—wait a darn minute."

"Take all the time you need."

"You weren't haggling me down," he said. "You were haggling me up. I never heard tell of such a thing."

"I'm willing to pay extra," I said, "so that you'll tell people the right story afterward. If anybody asks."

"What do you want me to tell 'em?"

"That somebody you never met before in your life paid you to fly over Graceland, hover over the mansion, lower your rope ladder, raise the ladder, and then fly away."

He thought about this for a full minute. "But that's what you said you wanted me to do," he said.

"I know."

"So you're fixing to pay me an extra three hundred dollars just to tell people the truth."

"If anybody should ask."

"You figure they will?"

"They might," I said. "It would be best if you said it in such a way that they thought you were lying."

"Nothing to it," he said. "Nobody ever believes a word I say. I'm a pretty honest guy, but I guess I don't look it."

"You don't," I said. "That's why I picked you."

That night Holly and I dressed up and took a cab downtown to the Peabody. The restaurant there was named Dux, and they had *canard aux cerises* on the menu, but it seemed curiously sacrilegious to have it there. We both ordered the blackened redfish. She had two dry Rob Roys first, most of the dinner wine, and a Stinger afterward. I had a Bloody Mary for openers, and my after-dinner drink was a cup of coffee. I felt like a cheap date.

Afterward we went back to my room and she worked on the scotch while we discussed strategy. From time to time she would put her drink down and kiss me, but as soon as things threatened to get interesting she'd draw away and cross her legs and pick up her pencil and notepad and reach for her drink.

"You're a tease," I said.

"I am not," she insisted. "But I want to, you know, save it."

"For the wedding?"

"For the celebration. After we get the pictures, after we carry the day. You'll be the conquering hero and I'll throw roses at your feet."

"Roses?"

"And myself. I figured we could take a suite at the Peabody and never leave the room except to see the ducks. You know, we never did see the ducks do their famous walk. Can't you just picture them waddling across the red carpet and quacking their heads off?"

"Can't you just picture what they go through cleaning that carpet?"

She pretended not to have heard me. "I'm glad we didn't have duckling," she said. "It would have seemed cannibalistic." She fixed her eyes on me. She'd had enough booze to induce coma in a six-hundred-pound gorilla, but her eyes looked as clear as ever. "Actually," she said, "I'm very strongly attracted to you, Bernie. But I want to wait. You can understand that, can't you?"

"I could," I said gravely, "if I knew I was coming back."

"What do you mean?"

"It would be great to be the conquering hero," I said, "and find you and the roses at my feet, but suppose I come home on my shield instead? I could get killed out there."

"Are you serious?"

"Think of me as a kid who enlisted the day after Pearl Harbor, Holly. And you're his girlfriend, asking him to wait until the war's over. Holly, what if that kid doesn't come home? What if he leaves his bones bleaching on some little hellhole in the South Pacific?"

"Oh my God," she said. "I never thought of that." She put down her pencil and notebook. "You're right, dammit. I *am* a tease. I'm worse than that." She uncrossed her legs. "I'm thoughtless and heartless. Oh, Bernie!"

"There, there," I said.

* * *

Graceland closes every evening at six. At precisely five-thirty Friday afternoon, a girl named Moira Beth Calloway detached herself from her tour group. "I'm coming, Elvis!" she cried, and she lowered her head and ran full speed for the staircase. She was over the gold rope and on the sixth step before the first guard laid a hand on her.

Bells rang, sirens squealed, and all hell broke loose. "Elvis is calling me," Moira Beth insisted, her eyes rolling wildly. "He needs me, he wants me, he loves me tender. Get your hands off me. Elvis! I'm coming, Elvis!"

I.D. in Moira Beth's purse supplied her name and indicated that she was seventeen years old, and a student at Mount St. Joseph Academy in Millington, Tennessee. This was not strictly true, in that she was actually twenty-two years old, a member of Actors Equity, and a resident of Brooklyn Heights. Her name was not Moira Beth Calloway, either. It was (and still is) Rona Jellicoe. I think it may have been something else in the dim dark past before it became Rona Jellicoe, but who cares?

While a variety of people, many of them wearing navy chinos and blue-and-white-striped shirts, did what they could to calm down Moira Beth, a middle-aged couple in the Pool Room went into their act. "Air!" the man cried, clutching at his throat. "Air! I can't breathe!" And he fell down, flailing at the wall, where Stacy had told us some 750 yards of pleated fabric had been installed.

"Help him," cried his wife. "He can't breathe! He's dying! He needs *air!*" And she ran to the nearest window and heaved it open, setting off whatever alarms hadn't already been shrieking over Moira Beth's assault on the staircase.

Meanwhile, in the TV room, done in the exact shades of yellow and blue used in Cub Scout uniforms, a gray squirrel had raced across the rug and was now perched on top of the jukebox. "Look at that awful squirrel!" a woman was screaming. "Somebody get that squirrel! He's gonna kill us all!"

Her fear would have been harder to credit if people had known that the poor rodent had entered Graceland in her handbag, and that she'd been able to release it without being seen because of the commotion in the other room. Her fear was contagious, though, and the people who caught it weren't putting on an act.

In the Jungle Room, where Elvis's *Moody Blue* album had actually been recorded, a woman fainted. She'd been hired to do just that, but other unpaid fainters were dropping like flies all over the mansion. And, while all of this activity was hitting its absolute peak, a helicopter made its noisy way through the sky over Graceland, hovering for several long minutes over the roof.

The security staff at Graceland couldn't have been better. Almost immediately two men emerged from a shed carrying an extension ladder, and in no time at all they had it propped against the side of the building. One of them held it while the other scrambled up it to the roof.

By the time he got there, the helicopter was going *pocketa-pocketa-pocketa*, and disappearing off to the west. The security man raced around the roof but didn't see anyone. Within the next ten minutes, two others joined him on the roof and searched it thoroughly. They found a tennis sneaker, but that was all they found.

At a quarter to five the next morning I let myself into my room at the Howard Johnson's and knocked on the door to Holly's room. There was no response. I knocked again, louder, then gave up and used the phone. I could hear it ringing in her room, but evidently she couldn't.

So I used the skills God gave me and opened her door. She was sprawled out on the bed, with her clothes scattered where she had flung them. The trail of clothing began at the scotch bottle on top of the television set. The set was on, and some guy with a sport jacket and an Ipana smile was explaining how you could get cash advances on your credit cards and buy penny stocks, an enterprise that struck me as a lot riskier than burglarizing mansions by helicopter.

Holly didn't want to wake up, but when I got past the veil of sleep she came to as if transistorized. One moment she was comatose and the next she was sitting up, eyes bright, an expectant look on her face. "Well?" she demanded.

"I shot the whole roll."

"You got in."

"Uh-huh."

"And you got out."

"Right again."

"And you got the pictures." She clapped her hands, giddy with glee. "I knew it," she said. "I was a positive genius to think of you. Oh, they ought to give me a bonus, a raise, a promotion, oh, I bet I get a company Cadillac next year instead of a lousy Chevy, oh, I'm on a roll, Bernie, I swear I'm on a roll!"

"That's great."

"You're limping," she said. "Why are you limping? Because you've only got one shoe on, that's why. What happened to your other shoe?"

"I lost it on the roof."

"God," she said. She got off the bed and began picking up her clothes from the floor and putting them on, following the trail back to the scotch bottle, which evidently had one drink left in it. "Ahhhh," she said, putting it down empty. "You know, when I saw them race up the ladder I thought you were finished. How did you get away from them?"

"It wasn't easy."

"I bet. And you managed to get down onto the second floor? And into his bedroom? What's it like?"

"I don't know."

"You don't *know*? Weren't you in there?"

"Not until it was pitch-dark. I hid in a hall closet and locked myself in. They gave the place a pretty thorough search but nobody had a key to the closet. I don't think there is one, I locked it by picking it. I let myself out somewhere around two in the morning and found my way into the bedroom. There was enough light to keep from bumping into things but not enough to tell what it was I wasn't bumping into. I just walked around pointing the camera and shooting."

She wanted more details, but I don't think she paid very much attention to them. I was in the middle of a sentence when she picked up the phone and made a plane reservation to Miami.

"They've got me on a ten-twenty flight," she said. "I'll get these right into the office and we'll get a check out to you as soon as they're developed. What's the matter?"

"I don't think I want a check," I said. "And I don't want to give you the film without getting paid."

"Oh, come on," she said. "You can trust us, for God's sake."

"Why don't you trust me instead?"

"You mean pay you without seeing what we're paying for? Bernie, you're a burglar. How can I trust you?"

"You're the *Weekly Galaxy*," I said. "*Nobody* can trust you."

"You've got a point," she said.

"We'll get the film developed here," I said. "I'm sure there are some good commercial photo labs in Memphis and that they can handle infrared film. First you'll call your office and have them wire cash here or set up an interbank transfer, and as soon as you see what's on the film you can hand over the money. You can even fax them one of the prints first to get approval, if you think that'll make a difference."

"Oh, they'll love that," she said. "My boss loves it when I fax him stuff."

"And that's what happened," I told Carolyn. "The pictures came out really beautifully. I don't know how Lucian Leeds turned up all those Egyptian pieces, but they looked great next to the 1940s Wurlitzer jukebox and the seven-foot statue of Mickey Mouse. I thought Holly was going to die of happiness when she realized the thing next to Mickey was a sarcophagus. She couldn't decide which tack to take—that he's mummified and they're keeping him in it or he's alive and really weird and uses it for a bed."

"Maybe they can have a reader poll. Call a nine hundred number and vote."

"You wouldn't believe how loud helicopters are when you're inside them. I just dropped the ladder and pulled it back in again. And tossed an extra sneaker on the roof."

"And wore its mate when you saw Holly."

"Yeah, I thought a little verisimilitude wouldn't hurt. The chopper pilot dropped me back at the hangar and I caught a ride down to the Burrell house in Mississippi. I walked around the room Lucian decorated for the occasion, admired everything, then turned out all the lights and took my pictures. They'll be running the best ones in the *Galaxy*."

"And you got paid."

"Twenty-five grand, and everybody's happy, and I didn't cheat anybody or steal anything. The *Galaxy* got some great pictures that'll sell a lot of copies of their horrible paper. The readers get a peek at a room no one has ever seen before."

"And the folks at Graceland?"

"They get a good security drill," I said. "Holly created a peach of a diversion to hide my entering the building. What it hid, of course, was my *not* entering the building, and that fact should stay hidden forever. Most of the Graceland people have never seen Elvis's bedroom, so they'll think the photos are legit. The few who know better will just figure my pictures didn't come out, or that they weren't exciting enough so the *Galaxy* decided to run fakes instead. Everybody with any sense figures the whole paper's a fake anyway, so what difference does it make?"

"Was Holly a fake?"

"Not really. I'd say she's an authentic specimen of what she is. Of course her little fantasy about a hot weekend watching the ducks blew away with the morning mist. All she wanted to do was get back to Florida and collect her bonus."

"So it's just as well you got your bonus ahead of time. You'll hear from her again the next time the *Galaxy* needs a burglar."

"Well, I'd do it again," I said. "My mother was always hoping I'd go into journalism. I wouldn't have waited so long if I'd known it would be so much fun."

"Yeah," she said.

"What's the matter?"

"Nothing, Bern."

"Come on. What is it?"

"Oh, I don't know. I just wish, you know, that you'd gone in there and got the real pictures. He could be in there, Bern. I mean, why else would they make such a big thing out of keeping people out of there? Did you ever stop to ask yourself that?"

"Carolyn—"

"I know," she said. "You think I'm nuts. But there are a lot of people like me, Bern."

"It's a good thing," I told her. "Where would the *Galaxy* be without you?"

AS GOOD AS A REST

Andrew says the whole point of a vacation is to change your perspective of the world. A change is as good as a rest, he says, and vacations are about change, not rest. If we just wanted a rest, he says, we could stop the mail and disconnect the phone and stay home: that would add up to more of a traditional rest than traipsing all over Europe. Sitting in front of the television set with your feet up, he says, is generally considered to be more restful than climbing the forty-two thousand steps to the top of Notre Dame.

Of course, there aren't forty-two thousand steps, but it did seem like it at the time. We were with the Dattners—by the time we got to Paris the four of us had already buddied up—and Harry kept wondering aloud why the genius who'd built the cathedral hadn't thought to put in an elevator. And Sue, who'd struck me earlier as unlikely to be afraid of anything, turned out to be petrified of heights. There are two staircases at Notre Dame, one going up and one coming down, and to get from one to the other you have to walk along this high ledge. It's really quite wide, even at its narrowest, and the view of the rooftops of Paris is magnificent, but all of this was wasted on Sue, who clung to the rear wall with her eyes clenched shut.

Andrew took her arm and walked her through it, while Harry and I looked out at the City of Light. "It's high open spaces that does it to her," he told me. "Yesterday, the Eiffel Tower, no problem, because the space was enclosed. But when it's open she starts getting afraid that she'll get sucked over the side or that she'll get this sudden impulse to jump, and, well, you see what it does to her."

While neither Andrew nor I have ever been troubled by heights, whether open or enclosed, the climb to the top of the cathedral wasn't the sort of thing we'd have done at home, especially since we'd already had a spectacular view of the city the day before from the Eiffel Tower. I'm not mad about walking up stairs, but it didn't occur to me to pass up the climb. For that matter, I'm not that mad about walking generally—Andrew says I won't go anywhere without a guaranteed parking space—but it seems to me that I walked from one end of Europe to the other, and didn't mind a bit.

When we weren't walking through streets or up staircases, we were parading through museums. That's hardly a departure for me, but for Andrew it is uncharacteristic behavior in the extreme. Boston's Museum of Fine Arts is one of the best in the country, and it's not twenty minutes from our house. We have a membership, and I go all the time, but it's almost impossible to get Andrew to go.

But in Paris he went to the Louvre, and the Rodin Museum, and that little museum in the 16th arrondissement with the most wonderful collection of Monets. And in London he led the way to the National Gallery and the National Portrait Gallery and the Victoria and Albert—and in Amsterdam he spent three hours in the Rijksmuseum and hurried us to the Van Gogh Museum first thing the next morning. By the time we got to Madrid, I was museumed out. I knew it was a sin to miss the Prado but I just couldn't face it, and I wound up walking around the city with Harry while my husband dragged Sue through galleries of El Grecos and Goyas and Velasquezes.

"Now that you've discovered museums," I told Andrew, "you may take a different view of the Museum of Fine Arts. There's a show of American landscape painters that'll still be running when we get back—I think you'll like it."

He assured me he was looking forward to it. But you know

he never went. Museums are strictly a vacation pleasure for him. He doesn't even want to hear about them when he's at home.

For my part, you'd think I'd have learned by now not to buy clothes when we travel. Of course, it's impossible not to—there are some genuine bargains and some things you couldn't find at home—but I almost always wind up buying something that remains unworn in my closet forever after. It seems so right in some foreign capital, but once I get it home I realize it's not me at all, and so it lives out its days on a hanger, a source in turn of fond memories and faint guilt. It's not that I lose judgment when I travel, or become wildly impulsive. It's more that I become a slightly different person during the course of the trip and the clothes I buy for that person aren't always right for the person I am in Boston.

Oh, why am I nattering on like this? You don't have to look in my closet to see how travel changes a person. For heaven's sake, just look at the Dattners.

If we hadn't all been on vacation together, we would never have come to know Harry and Sue, let alone spend so much time with them. We would never have encountered them in the first place—day-to-day living would not have brought them to Boston, or us to Enid, Oklahoma. But even if they'd lived down the street from us, we would never have become close friends at home. To put it as simply as possible, they were not our kind of people.

The package tour we'd booked wasn't one of those escorted ventures in which your every minute is accounted for. It included our charter flights over and back, all our hotel accommodations, and our transportation from one city to the next. We "did" six countries in twenty-two days, but what we did in each, and where and with whom, was strictly up to us. We could have kept to ourselves altogether, and have often done so when traveling, but by the time we checked into our hotel in London the first day we'd made arrangements to join the Dattners that night for dinner, and before we knocked off our after-dinner brandies that night it had been tacitly agreed that we would be a foursome throughout the trip—unless, of course, it turned out that we tired of each other.

"They're a pair," Andrew said that first night, unknotting

his tie and giving it a shake before hanging it over the doorknob. "That y'all-come-back accent of hers sounds like syrup flowing over corn cakes."

"She's a little flashy, too," I said. "But that sport jacket of his—"

"I know," Andrew said. "Somewhere, even as we speak, a horse is shivering, his blanket having been transformed into a jacket for Harry."

"And yet there's something about them, isn't there?"

"They're nice people," Andrew said. "Not our kind at all, but what does that matter? We're on a trip. We're ripe for a change. . . ."

In Paris, after a night watching a floor show at what I'm sure was a rather disreputable little nightclub in Les Halles, I lay in bed while Andrew sat up smoking a last cigarette. "I'm glad we met the Dattners," he said. "This trip would be fun anyway, but they add to it. That joint tonight was a treat, and I'm sure we wouldn't have gone if it hadn't been for them. And do you know something? I don't think *they'd* have gone if it hadn't been for *us*."

"Where would we be without them?" I rolled onto my side. "I know where Sue would be without your helping hand. Up on top of Notre Dame, frozen with fear. Do you suppose that's how the gargoyles got there? Are they nothing but tourists turned to stone?"

"Then you'll never be a gargoyle. You were a long way from petrification whirling around the dance floor tonight."

"Harry's a good dancer. I didn't think he would be, but he's very light on his feet."

"The gun doesn't weigh him down, eh?"

I sat up. "I *thought* he was wearing a gun," I said. "How on earth does he get it past the airport scanners?"

"Undoubtedly by packing it in his luggage and checking it through. He wouldn't need it on the plane—not unless he was planning to divert the flight to Havana."

"I don't think they go to Havana anymore. Why would he need it *off* the plane? I suppose tonight he'd feel safer armed. That place was a bit on the rough side."

"He was carrying it at the Tower of London, and in and out of a slew of museums. In fact, I think he carries it all the time except on planes. Most likely he feels naked without it."

"I wonder if he sleeps with it."

"I think he sleeps with her."

"Well, I know *that*."

"To their mutual pleasure, I shouldn't wonder. Even as you and I."

"Ah," I said.

And, a bit later, he said, "You like them, don't you?"

"Well, of course I do. I don't want to pack them up and take them home to Boston with us, but—"

"You like *him*."

"Harry? Oh, *I* see what you're getting at."

"Quite."

"And she's attractive, isn't she? You're attracted to her."

"At home I wouldn't look at her twice, but here—"

"Say no more. That's how I feel about him. That's exactly how I feel about him."

"Do you suppose we'll do anything about it?"

"I don't know. Do you suppose they're having this very conversation two floors below?"

"I wouldn't be surprised. If they *are* having this conversation, and if they had the same silent prelude to this conversation, they're probably feeling very good indeed."

"Mmmmm," I said dreamily. "Even as you and I."

I don't know if the Dattners had that conversation that particular evening, but they certainly had it somewhere along the way. The little tensions and energy currents between the four of us began to build until it seemed almost as though the air were crackling with electricity. More often than not we'd find ourselves pairing off on our walks, Andrew with Sue, Harry with me. I remember one moment when he took my hand crossing the street—I remember the instant but not the street, or even the city—and a little shiver went right through me.

By the time we were in Madrid, with Andrew and Sue trekking through the Prado while Harry and I ate garlicky shrimp and sipped a sweetish white wine in a little café on the Plaza Mayor, it was clear what was going to happen. We were almost ready to talk about it.

"I hope they're having a good time," I told Harry. "I just couldn't manage another museum."

"I'm glad we're out here instead," he said, with a wave at the plaza. "But I would have gone to the Prado if you went." And he reached out and covered my hand with his.

"Sue and Andy seem to be getting along pretty good," he said.

Andy! Had anyone else ever called my husband Andy?

"And you and me, we get along all right, don't we?"

"Yes," I said, giving his hand a little squeeze. "Yes, we do."

Andrew and I were up late that night, talking and talking. The next day we flew to Rome. We were all tired our first night there and ate at the restaurant in our hotel rather than venture forth. The food was good, but I wonder if any of us really tasted it.

Andrew insisted that we all drink *grappa* with our coffee. It turned out to be a rather nasty brandy, clear in color and quite powerful. The men had a second round of it. Sue and I had enough work finishing our first.

Harry held his glass aloft and proposed a toast. "To good friends," he said. "To close friendship with good people." And after everyone had taken a sip he said, "You know, in a couple of days we all go back to the lives we used to lead. Sue and I go back to Oklahoma, you two go back to Boston, Mass. Andy, you go back to your investments business and I'll be doin' what I do. And we got each other's addresses and phone, and we say we'll keep in touch, and maybe we will. But if we do or we don't, either way one thing's sure. The minute we get off that plane at JFK, that's when the carriage turns into a pumpkin and the horses go back to bein' mice. You know what I mean?"

Everyone did.

"Anyway," he said, "what me an' Sue were thinkin', we thought there's a whole lot of Rome, a mess of good restaurants, and things to see and places to go. We thought it's silly to have four people all do the same things and go the same places and miss out on all the rest. We thought, you know, after breakfast tomorrow, we'd split up and spend the day separate." He took a breath. "Like Sue and Andy'd team up for the day and, Elaine, you an' me'd be together."

"The way we did in Madrid," somebody said.

"Except I mean for the whole day," Harry said. A light film of perspiration gleamed on his forehead. I looked at his jacket and tried to decide if he was wearing his gun. I'd seen it on our afternoon in Madrid. His jacket had come open and I'd seen the gun, snug in his shoulder holster. "The whole day and then the evening, too. Dinner—and after."

There was a silence which I don't suppose could have lasted nearly as long as it seemed to. Then Andrew said he thought it was a good idea, and Sue agreed, and so did I.

Later, in our hotel room, Andrew assured me that we could back out. "I don't think they have any more experience with this than we do. You saw how nervous Harry was during his little speech. He'd probably be relieved to a certain degree if we did back out."

"Is that what you want to do?"

He thought for a moment. "For my part," he said, "I'd as soon go through with it."

"So would I. My only concern is if it made some difference between us afterward."

"I don't think it will. This is fantasy, you know. It's not the real world. We're not in Boston *or* Oklahoma. We're in Rome, and you know what they say. When in Rome, do as the Romans do."

"And is this what the Romans do?"

"It's probably what they do when they go to Stockholm," Andrew said.

In the morning, we joined the Dattners for breakfast. Afterward, without anything being said, we paired off as Harry had suggested the night before. He and I walked through a sun-drenched morning to the Spanish Steps, where I bought a bag of crumbs and fed the pigeons. After that—

Oh, what does it matter what came next, what particular tourist things we found to do that day? Suffice it to say that we went interesting places and saw rapturous sights, and everything we did and saw was heightened by anticipation of the evening ahead.

We ate lightly that night, and drank freely but not to excess. The trattoria where we dined wasn't far from our hotel and the night was clear and mild, so we walked back. Harry slipped an arm around my waist. I leaned a little against his shoulder. After we'd walked a way in silence, he said very softly, "Elaine, only if you want to."

"But I do," I heard myself say.

Then he took me in his arms and kissed me.

I ought to recall the night better than I do. We felt love and lust for each other, and sated both appetites. He was gentler than I might have guessed he'd be, and I more abandoned. I could probably remember precisely what happened if I put my mind to it, but I don't think I could make the memory seem real. Because it's as if it happened to someone else. It was vivid at the time, because at the time I truly was the person sharing her bed with Harry. But that person had no existence before or after that European vacation.

There was a moment when I looked up and saw one of Andrew's neckties hanging on the knob of the closet door. It struck me that I should have put the tie away, that it was out of place there. Then I told myself that the tie was where it ought to be, that it was Harry who didn't belong here. And finally I decided that both belonged, my husband's tie and my inappropriate Oklahoma lover. Now both belonged, but in the morning the necktie would remain and Harry would be gone.

As indeed he was. I awakened a little before dawn and was alone in the room. I went back to sleep, and when I next opened my eyes Andrew was in bed beside me. Had they met in the hallway? I wondered. Had they worked out the logistics of this passage in advance? I never asked. I still don't know.

Our last day in Rome, the Dattners went their way and we went ours. Andrew and I got to the Vatican, saw the Colosseum, and wandered here and there, stopping at sidewalk cafés for espresso. We hardly talked about the previous evening, beyond assuring each other that we had enjoyed it, that we were glad it had happened, and that our feelings for one another remained unchanged—deepened, if anything, by virtue of having shared this experience, if it could be said to have been shared.

We joined Harry and Sue for dinner. And in the morning we all rode out to the airport and boarded our flight to New York. I remember looking at the other passengers on the plane, few of whom I'd exchanged more than a couple of sentences with in the course of the past three weeks. There were almost certainly couples among them with whom we

ad more in common than we had with the Dattners. Had any
f them had comparable flings in the course of the trip?

At JFK we all collected our luggage and went through
customs and passport control. Then we were off to catch our
connecting flight to Boston while Harry and Sue had a four-
hour wait for their TWA flight to Tulsa. We said good-bye. The
men shook hands while Sue and I embraced. Then Harry and
kissed, and Sue and Andrew kissed. That woman slept with
my husband, I thought. And that man—I slept with him. I had
the thought that, were I to continue thinking about it, I would
start laughing.

Two hours later we were on the ground at Logan, and less
than an hour after that we were in our own house.

That weekend Paul and Marilyn Welles came over for
dinner and heard a play-by-play account of our three-week
vacation—with the exception, of course, of that second-last
night in Rome. Paul is a business associate of Andrew's and
Marilyn is a woman not unlike me, and I wondered to myself
what would happen if we four traded partners for an evening.

But it wouldn't happen and I certainly didn't want it to
happen. I found Paul attractive and I know Andrew had always
found Marilyn attractive. But such an incident among us
wouldn't be appropriate, as it had somehow been appropriate
with the Dattners.

I know Andrew was having much the same thoughts. We
didn't discuss it afterward, but one knows. . . .

I thought of all of this just last week. Andrew was in a
bank in Skokie, Illinois, along with Paul Welles and two other
men. One of the tellers managed to hit the silent alarm and
the police arrived as they were on their way out. There was
some shooting. Paul Welles was wounded superficially, as was
one of the policemen. Another of the policemen was killed.

Andrew is quite certain he didn't hit anybody. He fired his
gun a couple of times, but he's sure he didn't kill the police
officer.

But when he got home we both kept thinking the same
thing. It could have been Harry Dattner.

Not literally, because what would an Oklahoma state
trooper be doing in Skokie, Illinois? But it might as easily have
been the Skokie cop in Europe with us. And it might have been
Andrew who shot him—or been shot *by* him, for that matter.

I don't know that I'm explaining this properly. It's all so incredible. That I should have slept with a policeman while my husband was with a policeman's wife. That we had ever become friendly with them in the first place. I have to remind myself, and keep reminding myself, that it all happened over seas. It happened in Europe, and it happened to four other people. We were not ourselves, and Sue and Harry were not themselves. It happened, you see, in another universe altogether, and so, really, it's as if it never happened at all.

DEATH WISH

The cop saw the car stop on the bridge but didn't pay any particular attention to it. People were apt to pull over to the side in the middle of the span, especially late at night when the traffic was thin and they could stop for a moment without somebody's horn stabbing them in the back. The bridge was a graceful steel parabola over the deep channel of river that cut the city neatly in two, and the center of the bridge provided the best view of the city, with the old downtown buildings clustered together on the right, the flour mills downriver on the left, the gentle skyline, the gulls maneuvering over the river. The bridge was the best place to see it all. It wasn't private enough for the teenagers, who were given to long-term parking and preferred drive-in movie theaters or stretches of road along the north bank of the river, but sightseers stopped often, took in the view for a few moments, and then continued across.

Suicides liked the bridge, too. The cop didn't think of that at first, not until he saw the man emerge from the car, and walk slowly to the footpath at the edge, and place a hand tentatively upon the rail. There was something in his stance, something in the pose of the solitary figure upon the empty bridge in the after-midnight gloom, something about the grayness of the night, the way the fog was coming off the river. The cop looked at him and cursed and wondered if he could get to him in time.

He walked toward the man, headed over the bridge on the footpath. He didn't want to shout or blow his whistle at him because he knew what shock or surprise could do to a potential jumper. Once he saw the man's hands tense on the rail, his feet lifting up on the toes. At that moment he almost cried out, almost broke into a run, but then the man's feet came back into position, his hands loosened their grip, and he took out a cigarette and lit it. Then the cop knew he had time. They always smoked that last cigarette all the way down before they went over the edge.

When the cop was within ten yards of him the man turned, started slightly, then nodded in resignation. He appeared to be somewhere in his middle thirties, tall, with a long narrow face and deep-set eyes topped with thick black eyebrows.

"Nice night," the cop said.

"Yes."

"Having a look at the sights?"

"That's right."

"Saw you out here, thought I'd come out and have a talk with you. It can get lonely this hour at night." The cop patted his pockets, passed over his cigarettes. "Say, you don't happen to have a spare cigarette on you, do you? I must have run out."

The man gave him a cigarette. It was a filter, and the cop normally smoked nothing but regulars, but he wasn't about to complain. He thanked the man, accepted a light, thanked him again, and stood beside him, hands on the rail, leaning out over the water and looking at the city and the river.

"Looks pretty from here," he said.

"Does it?"

"Sure, I'd say so. Makes a man feel at peace with himself."

"It hasn't had that effect on me," the man said. "I was thinking about, oh, the ways a man could find peace for himself."

"I guess the best way is just to go on plugging away at life," the cop said. "Things generally have a way of straightening themselves out, sooner or later. Some of the time they take awhile, and I guess they don't look too good, but they work out."

"You really believe that?"

"Sure."

"With the things you see in your job?"

"Even with all of it," the cop said. "It's a tough world, but that's nothing new. It's the best we've got, the way I figure it. You're sure not going to find a better one at the bottom of a river."

The man said nothing for a long time, then he pitched his cigarette over the rail. He and the cop stood watching it as it shed sparks on the way down, then heard the tiny hiss as it met the water.

"It didn't make much of a splash," the man said.

"No."

"Few of us do," the man said. He paused for a moment, then turned to face the cop. "My name's Edward Wright," he added. The cop gave his own name. "I don't think I would have done it," the man went on. "Not tonight."

"No sense taking chances, is there?"

"I guess not."

"You're taking a chance yourself, aren't you? Coming out here, standing at the edge, thinking it over. Anyone who does that long enough, sooner or later gets a little too nervous and goes over the edge. He doesn't really want to and he's sorry long before he hits the water, but it's too late; he took too many chances and it's over for him. Tempt fate too much and fate gets you."

"I suppose you're right."

"Something in particular bothering you?"

"Not . . . anything special, no."

"Have you been seeing a doctor?"

"Off and on."

"That can help, you know."

"So they say."

"Want to go grab a cup of coffee?"

The man opened his mouth, started to say something, then changed his mind. He lit another cigarette and blew out a cloud of smoke, watching the way the wind dispersed it. "I'll be all right now," he said.

"Sure?"

"I'll go home, get some sleep. I haven't been sleeping so well, not since my wife—"

"Oh," the cop said.

"She died. She was all I had and, well, she died."

The cop put a hand on his shoulder. "You'll get over it, Mr. Wright. You just have to hold on, that's all. Hold on, and sooner or later you'll get over it. Maybe you think you can't live through it, nothing will be the same, but—"

"I know."

"You sure you don't want a cup of coffee?"

"No, I'd better get home," the man said. "I'm sorry to cause trouble. I'll try to relax, I'll be all right."

The cop watched him drive away and wondered whether he should have taken him in. No point, he decided. You went crazy enough hauling in every attempted suicide, and this one hadn't actually attempted anything, he had merely thought about it. Too, if you started picking up everyone who contemplated suicide you'd have your hands full.

He headed back for the other side of the bridge. When he reached his post he decided he should make a note of it, anyway, so he hauled out his pencil and his notebook and wrote down the name, *Edward Wright*. So he would remember what the name meant, he added *Big Eyebrows, Wife Dead, Contemplated Jumping*.

The psychiatrist stroked his pointed beard and looked over at the patient on the couch. The importance of beard and couch, as he had told his wife many times, lay in their property for enabling his patients to see him as a function of such outward symbols rather than as an individual, thus facilitating transference. His wife hated the beard and felt he used the couch for amorous dalliance. It was true, he thought, that he and his plump blond receptionist had on a few occasions occupied the couch together. A few memorable occasions, he amended, and he closed his eyes, savoring the memory of the delicious way he and Hannah had gone through Krafft-Ebing together, page by delirious page.

Reluctantly, he dragged himself back to his current patient. ". . . no longer seems worth living," the man said. "I drag myself through life a day at a time."

"We all live our lives a day at a time," the psychiatrist commented.

"But is it always an ordeal?"

"No."

"I almost killed myself last night. No, the night before last. I almost jumped from the Morrissey Bridge."

"And?"

"A policeman came along. I wouldn't have jumped anyway."

"Why not?"

"I don't know."

The interplay went on, the endless dialogue of patient and doctor. Sometimes the doctor could go through the whole hour without thinking at all, making automatic responses, reacting as he always did, but not really hearing a word that was said to him. *I wonder,* he thought, *whether I do these people any good at all. Perhaps they only wish to talk and need only the illusion of a listener. Perhaps the entire profession is no more than an intellectual confidence game. If I were a priest,* he thought wistfully, *I could go to my bishop when struck by doubts of faith, but psychiatrists do not have bishops. The only trouble with the profession is the unfortunate absence of an orderly hierarchy. Absolute religions could not be so democratically organized.*

He listened, next, to a dream. Almost all of his patients delighted in telling him their dreams, a source of unending frustration to the psychiatrist, who never in his life remembered having a dream of his own. From time to time he fantasied that it was all a gigantic put-on, that there were really no dreams at all. He listened to this dream with academic interest, glancing now and then at his watch, wishing the fifty-minute hour would end. The dream, he knew, indicated a diminishing enthusiasm for life, a development of the death wish, and a desire for suicide that was being tentatively held in check by fear and moral training. He wondered how long his patient would be able to refrain from taking his own life. In the three weeks he had been coming for therapy, he had seemed to be making only negative progress.

Another dream. The psychiatrist closed his eyes, sighed, and ceased listening. Five more minutes, he told himself. Five more minutes and then this idiot would leave, and perhaps he could persuade plump blond Hannah to do some further experimentation with him. There was a case of Stekel's he had read just the other night that sounded delicious.

* * *

The doctor looked up at the man, took in the heavy eyebrows, the deep-set eyes, the expression of guilt and fear. "I have to have my stomach pumped, Doctor," the man said. "Can you do it here or do we have to go to a hospital?"

"What's the matter with you?"

"Pills."

"What sort? Sleeping pills? Is that what you mean?"

"Yes."

"What sort? And how many did you take?"

The man explained the content of the pills and said that he had taken twenty. "Ten is a lethal dose," the doctor said. "How long ago did you take them?"

"Half an hour. No, less than that. Maybe twenty minutes."

"And then you decided not to act like a damned fool, eh? I gather you didn't fall asleep. Twenty minutes? Why wait this long?"

"I tried to make myself throw up."

"Couldn't do it? Well, we'll try the stomach pump," the doctor said. The operation of the pump was unpleasant, the analysis of the stomach's contents even less pleasant. The pumping had been in plenty of time, the doctor discovered. The pills had not yet been absorbed to any great degree by the bloodstream.

"You'll live," he said finally.

"Thank you, Doctor."

"Don't thank me. I'll have to report this, you know."

"I wish you wouldn't. I'm . . . I'm under a psychiatrist's care. It was more an accident than anything else, really."

"Twenty pills?" The doctor shrugged. "You'd better pay me now," he said. "I hate to send bills to potential suicides. It's risky."

"This is a fine shotgun for the price," the clerk said. "Now, if you want to get fancy, you can get yourself a weapon with a lot more range and accuracy. For just a few dollars more—"

"No, this will be satisfactory. And I'll need a box of shells."

The clerk put the box on the counter. "Or three boxes for—"

"Just the one."

"Sure thing," the clerk said. He drew the registry ledger from beneath the counter, opened it, set it on the top of the counter. "You'll have to sign right there," he said, "to keep the state happy." He checked the signature when the man had finished writing. "Now I'm supposed to see some identification, Mr. Wright. Just a driver's license if you've got it handy." He checked the license, compared the signatures, jotted down the license number, and nodded, satisfied.

"Thank you," said the man, when he had received his change. "Thank you very much."

"Thank *you*, Mr. Wright. I think you'll get a lot of use out of that gun."

"I'm sure I will."

At nine o'clock that night Edward Wright heard his back doorbell ring. He walked downstairs, glass in hand, finished his drink, and went to the door. He was a tall man, with sunken eyes topped by thick black eyebrows. He looked outside, recognized his visitor, hesitated only momentarily, and opened the door.

His visitor poked a shotgun into Edward Wright's abdomen.

"Mark—"

"Invite me in," the man said. "It's cold out here."

"Mark, I don't—"

"Inside."

In the living room Edward Wright stared into the mouth of the shotgun and knew that he was going to die.

"You killed her, Ed," the visitor said. "She wanted a divorce. You couldn't stand that, could you? I told her not to tell you. I told her it was dangerous, that you were nothing but an animal. I told her to run away with me and forget you but she wanted to do the decent thing and you killed her."

"You're crazy!"

"You made it good, didn't you? Made it look like an accident. How did you do it? You'd better tell me, or this gun goes off."

"I hit her."

"You hit her and killed her? Just like that?"

Wright swallowed. He looked at the gun, then at the man. "I hit her a few times. Quite a few times. Then I threw her down the cellar stairs. You can't go to the police with this, you know. They can't prove it and they wouldn't believe it."

"We won't go to the police," the man said. "I didn't go to them at the beginning. They didn't know of a motive for you, did they? I could have told them a motive, but I didn't go, Edward. Sit down at your desk, Edward. Now. That's right. Take out a sheet of paper and a pen. You'd better do as I say, Edward. There's a message I want you to write."

"You can't—"

"Write *I can't stand it any longer. This time I won't fail*, and sign your name."

"I won't do it."

"Yes, you will, Edward." He pressed the gun against the back of Edward Wright's shaking head.

"You wouldn't do it," Wright said.

"But I would."

"You'll hang for it, Mark. You won't get away with it."

"Suicide, Edward."

"No one would believe I would commit suicide, note or no note. They won't believe it."

"Just write the note, Edward. Then I'll give you the gun and leave you with your conscience. I definitely know what you'll do."

"You—"

"Just write the note. I don't want to kill you, Edward. I want you to write the note as a starter, and then I'll leave you here."

Wright did not exactly believe him, but the shotgun poised against the back of his head left him little choice. He wrote the note, signed his name.

"Turn around, Edward."

He turned, stared. The man looked very different. He had put on false eyebrows and a wig, and he had done something to his eyes, put makeup around them.

"Do you know who I look like now, Edward?"

"No."

"I look like *you*, Edward. Not exactly like you, of course. Not close enough to fool people who know you, but we're both about the same height and build. Add the character tags, the eyebrows and the hair and the hollow eyes, and put them on a man who introduces himself as Edward Wright and carries identification in that name, and what have you got? You've got a good imitation of you, Edward."

"You've been impersonating me."

"Yes, Edward."

"But why?"

"Character development," the man said. "You just told me you're not the suicidal type and no one will believe it when you kill yourself. However, you'd be surprised at your recent actions, Edward. There's a policeman who had to talk you out of jumping off the Morrissey Bridge. There's the psychiatrist who has been treating you for suicidal depression, complete with some classic dreams and fantasies. And there's the doctor who had to pump your stomach this afternoon." He prodded Edward's stomach with the gun.

"Pump my—"

"Yes, your stomach. A most unpleasant procedure, Edward. Do you see what I've gone through on your account? Sheer torture. You know, I was worried that my wig might slip during the ordeal, but these new epoxy resins are extraordinary. They say you can even wear a wig swimming, or in the shower." He rubbed one of the false eyebrows with his forefinger. "See how it stays on? And very lifelike, don't you think?"

Edward didn't say anything.

"All those things you've been doing, Edward. Funny you can't recall them. Do you remember buying this shotgun, Edward?"

"I—"

"You did, you know. Not an hour ago, you went into a store and bought this gun and a box of shells. Had to sign for it. Had to show your driver's license, too."

"How did you get my license?"

"I didn't. I created it." The man chuckled. "It wouldn't fool a policeman, but no policeman ever saw it. It certainly fooled the clerk, though. He copied that number very carefully. So you must have bought that gun after all, Edward."

The man ran his fingers through his wig. "Remarkably lifelike," he said again. "If I ever go bald, I'll have to get myself one of these." He laughed. "Not the suicidal type? Edward, this past week you've been the most suicidal man in town. Look at all the people who will swear to it."

"What about my friends? The people at the office?"

"They'll all help it along. Whenever a man commits suicide, his friends start to remember how moody he's been lately. Everybody always wants to get into the act, you know. I'm sure you've been acting very shocked and distraught over her death. You'd have to play the part, wouldn't you? Ah, you never should have killed her, Edward. I loved her, even if you didn't. You should have let her go, Edward."

Wright was sweating. "You said you weren't going to murder me. You said you would leave me alone with the gun—"

"Don't believe everything you hear," the man said, and very quickly, very deftly, he jabbed the gun barrel into Wright's mouth and pulled the trigger. Afterward he arranged things neatly enough, removed one of Wright's shoes, positioned his foot so that it appeared he had triggered the shotgun with his big toe. Then he wiped his own prints from the gun and managed to get Wright's prints all over the weapon. He left the note on top of the desk, slipped the psychiatrist's business card into Wright's wallet, stuffed the bill of sale for the gun into Wright's pocket.

"You shouldn't have killed her," he said to Wright's corpse. Then, smiling privately, he slipped out the back door and walked off into the night.

THE MERCIFUL
ANGEL OF DEATH

"**P**eople come here to die, Mr. Scudder. They check out of hospitals, give up their apartments, and come to Caritas. Because they know we'll keep them comfortable here. And they know we'll let them die."

Carl Orcott was long and lean, with a long sharp nose and a matching chin. Some gray showed in his fair hair and his strawberry-blond moustache. His facial skin was stretched tight over his skull, and there were hollows in his cheeks. He might have been naturally spare of flesh, or worn down by the demands of his job. Because he was a gay man in the last decade of a terrible century, another possibility suggested itself. That he was HIV-positive. That his immune system was compromised. That the virus that would one day kill him was already within him, waiting.

"Since an easy death is our whole reason for being," he was saying, "it seems a bit much to complain when it occurs. Death is not the enemy here. Death is a friend. Our people are in very bad shape by the time they come to us. You don't run to a hospice when you get the initial results from a blood test, or when the first purple K-S lesions show up. First you try everything, including denial, and everything works for a while, and finally nothing works, not the AZT, not the pentamidine, not the Louise Hay tapes, not the crystal healing. Not even the denial. When you're ready for it to be over, you come here and we see you out." He smiled thinly. "We hold the door for you. We don't boot you through it."

"But now you think—"

"I don't know what I think." He selected a briar pipe from a walnut stand that held eight of them, examined it, sniffed its bowl. "Grayson Lewes shouldn't have died," he said. "Not when he did. He was doing very well, relatively speaking. He was in agony, he had a CMV infection that was blinding him, but he was still strong. Of course he was dying, they're all dying, everybody's dying, but death certainly didn't appear to be imminent."

"What happened?"

"He died."

"What killed him?"

"I don't know." He breathed in the smell of the unlit pipe. "Someone went in and found him dead. There was no autopsy. There generally isn't. What would be the point? Doctors would just as soon not cut up AIDS patients anyway, not wanting the added risk of infection. Of course, most of our general staff are seropositive, but even so you try to avoid unnecessary additional exposure. Quantity could make a difference, and there could be multiple strains. The virus mutates, you see." He shook his head. "There's such a great deal we still don't know."

"There was no autopsy."

"No. I thought about ordering one."

"What stopped you?"

"The same thing that keeps people from getting the anti-body test. Fear of what I might find."

"You think someone killed Lewes."

"I think it's possible."

"Because he died abruptly. But people do that, don't they? Even if they're not sick to begin with. They have strokes or heart attacks."

"That's true."

"This happened before, didn't it? Lewes wasn't the first." He smiled ruefully. "You're good at this."

"It's what I do."

"Yes." His fingers were busy with the pipe. "There have been a few unexpected deaths. But there would be, as you've said. So there was no real cause for suspicion. There still isn't."

"But you're suspicious."

"Am I? I guess I am."

"Tell me the rest of it, Carl."

"I'm sorry," he said. "I'm making you drag it out of me, aren't I? Grayson Lewes had a visitor. She was in his room for twenty minutes, perhaps half an hour. She was the last person to see him alive. She may have been the first person to see him dead."

"Who is she?"

"I don't know. She's been coming here for months. She always brings flowers, something cheerful. She brought yellow freesias the last time. Nothing fancy, just a five-dollar bunch from the Korean on the corner, but they do brighten a room."

"Had she visited Lewes before?"

He shook his head. "Other people. Every week or so she would turn up, always asking for one of our residents by name. It's often the sickest of the sick that she comes to see."

"And then they die?"

"Not always. But often enough so that it's been remarked upon. Still, I never let myself think that she played a causative role. I thought she had some instinct that drew her to your side when you were circling the drain." He looked off to the side. "When she visited Lewes, someone joked that we'd probably have his room available soon. When you're on staff here, you become quite irreverent in private. Otherwise you'd go crazy."

"It was the same way on the police force."

"I'm not surprised. When one of us would cough or sneeze, another might say, 'Uh-oh, you might be in line for a visit from Mercy.'"

"Is that her name?"

"Nobody knows her name. It's what we call her among ourselves. The Merciful Angel of Death. Mercy, for short."

A man named Bobby sat up in bed in his fourth-floor room. He had short gray hair and a gray brush moustache and a gray complexion bruised purple here and there by Kaposi's

Sarcoma. For all of the ravages of the disease, he had a heart-breakingly youthful face. He was a ruined cherub, the oldest boy in the world.

"She was here yesterday," he said.

"She visited you twice," Carl said.

"Twice?"

"Once last week and once three or four days ago."

"I thought it was one time. And I thought it was yesterday." He frowned. "It all seems like yesterday."

"What does, Bobby?"

"Everything. Camp Arrowhead. *I Love Lucy*. The moon shot. One enormous yesterday with everything crammed into it, like his closet. I don't remember his name but he was famous for his closet."

"Fibber McGee," Carl said.

"I don't know why I can't remember his name," Bobby said languidly. "It'll come to me. I'll think of it yesterday."

I said, "When she came to see you—"

"She was beautiful. Tall, slim, gorgeous eyes. A flowing dove-gray robe, a blood-red scarf at her throat. I wasn't sure if she was real or not. I thought she might be a vision."

"Did she tell you her name?"

"I don't remember. She said she was there to be with me. And mostly she just sat there, where Carl's sitting. She held my hand."

"What else did she say?"

"That I was safe. That no one could hurt me anymore. She said—"

"Yes?"

"That I was innocent," he said, and he sobbed and let his tears flow.

He wept freely for a few moments, then reached for a Kleenex. When he spoke again his voice was matter-of-fact, even detached. "She *was* here twice," he said. "I remember now. The second time I got snotty, I really had the rag on, and I told her she didn't have to hang around if she didn't want to. And she said *I* didn't have to hang around if *I* didn't want to.

"And I said, right, I can go tap-dancing down Broadway with a rose in my teeth. And she said, no, all I have to do is let go and my spirit will soar free. And I looked at her, and I knew what she meant."

"And?"

"She told me to let go, to give it all up, to just let go and go to the light. And I said—this is strange, you know?"

"What did you say, Bobby?"

"I said I couldn't see the light and I wasn't ready to go to it. And she said that was all right, that when I was ready the light would be there to guide me. She said I would know how to do it when the time came. And she talked about how to do it."

"How?"

"By letting go. By going to the light. I don't remember everything she said. I don't even know for sure if all of it happened, or if I dreamed part of it. I never know anymore. Sometimes I have dreams and later they feel like part of my personal history. And sometimes I look back at my life and most of it has a veil over it, as if I never lived it at all, as if it were nothing but a dream."

Back in his office Carl picked up another pipe and brought its blackened bowl to his nose. He said, "You asked why I called you instead of the police. Can you imagine putting Bobby through an official interrogation?"

"He seems to go in and out of lucidity."

He nodded. "The virus penetrates the blood-brain barrier. If you survive the K-S and the opportunistic infections, the reward is dementia. Bobby is mostly clear, but some of his mental circuits are beginning to burn out. Or rust out, or clog up, or whatever it is that they do."

"There are cops who know how to take testimony from people like that."

"Even so. Can you see the tabloid headlines? MERCY KILLER STRIKES AIDS HOSPICE. We have a hard enough time getting by as it is. You know, whenever the press happens to mention how many dogs and cats the SPCA puts to sleep, donations drop to a trickle. Imagine what would happen to us."

"Some people would give you more."

He laughed. " 'Here's a thousand dollars—kill ten of 'em for me.' You could be right."

He sniffed at the pipe again. I said, "You know, as far as I'm concerned you can go ahead and smoke that thing."

He stared at me, then at the pipe, as if surprised to find

it in his hand. "There's no smoking anywhere in the building," he said. "Anyway, I don't smoke."

"The pipes came with the office?"

He colored. "They were John's," he said. "We lived together. He died . . . God, it'll be two years in November. It doesn't seem that long."

"I'm sorry, Carl."

"I used to smoke cigarettes, Marlboros, but I quit ages ago. But I never minded his pipe smoke, though. I always liked the aroma. And now I'd rather smell one of his pipes than the AIDS smell. Do you know the smell I mean?"

"Yes."

"Not everyone with AIDS has it but a lot of them do, and most sickrooms reek of it. You must have smelled it in Bobby's room. It's an unholy musty smell, a smell like rotted leather. I can't stand the smell of leather anymore. I used to love leather, but now I can't help associating it with the stink of gay men wasting away in fetid airless rooms.

"And this whole building smells that way to me. There's the stench of disinfectant over everything. We use tons of it, spray and liquid. The virus is surprisingly frail, it doesn't last long outside the body, but we leave as little as possible to chance, and so the rooms and halls all smell of disinfectant. But underneath it, always, there's the smell of the disease itself."

He turned the pipe over in his hands. "His clothes were full of the smell. John's. I gave everything away. But his pipes held a scent I had always associated with him, and a pipe is such a personal thing, isn't it, with the smoker's toothmarks in the stem." He looked at me. His eyes were dry, his voice strong and steady. There was no grief in his tone, only in the words themselves. "Two years in November, though I swear it doesn't seem that long, and I use one smell to keep another at bay. And, I suppose, to bridge the gap of years, to keep him a little closer to me." He put the pipe down. "Back to cases. Will you take a careful but unofficial look at our Angel of Death?"

I said I would. He said I'd want a retainer, and opened the top drawer of his desk. I told him it wouldn't be necessary.

"But isn't that standard for private detectives?"

"I'm not one, not officially. I don't have a license."

"So you told me, but even so—"

"I'm not a lawyer, either," I went on, "but there's no reason why I can't do a little *pro bono* work once in a while. If it takes too much of my time I'll let you know, but for now let's call it a donation."

The hospice was in the Village, on Hudson Street. Rachel Bookspan lived five miles north in an Italianate brownstone on Claremont Avenue. Her husband, Paul, walked to work at Columbia University, where he was an associate professor of political science. Rachel was a free-lance copy editor, hired by several publishers to prepare manuscripts for publication. Her specialties were history and biography.

She told me all this over coffee in her book-lined living room. She talked about a manuscript she was working on, the biography of a woman who had founded a religious sect in the late nineteenth century. She talked about her children, two boys, who would be home from school in an hour or so. Finally she ran out of steam and I brought the conversation back to her brother, Arthur Fineberg, who had lived on Morton Street and worked downtown as a librarian for an investment firm. And who had died two weeks ago at the Caritas Hospice.

"How we cling to life," she said. "Even when it's awful. Even when we yearn for death."

"Did your brother want to die?"

"He prayed for it. Every day the disease took a little more from him, gnawing at him like a mouse, and after months and months and months of hell it finally took his will to live. He couldn't fight anymore. He had nothing to fight with, nothing to fight *for*. But he went on living all the same."

She looked at me, then looked away. "He begged me to kill him," she said.

I didn't say anything.

"How could I refuse him? But how could I help him? First I thought it wasn't right, but then I decided it was his life, and who had a better right to end it if he wanted to? But how could I do it? How?

"I thought of pills. We don't have anything in the house except Midol for cramps. I went to my doctor and said I had trouble sleeping. Well, that was true enough. He gave me a prescription for a dozen Valium. I didn't even bother getting it filled. I didn't want to give Artie a handful of tranquilizers. I wanted to give him one of those cyanide capsules the spies always had in World War Two movies. You bite down and you're gone. But where do you go to get something like that?"

She sat forward in her chair. "Do you remember that man in the Midwest who unhooked his kid from a respirator? The doctors wouldn't let the boy die and the father went into the hospital with a gun and held everybody at bay until his son was dead. I think that man was a hero."

"A lot of people thought so."

"God, I wanted to be a hero! I had fantasies. There's a Robinson Jeffers poem about a crippled hawk and the narrator puts it out of its misery. 'I gave him the lead gift,' he says. Meaning a bullet, a gift of lead. I wanted to give my brother that gift. I don't have a gun. I don't even believe in guns. At least I never did. I don't know what I believe in anymore.

"If I'd had a gun, could I have gone in there and shot him? I don't see how. I have a knife, I have a kitchen full of knives, and believe me, I thought of going in there with a knife in my purse and waiting until he dozed off and then slipping the knife between his ribs and into his heart. I visualized it, I went over every aspect of it, but I didn't do it. My God, I never even left the house with a knife in my bag."

She asked if I wanted more coffee. I said I didn't. I asked her if her brother had had other visitors, and if he might have made the same request of one of them.

"He had dozens of friends, men and women who loved him. And yes, he would have asked them. He told everybody he wanted to die. As hard as he fought to live, for all those months, that's how determined he became to die. Do you think someone helped him?"

"I think it's possible."

"God, I hope so," she said. "I just wish it had been me."

"I haven't had the test," Aldo said. "I'm a forty-four-year-old gay man who led an active sex life since I was fifteen. I don't *have* to take the test, Matthew. I assume I'm seropositive. I assume everybody is."

He was a plump teddy bear of a man, with curly black hair and a face as permanently buoyant as a smile button. We were sharing a small table at a coffeehouse on Bleecker, just two doors from the shop where he sold comic books and baseball cards to collectors.

"I may not develop the disease," he said. "I may die a perfectly respectable death due to overindulgence in food and drink. I may get hit by a bus or struck down by a mugger. If I do get sick I'll wait until it gets really bad, because I love this life, Matthew, I really do. But when the time comes I don't want to make local stops. I'm gonna catch an express train out of here."

"You sound like a man with his bags packed."

"No luggage. Travelin' light. You remember the song?"

"Of course."

He hummed a few bars of it, his foot tapping out the rhythm, our little marble-topped table shaking with the motion. He said, "I have pills enough to do the job. I also have a loaded handgun. And I think I have the nerve to do what I have to do, when I have to do it." He frowned, an uncharacteristic expression for him. "The danger lies in waiting too long. Winding up in a hospital bed too weak to do anything, too addled by brain fever to remember what it was you were supposed to do. Wanting to die but unable to manage it."

"I've heard there are people who'll help."

"You've heard that, have you?"

"One woman in particular."

"What are you after, Matthew?"

"You were a friend of Grayson Lewes. And of Arthur Fineberg. There's a woman who helps people who want to die. She may have helped them."

"And?"

"And you know how to get in touch with her."

"Who says?"

"I forget, Aldo."

The smile was back. "You're discreet, huh?"

"Very."

"I don't want to make trouble for her."

"Neither do I."

"Then why not leave her alone?"

"There's a hospice administrator who's afraid she's murdering people. He called me in rather than start an official police inquiry. But if I don't get anywhere—"

"He calls the cops." He found his address book, copied out a number for me. "Please don't make trouble for her," he said. "I might need her myself."

I called her that evening, met her the following afternoon at a cocktail lounge just off Washington Square. She was as described, even to the gray cape over a long gray dress. Her scarf today was canary yellow. She was drinking Perrier, and I ordered the same.

She said, "Tell me about your friend. You say he's very ill."

"He wants to die. He's been begging me to kill him but I can't do it."

"No, of course not."

"I was hoping you might be able to visit him."

"If you think it might help. Tell me something about him, why don't you."

I don't suppose she was more than forty-five, if that, but there was something ancient about her face. You didn't need much of a commitment to reincarnation to believe she had lived before. Her facial features were pronounced, her eyes a graying blue. Her voice was pitched low, and along with her height it raised doubts about her sexuality. She might have been a sex change, or a drag queen. But I didn't think so. There was an Eternal Female quality to her that didn't feel like parody.

I said, "I can't."

"Because there's no such person."

"I'm afraid there are plenty of them, but I don't have one in mind." I told her in a couple of sentences why I was there. When I'd finished she let the silence stretch, then asked me if I thought she could kill anyone. I told her it was hard to know what anyone could do.

She said, "I think you should see for yourself what it is that I do."

She stood up. I put some money on the table and followed her out to the street.

We took a cab to a four-story brick building on Twenty-second Street west of Ninth. We climbed two flights of stairs, and the door opened when she knocked on it. I could smell the disease before I was across the threshold. The young black man who opened the door was glad to see her and unsurprised by my presence. He didn't ask my name or tell me his.

"Kevin's so tired," he told us both. "It breaks my heart."

We walked through a neat, sparsely furnished living room and down a short hallway to a bedroom, where the smell was stronger. Kevin lay in a bed with its head cranked up. He looked like a famine victim, or someone liberated from Dachau. Terror filled his eyes.

She pulled a chair up to the side of his bed and sat in it. She took his hand in hers and used her free hand to stroke his forehead. You're safe now, she told him. You're safe, you don't have to hurt anymore, you did all the things you had to do. You can relax now, you can let go now, you can go to the light.

"You can do it," she told him. "Close your eyes, Kevin, and go inside yourself and find the part that's holding on. Somewhere within you there's a part of you that's like a clenched fist, and I want you to find that part and be with that part. And let go. Let the fist open its fingers. It's as if the fist is holding a little bird, and if you open up the hand the bird can fly free. Just let it happen, Kevin. Just let go."

He was straining to talk, but the best he could do was make a sort of cawing sound. She turned to the black man, who was standing in the doorway. "David," she said, "his parents aren't living, are they?"

"I believe they're both gone."

"Which one was he closest to?"

"I don't know. I believe they're both gone a long time now."

"Did he have a lover? Before you, I mean."

"Kevin and I were never lovers. I don't even know him that well. I'm here 'cause he hasn't got anybody else. He had a lover."

"Did his lover die? What was his name?"

"Martin."

"Kevin," she said, "you're going to be all right now. All you have to do is go to the light. Do you see the light? Your mother's there, Kevin, and your father, and Martin—"

"Mark!" David cried. "Oh, God, I'm sorry, I'm so stupid, it wasn't Martin, it was Mark, Mark, that was his name."

"That's all right, David."

"I'm so damn stupid—"

"Look into the light, Kevin," she said. "Mark is there, and your parents, and everyone who ever loved you. Matthew, take his other hand. Kevin, you don't have to stay here anymore, darling. You did everything you came here to do. You don't have to stay. You don't have to hold on. You can let go, Kevin. You can go to the light. Let go and reach out to the light—"

I don't know how long she talked to him. Fifteen, twenty minutes, I suppose. Several times he made the cawing sound, but for the most part he was silent. Nothing seemed to be happening, and then I realized that his terror was no longer a presence. She seemed to have talked it away. She went on talking to him, stroking his brow and holding his hand, and I held his other hand. I was no longer listening to what she was saying, just letting the words wash over me while my mind played with some tangled thought like a kitten with yarn.

Then something happened. The energy in the room shifted and I looked up, knowing that he was gone.

"Yes," she murmured. "Yes, Kevin. God bless you, God give you rest. Yes."

"Sometimes they're stuck," she said. "They want to go but they can't. They've been hanging on so long, you see, that they don't know how to stop."

"So you help them."

"If I can."

"What if you can't? Suppose you talk and talk and they still hold on?"

"Then they're not ready. They'll be ready another time. Sooner or later everybody lets go, everybody dies. With or without my help."

"And when they're not ready—"

"Sometimes I come back another time. And sometimes they're ready then."

"What about the ones who beg for help? The ones like Arthur Fineberg, who plead for death but aren't physically close enough to it to let go?"

"What do you want me to say?"

"The thing you want to say. The thing that's stuck in your throat, the way his own unwanted life was stuck in Kevin's throat. You're holding on to it."

"Just let it go, eh?"

"If you want."

We were walking somewhere in Chelsea, and we walked a full block now without either of us saying a word. Then she said, "I think there's a world of difference between assisting someone verbally and doing anything physical to hasten death."

"So do I."

"And that's where I draw the line. But sometimes, having drawn that line—"

"You step over it."

"Yes. The first time I swear I acted without conscious intent. I used a pillow, I held it over his face and—" She breathed deeply. "I swore it would never happen again. But then there was someone else, and he just needed help, you know, and—"

"And you helped him."

"Yes. Was I wrong?"

"I don't know what's right or wrong."

"Suffering is wrong," she said, "unless it's part of His plan, and how can I presume to decide if it is or not? Maybe people can't let go because there's one more lesson they have to learn before they move on. Who the hell am I to decide it's time for somebody's life to end? How dare I interfere?"

"And yet you do."

"Just once in a while, when I just don't see a way around it. Then I do what I have to do. I'm sure I must have a choice in the matter, but I swear it doesn't feel that way. It doesn't feel as though I have any choice at all." She stopped walking, turned to look at me. She said, "Now what happens?"

"Well, she's the Merciful Angel of Death," I told Carl Orcott. "She visits the sick and dying, almost always at somebody's invitation. A friend contacts her, or a relative."

"Do they pay her?"

"Sometimes they try to. She won't take any money. She even pays for the flowers herself." She'd taken Dutch iris to Kevin's apartment on Twenty-second Street. Blue, with yellow centers that matched her scarf.

"She does it *pro bono*," he said.

"And she talks to them. You heard what Bobby said. I got

to see her in action. She talked the poor son of a bitch straight out of this world and into the next one. I suppose you could argue that what she does comes perilously close to hypnosis, that she hypnotizes people and convinces them to kill themselves psychically, but I can't imagine anybody trying to sell that to a jury."

"She just talks to them."

"Uh-huh. 'Let go, go to the light.' "

" 'And have a nice day.' "

"That's the idea."

"She's not killing people?"

"Nope. Just letting them die."

He picked up a pipe. "Well, hell," he said, "that's what we do. Maybe I ought to put her on staff." He sniffed the pipe bowl. "You have my thanks, Matthew. Are you sure you don't want some of our money to go with it? Just because Mercy works *pro bono* doesn't mean you should have to."

"That's all right."

"You're certain?"

I said, "You asked me the first day if I knew what AIDS smelled like."

"And you said you'd smelled it before. Oh."

I nodded. "I've lost friends to it. I'll lose more before it's over. In the meantime I'm grateful when I get the chance to do you a favor. Because I'm glad this place is here, so people have a place to come to."

Even I was glad she was around, the woman in gray, the Merciful Angel of Death. To hold the door for them, and show them the light on the other side. And, if they really needed it, to give them the least little push through it.

THE TULSA
EXPERIENCE

They were teasing me Friday at the office. Sharon told me to be sure and send her a postcard, the way she always does, and I said what I always say, that I'd be back before the postcard reached her. And Warren asked which airline I was flying, and when I told him he very solemnly pulled out a quarter and handed it to me, telling me to buy some flight insurance and put him down as beneficiary.

Lee said, "Where's it going to be this time, Dennis? Acapulco? Macao? The south of France?"

"Tulsa," I said.

"Tulsa," he said. "Would that be Tulsa, Spain, on the Costa Brava? Or do you mean Tulsa, Nepal, gateway to the Himalayas?"

"This will come as a shock to you," I said, "but it's Tulsa, Oklahoma."

"Tulsa, Oklahoma," he marveled. "So the Gold Dust Twins are going to glamorous Tulsa, Oklahoma. I suppose Harry is up to it, but are you sure your heart can handle the excitement?"

"I'll try to pace myself," I said.

Harry and I are not twins, Gold Dust or otherwise. He's my brother, two years older than I, and aside from our vacations we actually see very little of each other. Harry, who has never married, still lives in the row house in Woodside where we grew up. After college he helped in the store and took over the business when Dad retired. The house was left to both of us when our parents died, but we worked out a way for him to buy my share.

I was married for several years, but I've been divorced for longer than I was married, and I doubt I'll marry again. I have a nice apartment on East Eighty-third Street. It's small but it suits me, and it's rent-controlled. Work is a short bus ride away, a walk in good weather.

I had taken the bus that morning, although the weather was nice, because I had my suitcase with me. I worked right through lunch hour and then took the rest of the afternoon off and caught a cab to the airport. I got there over an hour before flight time and Harry was already there, his bag checked. "Well," he said, punching me affectionately on the shoulder. "You ready for the Tulsa experience, Denny?"

"I sure am," I said.

I've been at Langford Corporation for almost seventeen years. I had another job for a year and a half when I first got out of college, and then I came to Langford, and I've been with the company ever since. So for the past five years I've been entitled to four weeks of paid vacation a year. I take a week in the spring, a week in the summer, a week in the fall, and a week in the winter, and Harry arranges to close his store during those weeks. When we first started doing this he let his employees take over, but that didn't work out so well, and it's simpler and easier just to lock the doors for a week.

And that's really about the only time we see each other. Each season we pick a city, somewhere right here in the United States, and we take rooms in a nice hotel and make sure we experience the place to the hilt.

Boston was the third city we visited together, or maybe it was the fourth. I could stop and figure it out, but it doesn't matter; the point is that there was one of those multiscreen presentations in a theater near Quincy Market, giving you the history of the city and an armchair tour of the area. *The Boston Experience*, they called it, and ever since we've used that phrase to describe our travels to one another. After Boston we had the Atlanta experience. Now we were going to have the Tulsa experience, and three months ago, give or take a week, we were having the San Diego experience.

I can understand why Lee teases me. I have never been to London or Paris or Rome, and I don't know that I'll ever get out of this country at all. We've talked about it, Harry and I, but whenever it comes time to plan a trip we always wind up choosing an American city. I guess it's not glamorous, and maybe we're missing something, but we always have a great time, so why change?

Founded in 1879, Tulsa has a population of 360,919, and is the second-largest city in Oklahoma. (Oklahoma City, the capital, is larger by about forty thousand; we have not yet had the Oklahoma City experience.) Tulsa is 750 feet above sea level, located in the heart of a major oil- and gas-producing area. More than six hundred energy-oriented firms employ upward of thirty thousand people.

We reviewed this and other facts about Tulsa during our flight. Harry had done the planning, so he had the guidebooks, and we read passages aloud to one another. We both ordered martinis when the stewardess came around with the drinks cart. Harry's not a big drinker, and I hardly drink at all except when we travel. But the drinks are free in first class and it seems silly not to have one.

We always fly first class. The seats are more comfortable and they treat you with special care. It costs more, of course, and it may not really be worth the difference, but it helps make the trip special. And we can afford it. I earn a decent salary, and Harry has always done well with the store, and neither of us is given to high living. Harry has always lived alone, as I believe I mentioned, and my own marriage was childless, and my wife has long since remarried so I don't have any alimony to pay. That makes it easy enough for us to fly first class and stay at a good hotel and eat in the best restaurants. We don't throw money around like drunken sailors, or even like Tulsa oilmen, but we treat ourselves well.

There was an in-flight movie, but we didn't bother watching it. It was more interesting to read the guidebooks and discuss which attractions appealed and which we thought we could safely pass up. The average person would probably think that a week would be more than time enough to experience everything a city like Tulsa has to offer, but he would be very much mistaken.

You've probably heard jokes about Philadelphia, for example. That they had a contest, and first prize was a week in Philadelphia while second prize was two weeks. Well, we've had the Philadelphia experience, and a week was nowhere near enough to experience the city to the fullest. We did well, we went just about everywhere we really wanted to go, but there were still quite a few attractions we had to pass up with some regret.

The flight was enjoyable. Harry had the aisle seat this time, so he got to flirt a little with the stewardess. For my part, I was able to look out the window during our approach to Tulsa. It was still light out, but even on night flights I get a kick out of seeing the lights of the city below, as if they're all lit up just to welcome the two of us.

They delivered our rental car just minutes after our bags came off the luggage carousel. The car was a full-size Olds with a plush velour interior, very quiet and luxurious. Back home I don't even own a car, and all Harry has is the six-year-old panel truck with the name of the store painted on its sides. We could have managed just as well with a subcompact, but if you shop around you can usually get a really nice car for only a few dollars more. We'd had a great deal on a Lincoln Town Car in Denver, with free mileage and no charge for the full insurance coverage, for example.

We stayed downtown at the Westin on Second Street. Harry had booked us adjoining rooms on the luxury level. A double room or even a small suite would have been a lot less expensive, but we both like our privacy, as much as we enjoy being together on our vacations. And, as you probably have gathered by now, we don't stint on these trips. If we have one rule, it's to treat ourselves to what we want.

We made it an early night, unpacking, getting settled, and orienting ourselves in the hotel. First thing after breakfast the next day we took a Gray Line bus tour of Tulsa, which is what we always do when we can. It gives you a wonderful overview of the city and you don't have to find your own way around. You get to drive past some attractions that you might not be interested enough to see if they required a special trip, but that are certainly worth viewing through the window of the bus. And you pick up a familiarity with the place that makes it a lot easier to get around during the remainder of the stay. Harry and I are both sold on bus tours, and it's disappointing when a city doesn't have them.

The tour was a good one, and it took most of the morning. After lunch we went to the Thomas Gilcrease Institute of American History and Art. They have a wonderful collection of western art, with works by Remington, Moran, Charles Russell, and a great many others. The collection of Indian artifacts was also outstanding, but we spent so much time looking at the paintings that we didn't really have time to do the Indian collection justice.

"We'll get back during the week," Harry said.

We had dinner at a really nice restaurant just a short walk from our hotel. The menu was northern Italian, and they made their own pasta. We took a long walk afterward. When we got back to the hotel Harry wanted to have a swim in the pool, but I was ready to call it a night. I've found it's important to not try to do too much, especially the first couple of days. I took a long soak in the tub, watched a movie on HBO, and made an early night of it.

They brought in Tulsa's first oil well in 1901, and Tulsa invited oilmen to "come and make your homes in a beautiful little city that is high and dry, peaceful and orderly, where there are good churches, stores, schools and banks, and where our ordinances prevent the desolation of our homes and property by oil wells."

Sunday morning we went to services at Boston Avenue United Methodist Church, which had been pointed out to us on the Gray Line tour. Neither Harry nor I go to church as an ordinary thing, and we weren't raised as Methodists to begin with, but that's the whole point of vacation, to get away from the workaday world and experience something different. Why, I hardly ever go to museums in New York, where we have some of the best in the world, but when I am in another city I can't get enough of them.

That afternoon, though, we tried a different sort of cultural experience and drove over to Bell's Amusement Park. They had a big old wooden roller coaster, three water slides, a log ride and a sky ride and a pair of miniature golf courses. It was a little cold for the water slides but we did everything else, laughing and shouting and shoving each other like children. Harry threw darts at balloons until he won a stuffed panda, and then he gave it to the first little girl he saw.

"Now in the future," he told her, "don't you take pandas from strange men." And we laughed, and her mother and father laughed, and we went off to play miniature golf one more time.

There was a restaurant called Louisiane that we'd seen a few blocks from the church, and where we were planning to go for dinner. But after we got back to the hotel we arranged to meet in the bar downstairs, and when I got there Harry was knee-deep in conversation with a handsome woman with short dark hair and a full figure. He introduced her as Margaret Cummings, up from Fort Worth for the weekend.

I joined them for a quick drink, and then Harry took me aside and asked if I'd mind if he took Margaret to dinner. "I was talking to her at the pool last night," he said, "and the thing is, she's going back home tomorrow." I told him don't be silly, of course I didn't mind, and wished him luck.

So I ate right there in the hotel myself, and had a fine meal, and then went for a little walk after dinner. At breakfast the next day Harry grinned and said he'd had some fun with Margaret, and she'd given him her address and phone in case he ever got to Fort Worth. We've been to Dallas, and enjoyed that very much, and made a visit or two to Fort Worth at that time, taking in the Amon Carter Museum and some other attractions, so I doubt we'll be ready for the Fort Worth experience for quite a while yet.

"I was sorry to leave you stranded," Harry said, but I told him not to be silly. "You never know," I said. "Maybe we'll both get lucky here in Tulsa."

We started off the morning with an industrial tour of the Frankoma pottery. We both love industrial tours, and take advantage of them every chance we get. One of the highlights of the St. Louis experience was a tour of the Anheuser-Busch brewery, and we followed it up a day later with a half-hour tour of Bardenheier's Wine Cellars, followed by a half hour of wine-tasting. They didn't give you anything to drink at Frankoma, but it was very interesting to see how they made the pottery. Afterward they encouraged you to buy pottery in their shop, and they had some nice things for sale, but we didn't buy anything.

We almost never do. The National Park Service has a motto—"Take only snapshots, leave only footprints." (A side trip to Olympic National Park was one of the highlights of the Seattle experience.) We go them one better by not even taking snapshots. My apartment's too small to clutter it up with souvenirs, and Harry has the same attitude toward souvenirs, even though he has more than enough room for them at the house in Woodside.

As it is, I pick up one souvenir from every trip, a T-shirt with the name of the city we went to. My favorite so far is a fuchsia one from Indianapolis, with crossed black-and-white checkerboard racing flags on it to represent the Indianapolis 500. Most of the Tulsa T-shirts picture an oil well, and Thursday I finally picked out an especially nice one.

But I'm getting ahead of myself, aren't I?

Monday afternoon we went to the Tulsa Garden Center, and spent several hours there and nearby at the Park Department Conservatory. Tuesday we started out at the Historical Society Museum, then went to a synagogue to see the Gerson and Rebecca Fenster Gallery of Jewish Art, the largest collection of Judaica in the Southwest. From there we went to Oral Roberts University for a brief campus tour, and picked up tickets for a chamber music concert to be held the following evening.

We went to our rooms for a nap before dinner, arranging to meet in the cocktail lounge. This time I got there before Harry did, and I got into a conversation with a pretty young woman named Lylah. We were hitting it off pretty well, and then Harry joined us, and before you knew it a friend of Lylah's named Mary Eileen came by and made it a foursome. We had two rounds of drinks at a table and Harry said he hoped the two of them would join us for dinner.

Lylah and Mary Eileen exchanged glances, and then Mary Eileen said, "Why should a couple of nice fellows like you waste your money on dinner?"

Well, I won't say I was shocked, because I had the feeling that they were unusually quick to get friendly. Besides, this sort of thing has happened before. The Chicago experience, for example, included a couple of young ladies whose interest in us was purely professional, but we sure had a good time all the same.

The upshot of this was that Lylah came up to my room, and Mary Eileen went with Harry. I had some fun with Lylah, and she seemed happy with the hundred dollars I gave her. On her way out she gave me an engraved business card with just her first name and her phone number on it. Mary Eileen gave Harry one just like it, except with a different name, of course. They both had the same phone number.

"Take only snapshots," Harry said, tearing Mary Eileen's card in two. "Leave only footprints." And I did the same with Lylah's card. It wasn't likely we'd ever be back in Tulsa, and we wouldn't want to see those girls more than once this trip. The Gilcrease Institute might be worth a second visit, but not Lylah and Mary Eileen.

Wednesday we left town right after breakfast and drove fifty-five miles north to Bartlesville, where the founder of a big oil company set up a wildlife preserve with herds of bison, longhorn cattle, and all sorts of wild animals. We stayed right in the Olds and drove around, viewing them from the car. The complex includes a museum, and the western art and Plains Indian artifacts were magnificent, and just wonderfully displayed. They also had what was described as one of the finest collections of Colt weapons in the country, and I could believe it.

We wound up spending the whole day in Bartlesville, because there were other interesting attractions besides Woolaroc. We saw an exact replica of the state's first commercial drilling rig, we saw an exhibit on the development and uses of petroleum, and we saw a tower designed by Frank Lloyd Wright. North of Bartlesville in Dewey we paid a visit to the Tom Mix Museum and saw original costumes and cowboy gear from his movies along with film stills and other interesting items.

We finally got around to having dinner at Louisiane that night and just got to the concert on time at Oral Roberts. Afterward we roamed around the campus a bit, then took a lazy drive around Tulsa, just looking at people. There was a shopping mall Harry wanted to check out, but it was late by the time we got out of the concert so we decided we'd save that for tomorrow.

"We'll do some field work tomorrow afternoon and evening," Harry said, "and I figure Friday night we'll go for it."

I said that was fine with me. He'd been doing all the planning, and the Tulsa experience had been really fine so far.

When I had time to myself I'd read about Tulsa in the guidebook, or in some of the tourist brochures in the hotel room. I liked to pick up whatever information I could.

With the completion of the Arkansas River Navigation System, Tulsa has gained itself a water route to both the Great Lakes and the Gulf of Mexico. The port of Catoosa, three miles from Tulsa itself on Verdigris River, stands at the headwaters of the waterway and is presently America's westernmost inland water port.

Now you might think that a fact like that wouldn't stay with me, but it's funny how much of what we do and see and learn on these vacation trips remains in memory. It's a real education.

Thursday morning we went straight to the Philbrook Art Center after breakfast. It's set on over twenty acres and surrounded by gardens, and the collections ranged from Italian Renaissance paintings to Southeast Asian tradeware. It took the whole morning to do the place justice.

"I like Tulsa," I told Harry. "I really like it."

After lunch for a change of pace we went to the zoo in Mohawk Park. The performing elephants were the highlight, but just walking around and seeing the animals was enjoyable, too. Then toward the later part of the afternoon we went to that shopping mall and wandered around, and that was when I bought my souvenir T-shirt, a nice blue one with an oil well, of course, and the slogan "Progress and Culture." Harry thought it was a dopey slogan, but I liked the shirt. I still like it. The funny thing is nobody ever sees my T-shirts, because I wear a dress shirt and tie to the office every day, and even on weekends I'm afraid I'm not the T-shirt type. I wear them as undershirts beneath my dress shirts, or I'll wear them around the apartment, or to sleep in. I like having them, though, and you could say I'm developing quite a little collection, adding a new one every three months.

The Indianapolis shirt is my favorite so far, but I believe I mentioned that before.

We drove around Thursday night. We checked out the University of Tulsa campus and cruised around Mohawk Park. I was really glad we had the big car instead of an economy compact. I think it makes a difference.

I didn't sleep well Thursday night, and Harry said he was restless himself. We both had the impulse to skip the activity he had planned, but we stuck with it and I'm glad we did. We drove ten miles south of the city to the Allen Ranch, where we were booked for a half-day trail ride on horseback through some really pretty country. Neither of us is much of a rider, but we've been on horseback on other vacations, and the horses they give you are always gentle and well trained. I knew I'd be sore for the next week or so, but it seemed like a small price to pay. We had a really good time, and the weather was perfect for it, too.

I showered as soon as we got back, and then I went downstairs for a whirlpool and sauna. That wouldn't do anything about the saddle sores, but it took some of the ache out of muscles that don't get much use back in New York.

Then I took a long nap and left a call so I'd be up in time for dinner. Dinner was just a light bite at a coffee shop because we were both keyed up and a big meal wouldn't have been a good idea even if we'd been in the mood for it.

We went to the shopping mall and prowled around there for a while, but we didn't find what we were looking for. Then we drove to the hospital and waited in the parking lot for twenty minutes or so without any success. We went back to the University of Tulsa campus and came very close there, but we aborted the mission at the last minute and drove to a supermarket we had researched the day before.

We parked where we could watch people entering and leaving. We were there twenty minutes or so when Harry nudged my arm and pointed to a woman getting out of a Japanese compact. We watched as she walked past us and into the market. I nodded, smiling.

"Bingo," he said.

He parked our car right next to her. She wasn't in there long, maybe another ten minutes, and she came out carrying her groceries in a plastic bag.

Harry had the window rolled down, and he called her over. "Miss," he said, "maybe you can help me. Would you know where this address is?"

She came over for a look. I was by the side of the car and I stepped up behind her and got her in a chokehold and clapped my other hand over her mouth so she couldn't make a sound. I dragged her into the shadows and kept the pressure on her throat and Harry got out of the car and hurried over and hit her three times, once in the solar plexus and twice in the pit of the stomach.

We'd bought supplies yesterday, including a roll of tape. She was pretty much unconscious from the chokehold so it was easy to tape her mouth shut and get her hands behind her back and tape her wrists together. Harry opened the back door and I got in back with her and he got behind the wheel and drove. I had her groceries in the back of the car with me, and her purse.

Harry headed for Mohawk Park and we drove right out onto the golf course. She came to in the car but she was all trussed up and there wasn't a thing she could do. When he stopped the car we dragged her outside and got her clothes off, and we took turns having fun with her. We both had a really wonderful time with her, we really did.

Finally Harry asked me if I was done and I had to say I was, and he told me in that case to go ahead and finish up. I told him it was his turn, but then he reminded me that he had done the nurse in San Diego. Don't ask me how I'd managed to forget that.

So it was my turn after all, and I got the belt out of my pants and strangled her with it. Then I took her arms and Harry took her legs and we carried her off the fairway and left her deep in the rough. You'd have to hook your tee shot real bad to get anywhere near her.

We threw her purse in a Dumpster outside a restaurant on Lewis Avenue. There was a Goodwill Industries collection box a few blocks away, and that's where we left her clothes. I would have liked to keep something, an intimate garment of some sort, but we never did that. *Take no snapshots, leave no footprints*—that's the National Park Service motto as we've adapted it for our own use.

I'd bought a Dustbuster the day before and I used it to go over the interior of the Olds very thoroughly. They'd vacuum the car after we turned it in, but you don't want to leave anything to chance. The Dustbuster went in another Dumpster, along with the roll of tape. And her bag of groceries, except for a box of Wheat Thins. I was pretty hungry, so I took those back and ate them in the room.

Saturday we pretty much took it easy. I went back for a second visit to the Gilcrease Institute but Harry passed that up and hung around the hotel pool instead. We were planning on another concert that evening but we spent a long time over dinner and wound up taking in a movie instead. Then back to the hotel for a quick brandy in the bar, and then up to bed.

And Sunday morning we flew back to New York.

Monday morning I was at my desk by nine, which was more than some of my fellow workers could claim. Sharon said she hadn't received my postcard, and as always I told her to keep watching the mailbox. Of course I hadn't sent one. Warren breezed in at a quarter to ten and said he guessed he'd wasted another twenty-five cents on flight insurance. I told him he could try again in August. "I'll have to," he said. "I can't quit now, I've got too much money invested."

Lee asked me where I'd be going in August. "Baghdad? Timbuktu? Or someplace really exotic, like Newark?"

I'm not sure. Buffalo, possibly. I'd like to see Niagara Falls. Or maybe Minneapolis–St. Paul. It's the right time of year for either of those cities. It's my turn to plan the trip, so I'll take my time and make the right decision.

In the meantime I go to my office every morning and read guidebooks evenings and weekends. Sometimes when I sit at my desk I'll think about the T-shirt I'm wearing, invisible under my dress shirt. I'll remember which one it is, and I'll take a moment to relive the Denver experience, or the Baltimore experience, or the Tulsa experience. Depending on what shirt I'm wearing.

Lee can tease me all he wants. I don't mind. Tulsa was *wonderful.*

SOME DAYS YOU
GET THE BEAR

Beside him, the girl issued a soft grunt of contentment and burrowed closer under the covers. Her name was Karin, with the accent on the second syllable, and she worked for a manufacturer of floor coverings, doing something unfathomable with a computer. They'd had three dates, each consisting of dinner and a screening. On their first two dates he'd left her at her door and gone home to write his review of the film they'd just seen. Tonight she'd invited him in.

And here he was, happily exhausted at her side, breathing her smell, warmed by her body heat. Perhaps this will work, he thought, and closed his eyes, and felt himself drifting.

Only to snap abruptly awake not ten minutes later. He lay still at first, listening to her measured breathing, and then he slipped slowly out of the bed, careful not to awaken her.

She lived in one room, an L-shaped studio in a high rise on West Eighty-ninth Street. He gathered his clothes and dressed in darkness, tiptoed across the uncarpeted parquet floor.

There were five locks on her door. He unfastened them all, and when he tried the door it wouldn't open. Evidently she'd left one or more of them unlocked; thus, meddling with all five, he'd locked some even as he was unlocking the others. When this sort of dilemma was presented as a logic problem, to be attacked with pencil and paper, he knew better than to attempt its solution. Now, when he had to work upon real locks in darkness and in silence, with a sleeping woman not ten yards away, the whole thing was ridiculous.

"Paul?"

"I'm sorry," he said. "I didn't mean to wake you."

"Where are you going? I was planning to offer you breakfast in the morning. Among other things."

"I've got work to do first thing in the morning," he told her. "I'd really better get on home. But these locks—"

"I know," she said. "It's a Roach Motel I'm running here. You get in, but you can't get out." And, grinning, she slipped past him, turned this lock and that one, and let him out.

He hailed a taxi on Broadway, rode downtown to the Village. His apartment was a full floor of a brownstone on Bank Street. He had moved into it when he first came to New York and had never left it. It had been his before he was married and remained his after the divorce. "This is the one thing I'll miss," Phyllis had said.

"What about the screenings?"

"To tell you the truth," she said, "I've pretty much lost my taste for movies."

He occasionally wondered if that would ever happen to him. He contributed a column of film reviews to two monthly magazines; because the publications were mutually noncompetitive, he was able to use his own name on both columns. The columns themselves differed considerably in tone and content. For one magazine he tended to write longer and more thoughtful reviews, and leaned toward films with intellectual content and artistic pretension. His reviews for the other magazine tended to be briefer, chattier, and centered more upon the question of whether a film would be fun to see than if seeing it would make you a more worthwhile human being. In neither column, however, did he ever find himself writing something he did not believe to be the truth.

Nor had he lost his taste for movies. There were times, surely, when his perception of a movie was colored for the worse by his having seen it on a day when he wasn't in the mood for it. But this didn't happen that often, because he was usually in the mood for almost any movie. And screenings, whether in a small upstairs room somewhere in midtown or at a huge Broadway theater, were unquestionably the best way to see a film. The print was always perfect, the projectionist always kept his mind on what he was doing, and the audience, while occasionally jaded, was nevertheless respectful, attentive, and silent. Every now and then Paul took a busman's holiday and paid his way into a movie house, and the difference was astounding. Sometimes he had to change his seat three or four times to escape from imbeciles explaining the story line to their idiot companions; other times, especially at films with an enthusiastic teenage following, the audience seemed to have more dialogue than the actors.

Sometimes he thought that he enjoyed his work so much he'd gladly do it for free. Happily, he didn't have to. His two columns brought him a living, given that his expenses were low. Two years ago his building went co-op and he'd used his savings for the down payment. The mortgage payment and monthly maintenance charges were quite within his means. He didn't own a car, had no aged or infirm relatives to support, and had been blissfully spared a taste for cocaine, high-stakes gambling, and the high life. He preferred cheap ethnic restaurants, California zinfandel, safari jackets, and blue jeans. His income supported this sort of life-style quite admirably.

And, as the years went by, more opportunities for fame and fortune presented themselves. *The New York Times Book Review* wanted 750 words from him on a new book on the films of King Vidor. A local cable show had booked him half a dozen times to do capsule reviews, and there was talk of giving him a regular ten-minute slot. Last semester he'd taught a class, "Appreciating the Silent Film," at the New School for Social Research; this had increased his income by fifteen hundred dollars and he'd slept with two of his students, a thirty-three-year-old restless housewife from Jamaica Heights and a thirty-eight-year-old single mother who lived with her single child in three very small rooms on East Ninth Street.

Now, home again, he shucked his clothes and showered. He dried off and turned down his bed. It was a queen-size platform bed, with storage drawers underneath it and a bookcase headboard, and he made it every morning. During his marriage he and Phyllis generally left the bed unmade, but the day after she moved out he made the bed, and he'd persisted with this discipline ever since. It was, he'd thought, a way to guard against becoming one of those seedy old bachelors you saw in British spy films, shuffling about in slippers and feeding shillings to the gas heater.

He got into bed, settled his head on the pillow, closed his eyes. He thought about the film he'd seen that night, and about the Ethiopian restaurant at which they'd dined afterward. Whenever a country had a famine, some of its citizenry escaped to the United States and opened a restaurant. First the Bangladeshi, now the Ethiopians. Who, he wondered, was next?

He thought about Karin—whose name, he suddenly realized, rhymed with Marin County, north of San Francisco. He'd first encountered Marin County in print and had assumed it was pronounced with the accent on the first syllable, and he had accordingly mispronounced it for some time until Phyllis had taken it upon herself to correct him. He'd had no opportunity to make the same mistake with Karin; he had met her in the flesh, so to speak, before he knew how her name was spelled, and thus—

No, he thought. This wasn't going to work. What was he trying to prove? Who (or, more grammatically, whom) was he kidding?

He got out of bed. He went to the closet and took the bear down from the top shelf. "Well, what the hell," he said to the bear. (If you could sleep with a bear, you could scarcely draw the line at talking to it.) "Here we go again, fella," he said.

He got into bed again and took the bear in his arms. He closed his eyes. He slept.

The whole thing had taken him by surprise. It was not as though he had intentionally set out one day to buy himself a stuffed animal as a nocturnal companion. He supposed there were grown men who did this, and he supposed there was nothing necessarily wrong with their so doing, but that was not what had happened. Not at all.

He had bought the bear for a girl. Sibbie was her name, short for Sybil, and she was a sweet and fresh young thing just a couple of years out of Skidmore, a junior assistant production person at one of the TV nets. She was probably a little young for him, but not *that* young, and she seemed to like screenings and ethnic restaurants and guys who favored blue jeans and safari jackets.

For a couple of months they'd been seeing each other once or twice a week. Often, but not always, they went to a screening. Sometimes he stayed over at her place just off Gramercy Park. Now and then she stayed over at his place on Bank Street.

It was at her apartment that she'd talked about her stuffed animals. How she'd slept with a whole menagerie of them as a child, and how she'd continued to do so all through high school. How, when she'd gone off to college, her mother had exhorted her to put away childish things. How she had valiantly and selflessly packed up all her beloved plush pets and donated them to some worthy organization that recycled toys to poor children. How she'd held back only one animal, her beloved bear Bartholomew, intending to take him along to Skidmore. But at the last minute she'd been embarrassed ("Em*bear*assed?" Paul wondered) to pack him, afraid of how her roommates might react, and when she got home for Thanksgiving break she discovered that her mother had given the bear away, claiming that she'd thought that was what Sibbie had wanted her to do.

"So I started sleeping with boys," Sibbie explained. "I thought, 'All right, bitch, I'll just show you,' and I became, well, not promiscuous exactly, but not antimiscuous either."

"All for want of a bear."

"Exactly," she'd said. "So do you see what that makes you? You're just a big old bear substitute."

The next day, though, he found himself oddly touched by her story. There was hurt there, for all the brittle patter, and when he passed the Gingerbread House the next afternoon and saw the bear in the window he never even hesitated. It cost more than he would have guessed, and more than he really felt inclined to spend on what was a sort of half-joke, but they took credit cards, and they took his.

The next night they spent together he almost gave her the bear, but he didn't want the gift to follow that quickly upon their conversation. Better to let her think her story had lingered in his consciousness awhile before he'd acted on it. He'd wait another few days and say something like, "You know, that story you told me, I couldn't get it out of my mind. What I decided, I decided you need a bear." And so they'd spent that night in his bed, with only each other for company, while the bear spent the night a few yards away on the closet shelf.

He next saw her five days later, and he'd have given her the bear then but they wound up at her apartment, and of course he hadn't dragged the creature along to the Woody Allen screening, or to the Thai restaurant. A week later, just to set the stage, he'd made his bed that morning with the bear in it, its head resting on the middle pillow, its fat little arms outside the bedcovers.

"Oh, it's a *bear*!" she would say. And he would say, "The thing is, I've got a no-bears clause in my lease. Do you think you could give it a good home?"

Except it didn't work that way. They had dinner, they saw a movie, and then when he suggested they repair to his place she said, "Could we go someplace for a drink, Paul? There's a conversation we really ought to have."

The conversation was all one-sided. He sat there, holding but not sipping his glass of wine, while she explained that she'd been seeing someone else once or twice a week, since theirs had not been designed to be an exclusive relationship, and that the other person she was seeing, well, it seemed to be getting serious, see, and it had reached the point where she didn't feel it was appropriate for her to be seeing other people. Such as Paul, for example.

It was, he had to admit, not a bad kissoff, as kissoffs go. And he'd expected the relationship to end sooner or later, and probably sooner.

But he hadn't expected it to end quite yet. Not with a bear in his bed.

He put her in a cab, and then he put himself in a cab, and he went home and there was the bear. Now what? Send her the bear? No, the hell with that; she'd be convinced he'd bought it *after* she dumped him, and the last thing he wanted her to think was that he was the kind of dimwit who would do something like that.

The bear went back into the closet.

* * *

And stayed there.

It was surprisingly hard to give the bear away. It was not, after all, like a box of candy or a bottle of cologne. You could not give a stuffed bear to just anyone. The recipient had to be the right sort of person, and the gift had to be given at the right stage of the relationship. And many of his relationships, it must be said, did not survive long enough to reach the bear-giving stage.

Once he had almost made a grave mistake. He had been dating a rather abrasive woman named Claudia, a librarian who ran a research facility for a Wall Street firm, and one night she was grousing about her ex-husband. "He didn't want a wife," she said. "He wanted a daughter, he wanted a child. And that's how he treated me. I'm surprised he didn't buy me Barbie dolls and teddy bears."

And he'd come within an inch of giving her the bear! That, he realized at once, would have been the worst possible thing he could have done. And he realized, too, that he didn't really want to spend any more time with Claudia. He couldn't say exactly why, but he didn't really feel good about the idea of having a relationship with the sort of woman you couldn't give a bear to.

There was one of those cardboard signs over the cash register of a hardware store on Hudson Street. SOME DAYS YOU GET THE BEAR, it said. SOME DAYS THE BEAR GETS YOU.

He discovered an addendum: Sooner or later, you sleep with the bear.

It happened finally on an otherwise unremarkable day. He'd spent the whole day working on a review of a biography (*Sydney Greenstreet: The Untold Story*), having a lot of trouble getting it the way he wanted it. He had dinner alone at the Greek place down the street and rented the video of *Casablanca*, sipping jug wine and reciting the lines along with the actors. The wine and the film ran out together.

He got undressed and went to bed. He lay there, waiting for sleep to come, and what came instead was the thought that he was, all things considered, the loneliest and most miserable son of a bitch he knew.

He sat up, astonished. The thought was manifestly untrue. He liked his life, he had plenty of companionship whenever he wanted it, and he could name any number of sons of bitches who were ever so much lonelier and more miserable than he. A wine thought, he told himself. *In vino stupiditas*. He dismissed the thought, but sleep remained elusive. He tossed around until something sent him to the closet. And there, waiting patiently after all these months, was the bear.

"Hey, there," he said. "Time to round up the usual suspects. Can't sleep either, can you, big fellow?"

He took the bear and got back into bed with it. He felt a little foolish, but he also felt oddly comforted. And he felt a little foolish *about* feeling comforted, but that didn't banish the comfort.

With his eyes closed, he saw Bogart clap Claude Rains on the back. "This could be the start of a beautiful friendship," Bogart said.

And, before he could begin to figure it all out, Paul fell asleep.

Every night since, with only a handful of exceptions, he had slept with the bear.

Otherwise he slept poorly. On a couple of occasions he had stayed overnight with a woman, and he had learned not to do this. He had explained to one woman (the single mother on East Ninth Street, as a matter of fact) that he had this quirk, that he couldn't fall fully asleep if another person was present.

"That's more than a quirk," she'd told him. "Not to be obnoxious about it, but that sounds pretty neurotic, Paul."

"I know," he'd said. "I'm working on it in therapy."

Which was quite untrue. He wasn't in therapy. He had indeed thought of checking in with his old therapist and examining the whole question of the bear, but he couldn't see the point. It was like the old Smith-and-Dale routine: "Doctor, it hurts when I do this." "So don't do that!" If it meant a sleepless night to go to bed without the bear, then don't go to bed without the bear!

A year ago he'd gone up to Albany to participate in an Orson Welles symposium. They put him up at the Ramada for two nights, and after the first sleepless night he actually thought of running out to a store and buying another bear. Of course he didn't, but after the second night he wished he had.

There was, thank God, no third night; as soon as the program ended he glanced at the honorarium check to make sure the amount was right, grabbed his suitcase, and caught the Amtrak train back to the city, where he slept for twelve solid hours with the bear in his arms.

And, several months later when he flew out to the Palo Alto Film Festival, the bear rode along at the bottom of his duffel bag. He felt ridiculous about it, and every morning he stowed the bear in his luggage, afraid that the chambermaids might catch on otherwise. But he slept nights.

The morning after the night with Karin, he got up, made the bed, and returned the bear to the closet. As he did so, for the first time he felt a distinct if momentary pang. He closed the door, hesitated, then opened it. The bear sat uncomplaining on its shelf. He closed the door again.

This was not, he told himself, some Stephen King movie, with the bear possessed of some diabolical soul, screaming to be let out of the closet. He could imagine such a film, he could just about sit down and write it. The bear would see itself as a rival for Paul's affections, it would be jealous of the women in his life, and it would find some bearish way to kill them off. Hugging them to death, say. And in the end Paul would go to jail for the murders, and his chief concern would be the prospect of spending life in prison without the possibility of either parole or a good night's sleep. And the cop, or perhaps the prosecuting attorney, would take the bear and toss it in the closet, and then one night, purely on a whim, would take it to bed.

And the last shot would be an ECU of the bear, and you'd swear it was smiling.

No, scratch that. Neither he nor the bear inhabited a Stephen King universe, for which he gave thanks. The bear was not alive. He could not even delude himself that it had been made by some craftsman whose subtle energies were locked in the bear, turning it into more than the inanimate object it appeared to be. It had been made, according to its tag, in Korea, at a factory, by workers who couldn't have cared less whether they were knocking out bears or bow ties or badminton sets. If he happened to sleep better with it in his bed, if he indeed took comfort in its presence, that was his eccentricity, and a remarkably harmless one at that. The bear was no more than an inanimate participant in it all.

Two days later he made the bed and tucked the bear under the covers, its head on a pillow, its arms outside the blankets.

Not, he told himself, because he fancied that the bear didn't like it in the closet. But because it seemed somehow inappropriate to banish the thing with daylight. It was more than inappropriate. It was dishonest. Why, when people all over America were emerging from their closets, should the bear be tucked into one?

He had breakfast, watched *Donahue*, went to work. Paid some bills, replied to some correspondence, labored over some revisions on an essay requested by an academic quarterly. He made another pot of coffee, and while it was brewing he went into the bedroom to get something, and there was the bear.

"Hang in there," he said.

He found he was dating less.

This was not strictly true. He no less frequently took a companion to a screening, but more and more of these companions tended to be platonic. Former lovers with whom he'd remained friendly. Women to whom he was not attracted physically. Male friends, colleagues.

He wondered if he was losing interest in sex. This didn't seem to be the case. When he was with a woman, his lovemaking was as ardent as ever. Of course, he never spent the night, and he had ceased to bring women back to his own apartment, but it seemed to him that he took as much pleasure as ever in the physical embrace. He didn't seek it as often, wasn't as obsessed with it, but couldn't that just represent the belated onset of maturity? If he was at last placing sex in its proper proportion, surely that was not cause for alarm, was it?

In February, another film festival.

This one was in Burkina Faso. He received the invitation in early December. He was to be a judge, and would receive a decent honorarium and all expenses, including first-class travel on Air Afrique. This last gave him his first clue as to where Burkina Faso was. He had never previously heard of it, but now guessed it was in Africa.

A phone call unearthed more information. Burkina Faso

had earlier been Upper Volta. Its postage stamps, of which his childhood collection had held a handful, bore the name Haute-Volta; the place had been a French colony, and French remained the prevailing language, along with various tribal dialects. The country was in West Africa, north of the Equator but south of the Sahel. The annual film festival, of which this year's would be the third, had not yet established itself as terribly important cinematically, but the Burkina Fasians (or whatever you called them) had already proved to be extremely gracious hosts, and the climate in February was ever more hospitable than New York's. "Marisa went last year," a friend told him, "and she hasn't left off talking about it yet. Not to be missed. *Emphatically* not to be missed."

But how to bring the bear?

He obtained a visa, he got a shot for yellow fever (providing ten years of immunity; he could go to no end of horrid places before the shot need be renewed) and began taking chloroquine as a malaria preventative. He went to Banana Republic and bought clothing he was assured would be appropriate. He made a couple of phone calls and landed a sweet assignment, thirty-five hundred words plus photos for an airline in-flight magazine. The airline in question didn't fly to Burkina Faso, or anywhere near it, but they wanted the story all the same.

But he couldn't take the bear. He had visions of uniformed Africans going through his luggage, holding the bear aloft and jabbering, demanding to know what it was and why he was bringing it in. He saw himself, flushing crimson, surrounded by other festival-goers, all either staring at him or pointedly *not* staring at him. He could imagine Cary Grant, say, or Michael Caine, playing a scene like that and coming out of it rather well. He could not envision himself coming out of it well at all.

Nor did he have room for a stuffed animal that measured twenty-seven inches end to end. He intended to make do with carry-on luggage, not much wanting to entrust his possessions to the care of Air Afrique, and if he took the bear he would have to check a bag. If they did not lose it in the first leg of the flight, from New York to Dakar, surely it would vanish somewhere between Dakar and Ouagadougou, Burkina Faso's unpronounceable capital.

He went to a doctor and secured a prescription for Seconal. He flew to Dakar, and on to Ouagadougou. The bear stayed at home.

The customs check upon arrival was cursory at best. He was given VIP treatment, escorted through customs by a giant of a woman who so intimidated the functionaries that he was not even called upon to open his bag. He could have brought the bear, he could have brought a couple of Uzis and a grenade launcher, and no one would have been the wiser.

The Seconal, the bear substitute, was a total loss. His only prior experience with sleeping pills was when he was given one the night before an appendectomy. The damned pill had kept him up all night, and he learned later that this was known as a paradoxical effect, and that it happened with some people. It still happened years later, he discovered. He supposed it might be possible to override the paradoxical effect by increasing the dosage, but the Burkina Fasians were liberal suppliers of wine and stronger drinks, and the local beer was better than he would ever have guessed it might be, and he knew about the synergy of alcohol and barbiturates. Enough film stars had been done in by the combination; there was no need for a reviewer to join their company.

He might not have slept anyway, he told himself, even with the bear. There were two distractions, a romance with a Polish actress who spoke no more English than he spoke Polish ("The Polish starlet," he would tell friends back home. "Advancing her career by sleeping with a writer.") and a case of dysentery, evidently endemic in Burkina Faso, that was enough to wake a bear from hibernation.

"They didn't paw through my bag at Ooogabooga," he told the bear upon his return, "but they sure did a number at JFK. I don't know what they think anybody could bring back from Burkina Faso. There's nothing there. I bought a couple of strands of trading beads and a mask that should look good on the wall, if I can find the right spot for it. But just picture that clown at Customs yanking you out of the suitcase!"

They might have cut the bear open. They did things like that, and he supposed they had to. People smuggled things all the time, drugs and diamonds and state secrets and God knew what else. A hardened smuggler would hardly forbear (for-

bear!) to use a doll or a stuffed animal to conceal contraband. And a bear that had been cut open and probed could, he supposed, be stitched back together, and be none the worse for wear.

Still, something within him recoiled at the thought.

One night he dreamed about the bear.

He rarely dreamed, and what dreams he had were fragmentary and hazy. This one, though, was linear, and remarkably detailed. It played on his mind's retina like a movie on a screen. In fact dreaming it was not unlike watching a movie, one in which he was also a participant.

The story line fell somewhere between *Pygmalion* and "The Frog Prince." The bear, he was given to understand, was enchanted, under a spell. If the bear could win the unconditional love of a human being it would cast off its ursine form and emerge as the ideal partner of the person who loved it. And so he gave his heart to the bear, and fell asleep clutching it, and woke up with his arms around the woman of his, well, dreams.

Then he woke up in fact, and it was a bear he was clutching so desperately. Thank God, he thought.

Because it had been a nightmare. Because he didn't *want* the bear to transform itself into anything, not even the woman of his dreams.

He rose, made the bed, tucked the bear in. And chucked the bear under its chin.

"Don't ever change," he told it.

The woman was exotic. She'd been born in Ceylon, her mother a Sinhalese, her father an Englishman. She had grown up in London, went to college in California, and had lately moved to New York. She had high cheekbones, almond-shaped eyes, a sinuous figure, and a general appearance that could have been described as Nonspecific Ethnic. Whatever restaurant Paul took her to, she looked as though she belonged there. Her name was Sindra.

They met at a lecture at NYU, where he talked about Hitchcock's use of comic relief and where she asked the only really provocative question. Afterward, he invited her to a screening. They had four dates, and he found that her enthusiasm for film matched his own. So, more often than not, did her taste and her opinions.

Four times at the evening's end she went home alone in a taxi. At first he was just as glad, but by the fourth time his desire for her was stronger than his inclination to end the evening alone. He found himself leaning in the window of her cab, asking her if she wouldn't like a little company.

"Oh, I would," she assured him. "But not tonight, Paul."

Not tonight, darling, I've got a . . . what? A headache, a husband? What?

He called her the next morning, asked her out to yet another screening two days hence. The movie first, then a Togolese restaurant. The food was succulent, and fiery hot. "I guess there's a famine in Togo," he told her. "I hadn't heard about it."

"It's hard to keep up. This food's delicious."

"It is, isn't it?" His hand covered hers. "I'm having a wonderful time. I don't want the night to end."

"Neither do I."

"Shall I come up to your place?"

"It would be so much nicer to go to yours."

They cabbed to Bank Street. The bear, of course, was in the bed. He settled Sindra with a drink and went to stow the bear in the closet, but Sindra tagged after him. "Oh, a teddy bear!" she cried, before he could think what to do.

"My daughter's," he said.

"I didn't even know you had a daughter. How old is she?"

"Seven."

"I thought you'd been divorced longer than that."

"What did I say, seven? I meant eleven."

"What's her name?"

"Doesn't have one."

"Your daughter doesn't have a name?"

"I thought you meant the bear. My daughter's name is uh Paula."

"Apolla? The feminine of Apollo?"

"That's right."

"It's an unusual name. I like it. Was it your idea or your wife's?"

Christ! "Mine."

"And the bear doesn't have a name?"

"Not yet," he said. "I just bought it for her recently, and she sleeps with it when she stays over. I sleep in the living room."

"Yes, I should think so. Do you have any pictures?"

"Of the bear? I'm sorry, of course you meant of my daughter."

"Quite," she said. "I already know what the bear looks like."

"Right."

"Do you?"

"Shit."

"I beg your—"

"Oh, the *hell* with it," he said. "I don't have a daughter, the marriage was childless. I sleep with the bear myself. The whole story's too stupid to go into, but if I don't have the bear in bed with me I don't sleep well. Believe me, I know how ridiculous that sounds."

Something glinted in her dark almond eyes. "I think it sounds sweet," she said.

He felt curiously close to tears. "I've never told anyone," he said. "It's all so silly, but—"

"It's not silly. And you never named the bear?"

"No. It's always been just The Bear."

"*It?* Is it a boy bear or a girl bear?"

"I don't know."

"May I see it? No clothing, so there's no help there. Just a yellow ribbon at the throat, and that's a sexually neutral color, isn't it? And of course it's not anatomically correct, in the manner of those nasty dolls they're selling for children who haven't the ingenuity to play doctor." She sighed. "It would appear your bear is androgynous."

"We, on the other hand," he said, "are not."

"No," she said. "We're not, are we?"

The bear remained in the bed with them. It was absurd to make love in the bear's company, but it would have been more absurd to banish the thing to the closet. No matter; they soon became sufficiently aware of one another as to be quite unaware of the bear.

Then two heartbeats returning to normal, and the air cool on sweat-dampened skin. A few words, a few phrases.

Drowsiness. He lay on his side, the bear in his arms. She twined herself around him.

Sleep, blissful sleep.

He woke, clutching the bear but unclutched in return. The bed was full of her scent. She, however, was gone. Sometime during the night she had risen and dressed and departed.

He called her just before noon. "I can't possibly tell you," he said, "how much I enjoyed being with you last night."

"It was wonderful."

"I woke up wanting you. But you were gone."

"I couldn't sleep."

"I never heard you leave."

"I didn't want to disturb you. You were sleeping like a baby."

"Hugging my bear."

"You looked so sweet," she said.

"Sindra, I'd like to see you. Are you free tonight?"

There was a pause, time enough for him to begin to regret having asked. "Let me call you after lunch," she said.

A colleague had just published an insufferably smug piece on Godard in a quarterly with a circulation in the dozens. He was reading it and clucking his tongue at it when she called. "I'm going to have to work late," she said.

"Oh."

"But you could come over to my place around nine-thirty or ten, if that's not too late. We could order a pizza. And pretend there's a famine in Italy."

"Actually, I believe they've been having a drought."

She gave him the address. "I hope you'll come," she said, "but you may not want to."

"Of course I want to."

"The thing is," she said, "you're not the only one with a nocturnal eccentricity."

He tried to think what he had done that might have been characterized as eccentric, and tried to guess what eccentricity she might be about to confess. Whips and chains? Rubber attire? Enemas?

"Oh," he said, light dawning. "You mean the bear."

"I also sleep with an animal, Paul. And sleep poorly without it."

His heart cast down its battlements and surrendered. "I should have known," he said. "Sindra, we were made for each other. What kind of animal?"

"A snake."

"A snake," he echoed, and laughed. "Well, that's more exotic than a bear, isn't it? Although I suppose they're more frequently encountered than bears in Sri Lanka. Do you know something? I don't think I've ever even seen a stuffed snake."

"Paul, I—"

"Squirrels, raccoons, beavers, all of those. Little cuddly furry creatures. And bears, of course. But—"

"Paul, it's not a stuffed snake."

"Oh."

"It's a living snake. I got it in California, I had the deuce of a time shipping it when I moved. It's a python."

"A python," he said.

"A reticulated python."

"Well, if you were going to have a python," he said, "you would certainly want to have it reticulated."

"That refers to its markings. It's twelve feet long, Paul, although in time it will grow to be considerably larger. It eats mice, but it doesn't eat very often or very much. It sleeps in my bed, it wraps itself around me. For warmth, I'm sure, although it seems to me that there's love in its embrace. But I may very well be imagining that."

"Uh," he said.

"You're the first person I've ever told. Oh, my friends in L.A. knew I had a snake, but that was before I started sleeping with it. I never had that intention when I bought it. But then one night it crawled into the bed. And I felt truly safe for the first time in my life."

An army of questions besieged his mind. He picked one. "Does it have a name?"

"Its name is Sunset. I bought it in a pet shop on Sunset Boulevard. They specialize in reptiles."

"Sunset," he said. "That's not bad. I mean, there but for the grace of God goes Harbor Freeway. Is Sunset a boy snake or a girl snake? Or aren't pythons anatomically correct?"

"The pet-shop owner assured me Sunset was female. I haven't figured out how to tell. Paul, if the whole thing puts you off, well, I can understand that."

"It doesn't."

"If it disgusts you, or if it just seems too weird by half."

"Well, it seems weird," he allowed. "You said nine-thirty, didn't you? Nine-thirty or ten?"

"You still want to come?"

"Absolutely. And we'll call out for a pizza. Will they toss in a side order of mice?"

She laughed. "I fed her just this morning. She won't be hungry for days."

"Thank God. And Sindra? Will it be all right if I stay over? I guess what I'm asking is should I bring the bear?"

"Oh, yes," she said. "By all means bring the bear."

PASSPORT IN ORDER

Marcia stood up, yawned, and crushed out a cigarette in the round glass ashtray. "It's late," she said. "I should be getting home. How I hate to leave you!"

"You said it was his poker night."

"It is, but he might call me. Sometimes, too, he loses a lot of money in a hurry and comes home early, and in a foul mood, naturally." She sighed, turned to look at him. "I wish it didn't have to be secretive like this—hotel room, motels."

"It can't stay this way much longer."

"Why not?"

Bruce Farr ran a hand through his wavy hair, groped for a cigarette, and lit it. "Inventory is scheduled in a month," he said. "It won't be ten minutes before they discover I'm into them up to the eyes. They're a big firm, but a quarter of a million dollars' worth of jewelry can't be eased out of the vaults without someone noticing it sooner or later."

"Did you take that much?"

He grinned. "That much," he said, "a little at a time. I picked pieces no one would ever look for, but the inventory will show them gone. I made out beautifully on the sale, honey; peddled some of the goods outright and borrowed on the rest.

Got a little better than a hundred thousand dollars, safely stowed away."

"All that money," she said. She pursed her lips as if to whistle. "A hundred thousand . . ."

"Plus change." His smile spread and she thought how pleased he was with himself. Then he became serious. "Close to half the retail value. It went pretty well, Marcia, but we can't sit on it. We have to get out, out of the country."

"I know, but I'm afraid," Marcia said.

"They won't get us. Once we're out of the country, we don't have a thing to worry about. There are countries where you can buy yourself citizenship for a few thousand U.S. dollars, and beat extradition forever. They can't get us."

She was silent for a moment. When he took her hand and asked her what was wrong, she turned away, then met his eyes. "I'm not that worried about the police. If you say we can get away with it, well, I believe you."

"Then what's scaring you?"

"It's Ray," she said and dropped her eyes. "Ray, my sweet loving husband. He'll find us, darling. I know he will. He'll find us, and he won't care whether we're citizens of Patagonia or Cambodia or wherever we go. He won't try to extradite us. He'll . . ." Her voice broke. "He'll kill us," she finished.

"How can he find us? And what makes you think . . ."

She was shaking her head. "You don't know him."

"I don't particularly want to. Honey. . . ."

"You don't know him," she repeated. "I do. I wish I didn't, I wish I'd never met him. I'm one of his possessions, I belong to him, and he wouldn't let me get away from him, not in a million years. He knows all kinds of people, terrible people. Criminals, gangsters." She gnawed her lip. "Why do you think I never left him? Why do you think I stay with him? Because I know what would happen if I didn't. He'd find me, one way or another, and he'd kill me, and . . ."

She broke. His arms went around her and held her, comforted her.

"I'm not giving you up," he said, "and he won't kill us. He won't kill either of us."

"You don't *know* him." Panic rose in her voice. "He's vicious, ruthless. He . . ."

"Suppose we kill him first, Marcia?"

He had to go over it with her a long time before she would even listen to him. They had to leave the country anyway. Neither of them was ready to spend a lifetime, or part of it, in jail. Once they were out they could stay out. So why not burn an extra bridge on the way? If Ray was really a threat to them, why not put him all the way out of the picture?

"Besides," he told her, "I'd like to see him dead. I really would. For months now you've been mine, yet you always have to go home to him."

"I'll have to think about it," she said.

"You wouldn't have to do a thing, baby. I'd take care of everything."

She nodded, got to her feet. "I never thought of—murder," she said. "Is this how murders happen? When ordinary people get caught up over their heads? Is that how it starts?"

"We're not ordinary people, Marcia. We're special. And we're not in over our heads. It'll work."

"I'll think about it," she said. "I'll—I'll think about it."

Marcia called Bruce two days later. She said, "Do you remember what we were talking about? We don't have a month anymore."

"What do you mean?"

"Ray surprised me last night. He showed me a pair of airline tickets for Paris. We're set to fly in ten days. Our passports are still in order from last year's trip. I couldn't stand another trip with him, dear. I couldn't live through it."

"Did you think about . . . ?"

"Yes, but this is no time to talk about it," she said. "I think I can get away tonight."

"Where and when?"

She named a time and place. When she placed the receiver back on its cradle she was surprised that her hand did not tremble. So easy, she thought. She was deciding a man's fate, planning the end of a man's life, and her hand was as steady as a surgeon's. It astonished her that questions of life and death could be so easily resolved.

She was a few minutes late that night. Bruce was waiting for her in front of a tavern on Randolph Avenue. As she approached, he stepped forward and took her arm.

"We can't talk here," he said. "I don't think we should

chance being seen together. We can drive around. My car's across the street."

He took Claibourne Drive out to the east end of town. She lit a cigarette with the dashboard lighter and smoked in silence. He asked her what she had decided.

"I tried not to think about it," she told him. "Then last night he sprang this jaunt on me, this European tour. He's planning on spending three weeks over there. I don't think I could endure it."

"So?"

"Well, I got this wild idea. I thought about what you said, about—about killing him. . . ."

"Yes?"

She drew a breath, let it out slowly. "I think you're right. We have to kill him. I'd never rest if I knew he was after us. I'd wake up terrified in the middle of the night. I know I would. So would you."

He didn't say anything. His eyes were on hers and he clasped her hands.

"I guess I'm a worrier. I'd worry about the police, too. Even if we managed to do what you said, to buy our way out of extradition. The things you read, I don't know. I'd hate to feel like a hunted animal for the rest of my life. I'd rather have the police hunting me than Ray, but even so, I don't think I'd like it."

"So?"

She lit another cigarette. "It's probably silly," she said. "I thought there might be a way to keep them from looking for you, and to get rid of him at the same time. Last night it occurred to me that you're about his build. About six-one, aren't you?"

"Just about."

"That's what I thought. You're younger, and you're much better-looking than he is, but you're both about the same height and weight. And I thought—oh, this is silly!"

"Keep going."

"Oh, this is the kind of crazy thing you see on television. I don't know what kind of a mind I must have to think of it. But I thought that you could leave a note. You'd go to sleep at your house, then get up in the middle of the night and leave a long note explaining how you stole jewelry from your company and lost the money gambling and kept stealing more money and getting in deeper and deeper until there's no way out. And that you're doing the only thing you can do, that you've decided, well, to commit suicide."

"I think I'm beginning to get it."

Her eyes lowered. "It doesn't make any sense, does it?"

"It sure does. You're about as crazy as a fox. Then we kill Ray and make it appear to be me."

She nodded. "I thought of a way we could do it. I can't believe it's really me saying all of this! I thought we could do it that same night. You would come over to the house and I would let you in. We could get Ray in his sleep. Press a pillow over his face or something like that. I don't know. Then we could load him into your car and drive somewhere and . . ."

"And put him over a cliff." His eyes were filled with frank admiration. "Beautiful, just beautiful."

"Do you really think so?"

"It couldn't be better. They'll have a perfect note, in my handwriting. They'll have my car over a cliff and a burned body in it. And they'll have a good motive for suicide. You're a wonder, honey."

She managed a smile. "Then your company won't be hunting you, will they?"

"Not me or their money. *Gambled every penny away*—that'll throw 'em a curve. I haven't bet more than two bucks on a horse in my life. But your sweetheart of a husband will be gone, and somebody might start wondering where he is. Oh, wait a minute. . . ."

"What?"

"This gets better the more I think about it. He'll take my place in the car and I'll take his on that plane to Europe. We're the same build, his passport is in good order, and the reservations are all made. We'll use those tickets to take the Grand Tour, except that we won't come back. Or if we do, we'll wind up in some other city where nobody knows us, baby. We'll have every bridge burned the minute we cross over. When are you scheduled to take that trip?"

She closed her eyes, thought it through. "A week from Friday," she said. "We fly to New York in the morning, and then on to Paris the next afternoon."

"Perfect. You can expect company Thursday night. Slip

downstairs after he goes to bed and let me into the house. I'll have the note written. We'll take care of him and go straight to the airport. We won't even have to come back to the house."

"The money?"

"I'll have it with me. You can do your packing Thursday so we'll have everything ready, passports and all." He shook his head in disbelief. "I always knew you were wonderful, Marcia. I didn't realize you were a genius."

"You really think it will work?"

He kissed her and she clung to him. He kissed her again, then grinned down at her. "I don't see how it can miss," he said.

The days crawled. They couldn't risk seeing each other until Thursday night, but Bruce assured Marcia that it wouldn't be long.

But it *was* long. Although she found herself far calmer than she had dared to expect, Marcia was still anxious, nervous about the way it might go.

Oh, it was long, very long. Bruce called Wednesday afternoon to make final plans. They arranged a signaling system. When Ray was sleeping soundly, she would slip out of bed and go downstairs. She would dial his phone number. He would have the note written, the money stowed in the trunk of his car. As soon as she called he would drive over to her house, and she would be waiting downstairs to let him in.

"Don't worry about what happens then," he said. "I'll take care of the details."

That night and the following day consumed at least a month of subjective time for her. She called him, finally, at twenty minutes of three Friday morning. He answered at once.

"I thought you weren't going to call at all," he said.

"He was up late, but he's asleep now."

"I'll be right over."

She waited downstairs at the front door, heard his car pull to a stop, had the door open for him before he could knock. He stepped quickly inside and closed the door.

"All set," he said. "The note, everything."

"The money?"

"It's in the trunk, in an attaché case, packed to the brim."

"Fine," she said. "It's been fun, darling."

But Bruce never heard the last sentence. Just as her lips

framed the words, a form moved behind him and a leather-covered sap arced downward, catching him deftly and decisively behind the right ear. He fell like a stone and never made a sound.

Ray Danahy straightened up. "Out cold," he said. "Neat and sweet. Take a look outside and check the traffic. This is no time for nosy neighbors."

She opened the door, stepped outside. The night was properly dark and silent. She filled her lungs gratefully with fresh air.

Ray said, "Pull his car into the driveway alongside the house. Wait a sec, I think he's got the keys on him." He bent over Farr, dug a set of car keys out of his pocket. "Go ahead," he said.

She brought the car to the side door. Ray appeared in the doorway with Bruce's inert form over one shoulder. He dumped him onto the backseat and walked around the car to get behind the wheel.

"Take our buggy," he told Marcia. "Follow me, but not too close. I'm taking 32 north of town. There's a good drop about a mile and a half past the county line."

"Not too good a drop, I hope," she said. "He could be burned beyond recognition."

"No such thing. Dental X rays—they can't miss. It's a good thing he didn't have the brains to think of that."

"He wasn't very long on brains," she said.

"*Isn't*," he corrected. "He's not dead yet."

She followed Ray, lagging about a block and a half behind him. At the site he had chosen, she stood by while he took the money from the trunk and checked Farr's pockets to make sure he wasn't carrying anything that might tip anybody off. Ray propped him behind the wheel, put the car in neutral, and braced Farr's foot on the gas pedal. Farr was just beginning to stir.

"Good-bye, Brucie," Marcia said. "You don't know what a bore you were."

Ray reached inside and popped the car into gear, then jumped aside. The heavy car hurtled through an ineffective guard rail, hung momentarily in the air, then began the long fast fall. First, there was the noise of the impact. Then there was another loud noise, an explosion, and the vehicle burst into flames.

They drove slowly away, the suitcase full of money between them on the seat of their car. "Scratch one fool," Ray said pleasantly. "We've got two hours to catch our flight to New York, then on to Paris."

"Paris," she sighed. "Not on a shoestring, the way we did it last time. This time we'll do it in style."

She looked down at her hands, her steady hands. How surprisingly calm she was, she thought, and a slow smile spread over her face.

SOMETHING TO
REMEMBER YOU BY

He picked her up at her dorm. She was out in front with her suitcases and her duffel bag and he pulled up right on time and helped her load everything. She got in front with him and he waited until she had fastened her seat belt before pulling away from the curb.

"I'll be glad to get home," she said. "I didn't think I was going to live through finals."

"Well, you made it."

"Uh-huh. This is a nice car. What is it, a Plymouth?"

"That's right."

"Almost new, too."

"Two years old. Three in a couple of months when the new cars come out."

"That's still pretty new. Does the radio work?"

He turned it on. "Find something you like," he said.

"You're driving. What kind of music do you like?"

"It doesn't matter."

She found a country station and asked if that was all right. He said it was. "I'll probably just fall asleep anyway," she said. "I was up most of the night. Will that bother you?"

"If you fall asleep? Why should it?"

"I won't be much company."

"That's okay," he said.

When they got out onto the interstate she let her eyes close and slumped a little in her seat. The car rode comfortably and she thought how lucky she was to be in it. She'd put a notice up on the bulletin board outside the cafeteria, RIDE WANTED TO CHICAGO END OF TERM, and just when she was beginning to think no one would respond he had called. All she had to do was pay half the gas money and she had her ride.

She drifted then, and her mind wandered up one path and down another, and then she came to with a start when he turned off the radio in the middle of a song. She opened her eyes and saw that it was getting dark out. And they had left the interstate.

"I was sleeping," she said.

"Like a log. Where do you suppose that expression comes from?"

"I don't know. I never thought about it. Where are we?"

"On our way to Chicago."

"What happened to the interstate?"

"It was putting me to sleep," he said. "Too much traffic, too little scenery. Too many troopers, too. It's the end of the month and they've all got their quotas to make."

"Oh."

"I like back roads better," he said. "Especially at night. You're not afraid, are you?"

"Why should I be afraid?"

"I just wondered if you were. Some people get agoraphobic, and just being out in wide open spaces bothers them."

"Not me."

"I guess you're not scared of anything, huh?"

She looked at him. His eyes were on the road, his hands steady on the wheel. "What's that supposed to mean?"

"Nothing in particular. It's pretty daring of you, though, when you stop to think of it."

"What is?"

"Being here. In this car, out in the middle of nowhere with someone you don't know from Adam."

"You're a college student," she said.

"Am I? You don't know that for sure. I said I was, that's all. I'm the right age, more or less, but that doesn't make me a student."

"You've got a KU decal on your window."

"You don't have to pay tuition to get one." She tried to look at him, but his face was hard to read in the dim light. "You were the one who put the notice up," he reminded her. "I called you. I gave you a name and said I was a student and I'd be heading for Chicago when the term ended, but I never gave you my phone number or told you where I lived. Did you check up on me at all, find out if there was a student registered under the name I gave you?"

"Hey, cut it out," she said.

"Cut what out?"

"Cut out trying to freak me out."

"You're not scared, are you?"

"No, but—"

"But you're wondering if maybe you should be. You're in a car with someone you don't know on a lonely road you don't know either, and you're starting to realize that you don't have much control over the situation. In fact you don't really have any control at all, do you?"

"Stop it."

"Okay," he said. "Hey, I'm sorry. I didn't mean to upset you."

"I'm not upset."

"Well, whatever. I'm a psych major and sometimes I tend to get into head games. It's nothing serious, but if I increased your anxiety level I want to apologize."

"It's all right."

"I'm forgiven?"

"There's nothing to forgive."

"Fair enough," he said. He yawned.

"Are you tired? Do you want me to drive?"

"No, I'm fine," he said. "And I'm the kind of control freak who uses up twice as much energy when somebody else is driving."

"My dad's like that."

"I guess lots of men are. Could you do me a favor? Could you get me something from the glove compartment?"

"What?"

"Right next to the flashlight there. That leather pouch. Could you hand it to me?"

It was a black leather pouch with a drawstring. She gave

it to him and he weighed it in his hand. "What do you suppose is in this?" he asked her.

"I have no idea."

"Not even a farfetched one? Take a guess."

"I couldn't."

"Drugs, do you suppose?"

"Maybe."

"Not drugs," he said. "I don't use drugs. Don't approve of them."

"Good."

He reached to set the pouch on top of the dashboard. "You were scared before," he said.

"A little."

"But not anymore."

"No."

"Why not?"

"Well, because—"

"When you stop to think about it," he said, "nothing's changed. The situation's the same as it was. You're alone with a stranger in a dangerous place, and you don't know anything about the man you're with, and what could you do if I tried something? You've got a purse. Do you happen to have a gun in it?"

"Of course not."

"Don't say it that way. Lots of people have guns. But not you, evidently. How about some chemical Mace? Paralyze attackers with no loss of life. Got any of that stuff?"

"You know I don't."

"How would I know that? It's not as though I searched your purse. But I'm willing to take your word for it. No gun and no Mace. What else? A nail file? Some pepper to throw in my eyes?"

"I have an emery board."

"That's something. You could sort of saw me in half with it, I suppose, but it'd take a long time. You're really essentially defenseless, though, aren't you?"

"Stop it."

"It's true, though, isn't it? If I tried something—"

"What do you mean, tried something?"

"Want me to come right out and say it, huh? Okay. I could

stop the car and overpower you and rape you and you couldn't do a thing about it, could you?"

"I could put up a fight."

"What would that get you? I'd just have to hurt you and that would take the fight right out of you. You'd be better off giving in from the start and hoping I'd take it easy on you."

"Look," she said, "cut it out, huh?"

"Cut what out?"

"You know damn well what you should cut out. Quit doing a number on my mind."

"It's getting to you, isn't it?"

"Look, I told you—"

"I know what you told me. Maybe you ought to consider the possibility that I don't much care what you want."

"I don't like this," she said. "I just want to get out, okay? Just stop the car and let me out."

"Are you sure you want me to stop the car?"

"I—"

"Of course it's not a good idea to get out while we're sailing along at fifty miles an hour, but you're safe as long as the car's moving, aren't you? If I was going to do anything, I'd really have to stop the car first."

"Why would you want to—"

"To rape you? I'm a man and you're a woman. An attractive one, too. Isn't that enough of a reason?"

"Is it?"

"I don't know," he said. "What do you think?"

"I think you're not being very nice."

"No," he agreed, "I guess I'm not. You're really scared now, aren't you?"

"Stop it."

"Why do you have so much trouble answering that question? 'Cut it *out. Stop* it.' What's such a big deal about admitting that you're scared?"

"I don't know."

"You *are* scared, though. Aren't you?"

"You're trying to scare me."

"Uh-huh, and it seems to be working. You're terrified, aren't you? I guess you have a right to be. I mean, there's a very good chance that you're going to be raped. At least you think there is, and all on the basis of a brief conversation. You're beginning to see just how powerless you are. I could do whatever I want with you and you couldn't do a thing about it."

"You'd be punished," she said.

"They wouldn't know who to punish."

"I could tell them."

"You don't even know my name."

"You're a student."

"Are you sure of that?"

"I could describe you," she said. "I could describe the car, I could give them the license number."

"Maybe it's stolen."

"I bet it's not. I could work with a police artist, I could have him make up a sketch of you. You really wouldn't get away with it."

"Hmmmm," he said. "I guess you're right."

"So there's no point in doing anything, and you can stop playing mind games, okay?"

"You could describe me," he said. "I guess I'd have to kill you."

"Don't even say that."

"Why not? That's the best policy anyway, and it's part of the fun, isn't it? If it weren't so much fun there wouldn't be so many people doing it, would there?"

"Stop."

" 'Stop, stop, stop.' You don't look very strong. I bet you'd be easy to kill."

"Why kill me?"

"Why not?"

"The police would be after you. People don't get away with murder."

"Are you kidding? People get away with murder every day. And they wouldn't have any idea who to look for."

"You'd leave evidence behind. They have these new techniques, matching the DNA."

"Maybe I'll practice safe sex."

"Even so, there's always physical evidence."

"They could use it to convict me after they caught me, but it wouldn't help them catch me. And I don't intend to be caught. They haven't caught me so far."

"What?"

"Did you think you were the first?"

She closed her eyes and tried to breathe evenly, regularly. Her heart was racing. Evenly she said, "All right, you've got me frightened. I suppose that's what you wanted."

"It's part of it."

"Are you satisfied now?"

"Oh, I wouldn't say I was satisfied," he said. "I wouldn't use that word. I won't be satisfied until I've got you raped and strangled and lying in a ditch. And incidentally there's not a lot of physical evidence unless they find you fairly quickly, and I'm pretty good at hiding things. They may not find you for months."

"Oh, don't do this to me—"

"By then you'll be nothing but a memory to me," he said. "That's all I'll have of you, that and your little finger."

"My little finger?"

"The little finger of your left hand." He shrugged. "I'm the kind of sentimental fool who likes to take a souvenir. I won't cut it off until afterward. You won't feel a thing."

"My God," she said. "You're crazy."

"Do you really think so? Maybe this is just a joke."

"It's not a funny one."

"We could argue the point. But if it's not a joke, if I'm serious, does that necessarily mean I'm crazy? And what act would serve to identify me as crazy? Am I crazy if I rape you? Crazy if I kill you? Or only crazy if I cut off your finger?"

"Don't do this."

"I don't see anything fundamentally wacko in wanting a souvenir. Something to remember you by. Remember the song?"

"Please. Please."

"Now I'll ask you a question I asked you before. What do you think's in the pouch?"

"The pouch?"

He took it from the dashboard, held it in the palm of his hand. "Guess the contents," he said, "and you win the prize. What's in the bag?"

"Oh, God. I'm going to be sick."

"Want to see for yourself?"

She shrank from it.

"Suit yourself," he said, returning it to the dashboard. "Because of our conversation, because of a chance remark about little fingers, you've jumped to the conclusion that the pouch contains something grisly. It could be full of cowrie shells, or horse chestnuts, or jelly beans, but that's not what you think, is it? I think it's time to stop and pull off the road, don't you think?"

"No!"

"You want me to keep driving?"

"Yes."

"Then take off your sweater." She stared at him. "Your choice," he said. "Take off the sweater or I put on the brakes. Come on. Take it off."

"Why are you making me do this?"

"The same reason some people make other people dig their own graves. It saves time and effort. First unhook your seat belt, make it easier for yourself. Oh, very pretty, very pretty. You're terrified now, aren't you? Say it."

"I'm terrified."

"You're scared to death. Say it."

"I'm scared to death."

"And now I think it's time to find a parking place."

"No!" she cried. Her foot found his and pressed the accelerator flat against the floorboards, while her hand wrenched the wheel hard to the right. The car took flight. Then there was impact, and then there was noise, and then there was nothing.

She came to suddenly, abruptly. She had a headache and she'd hurt her shoulder badly and she could taste blood in the back of her throat. But she was alive. God, she was alive!

The car was upside down, its top crushed. And he was behind the wheel, his head bent at an impossible angle. Blood trailed from the corner of one eye, and more blood leaked from between his lips. His eyes were wide open, staring, and rolled up in their sockets.

The passenger door wouldn't open. She had to roll down the window and wriggle out through it. She felt faint when she stood up, and she had to hold on to the side of the car for support. She looked in the window she had just crawled through, and there, within reach, was the leather drawstring pouch.

She had not willed her foot to press down on the gas pedal, or her hand to yank the steering wheel. She did not now will her hand to reach through the window and extract the leather pouch. It did so of its own accord.

You don't have to open it, she told herself.

She took a breath. *Yes you do*, she thought, and loosened the drawstring.

Inside, she found a small bottle of aspirin, a package of cheese-and-peanut-butter crackers, a small tin of nonprescription stay-awake pills, a bank-wrapped roll of quarters, and a nail clipper. She looked at all of this and shook her head.

But he'd made her take her sweater off. And it was still off, she was bare to the waist.

She couldn't find her sweater, couldn't guess where it had landed after the car flipped and bounced around. She tried one of the rear doors and managed to open it. When she did so the dome light went on, which made it easier for her to see what she was doing.

She found a sweatshirt in one of her bags and put it on. She found her purse—it had somehow ended up in the backseat—and she set that aside. And something made her open one of his bags and go through it, not certain what she was looking for.

She had to go through a second bag before she found it. A three-blade pocketknife with a simulated stag handle.

She cut off the little finger of his left hand. This was harder than it sounded, but she kept at it, and she seemed to have all the time in the world. Not a single car had passed on that desolate road.

When she was done she closed his knife and put it in her purse. She dumped everything else from the drawstring pouch, put the finger inside it, and tucked the pouch into her purse. Then, her purse on her shoulder, she made her way to the road and began walking along it, toward whatever came next.

HILLIARD'S CEREMONY

The old man sat on a low three-legged stool in the courtyard. He had removed his caftan and sandals. Hilliard had thought he'd be wearing a loincloth beneath the caftan, but in fact the old man was wearing a pair of boxer shorts, light blue in color. The incongruity struck Hilliard for a moment, but it did not linger; he had already learned that incongruity was to be expected in West Africa. Hilliard, nominally a cultural attaché, was in fact a coordinator of intelligence-gathering in the region, running a loose string of part-time agents and trying to make sense of their reports. Incongruity was his stock-in-trade.

He watched as two women—girls, really—dipped sponges in a large jar of water and sluiced the old man down with them. One knelt to wash the old fellow's feet with near-biblical ardor. When she had finished she stood up, and her companion indicated to the old man that he should lean forward with his head between his knees. When he was arranged to her satisfaction she upended the clay jar and poured the remaining water over his head. He remained motionless, allowing the water to drain from him onto the hard-packed dirt floor.

"They are washing him," Atuele said. "For the ceremony.

Now he will go into a room and light a candle and observe its flame. Then he will have his ceremony."

Hilliard waited for Donnelly to say something, but his companion was silent. Hilliard said, "What's the ceremony for?"

Atuele smiled. He had a well-shaped oval head, regular features, an impish white-toothed grin. He had one white grandparent, and was dark enough to be regarded as a black man in America. Here in Togo, where mixed blood was a rarity, he looked to be of another race altogether.

"The ceremony," he said, "is to save his life. Did you see his eyes?"

"Yes."

"The whites are yellow. There is no life in them. His skin has an ashen cast to it. He has a stone in his liver. Without a ceremony, it will kill him in a month. Perhaps sooner. Perhaps a week, perhaps a matter of days."

"Shouldn't he be—"

"Yes?"

"In a hospital, I was going to say."

Atuele took a cigarette from the pack Donnelly had given him earlier. He inhaled deeply, exhaled slowly, watching the smoke rise. Tall poles supported a thatch woven of palm fronds, and the three of them sat in its shade. Atuele stared, seemingly fascinated, as the smoke rose up into the thatch.

"American cigarettes," he said. "The best, eh?"

"The best," Hilliard agreed.

"He came from the hospital. He was there a week. More, ten days. They ran tests, they took pictures, they put his blood under a microscope. They said they could do nothing for him." He puffed on his cigarette. "So," he said, "he comes here."

"And you can save him?"

"We will see. A stone in the liver—without a ceremony it is certain he will die. With a ceremony?" The smiled flashed. "We will see."

The ceremony was doubly surprising. Hilliard was surprised that he was allowed to witness it, and surprised that its trappings were so mundane, its ritual so matter-of-fact. He had expected drums, and dancers with their eyes rolling in their heads, and a masked witch doctor stamping on the ground and shaking his dreadlocks at unseen spirits. But there were no drums and no dancers, and Atuele was a far cry from the stereotypical witch doctor. He wore no mask, his hair was cropped close to his skull, and he never raised his voice or shook a fist at the skies.

At the far end of the walled compound, perhaps twenty yards from where they had been sitting, there was a small area reserved for ceremonies, its perimeter outlined by white-washed stones. Within it, the old man knelt before a carved wooden altar. He was dressed again, but in a pure white caftan, not his original garment. Atuele, too, had changed to a white caftan, but his had gold piping on the shoulders and down the front.

To one side, two men and a woman, Africans in Western dress, stood at rapt attention. "His relatives," Donnelly whispered. Alongside Atuele stood the two girls who had washed the old man. They were also dressed in white, and their feet were bare. One of them, Hilliard noticed, had her toenails painted a vivid scarlet.

She was holding an orange and a knife. The knife looked to be ordinary kitchen cutlery, the sort of thing you'd use to bone a roast. Or to quarter an orange, which was what Atuele had the old man do with it. Having done so, he placed the four sections of fruit upon the altar, whereupon Atuele lit the four white candles that stood upon the altar, two at either end. Hilliard noticed that he employed the same disposable lighter he'd used earlier to light his American cigarette.

Next the girl with the red toenails covered the old man's head with a white handkerchief. Then the other girl, who had been holding a white chicken, handed the bird to Atuele. The chicken—pure white, with a red comb—struggled at first, and tried to flap a wing. Atuele said something to it and it calmed down. He placed it on the altar and placed the old man's hands on top of the bird.

"A lot of the ceremonies involve a chicken," Donnelly whispered.

No one moved. The old man, his head bent, the handkerchief covering his head, rested his hands upon the white chicken. The chicken remained perfectly still and did not let out a peep. The girl, the old man's relatives, all stood still and silent. Then the old man let out a sigh and Hilliard sensed that something had happened.

Atuele bent over the altar and drew the chicken out from under the man's grasp. The chicken remained curiously docile. Atuele straightened up, holding the bird in both hands, then inclined his head and seemed to be whispering into its ear. Did chickens have ears? Hilliard wasn't sure, but evidently the message got through, because the bird's response was immediate and dramatic. Its head fell forward, limp, apparently lifeless.

"It's dead," Donnelly said.

"How—"

"I've seen him do this before. I don't know what it is he says. I think he tells them to die. Of course, he doesn't speak English to them."

"What does he speak? Chicken?"

"Ewé, I suppose." He pronounced it *Eh-veh*. "Or some tribal dialect. Anyway, the chicken's dead."

Maybe he's hypnotized it, Hilliard thought. A moment later he had to discard the notion when Atuele took up the knife and severed the chicken's head. No blood spurted. Indeed, Atuele had to give the bird a good shake in order to get some of its blood to dribble out onto the dirt in front of the altar. If Atuele had hypnotized the bird, he'd hypnotized its bloodstream, too.

Atuele handed the bird to one of the girls. She walked off with it. He leaned forward and snatched the handkerchief from the old man's head. He said something, presumably in Ewé, and the old man stood up. Atuele gathered up the sections of orange and gave one each to the old man and his relatives. All, without hesitation, commenced eating the fruit.

The old man embraced one of his male relatives, stepped back, let out a rich laugh, then embraced the other man and the woman in turn. He held himself differently now, Hilliard noticed. And his eyes were clear. Still—

Atuele took Hilliard and Donnelly by the arm and led them back into the shade. He motioned them to their chairs, and a male servant came and poured out three glasses of palm wine. "He is well," Atuele announced. "The stone has passed from his liver into the liver of the chicken. He is lively now, see how he walks with a light step. In an hour he will lie down and sleep the clock around. Tomorrow he will feel fine. He is healed."

"And the chicken?"

"The chicken is dead, of course."

"What will happen to the chicken?"

"What should happen to a dead chicken? The women will cook him." He smiled. "Togo is not a rich country, you know. We cannot be throwing away perfectly good chickens. Of course, the liver will not be eaten."

"Because there is a stone in it."

"Exactly."

"I should have asked," Hilliard said, "to see the chicken cut open. To examine the liver."

"And if there wasn't a stone in it? Alan, you saw the old man, you shook his hand and looked him in the eye. He had eyes like egg yolks when he walked in there. His shoulders were slumped, his gut sagged. When Atuele was done with him he was a new man."

"Power of suggestion."

"Maybe."

"What else?"

Donnelly started to say something, held off while the waiter set drinks and a bowl of crisp banana chips before them. They were at the Hotel de la Paix in Lomé, the capital and the only real city in Togo. Atuele's hamlet, twenty minutes distant in Donnelly's Renault, seemed a world away.

"You know," Donnelly said, "he has an interesting story. His father's father was German. Of course, the whole place was a German colony until the First World War. Togoland, they called it."

"I know."

"Then the French took it over, and now of course it's independent." Donnelly glanced involuntarily at the wall, where the ruler's portrait was to be seen. It was a rare public room in Togo that did not display the portrait. A large part of Hilliard's job lay in obtaining foreknowledge of the inevitable coup that would one day dislodge all those portraits from all those walls. It would not happen soon, he had decided, and whenever it did happen, it would come as a surprise to businessmen like Donnelly, as well as to everyone like Hilliard whose job it was to predict such things.

"Atuele was brought up Christian," Donnelly went on. "A modern family, Western dress, a good education at church schools. Further education at the Sorbonne."

"In Paris?"

"Last I looked. You're surprised? He graduated from there and studied medicine in Germany. Frankfurt, I think it was."

"The man's a physician?"

"He left after two years. He became disenchanted with Western medicine. Nothing but drugs and surgery, according to him, treating the symptoms and overlooking the underlying problem. The way he tells it, a spirit came to him one night and told him his path called for a return to the old ways."

"A spirit," Hilliard said.

"Right. He quit med school, flew home, and looked for people to study with. Apprenticed himself to the best herbalist he could find. Then went upcountry and spent months with several of the top shamans. He'd already begun coming into his powers back in Germany, and they increased dramatically once he channeled his energies in the right direction."

Donnelly went on, telling Atuele's story. How he'd gathered a few dozen people around him; they served him, and he saw to their welfare. How several of his brothers and sisters had followed him back to the old ways, much to the despair of their parents.

"There are shamans behind every bush in this country," Donnelly said. "Witch doctors, charlatans. Even in the Moslem north they're thicker than flies. Down here, where the prevailing religion is animist, they're all over the place. But most of them are a joke. This guy's the real tinsel."

"A stone in the liver," Hilliard said. "What do you suppose that means, anyway? I've heard of kidney stones, gallstones. What the hell is a stone in the liver?"

"What's the difference? Maybe the old guy had some calcification of the liver. Cirrhosis, say."

"And Atuele cured cirrhosis by giving it to the chicken?"

Donnelly smiled gently. "Atuele wouldn't say he cured it. He might say that he got a spirit to move the stone from the man to the chicken."

"A spirit again."

"He works with spirits. They do his bidding."

Hilliard looked at his friend. "I'm not sure what happened back there," he said, "but I can live without knowing. I was in Botswana before they sent me here, and in Chad before that. You see things, and you hear of things. But what I'd really like to know is how seriously you take this guy."

"Pretty seriously."

"Why? I mean, I'm willing to believe he cures people, including some specimens the doctors have given up on. Powers of the mind and all that, and if he wants to think it's spirits, and if his clients believe it, that's fine for them. But you're saying it's more than that, aren't you?"

"Uh-huh."

"Why?"

Donnelly drank his drink. "They say seeing is believing," he said, "but that's crap. This afternoon didn't make a believer out of you, and why should it? But think what an impact it must have had on the old man."

"What's your point?"

"I had a ceremony," Donnelly said. "Nine, ten months ago, just before the July rains. Atuele summoned a spirit and ordered it to enter into me." He smiled almost apologetically. "It worked," he said.

The Hilliards' dinner was guinea fowl with a rice stuffing, accompanied by sautéed green beans and a salad. Hilliard wished his wife would get their cook to prepare some of the native specialties. The hotels and all of the better restaurants served a watered-down French cuisine, but he'd eaten a fiery stew at an unassuming place down the street from the embassy that made him want more. Marilyn had passed on his request to the cook, and reported that the woman did not seem to know how to cook Togolese dishes.

"She said they're very common anyway," she told him. "Not to Western tastes. You wouldn't like them, she said."

"But I do like them. We already know that much."

"I'm just telling you what she said."

They ate on the screened patio, with moths buzzing against the screens. Hilliard wondered what moths had done ages ago, before electric lights, before candles, before human campfires. What did their phototropism do for them when the only lights at night were the stars?

"I had lunch with Donnelly," he said. "I never did get back to the office. He dragged me out of town to see a witch doctor with a college education."

"Oh?"

He described Atuele briefly, and the ritual they had witnessed. "I don't know if he was really cured," he concluded, "or what was wrong with him in the first place, but the change in him was pretty dramatic."

"He was probably the witch doctor's uncle."

"I never thought of that."

"More likely he believed he was sick, and the witch doctor got him to believe himself well. You know how superstitious they are in places like this."

"I guess the chicken was superstitious, too."

She rang for the serving girl, told her to bring more iced tea. To Hilliard she said, "I don't suppose you'd have to study at the Sorbonne to learn how to kill a chicken."

He laughed. The girl brought the tea. Hilliard normally drank his unsweetened, but tonight he added two spoons of sugar. He'd been doing this lately. Because life needs a little sweetness, he told himself.

He did not say anything to Marilyn about Donnelly's ceremony.

"I wasn't getting anywhere," Donnelly had explained. "I was the kind of guy never got fired and never got promoted. What I was, I was never a take-charge kind of a guy."

"That's not how you seem."

The smile again. "Alan, you never knew me before my ceremony. That's the whole point. I'm changed."

"A new man."

"You could say that."

"Tell me about it," he'd said, and Donnelly had done just that. Reluctantly, he'd let it drop to Atuele that he'd been overlooked for promotion. Before he knew what was happening, he was admitting things to the shaman he'd never even admitted to himself. That he was ineffectual. That something always held him back. That his timing was off, that he never did the right thing or said the right thing, that when the going got tough he invariably shot himself in the foot.

"He told me I was afflicted," Donnelly recalled. "That there was an imbalance that ought to be set right. That I needed a spirit."

"And what happened?"

Donnelly shook his head. "I can't really talk about that," he said.

"You're not allowed? If you talk about it your wish won't come true?"

"Nothing like that. I mean I literally cannot talk about it. I can't fit words to the tune. I don't know exactly what happened."

"Well, what did you do? You put your hands on a chicken and the poor thing couldn't peck straight anymore?"

"Nothing like that."

"Then what? I'm not making fun of you, I'm just trying to get the picture. What happened?"

"There was a ceremony," Donnelly said. "Lots of people, lots of dancing and drumming. He gave me an herbal preparation that I had to swallow."

"Uh-huh."

"It didn't get me high, if that's what you're thinking. It tasted like grass. Not dope, not that kind of grass. The kind cows eat. It tasted like lawn clippings that had started to compost."

"Yum."

"It wasn't that terrible, but not your standard gourmet treat, either. I didn't get a buzz from it. At least I don't think I did. Later on I was dancing, and I think I went into a trance."

"Really."

"And there was a ritual in which I had to break an egg into a clean white cotton handkerchief, and Atuele rubbed the yolk of the egg into my hair."

"It sounds like a conditioning treatment."

"I know. Then they took me into one of the huts and let me go to sleep. I was exhausted, and I slept like a corpse for two or three hours. And then I woke up."

"And?"

"And I went home."

"That's all?"

"And I've never been the same again."

Hilliard looked at him. "You're serious."

"Utterly."

"What happened?"

"I don't know what happened. But something happened. I was different. I acted differently and people reacted to me differently. I had confidence. I commanded respect. I—"

"*Wizard of Oz* stuff," Hilliard said. "All he could give you was what you had all along, but the mumbo jumbo made you think you had confidence, and therefore you had it."

But Donnelly was shaking his head. "There's no way I can expect you to believe this," he said, "because seeing isn't believing, and neither is hearing. Let me tell you how I experienced it, all right?"

"By all means."

"I woke up the next morning and nothing was different, I felt the same, except I'd slept very deeply and felt refreshed. But I also felt like an idiot, because I'd danced around like a savage and paid five hundred dollars for the privilege, and—"

"Five hundred dollars!"

"Yes, and—"

"Is that what it costs?"

"It varies, but it's never cheap. It's a lot higher relatively for the Togolese who must make up ninety-five percent of his regular clients. I'm sure that old man this afternoon must have paid a hundred dollars, and likely more. What do you give your house servants, twenty-five bucks a month? Believe me, it's less of a sacrifice for me to come up with five hundred dollars than for a native to part with several months' wages."

"It still seems high."

"It seemed high the morning after, take my word for it. I felt bloody stupid. I blamed myself six ways and backwards—for falling for it in the first place, and for not getting anything out of it, as if there was something there to be gotten and it was my fault it hadn't worked. And then, it must have been ten days later and I'd put the whole thing out of my mind, and I was in a meeting with my then-boss and that old bastard Kostler. Do you know him?"

"No."

"Consider yourself lucky. I was in there, and Kostler was

kicking our brains in, really killing us. And something clicked in. I felt the presence of a power within me that had not been there before. I took a breath, and I literally felt the energy shift in the room, the whole balance among the three of us. And I started talking, and the words were just *there*, Alan. I could have charmed the birds out of the trees, I could have talked a dog off a meat wagon."

"You were on," Hilliard suggested. "Everybody has days like that, when the edges just line up for you. I had it one night playing pool at the Harcourt Club in Nairobi. I couldn't miss a shot. Bank shots, combinations—everything worked. And the next day I was the same klutz I'd always been."

"But I wasn't," Donnelly said. "I had something extra, something I hadn't had before, and it didn't go away the next day or the next week or the next month. It can't go away now. It's not a lucky charm, something you could pick up downtown at the fetish market. It's a part of who I am, but it's a part that never existed before I ate Atuele's lawn clippings and had an egg rubbed in my scalp."

Hilliard thought about this. "You don't think it's all in your mind, then," he said.

"I think it's all in my self. I think, if you will, that my self has been enlarged by the addition of a spirit that wasn't there before, and that this spirit has incorporated itself into my being, and—" He broke off abruptly, gave his head a shake. "Do you know something? I don't *know* what I believe, or what happened, or how or why, either. I know that a month after my ceremony I got a five-thousand-dollar raise without asking for it, which makes Atuele look like a damned good investment. I've had two raises since then, and a promotion to the second desk in the Transcorporate Division. And they're right to promote me, Alan. Before they were carrying me. Now I'm worth every penny they pay me."

After dinner Hilliard and his wife watched a movie on the VCR. He couldn't keep his mind on it. All he could think about was what he had seen in Atuele's compound, and what Donnelly had told him at the hotel bar.

In the shower, he tried to picture the ceremony Donnelly had described. The roar of the shower became the relentless drumming of a quartet of grinning sweating half-naked blacks.

He dried off, made himself a d..ink, carried it into the air-conditioned bedroom. The lights were out and his wife was already sleeping, or putting on a good act. He got into bed and sipped his drink in the darkness. His heart welled up with the mixture of tenderness and desire that she always inspired in him. He set down his drink half-finished and laid a hand on her exposed shoulder.

His hand moved on her body. For a while she made no response, although he knew she was awake. Then she sighed and rolled over and he moved to take her.

Afterward he kissed her and told her that he loved her.

"It's late," she said. "I have an early day tomorrow."

She rolled over and lay as she had lain when he came into the room. He sat up and took his drink from the nightstand. The ice had melted but the whiskey was cool. He sipped the drink slowly, but when the glass was empty he was still not sleepy. He thought of fixing himself another but he didn't want to risk disturbing her.

He had the urge to put his hand on her bare shoulder again, not as a sexual overture but just to touch her. But he did not do this. He sat up, his hand at his side. After a while he lay down and put his head on the pillow, and after a while he slept.

Two days later he lunched with Donnelly at the native restaurant. Hilliard had chicken with yams with some sort of red sauce. It brought tears to his eyes and beaded his forehead with sweat. It was, he decided, even better than the stew he'd had there earlier.

To Donnelly he said, "The thing is, my life works fine just as it is. I'm happily married, I love my wife, and I'm doing well at the embassy. So why would I want a ceremony?"

"Obviously you don't."

"But the thing is I do, and I couldn't tell you why. Silly, isn't it?"

"You could talk with Åtuele," Donnelly offered.

"Talk with him?"

"He may tell you you don't need a ceremony. One woman came to him with a list of symptoms a yard long. She was all primed to pay a fortune and be ordered to smear herself with palm oil and dance naked in the jungle. Atuele told her to cut back on starches and take a lot of vitamin C." Donnelly poured the last of his beer into his glass. "I thought I'd take a run out there this afternoon myself," he said. "Do you want to come along and talk with him?"

"I'm actually a very happy man," he told Atuele. "I love my job, I love my wife, we have a pleasant, well-run home—"

Atuele listened in silence. He was smoking one of the cigarettes Hilliard had brought him. Donnelly had said it was customary to bring a gift, so Hilliard had picked up a carton of Pall Malls. For his part, Donnelly had brought along a liter of good scotch.

When Hilliard had run out of things to say, Atuele finished his cigarette and put it out. He gazed at Hilliard. "You are walking on the beach," he said suddenly, "and you stop and turn around, and what do you see?"

What kind of nonsense was this? Hilliard tried to think of an answer. His own voice, unbidden, said: "I have left no footprints."

And, quite unaccountably, he burst into tears.

He sobbed shamelessly for ten minutes. At last he stopped and looked across at Atuele, who had smoked half of another cigarette. "You ought to have a ceremony," Atuele said.

"Yes."

"The price will be four hundred dollars U.S. You can manage this?"

"Yes."

"Friday night. Come here before sundown."

"I will. Uh. Is it all right to eat first? Or should I skip lunch that day?"

"If you do not eat you will be hungry."

"I see. Uh, what should I wear?"

"What you wish. Perhaps not a jacket, not a tie. You will want to be comfortable."

"Casual clothes, then."

"Casual," Atuele said, enjoying the word. "Casual, casual. Yes, casual clothes. We are casual here."

"Friday night," Hilliard said. "How long do these things last?"

"Figure midnight, but it could go later."

"That long."

"Or you could be home by ten. It's hard to say."

Hilliard was silent for a moment. Then he said, "I don't think I would want Marilyn to know about this."

"She's not going to hear it from me, Alan."

"I'll say there's an affair at the Gambian embassy."

"Won't she want to go?"

"God, have you ever been to anything at the Gambian embassy? No, she won't want to go." He looked out the car window. "I could tell her. It's not that I have to ask her permission to do anything. It's just—"

"Say no more," said Donnelly. "I was married once."

The lie was inconvenient in one respect. In order to appear suitably dressed for the mythical Gambian party, Hilliard left his house in black tie. At Donnelly's office he changed into khakis and a white safari shirt and a pair of rope sandals.

"Casual," Donnelly said, approvingly.

They took two cars and parked side by side at the entrance to Atuele's compound. Inside, rows of benches were set up to accommodate perhaps three dozen Africans, ranging from very young to very old. Children were free to run around and play in the dirt, although most of them sat attentively beside their parents. Most of the Africans wore traditional garb, and all but a few were barefoot.

To the side of the benches ranged half a dozen mismatched armchairs with cushioned bottoms. Two of these were occupied by a pair of sharp-featured angular ladies who could have been sisters. They spoke to each other in what sounded a little like German and a little like Dutch. Hilliard guessed that they were Belgian, and that the language was Flemish. A third chair held a fat red-faced Australian whose name was Farquahar. Hilliard and Donnelly each took a chair. The sixth chair remained vacant.

At the front, off to one side, six drummers had already begun playing. The rhythm they laid down was quite complicated, and unvarying. Hilliard watched them for a while, then looked over at Atuele, who was sitting in an armchair and chatting with a black woman in a white robe. He was smoking a cigarette.

"For a spiritual guy," Hilliard said, "he sure smokes a lot."

"He has a taste for good scotch, too," Farquahar said. "Puts a lot of it away, though you won't see him drink tonight. Says alcohol and tobacco help keep him grounded."

"You've been here before?"

"Oh, I'm an old hand," Farquahar said. "I'm here every month or so. Don't always have a personal ceremony, but I come just the same. He's one of a kind, is our Atuele."

"Really."

"How old do you think he is?"

Hilliard hadn't really thought about it. It was hard to tell with Africans. "I don't know," he said. "Twenty-eight?"

"You'd say that, wouldn't you? He's my age exactly and I'm forty-two. And he drinks like a fish and smokes like a chimney. Makes you think, doesn't it?"

One of the girls who'd assisted at the old man's ceremony collected money from Hilliard and Donnelly and the Belgian ladies. Then Atuele came over and gave each of the four a dose of an herbal preparation. Farquahar, who was not having a ceremony this evening, did not get an herb to eat. Hilliard's portion was a lump the size of a pigeon's egg, and it did taste much as Donnelly had described it. Lawn clippings left in a pile for a few days, with an aftertaste of something else. Dirt, say.

He sat with it on his tongue like a communion wafer, wondering if he was supposed to chew it. Tasty, he thought, and he considered voicing the thought to either Donnelly or Farquahar, but something told him not to say anything to anyone from this point on but to be silent and let this happen, whatever it was. He chewed the stuff and swallowed it, and if anything the taste got worse the more you chewed it, but he had no trouble getting it down.

He waited for it to hit him.

Nothing happened. Meanwhile, though, the drumming was beginning to have an effect on a couple of the women in the crowd. Several of them had risen from the benches and were standing near the drummers, shuffling their feet to the intricate beat.

Then one of them went into an altered state. It happened

quite suddenly. Her movements became jerky, almost spastic, and her eyes rolled up into her head, and she danced with great authority, her whole body taken over by the dance. She made her way throughout the assembly, pausing now and then in front of someone. The person approached would extend a hand, palm up, and she would slap palms forcefully before dancing on.

The people whose palms were slapped mostly stayed where they were and went on as before, but periodically the slappee would be immediately taken over by whatever was in possession of the dancer. Then he or she—it was mostly women, but not exclusively so—he or she would rise and go through the same sort of fitful gyrations as the original dancer, and would soon be approaching others and slapping their palms.

Like vampires making new vampires, Hilliard thought.

One woman, eyes rolling, brow dripping sweat, danced over to the row of armchairs. Hilliard at once hoped and feared he'd get his palm slapped. Instead it was Donnelly she approached, Donnelly whose palm received her slap. Hilliard fancied that electricity flowed from the woman into the man beside him, but Donnelly did not react. He went on sitting there.

Meanwhile, Atuele had taken one of the Belgian women over to the drummers. He had her holding a white metal basin on top of her head. A group of Africans were dancing around her, dancing *at* her, it seemed to Hilliard. The woman just stood there balancing the dishpan on her head and looking uncomfortable about it.

Her companion, Hilliard saw, was dancing by herself, shuffling her feet.

Another dancer approached. She went down the row, a dynamo of whatever energy the dance generated, and she slapped palms with Donnelly, with Hilliard, with Farquahar. Donnelly received the slap as he'd received the first. Hilliard felt something, felt energy leap from the dancer into his hand and up his arm. It was like getting an electrical shock, and yet it wasn't.

Donnelly was on his feet now. He was not dancing like the Africans, he was sort of stomping in a rhythm all his own, and Hilliard looked at him and thought how irremediably white the man was.

What, he wondered, was he doing here? What were any of them doing here? Besides having a grand cross-cultural experience, something to wow them with next time he got Stateside, what in God's name was he doing here?

Farquahar was up, dancing. Bouncing around like a man possessed, or at least like a man determined to appear possessed. The bastard hadn't even paid for a private ceremony and here he was caught up in something, or at any rate uninhibited enough to pretend to be, while Hilliard himself was sitting here, unaffected by the gloppy lawn clippings, unaffected by the slapped palm, unaffected by the goddamned drums, unaffected by any damn thing, and four hundred dollars poorer for it.

Wasn't he supposed to have a private ceremony, a ritual all his own? Wasn't something supposed to happen? Maybe Atuele had forgotten him. Or maybe, because he had come here without a goal, he was not supposed to get anything. Maybe it was a great joke.

He got up and looked around for Atuele. A man danced over, behaving just as weirdly as the women, and slapped Hilliard's palm, then held out his own palm. Hilliard slapped him back. The man danced away.

Hilliard, feeling foolish, began to shuffle his feet.

A little after midnight Hilliard had the thought that it was time to go home. He had danced for a while—he had no idea how long—and then he had returned to his chair. He had been sitting there lost in thought ever since. He could not recall what he had been thinking about, any more than he could remember a dream once he'd fully awakened from it.

He looked around. The drummers were still at it. They had been playing without interruption for five hours. A few people were dancing, but none were twitching as if possessed. The ones who had done that had not seemed to remain in trance for very long. They would go around slapping palms and spreading energy for ten frenzied minutes or so; then someone would lead them away, and later they'd return, dressed in clean white robes and much subdued.

The Belgian women were nowhere to be seen. Donnelly, too, was missing. Farquahar was up front chatting with Atuele. Both men were smoking, and drinking what Hilliard assumed was whiskey.

Time to go.

He got to his feet, swayed, before catching his balance. What was protocol? Did you shake hands with your host, thank your hostess? He took a last look around, then walked off toward where they'd left the cars.

Donnelly's car was gone. Hilliard's evening clothes were in the backseat of his own car. Marilyn would be sleeping, it was pointless to change, but he did so anyway, stowing his khakis and safari shirt in the trunk. It wasn't until he was putting on his socks and black pumps that he realized his sandals were missing. Evidently he'd kicked them off earlier. He couldn't recall doing it, but he must have.

He didn't go back for them.

In the morning he waited for Marilyn to ask about the party. He had a response ready but was never called upon to deliver it. She went out for a tennis date right after breakfast, and she never did ask him about his evening.

They played bridge the following night with a British couple. The husband was some sort of paper shuffler, the wife an avid amateur astrologer who, unless she was playing cards, became quite boring on the subject.

Sunday was quiet. Hilliard drank a bit more than usual Sunday night, and he thought of telling his wife how he'd actually spent Friday evening. The impulse was not a terribly urgent one and he had the good sense to suppress it.

Monday he lunched with Donnelly.

"Well, it was an experience," he said.

"It always is."

"I'm not sorry I went."

"I'm not surprised," Donnelly said. "You went really deep, didn't you?"

"Deep? What do you mean?"

"Your trance. Or don't you even know you were in one?"

"I wasn't."

Donnelly laughed. "I wish I had a film of you dancing," he said. "I wondered if you were even aware of how caught up you were in it."

"I remember dancing. I wasn't leaping around like an acrobat or anything. Was I?"

"No, but you were . . . what's the word I want?"

"I don't know."

"Abandoned," Donnelly said. "You were dancing with abandon."

"That's hard to believe."

"And then you sat down and stared at nothing at all for hours on end."

"Maybe I fell asleep."

"You were in a trance, Alan."

"It didn't feel like a trance."

"Yes it did. That's what a trance feels like. It can be disappointing, because it feels like a normal state while it's going on, but it isn't."

He nodded, but he didn't speak right away. Then he said, "I thought I'd get something special for my money. An egg to rub into my scalp or something. A pot to hold on my head. A private ceremony—"

"The herb was your private ceremony."

"What did it do? Drug me so that I went into the trance-that-didn't-feel-like-a-trance? Farquahar got the same thing for free."

"The herb contained your spirit, or allowed the spirit to enter into you. Or whatever. I'm not too clear on how it works."

"So I've got a spirit in me now?"

"That's the theory."

"I don't feel different."

"You probably won't. And then one day something will click in, and you'll realize that you're different, that you've changed."

"Changed how?"

"I don't know. Look, maybe nothing will happen and you're out whatever it was. Four hundred dollars?"

"That's right. How about you? What did it cost you?"

"A thousand."

"My God."

"It was five hundred the first time, three hundred the

second, and this time it was an even thousand. I don't know how he sets the prices. Maybe a spirit tells him what to charge."

"Maybe if I'd paid more—" Hilliard began, and then he caught himself and started laughing. "Did you hear that? My God, I'm the original con man's dream. No sooner do I decide I've wasted my money than I start wondering if I shouldn't have wasted a little more of it."

"Give it a while," Donnelly said. "Maybe you didn't waste it. Wait and see."

Nothing was changed. Hilliard went to his office, did his work, lived his life. Evenings he went to diplomatic functions or played cards or, more often, sat home watching films with Marilyn.

On one such evening, almost a month after his ceremony, Hilliard frowned at his dish of *poulet rôti avec pommes frites et haricots verts*. "I'll be a minute," he told his wife, and he got up and went into the kitchen.

The cook was a tall woman, taller than Hilliard. She had glossy black skin and a full figure. Her cheekbones were high, her smile blinding.

"Liné," he said, "I'd like you to try something different for tomorrow night's dinner."

"Dinner is not good?"

"Dinner is fine," he said, "but it's not very interesting, is it? I would like you to prepare Togolese dishes for us."

"Ah," she said, and flashed her smile. "You would not like them."

"I would like them very much."

"No," she assured him. "Americans not like Togolese food. Is very simple and common, not good. I know what you like. I cook in the hotels, I cook for American people, for French people, for Nor, Nor—"

"Norwegian," he supplied.

"For Norjian people, yes. I know what you like."

"No," he said with conviction. "*I* know what I like, Liné, and I like Togolese dishes very much. I like chicken and yams with red sauce, and I like Togolese stew, I like them very hot and spicy, very fiery."

She looked at him, and it seemed to him that she had

never actually looked at him before. She extended the tip of her tongue and ran it across her upper lip. She said, "You want this tomorrow?"

"Yes, please."

"Real Togolese food," she said, and all at once her smile came, but now it was in her eyes as well. "Oh, I cook you some meal, boss! You see!"

That night, showering, he felt different. He couldn't define the difference but it was palpable.

He dried off and went to the bedroom. Marilyn was already asleep, lying on her side facing away from him. He got into bed and felt himself fill with desire for her.

He put a hand on her shoulder.

She rolled over to face him, as if she'd been waiting for his touch. He began to make love to her and her response had an intensity it had never had before. She cried out at climax.

"My God," she said afterward. She was propped up on one arm and her face was glowing. "What was that all about?"

"It's the Togolese food," he told her.

"But that's tomorrow night. If she actually cooks it."

"She'll cook it. And it's the expectation of the Togolese food. It heats the blood."

"Something sure did," she said.

She turned over and went to sleep. Moments later, so did Hilliard.

In the middle of the night he came half-awake. He realized that Marilyn had shifted closer to him in sleep, and that she had thrown an arm across his body. He liked the feeling. He closed his eyes and drifted off again.

The following evening Liné laid on a feast. She had produced a beef stew with yams and served it on a bed of some grain he'd never had before. It was not quite like anything he'd eaten at the native restaurant, and it was hotter than anything he'd ever eaten anywhere, but with all the flavors in good proportion. Midway through the meal Liné came out to the patio and beamed when they praised the food.

"I cook terrific every night now," she said. "You see!"

When the serving girl cleared the dishes, her little breast brushed Hilliard's arm. He could have sworn it was deliberate.

Later, when she brought the coffee, she grinned at him as if they shared a secret. He glanced at Marilyn, but if she caught it she gave no indication.

Later, they watched *Dr. Zhivago* on the VCR. Midway through it Marilyn got up from her chair and sat next to him on the couch. "This is the most romantic movie ever made," she told him. "It makes me want to cuddle."

"It's the spicy food," he said, slipping an arm around her.

"No, it's the movie," she said. She stroked his cheek, breathed kisses against the side of his neck. "Now *this*," she said, dropping a hand into his lap, "*this*," she said, fondling him, "*this* is an effect of the spicy food."

"I see the difference."

"I thought you would," she said.

"Good morning, Peggy," he said to Hank Suydam's secretary.

"Why, good morning, Mr. Hilliard," she said, a hitherto unseen light dancing in her brown eyes.

"Alan," he said.

"Alan," she said archly. "Good morning, Alan."

He called Donnelly, arranging to meet him for lunch. "And you can pay for lunch," Donnelly said.

"I was planning on it," he said, "but how did you know that?"

"Because it clicked in and you're eager to express your gratitude. I know it happened, I can hear it in your voice. How do you feel?"

"How do you think I feel?"

He hung up and started to go through the stack of letters on his desk. After a few minutes he realized he was grinning hugely. He got up and closed his office door.

Then, tentatively, he began to do a little dance.

THE EHRENGRAF
NOSTRUM

Gardner Bridgewater paced to and fro over Martin Ehrengraf's office carpet, reminding the little lawyer rather less of a caged jungle cat than—what? He doth bestride the narrow world like a Colossus, Ehrengraf thought, echoing Shakespeare's Cassius. But what, really, did a Colossus look like? Ehrengraf wasn't sure, but the alleged uxoricide was unquestionably colossal, and there he was, bestriding all over the place as if determined to wear holes in the rug.

"If I'd wanted to kill the woman," Bridgewater said, hitting one of his hands with the other, "I'd have damn well done it. By cracking her over the head with something heavy. A lamp base. A hammer. A fireplace poker."

An anvil, Ehrengraf thought. A stove. A Volkswagen.

"Or I might have wrung her neck," said Bridgewater, flexing his fingers. "Or I might have beaten her to death with my hands."

Ehrengraf thought of Longfellow's village blacksmith. "'The smith, a mighty man is he, with large and sinewy hands,'" he murmured.

"I beg your pardon?"

"Nothing important," said Ehrengraf. "You're saying, I gather, that if murderous impulses had overwhelmed you, you would have put them into effect in a more spontaneous and direct manner."

"Well, I certainly wouldn't have poisoned her. Poison's sneaky. It's the weapon of the weak, the devious, the cowardly."

"And yet your wife was poisoned."

"That's what they say. After dinner Wednesday she complained of headache and nausea. She took a couple of pills and lay down for a nap. She got up feeling worse, couldn't breathe. I rushed her to the hospital. Her heart ceased beating before I'd managed to fill out the questionnaire about medical insurance."

"And the cause of death," Ehrengraf said, "was a rather unusual poison."

Bridgewater nodded. "Cydonex," he said. "A tasteless, odorless, crystalline substance, a toxic hydrocarbon developed serendipitously as a by-product in the extrusion-molding of plastic dashboard figurines. Alyssa's system contained enough Cydonex to kill a person twice her size."

"You had recently purchased an eight-ounce canister of Cydonex."

"I had," Bridgewater said. "We had squirrels in the attic and I couldn't get rid of the wretched little beasts. The branches of several of our trees are within leaping distance of our roof and attic windows, and squirrels have quite infested the premises. They're noisy and filthy creatures, and clever at avoiding traps and poisoned baits. Isn't it extraordinary that a civilization with the capacity to devise napalm and Agent Orange can't come up with something for the control of rodents in a man's attic?"

"So you decided to exterminate them with Cydonex?"

"I thought it was worth a try. I mixed it into peanut butter and put gobs of it here and there in the attic. Squirrels are mad for peanut butter, especially the crunchy kind. They'll eat the creamy, but the crunchy really gets them."

"And yet you discarded the Cydonex. Investigators found the almost full canister near the bottom of your garbage can."

"I was worried about the possible effects. I recently saw a neighbor's dog with a squirrel in his jaws, and it struck me that a poisoned squirrel, reeling from the effects of the Cydonex, might be easy prey for a neighborhood pet, who would in turn be the poison's victim. Besides, as I said, poison's a sneak's weapon. Even a squirrel deserves a more direct approach."

A narrow smile blossomed for an instant on Ehrengraf's thin lips. Then it was gone. "One wonders," he said, "how the Cydonex got into your wife's system."

"It's a mystery to me, Mr. Ehrengraf. Unless poor Alyssa ate some peanut butter off the attic floor, I'm damned if I know where she got it."

"Of course," Ehrengraf said gently, "the police have their own theory."

"The police."

"Indeed. They seem to believe that you mixed a lethal dose of Cydonex into your wife's wine at dinner. The poison, tasteless and odorless as it is, would have been undetectable in plain water, let alone wine. What sort of wine was it, if I may ask?"

"Nuits-St.-Georges."

"And the main course?"

"Veal, I think. What difference does it make?"

"Nuits-St.-Georges would have overpowered the veal," Ehrengraf said thoughtfully. "No doubt it would have overpowered the Cydonex as well. The police said the wineglasses had been washed out, although the rest of the dinner dishes remained undone."

"The wineglasses are Waterford. I always do them up by hand, while Alyssa put everything else in the dishwasher."

"Indeed." Ehrengraf straightened up behind his desk, his hand fastening upon the knot of his tie. It was a small precise knot, and the tie itself was a two-inch-wide silk knit the approximate color of a bottle of Nuits-St.-Georges. The little lawyer wore a white-on-white shirt with French cuffs and a spread collar, and his suit was navy with a barely perceptible scarlet stripe. "As your lawyer," he said, "I must raise some unpleasant points."

"Go right ahead."

"You have a mistress, a young woman who is expecting your child. You and your wife were not getting along. Your wife refused to give you a divorce. Your business, while extremely profitable, has been experiencing recent cash-flow problems. Your wife's life was insured in the amount of five hundred thousand dollars with yourself as beneficiary. In addition, you are her sole heir, and her estate after taxes will still be considerable. Is all of that correct?"

"It is," Bridgewater admitted. "The police found it significant."

"I'm not surprised."

Bridgewater leaned forward suddenly, placing his large and sinewy hands upon Ehrengraf's desk. He looked capable of yanking the top off it and dashing it against the wall. "Mr. Ehrengraf," he said, his voice barely above a whisper, "do you think I should plead guilty?"

"Of course not."

"I could plead to a reduced charge."

"But you're innocent," Ehrengraf said. "My clients are always innocent, Mr. Bridgewater. My fees are high, sir. One might even pronounce them towering. But I collect them only if I win an acquittal or if the charges against my client are peremptorily dismissed. I intend to demonstrate your innocence, Mr. Bridgewater, and my fee system provides me with the keenest incentive toward that end."

"I see."

"Now," said Ehrengraf, coming out from behind his desk and rubbing his small hands briskly together, "let us look at the possibilities. Your wife ate the same meal you did, is that correct?"

"It is."

"And drank the same wine?"

"Yes. The residue in the bottle was unpoisoned. But I could have put Cydonex directly into her glass."

"But you didn't, Mr. Bridgewater, so let us not weigh ourselves down with what you could have done. She became ill after the meal, I believe you said."

"Yes. She was headachy and nauseous."

"Headachy and nauseated, Mr. Bridgewater. That she was nauseous in the bargain would be a subjective conclusion of your own. She lay down for a nap?"

"Yes."

"But first she took something."

"Yes that's right."

"Aspirin, something of that sort?"

"I suppose it's mostly aspirin," Bridgewater said. "It's a

patent medicine called Darnitol. Alyssa took it for everything from cramps to athlete's foot."

"Darnitol," Ehrengraf said. "An analgesic?"

"An analgesic, an anodyne, an antispasmodic, a panacea, a catholicon, a cure-all, a nostrum. Alyssa believed in it, Mr. Ehrengraf, and my guess would be that her belief was responsible for much of the preparation's efficacy. I don't take pills, never have, and my headaches seemed to pass as quickly as hers." He laughed shortly. "In any event, Darnitol proved an inadequate antidote for Cydonex."

"Hmm," said Ehrengraf.

"To think it was the Darnitol that killed her."

Five weeks had passed since their initial meeting, and events in the interim had done a great deal to improve both the circumstances and the spirit of Ehrengraf's client. Gardner Bridgewater was no longer charged with his wife's murder.

"It was one of the first things I thought of," Ehrengraf said. "The police had their vision clouded by the extraordinary coincidence of your purchase and use of Cydonex as a vehicle for the extermination of squirrels. But my view was based on the presumption of your innocence, and I was able to discard this coincidence as irrelevant. It wasn't until other innocent men and women began to die of Cydonex poisoning that a pattern began to emerge. A schoolteacher in Kenmore. A retired steelworker in Lackawanna. A young mother in Orchard Park."

"And more," Bridgewater said. "Eleven in all, weren't there?"

"Twelve," Ehrengraf said. "But for diabolical cleverness on the part of the poisoner, he could never have gotten away with it for so long."

"I don't understand how he managed it."

"By leaving no incriminating residue," Ehrengraf explained. "We've had poisoners of this sort before, tainting tablets of some nostrum or other. And there was a man in Boston, I believe it was, who stirred arsenic into the sugar in coffeeshop dispensers. With any random mass murder of that sort, sooner or later a pattern emerges. But this killer only tampered with a single capsule in each bottle of Darnitol. The victim might consume capsules with impunity until the one fatal pill was swallowed, whereupon there would be no evidence remaining in the bottle, no telltale leftover capsule to give the police a clue."

"Good heavens."

"Indeed. The police did in fact test as a matter of course the bottles of Darnitol which were invariably found among the victims' effects. But the pills invariably proved innocent. Finally, when the death toll mounted high enough, the fact that Darnitol was associated with every single death proved indismissable. The police seized drugstore stocks of the painkiller, and again and again bottles turned out to have a single tainted capsule in with the legitimate pills."

"And the actual killer—"

"Will be found, I shouldn't doubt, in the course of time." Ehrengraf straightened his tie, a stylish specimen showing a half-inch stripe of royal blue flanked by two narrower stripes, one of gold and the other of a vivid green, all displayed on a field of navy. The tie was that of the Caedmon Society, and it brought back memories. "Some disgruntled employee of the Darnitol manufacturer, I shouldn't wonder," said Ehrengraf carelessly. "That's usually the case in this sort of affair. Or some unbalanced chap who took the pill himself and was unhappy with the results. Twelve dead, plus your wife of course, and a company on the verge of ruin, because I shouldn't think too many people are rushing down to their local pharmacy and purchasing Extra-Strength Darnitol."

"There's a joke going round," Bridgewater said, flexing his large and sinewy hands. "Patient calls his doctor, says he's got a headache, an upset stomach, whatever. Doctor says, 'Take two Darnitol and call me in the Hereafter.' "

"Indeed."

Bridgewater sighed. "I suppose," he said, "the real killer may never be found."

"Oh, I suspect he will," Ehrengraf said. "In the interests of rounding things out, you know. And, speaking of rounding things out, sir, if you've your checkbook with you—"

"Ah, yes," said Bridgewater. He made his check payable to Martin H. Ehrengraf and filled in the sum, which was a large one. He paused then, his pen hovering over the space for his signature. Perhaps he reflected for a moment on the curious business of paying so great an amount to a person who, on the face of it, had taken no concrete action on his behalf.

But who is to say what thoughts go through a man's mind? Bridgewater signed the check, tore it from the checkbook, and presented it with a flourish.

"What would you drink with veal?" he demanded.

"I beg your pardon?"

"You said the Nuits-St.-Georges would be overpowering with veal. What would you choose?"

"I shouldn't choose veal in the first place. I don't eat meat."

"Don't eat meat?" Bridgewater, who looked as though he might cheerfully consume a whole lamb at a sitting, was incredulous. "What *do* you eat?"

"Tonight I'm having a nut-and-soybean casserole," the little lawyer said. He blew on the check to dry the ink, folded it, and put it away. "Nuits-St.-Georges should do nicely with it," he said. "Or perhaps a good bottle of Chambertin."

The Chambertin and the nut-and-soybean casserole that it had so superbly complemented were but a memory four days later when a uniformed guard ushered the little lawyer into the cell where Evans Wheeler awaited him. The lawyer, neatly turned out in a charcoal-gray-flannel suit with a nipped-in waist, a Wedgwood-blue shirt, and a navy tie with a below-the-knot design, contrasted sharply in appearance with his prospective client. Wheeler, as awkwardly tall and thin as a young Lincoln, wore striped overalls and a denim shirt. His footwear consisted of a pair of chain-store running shoes. The lawyer wore highly polished cordovan loafers.

And yet, Ehrengraf noted, the young man was poised enough in his casual costume. It suited him, even to the stains and chemical burns on the overalls and the ragged patch on one elbow of the workshirt.

"Mr. Ehrengraf," said Wheeler, extending a bony hand. "Pardon the uncomfortable surroundings. They don't go out of their way to make suspected mass murderers comfortable." He smiled ruefully. "The newspapers are calling it the crime of the century."

"That's nonsense," said Ehrengraf. "The century's not over yet. But the crime's unarguably a monumental one, sir, and the evidence against you would seem to be particularly damning."

"That's why I want you on my side, Mr. Ehrengraf."

"Well," said Ehrengraf.

"I know your reputation, sir. You're a miracle worker, and it looks as though that's what I need."

"What you very likely need," Ehrengraf said, "is a master of delaying tactics. Someone who can stall your case for as long as possible to let some of the heat of the moment be discharged. Then, when public opinion has lost some of its fury, he can arrange for you to plead guilty to homicide while of unsound mind. Some sort of insanity defense might work, or might at least reduce the severity of your sentence."

"But I'm innocent, Mr. Ehrengraf."

"I wouldn't presume to say otherwise, Mr. Wheeler, but I don't know that I'd be the right person to undertake your defense. I charge high fees, you see, which I collect only in the event that my clients are entirely exonerated. This tends to limit the nature of my clients."

"To those who can afford you."

"I've defended paupers. I've defended the poor as a court-appointed attorney and I volunteered my services on behalf of a penniless poet. But in the ordinary course of things, my clients seem to have two things in common. They can afford my high fees. And, of course, they're innocent."

"I'm innocent."

"Indeed."

"And I'm a long way from being a pauper, Mr. Ehrengraf. You know that I used to work for Triage Corporation, the manufacturer of Darnitol."

"So I understand."

"You know that I resigned six months ago."

"After a dispute with your employer."

"Not a dispute," Wheeler said. "I told him where he could resituate a couple of test tubes. You see, I was in a position to make the suggestion, although I don't know that he was in a position to follow it. On my own time I'd developed a process for extenuating lapiform polymers so as to produce a variable-stress oxypolymer capable of withstanding—"

Wheeler went on to explain just what the oxypolymer was capable of withstanding, and Ehrengraf wondered what the young man was talking about. He tuned in again to hear him say, "And so my royalty on the process in the first year will be in excess of six hundred fifty thousand dollars, and I'm told that's only the beginning."

"Only the beginning," said Ehrengraf.

"I haven't sought other employment because there doesn't seem to be much point in it, and I haven't changed my lifestyle because I'm happy as I am. But I don't want to spend the rest of my life in prison, Mr. Ehrengraf, nor do I want to escape on some technicality and be loathed by my neighbors for the remainder of my days. I want to be exonerated and I don't care what it costs me."

"Of course you do," said Ehrengraf, drawing himself stiffly erect. "Of course you do. After all, son, you're innocent."

"Exactly."

"Although," Ehrengraf said with a sigh, "your innocence may be rather tricky to prove. The evidence—"

"Is overpowering."

"Like Nuits-St.-Georges with veal. A search of your workroom revealed a half-full container of Cydonex. You denied ever having seen it before."

"Absolutely."

Ehrengraf frowned. "I wonder if you mightn't have purchased it as an aid to pest control. Rats are troublesome. One is always being plagued by rats in one's cellar, mice in one's pantry, squirrels in one's attic—"

"And bats in one's belfry, I suppose, but my house has always been comfortingly free of vermin. I keep a cat. I suppose that helps."

"I'm sure it must, but I don't know that it helps your case. You seem to have purchased Cydonex from a chemical-supply house on North Division Street, where your signature appears in the poison-control ledger."

"A forgery."

"No doubt, but a convincing one. Bottles of Darnitol, some unopened, others with a single Cydonex-filled capsule added, were found on a closet shelf in your home. They seem to be from the same lot as those used to murder thirteen people."

"I was framed, Mr. Ehrengraf."

"And cleverly so, it would seem."

"I never bought Cydonex. I never heard of Cydonex—not until people started dying of it."

"Oh? You worked for the plastics company that discovered the substance. That was before you took employment with the Darnitol people."

"It was also before Cydonex was invented. You know those dogs people mount on their dashboards and the head bobs up and down when you drive?"

"Not when I drive," Ehrengraf said.

"Nor I either, but you know what I mean. My job was finding a way to make the dogs' eyes more realistic. If you had a dog bobbing on your dashboard, would you even *want* the eyes to be more realistic?"

"Well," said Ehrengraf.

"Exactly. I quit that job and went to work for the Darnitol folks, and then my previous employer found a better way to kill rats, and so it looks as though I'm tied into the murders in two different ways. But actually I've never had anything to do with Cydonex and I've never so much as swallowed a Darnitol, let alone paid good money for that worthless snake oil."

"*Someone* bought those pills."

"Yes, but it wasn't—"

"And someone purchased that Cydonex. And forged your name to the ledger."

"Yes."

"And planted the bottles of Darnitol on drugstore and supermarket shelves after fatally tampering with their contents."

"Yes."

"And waited for the random victims to buy the pills, to work their way through the bottle until they ingested the deadly capsule, and to die in agony. And planted evidence to incriminate you."

"Yes."

"And made an anonymous call to the police to put them on your trail." Ehrengraf permitted himself a slight smile, one that did not quite reach his eyes. "And there he made his mistake," he said. "He could have waited for nature to take its course, just as he had already waited for the Darnitol to do its deadly work. The police were checking on ex-employees of

Triage Corporation. They'd have gotten to you sooner or later.
But he wanted to hurry matters along, and that proves you
were framed, sir, because who but the man who framed you
would ever think to have called the police?"

"So the very phone call that got me on the hook serves to
get me off the hook?"

"Ah," said Ehrengraf, "would that it were that easy."

Unlike Gardner Bridgewater, young Evans Wheeler proved
a model of repose. Instead of pacing back and forth across
Ehrengraf's carpet, the chemist sat in Ehrengraf's overstuffed
leather chair, one long leg crossed over the other. His costume
was virtually identical to the garb he had worn in prison,
although an eye as sharp as Ehrengraf's could detect a different pattern to the stains and acid burns that gave character to
the striped overalls. And this denim shirt, Ehrengraf noted,
had no patch upon its elbow. Yet.

Ehrengraf, seated at his desk, wore a Dartmouth-green
blazer over tan flannel slacks. As was his custom on such
occasions, his tie was once again the distinctive Caedmon
Society cravat.

"Ms. Joanna Pellatrice," Ehrengraf said. "A teacher of sev-
enth- and eighth-grade social studies at Kenmore Junior High
School. Unmarried, twenty-eight years of age, and living alone
in three rooms on Deerhurst Avenue."

"One of the killer's first victims."

"That she was. The very first victim, in point of fact, although Ms. Pellatrice was not the first to die. Her murderer
took one of the capsules from her bottle of Darnitol, pried it
open, disposed of the innocent if ineffectual powder within
and replaced it with the lethal Cydonex. Then he put it back
in her bottle, returned the bottle to her medicine cabinet or
purse, and waited for the unfortunate woman to get a headache or cramps or whatever impelled her to swallow the capsules."

"Whatever it was," Wheeler said, "they wouldn't work."

"This one did, when she finally got to it. In the meantime
her intended murderer had already commenced spreading little bottles of joy all over the metropolitan area, one capsule
to each bottle. There was danger in doing so, in that the toxic
nature of Darnitol might come to light before Ms. Pellatrice

took her pill and went to that big classroom in the sky. But he reasoned, correctly it would seem, that a great many persons would die before Darnitol was seen to be the cause of death. And indeed this proved to be the case. Ms. Pellatrice was the fourth victim, and there were to be many more."

"And the killer—"

"Refused to leave well enough alone. His name is George Grodek, and he'd had an affair with Ms. Pellatrice, although married to another teacher all the while. The affair evidently meant rather more to Mr. Grodek than it did to Ms. Pellatrice. He had made scenes, once at her apartment, once at her school during a midterm examination. The newspapers describe him as a disappointed suitor, and I suppose the term's as apt as any."

"You say he refused to leave well enough alone."

"Indeed," said Ehrengraf. "If he'd been content with depopulating the area and sinking Triage Corporation, I'm sure he'd have gotten away with it. The police would have had their hands full checking people with a grudge against Triage, known malcontents and mental cases, and the sort of chaps who get themselves into messes of that variety. But he has a neat sort of mind, has Mr. Grodek, and so he managed to learn of your existence and decided to frame you for the chain of murders."

Ehrengraf brushed a piece of lint from his lapel. "He did a workmanlike job," he said, "but it broke down on close examination. That signature in the poison-control book did turn out to be a forgery, and matching forgeries of your name—trials, if you will—turned up in a notebook hidden away in a dresser drawer in his house."

"That must have been hard for him to explain."

"So were the bottles of Darnitol in another drawer of the dresser. So was the Cydonex, and so was the little machine for filling and closing the capsules, and a whole batch of broken capsules which evidently represented unsuccessful attempts at pill-making."

"Funny he didn't flush it all down the toilet."

"Successful criminals become arrogant," Ehrengraf explained. "They believe themselves to be untouchable. Grodek's arrogance did him in. It led him to frame you, and to tip the police to you."

"And your investigation did what no police investigation could do."

"It did," said Ehrengraf, "because mine started from the premise of your innocence. If you were innocent, someone else was guilty. If someone else was guilty and had framed you, that someone must have had a motive for the crime. If the crime had a motive, the murderer must have had a reason to kill one of the specific victims. And if that was the case, one had only to look to the victims to find the killer."

"You make it sound so simple," said Wheeler. "And yet if I hadn't had the good fortune to engage your services, I'd be spending the rest of my life in prison."

"I'm glad you see it that way," Ehrengraf said, "because the size of my fee might otherwise seem excessive." He named a figure, whereupon the chemist promptly uncapped a pen and wrote out a check.

"I've never written a check for so large a sum," he said reflectively.

"Few people have."

"Nor have I ever gotten greater value for my money. How fortunate I am that you believed in me, in my innocence."

"I never doubted it for a moment."

"You know who else claims to be innocent? Poor Grodek. I understand the madman's screaming in his cell, shouting to the world that he never killed anyone." Wheeler flashed a mischievous smile. "Perhaps he should hire you, Mr. Ehrengraf."

"Oh, dear," said Ehrengraf. "No, I think not. I can sometimes work miracles, Mr. Wheeler, or what have the appearance of miracles, but I can work them only on behalf of the innocent. And I don't think the power exists to persuade me of poor Mr. Grodek's innocence. No, I fear the man is guilty, and I'm afraid he'll be forced to pay for what he's done." The little lawyer shook his head. "Do you know Longfellow, Mr. Wheeler?"

"Old Henry Wadsworth, you mean? 'By the shores of Gitche Gumee, by the something Big-Sea-Water?' That Longfellow?"

"The shining Big-Sea-Water," said Ehrengraf. "Another client reminded me of 'The Village Blacksmith,' and I've been looking into Longfellow lately. Do you care for poetry, Mr. Wheeler?"

"Not too much."

" 'In the world's broad field of battle,' " Ehrengraf said,

" 'In the bivouac of Life,

" 'Be not like dumb, driven cattle!

" 'Be a hero in the strife!' "

"Well," said Evans Wheeler, "I suppose that's good advice, isn't it?"

"None better, sir. 'Let us then be up and doing, with a heart for any fate; still achieving, still pursuing, learn to labor and to wait.' "

"Ah, yes," said Wheeler.

" 'Learn to labor and to wait,' " said Ehrengraf. "That's the ticket, eh? 'To labor and to wait.' Longfellow, Mr. Wheeler. Listen to the poets, Mr. Wheeler. The poets have the answers, haven't they?" And Ehrengraf smiled, with his lips and with his eyes.

LIKE A BUG
ON A WINDSHIELD

There are two Rodeway Inns in Indianapolis, but Waldron only knew the one on West Southern Avenue, near the airport. He made it a point to break trips there if he could do so without going out of his way or messing up his schedule. There were eight or ten motels around the country that were favorites of his, some of them chain affiliates, a couple of them independents. A Days Inn south of Tulsa, for example, was right across the street from a particularly good restaurant. A Quality Court outside of Jacksonville had friendly staff and big cakes of soap in the bathroom. Sometimes he didn't know exactly why a motel was on his list, and he thought that it might be habit, like the brand of cigarettes he smoked, and that habit in turn might be largely a matter of convenience. Easier to buy Camels every time than to stand around deciding what you felt like smoking. Easier to listen to WJJD out of Chicago until the signal faded, then dial on down to KOMA in Omaha, than to hunt around and try to guess what kind of music you wanted to hear and where you were likely to find it.

It was more than habit, though, that made him stop at the Indianapolis Rodeway when he was in the neighborhood. They made it nice for a trucker without running a place that felt like a truck stop. There was a separate lot for the big rigs, of course, but there was also a twenty-four-hour check-in area around back just for truckers, with a couple of old boys sitting around in chairs and country music playing on the radio. The coffee was always hot and always free, and it was real coffee out of a Silex, not the brown dishwater the machines dispensed.

Inside, the rooms were large and clean and the beds comfortable. There was a huge indoor pool with Jacuzzi and sauna. A good bar, an okay restaurant—and, before you hit the road again, there was more free coffee at the truckers' room in back.

Sometimes a guy could get lucky at the bar or around the pool. If not, well, there was free HBO on the color television and direct-dial phones to call home on. You wouldn't drive five hundred miles out of your way, but it was worth planning your trip to stop there.

He walked into the Rodeway truckers' room around nine on a hot July night. The room was air-conditioned but the door was always open, so the air-conditioning didn't make much difference. Lundy rocked back in his chair and looked up at him. "Hey, boy," Lundy said. "Where you *been*?"

"Drivin'," he said, giving the ritual response to the ritual question.

"Yeah, I guess. You look about as gray as this desk. Get yourself a cup of coffee, I think you need it."

"What I need is about four ounces of bourbon and half an hour in the Jacuzzi."

"And two hours with the very best TWA has to offer," Lundy said. "What we all need, but meantime grab some coffee."

"I guess," Waldron said, and poured himself a cup. He blew on the surface to cool it and glanced around the room. Besides Lundy, a chirpy little man with wire-rimmed glasses and a built-up shoe, there were three truckers in the room. Two, like Waldron, were drinking coffee out of Styrofoam cups. The third man was drinking Hudepohl beer out of the can.

Waldron filled out the registration card, paid with his Visa card, pocketed his room key and receipt. Then he sat down and took another sip of his coffee.

"The way some people drive," he said.

There were murmurs of agreement.

"About forty miles out of here," he said, "I'm on the Interstate—what's the matter with me, I can't even think of the goddamned number—"

"Easy, boy."

"Yeah, easy." He took a breath, sipped at his coffee, blew at the surface. It was cool enough to drink, but blowing on it was reflexive, habitual. "Two kids in a Toyota. I thought at first it was two guys, but it was a guy and a girl. I'm going about five miles over the limit, not pushing it, and they pass me on a slight uphill and then they cut in tight. I gotta step on my brake or I'm gonna walk right up their back bumper."

"These people don't know how to drive," one of the coffee drinkers said. "I don't know where they get their licenses."

"Through the mails," the beer drinker said. "Out of the Monkey Ward catalog."

"So I tapped the horn," Waldron said. "Just a tap, you know? And the guy was driving, he taps back."

"Honks his horn."

"Right. And slows down. Sixty-two, sixty, fifty-eight, he's dying out there in front of me. So I wait, and I flip the brights on and off to signal him, and then I go around him and wait until I'm plenty far ahead of him before I move back in."

"And he passes you again," said the other coffee drinker, speaking for the first time.

"How'd you know?"

"He cut in sharp again?"

Waldron nodded. "I guess I was expecting it once he moved out to pass me. I eased up on the gas, and when he cut in I had to touch the brake, but it wasn't close, and this time I didn't bother hitting the horn."

"I'da used the horn," the beer drinker said. "I'da *stood up* on the horn."

"Then he slowed down again," the second coffee drinker said. "Am I right?"

"What are these guys, friends of yours?"

"They slow down again?"

"To a crawl. And then I *did* use the horn, and the girl turned around and gave me the finger." He drank the rest of the coffee. "And I got angry," he said. "I pulled out. I put the pedal on the floor and I moved out in front of them—and this time they're not gonna let me pass, you know, they're gonna pace me, fast when I speed up, slow when I lay off. And they're looking up at me, and they're laughing, and she's leaning across his lap and she's got her blouse or the front of her dress, whatever it is, she's got it pushed down, you know, like I've never seen it before and my eyeballs are gonna go out on stalks—"

"Like in a cartoon."

"Right. And I thought, You idiots, because all I had to do, you know, was turn the wheel. Because where are they gonna go? The shoulder? They won't have time to get there. I'll run right over them, I'll smear 'em like a bug on the windshield. Splat, and they're gone."

"I like that," Lundy said.

Waldron took a breath. "I almost did it," he said.

"How much is almost?"

"I could feel it in my hands," he said. He held them out in front of him, shaped to grip a steering wheel. "I could feel the thought going into my hands, to turn that wheel and flatten them. I could see it all happening. I had the picture in my mind, and I was seeing myself driving away from them, just driving off, and they're wrecked and burning."

Lundy whistled.

"And I had the thought, That's murder! And the thought like registered, but I was still going to do it, the hell with it. My hands"—he flexed his fingers—"my hands were ready to move on the wheel, and then it was gone."

"The Toyota was gone?"

"The *thought* was gone. I hit the brake and I got behind them and a rest area came up and I took it, fast. I pulled in and cut the engine and had a smoke. I was all alone there. It was empty and I was thinking that maybe they'd come back and pull into the rest area, too, and if they did I was gonna take him on with a tire iron. There's one I keep in the front seat with me and I actually got it down from the rig and walked around with it in one hand, smoking a cigarette and swinging the tire iron just so I'll be ready."

"You see 'em again?"

"No. They were just a couple of kids clowning around, probably working themselves up. Now they'll get into the backseat and have themselves a workout."

"I don't envy them," Lundy said. "Not in the backseat of an effing Toyota."

"What they don't know," said Waldron, "is how close they came to being dead."

They were all looking up at him. The second coffee drinker, a dark-haired man with deep-set brown eyes, smiled. "You really think it was close?"

"I told you, I almost—"

"So how close is almost? You thought about it and then you didn't do it."

"I thought about making it with Jane Fonda," Lundy said, "but then I didn't do it."

"I was going to do it," Waldron said.

"And then you didn't."

"And then I didn't." He shook a cigarette out of his pack and picked up Lundy's Zippo and lit it. "I don't know where the anger came from. I was angry enough to kill. Why? Because the girl shot me a bone? Because she waggled her—?"

"Because you were afraid," the first coffee drinker suggested.

"Afraid of what? I got eighteen wheels under me, I'm hauling building materials, how'm I afraid of a Toyota? It's not my ass if I hit them." He took the cigarette out of his mouth and looked at it. "But you're right," he said. "I was scared I'd hit them and kill them, and that turned into anger, and I almost *did* kill them."

"Maybe you should have," someone said. Waldron was still looking at his cigarette, not noticing who was speaking. "Whole road's full of amateurs and people thinking they're funny. Maybe you got to teach 'em a lesson."

"Swat 'em," someone else said. "Like you said, bug on the windshield."

" 'I'm just a bug on the windshield of life,' " Lundy sang in a tuneless falsetto whine. "Now who was it sang that or did I just make it up?" Dolly Parton, the beer drinker suggested. "Now wouldn't I just love to be a bug on her windshield?" Lundy said.

Waldron picked up his bag and went to look for his room.

* * *

Eight, ten weeks later, he was eating eggs and scrapple in a diner on Route 1 outside of Bordentown, New Jersey. The diner was called the Super Chief and was designed to look like a diesel locomotive and painted with aluminum paint. Waldron was reading a paper someone else had left in the booth. He almost missed the story, but then he saw it.

A camper had plunged through a guardrail and off an embankment on a branch of the Interstate near Gatlinburg, Tennessee. The driver, an instructor at Ozark Community College in Pine Bluff, Arkansas, had survived with massive chest and leg injuries. His wife and infant son had died in the crash.

According to the driver, an eighteen-wheeler had come up "out of nowhere" and shoved the little RV off the road. "It's like he was a snowplow," he said, "and he was clearing us out of the way."

Like a bug on a windshield, thought Waldron.

He read the story again, closed the paper. His hand was shaking as he picked up his cup of coffee. He put the cup down, took a few deep breaths, then picked up the cup again without trembling.

He pictured them in the truckers' room at the Rodeway, Lundy rocking back in his chair with his feet up, built-up shoe and all. The beer drinker, the two coffee drinkers. Had he even heard their names? He couldn't remember, nor could he keep their images in focus in his memory. But he could hear their voices. And he could hear his own, suggesting an act not unlike the one he had just read about.

My God, had he given someone an idea?

He sipped his coffee, left the rest of his food untouched on the plate. Scrapple was a favorite of his and you could only find it in and around Philadelphia, and they did it right here, fried it crisp and served it with maple syrup, but he was letting the grease congeal around it now. That one coffee drinker, the one with the deep-set eyes, was he the one who'd spoken the words, but he remembered the anger in them, and something else, too, something like a blood lust.

Of course, the teacher could have dreamed the part about the eighteen-wheeler. Could have gone to sleep at the wheel and made up a story to keep him from seeing he'd driven off the road and killed his own family. Pin it on the Phantom Trucker and keep the blame off your own self.

Probably how it happened.

Still, from that morning on, Waldron kept an eye on the papers.

"Hey, boy," Lundy said. "Where *you* been?"

It was a cold December afternoon, overcast, with a raw wind blowing out of the northwest. The daylight ran out early this time of year but there were hours of it left. Waldron had broken his trip early just to stop at the Rodeway.

"Been up and down the Seaboard," he said. "Mostly. Hauling a lot of loads in and out of Baltimore." Of course there'd been some cross-country trips, too, but he'd managed to miss Indianapolis each time, once or twice distorting his schedule as much to avoid Indy as he'd fooled with it today to get here.

"Been a while," Lundy said.

"Six months."

"That long?"

"July, last I was here."

"Makes five months, don't it?"

"Well, early July. Say five and a half."

"Say a year and a half if you want. Your wife asks, I'll swear you was never here at all. Get some coffee, boy."

There was another trucker sitting with a cup of coffee, a bearded longhair with a fringed buckskin jacket, and he'd laughed at Lundy's remark. Waldron poured himself a cup of coffee and sat down with it, sitting quietly, listening to the radio and the two men's light banter. When the fellow in buckskin left, Waldron leaned forward.

"The last time I was here," he said.

"July, if we take your word for it."

"I was wired that night, I'd had a clown playing tag with me on the road."

"If you say so."

"There were three truckers in here plus yourself. One was drinking beer and the other two were drinking coffee."

Lundy looked at him.

"What I need to know," Waldron said, "is their names."

"You must be kidding."

"It wouldn't be hard to find out. You'd have the registrations. I checked the date, it was the ninth of July."

"Wait a minute." Lundy rocked his chair back and put both feet on the metal desk. Waldron glanced at the built-up shoe. "A night in July," Lundy said. "What in hell happened?"

"You must remember. I almost had an accident with a wise-ass, cut me off, played tag, made a game of it. I was saying how angry I was, how I wanted to kill him."

"So?"

"I wanted to kill him with the truck."

"So?"

"Don't you remember? Something I said, you made a song out of it. I said I could have killed him like a bug on the windshield."

"Now I remember," Lundy said, showing interest. "Just a bug on the windshield of life, that's the song that came to me, I couldn't get it out of my head for the next ten or twelve days. Now I'll be stuck with it for the *next* ten or twelve days, like as not. Don't tell me you want to haul my ass down to Nashville and make me a star."

"What I want," Waldron said evenly, "is for you to check the registrations and figure out who was in the room that night."

"Why?"

"Because somebody's doing it."

Lundy looked at him.

"Killing people. With trucks."

"Killing people with trucks? Killing drivers or owners or what?"

"Using trucks as murder weapons," Waldron said. On the radio, David Allen Coe insisted he was an outlaw like Waylon and Willie. "Running people off the road. Flyswatting 'em."

"How d'you know all this?"

"Look," Waldron said. He took an envelope from his pocket, unfolded it, and spread newspaper clippings on the top of Lundy's desk. Without removing his feet from the desk, Lundy leaned forward to scan the clips. "These are from all over," he said after a moment.

"I know."

"Any of these here could be an accident."

"Then somebody's leaving the scene of a lot of accidents. Last I heard, there was a law against it."

"Could be a whole lot of different accidents."

"It could," Waldron admitted. "But I don't believe it. It's murder and it's one man doing it and I know who he is."

"Who?"

"At least I think I know."

"You gonna tell me or is it a secret?"

"Not the beer drinker," Waldron said. "One of the two fellows who were drinking coffee."

"Narrows it down. Not too many old boys drive trucks and drink coffee."

"I can almost picture him. Deep-set eyes, dark hair, sort of a dark complexion. He had a way of speaking. I can about hear his voice."

"What makes you think he's the one?"

"I don't know. You want to get those registrations?"

He didn't, and Waldron had to talk him into it. Then there were three check-ins, one right after the other, and two of the men lingered with their coffee. When they left, Lundy heaved a sigh and told Waldron to mind the store. He limped off and came back ten minutes later with a stack of index cards.

"July the ninth," he announced, sinking into his chair and slapping the cards onto the desk. "You want to deal those, we can play some Five Hundred Rummy. You got enough cards for it."

Not quite. There were forty-three registrations that had come through the truckers' check-in room for that date. Just over half were names that one of the two men recognized and could rule out as the possible identity of the dark-eyed coffee drinker. But there were still twenty possibles, names that meant nothing to either man—and Lundy explained that their man might not have filled in a card.

"He could of shared a room and the other man registered," he said, "or he could have just come by for the coffee and the company. There's old boys every night that pull in for half an hour and the free coffee, or maybe they're taking a meal break and they come around back to say hello. So what you got, you got it narrowed down to twenty, but he might not be one of the twenty anyway. You get tired of driving a truck, boy, you can get a job with Sherlock Holmes. Get you the cap and the pipe, nobody'll know the difference."

Waldron was going through the cards, reading the names and addresses.

"Looking through a stack of cards for a man who maybe isn't there in the first place and who probably didn't do anything anyway. And what are you gonna do if you find him?"

"I don't know."

"Where's it your business, come to that?"

Waldron didn't say anything at first. Then he said, "I gave him the idea."

"With what you said? Bug on the windshield?"

"That's right."

"Oh, that's crazy," Lundy said. "Where you been, boy? I hear that same kind of talk four days out of seven. Guy walks in, hot about some fool who almost made him lose it, next thing you know he's saying how instead of driving off the road, next time he'll drive right *through* the mother. Even if somebody's doin' this"—he tapped Waldron's clippings— "which I don't think they are, there's no way it's you gave him the idea. My old man, he'd wash his car and then it'd rain and he'd swear it was him brought the rain on. You're startin' to remind me of him, you know that?"

"I can picture him," Waldron said. "Sitting up behind the wheel, a light rain coming down, the windshield wipers working at the low speed. And he's smiling."

"And about to run some sucker off the road."

"I can just see it so clear. This one time"—he sorted through the newspaper clippings—"downstate Illinois, this sportscar. Witness said a truck just ran right *over* it."

"Like steppin' on it," Lundy said thoughtfully.

"And when I think about it—"

"You don't know it's on purpose," Lundy said. "All the pills some of you old boys take. And you don't know it's one man doing it, and you don't know it's him, and you don't know who he is anyway. And you don't know you gave him the idea, and if there's a God or not you ain't It, so why are you makin' yourself crazy over it?"

"Well, you got a point," Waldron said.

* * *

He went to his room, showered, put on swim trunks, and picked up a towel. He went back and forth from the sauna to the pool and into the Jacuzzi and back into the pool again. He swam some laps, then stretched out on a chaise next to the pool. He listened, eyes closed, while a man with a soft hill-country accent was trying to teach his young son to swim. Then he must have dozed off, and when he opened his eyes he was alone in the pool area. He returned to his room, showered, shaved, put on fresh clothes, and went to the bar.

It was a nice room—low lighting, comfortable chairs, and barstools. Some decorator had tricked it out with a library motif, and there were bookshelves here and there with real books in them. At least Waldron supposed they were real books. He'd never seen anyone reading one of them.

He settled in at the bar with bourbon and dry-roast peanuts from the dish on the bartop. An hour later he was in a conversation, and thirty minutes after that he was back in his room, bedded down with an old girl named Claire who said she was assistant manager of the gift shop at the airport. She was partial to truckers, she told him. She'd even married one, and although it hadn't worked out they remained good friends. "Man drives for a living, chances are he's thoughtful and considerate and sure of himself, you know what I mean?"

Waldron saw those deep-set brown eyes looking over the steering wheel. And that slow smile.

After that he seemed to catch a lot of cross-country hauling and he stopped pretty regularly at the Rodeway. It was convenient enough, and the Jacuzzi was a big attraction during the winter months. It really took the road-tension out of you.

Claire was an attraction, too. He didn't see her every visit, but if the hour was right he sometimes gave her a call and they sometimes got together. She'd come by for a drink or a swim, and one night he put on a jacket and took her to dinner in town at the King Cole.

She knew he was married and felt neither jealousy nor guilt about it. "Me and my ex," she said, "it wasn't what he did on the road that broke us up. It was what he didn't do when he was home."

It was mid-March when he finally found the man. And it was nowhere near Indianapolis.

It was a truck stop just east of Tucumcari, New Mexico, and he'd had no intention of stopping there. He'd had breakfast a while back in a Tex-Mex diner midway between Gallup and Albuquerque, and by the time he hit Tucumcari his gut was rumbling and he was ready for an unscheduled pit stop. He picked a place he'd never stopped at. If it had a name he didn't know what it was. The signs said nothing but DIESEL FUEL and TRUCKERS WELCOME. He clambered down from the cab and used the john, then went in for a cup of coffee he didn't particularly want.

And saw the man right away.

He'd been able to picture the eyes and the smile, and a pair of hands on a wheel. Now the image enlarged to include a round, close-cropped head with a receding hairline, a bulldog jaw, a massive pair of shoulders. The man sat on a stool at the counter, drinking coffee and reading a magazine, and Waldron just stood for a moment, looking at him.

There was a point where he almost turned and walked out. It passed, and instead he took the adjoining stool and ordered coffee. When the girl brought it, he let it sit there. Beside him, the man with the deep-set eyes was reading an article about bonefishing in the Florida Keys.

"Nice day out there," Waldron said.

The man raised his eyes, nodded.

"I think I met you sometime last summer. Indianapolis, the Rodeway Inn."

"I've been there."

"I met you in Lundy's room in the back. There were three men there beside Lundy. One of them was drinking a can of Hudepohl."

"You got a memory," the man said.

"Well, the night stuck in my mind. I had a close one out on the highway, I came in jawing about it. A jerk in a car playing tag with me and I came in mad enough to talk about running him off the road, killing him."

"I remember that night," the man said, and he smiled the way Waldron remembered. "Now I remember you."

Waldron sipped his coffee.

" 'Like a bug on a windshield,' " the man said. "I remember you saying that. Next little while, every time some insect went and gummed up the glass, it came to me, you saying that. You ever find them?"

"Find who?"

"Whoever was playing tag with you."

"I never looked for them."

"You were mad enough to," the man said. "That night you were."

"I got over it."

"Well, people get over things."

There was a whole unspoken conversation going on and Waldron wanted to cut through and get to it. "Who I been looking for," he said, "is I been looking for you."

"Oh?"

"I get things in my mind I can't get rid of," Waldron said. "I'll get a thought working and I won't be able to let go of it for a hundred miles. And my stomach's been turning on me."

"You lost me on a curve there."

"What we talked about. What I said that night, just running my mouth, and you picked up on it." Waldron's hands worked, forming into fists, opening again. "I read the papers," he said. "I find stories, I clip them out of the papers." He met the man's eyes. "I know what you're doing," he said.

"Oh?"

"And I gave you the idea," he said.

"You think so, huh?"

"The thought keeps coming to me," Waldron said. "I can't shake it off. I drop it and it comes back."

"You want the rest of that coffee?" Waldron looked at his cup, put it down unfinished. "C'mon then," the man said and put money on the counter to cover both their checks.

Waldron kept his newspaper clippings in a manila envelope in the zippered side pocket of his bag. The bag rode on the floor of the cab in front of the passenger seat. They were standing beside the cab now, facing away from the sun. The man was going through some of the clippings and Waldron was holding the rest of them.

"You must read a lot of papers," the man said.

Waldron didn't say anything.

"You think I been killing people. With my truck."

"I thought so, all these months."

"And now?"

"I still think so."

"You think I did all these here. And you think you started it all by getting mad at some fool driver in Indiana."

Waldron felt the sun on the back of his neck. The world had gone silent and all he could hear was his own breathing.

Then the man said, "This here one was mine. Little panel truck, electrical contractor or some damn thing. Rode him right off a mountain. I didn't figure he'd walk away from it, but then I didn't stay around to find out, you know, and I don't get around to reading the papers much." He put the clipping on the pile. "A few of these are mine," he said.

Waldron felt a pressure in his chest, as if his heart had turned to iron and was being drawn by a magnet.

"But most of these," the man went on, "the hell, I'd have to work night and day doing nothing else. I mean, figure it out, huh? Some of these are accidents, just like they're written up."

"And the rest?"

"The rest are a whole lot of guys like you and me taking a whack at somebody once in a while. You think it's one man doing all of it and you said something to get him started, hell, put your mind to rest. I did it a couple of times before you ever said a word. And I wasn't the first trucker ever thought of it, or the first ever did it."

"Why?"

"Why do it?"

Waldron nodded.

"Sometimes to teach some son of a bitch a lesson. Sometimes to get the anger out. And sometimes—look, you ever go hunting?"

"Years ago, with my old man."

"You remember what it felt like?"

"Just that I was scared all the time," Waldron said, remembering. "That I'd do something wrong, miss a shot or make noise or something, and my dad would get mad at me."

"So you never got to like it."

"No."

"Well, it's like hunting," the man said. "Seeing if you can do it. And there's you and him, and it's like you're dancing, and then he's gone and you're all that's left. It's like a bullfight, it's like shooting a bird on the wing. There's something about it that's beautiful."

Waldron couldn't speak.

"It's just a once-in-a-while thing," the man said. "It's a way to have fun, that's all. It's no big deal."

He drove all day, eastbound on 66, his mind churning and his stomach a wreck. He stopped often for coffee, sitting by himself, avoiding conversations with other drivers. Any of them could be a murderer, he thought, and once he fancied that they were all murderers, unpunished killers racing back and forth across the country, running down anyone who got in their way.

He knew he ought to eat, and twice he ordered food only to leave it untouched on his plate. He drank coffee and smoked cigarettes and just kept going.

At a diner somewhere he reached for a newspaper someone else had left behind. Then he changed his mind and drew away from it. When he returned to his truck he took the manila envelope of newspaper clippings from his bag and dropped it into a trash can. He wouldn't clip any more stories, he knew, and for the next little while he wouldn't even read the papers. Because he'd only be looking for stories he didn't want to find.

He kept driving. He thought about stopping when the sky darkened but he decided against it. Sleep just seemed out of the question. Being off the highway for longer than it took to gulp a cup of coffee seemed impossible. He played the radio once or twice but turned it off almost immediately; the country music he normally liked just didn't sound right to him. At one point he switched on the CB—he hardly ever listened to it these days, and now the chatter that came over it sounded like a mockery. They were out there killing people for sport, he thought, and they were chatting away in that hokey slang and he couldn't stand it. . . .

Four in the morning, or close to it, he was on a chunk of Interstate in Missouri or maybe Iowa—he wasn't too sure where he was, his mind was running all over the place. The median strip was broad here and you couldn't see the lights of cars in the other lane. The traffic was virtually nonexistent—it was like he was the only driver on the road, a trucker's Flying Dutchman or something out of a Dave Dudley song, doomed to ride empty highways until the end of time.

Crazy.

There were lights in his mirror. High beams, somebody coming up fast. He moved to his right, hugging the shoulder.

The other vehicle moved out and hovered alongside him. For a mindless instant he had the thought that it was the man with the deep-set eyes, the killer come to kill him. But this wasn't even a truck, this was a car, and it was just sort of dipsy-doodling along next to Waldron. Waldron wondered what was the matter with the damn fool.

Then the car passed him in a quick burst of speed and Waldron saw what it was.

The guy was drunk.

He got past Waldron's rig, cut in abruptly, then almost drove off the road before he got the wheel straightened out again. He couldn't keep the car in line, he kept wandering off to the left or the right, he was all over the road.

A fucking menace, Waldron thought.

He took his own foot off the gas and let the car pull away from him, watching the taillights get smaller in the distance. Only when the car was out of sight did Waldron bring his truck back up to running speed.

His mind wandered then, drifting along some byway, and he came back into present time to note that he was driving faster than usual, pushing past the speed limit. He found he was still doing it even after he noticed it.

Why?

When the taillights came into view, he realized what he'd subconsciously been doing all along. He was looking for the drunk driver, and there he was. He recognized the taillights. Even if he hadn't, he'd recognize the way the car swung from side to side, raising gravel on the shoulder, then wandering way over into the left-hand lane and back again.

Drivers like that were dangerous. They killed people every day and the cops couldn't keep the bastards off the roads. Look at this crazy son of a bitch, look at him, for God sake, he was all over the place, he was sure to kill himself if he didn't kill someone else first.

Downhill stretch coming up. Waldron was loaded up with kitchen appliances, just a hair under his maximum gross weight. Give him a stretch of downhill loaded like that, hell, wasn't anyone could run away from him going downhill.

He looked at the weaving car in front of him. Nobody else out in front, nobody in his mirror. Something quickened in his chest. He got a flash of deep-set eyes and a knowing smile.

He put the gas pedal on the floor.

A BLOW FOR FREEDOM

The gun was smaller than Elliott remembered. At Kennedy, waiting for his bag to come up on the carousel, he'd been irritated with himself for buying the damned thing. For years now, ever since Pan Am had stranded him in Milan with the clothes he was wearing, he'd made an absolute point of never checking luggage. He'd flown to Miami with his favorite carry-on bag; returning, he'd checked the same bag, all because it now contained a Smith & Wesson revolver and a box of fifty .38-caliber shells.

At least he hadn't had to take a train. "Oh, for Christ's sake," he'd told Huebner, after they'd bought the gun together. "I'll have to take the train back, won't I? I can't get on the plane with a gun in my pocket."

"It's not recommended," Huebner had said. "But all you have to do is check your bag with the gun and shells in it."

"Isn't there a regulation against it?"

"Probably. There's rules against everything. All I know is, I do it all the time, and I never heard of anyone getting into any trouble over it. They scope the checked bags, or at least they're supposed to, but they're looking for bombs. There's nothing very dangerous about a gun locked away in the baggage compartment."

"Couldn't the shells explode?"

"In a fire, possibly. If the plane goes down in flames, the bullets may go off and put a hole in the side of your suitcase."

"I guess I'm being silly."

"Well, you're a New Yorker. You don't know a whole lot about guns."

"No." He'd hesitated. "Maybe I should have bought one of those plastic ones."

"The Glock?" Huebner smiled. "It's a nice weapon, and it's probably the one I'll buy next. But you couldn't carry it on a plane."

"But I thought—"

"You thought it would fool the scanners and metal detectors at airport security. It won't. That's hardly the point of it, a big gun like that. No, they replaced a lot of the metal with high-impact plastic to reduce the weight. It's supposed to lessen recoil slightly, too, but I don't know if it does. Personally, I like the looks of it. But it'll show up fine on a scanner if you put it in a carry-on bag, and it'll set off alarms if you walk it through a metal detector." He snorted. "Of course, that didn't keep some idiots from introducing bills banning it in the United States. Nobody in politics likes to let a fact stand in the way of a grandstand play."

His bag was one of the last ones up. Waiting for it, he worried that there was going to be trouble about the gun. When it came, he had to resist the urge to open the bag immediately and make sure the gun was still there. The bag felt light, and he decided some baggage handler had detected it and appropriated it for his own use.

Nervous, he thought. Scared it's there, scared it's not.

He took a cab home to his Manhattan apartment and left the bag unopened while he made himself a drink. Then he unpacked, and the gun was smaller than he remembered it. He picked it up and felt its weight, and that was greater than he recalled. And it was empty. It would be even heavier fully loaded.

After Huebner had helped him pick out the gun, they'd driven way out on Route 27, where treeless swamps extended for miles in every direction. Huebner pulled off the road a few yards from a wrecked car, its tires missing and most of its window glass gone.

"There's our target," he said. "You find a lot of cars abandoned along this stretch, but you don't want to start shooting up the newer ones."

"Because someone might come back for them?"

Huebner shook his head. "Because there might be a body in the trunk. This is where the drug dealers tend to drop off the unsuccessful competition, but no self-respecting drug dealer would be caught dead in a wreck like this one. You figure it'll be a big enough target for you?"

Embarrassingly enough, he missed the car altogether with his first shot. "You pulled up on it," Huebner told him. "Probably anticipating the recoil. Don't waste time worrying where the bullets are going yet. Just get used to pointing and firing."

And he got used to it. The recoil was considerable and so was the weight of the gun, but he did get used to both and began to be able to make the shots go where he wanted them to go. After Elliott had used up a full box of shells, Huebner got a pistol of his own from the glove compartment and put a few rounds into the fender of the ruined automobile. Huebner's gun was a nine-millimeter automatic with a clip that held twelve cartridges. It was much larger, noisier, and heavier than the .38, and it did far more damage to the target.

"Got a whole lot of stopping power," Huebner said. "Hit a man in the arm with this, you're likely to take him down. Here, try it. Strike a blow for freedom."

The recoil was greater than the .38's, but less so than he would have guessed. Elliott fired off several rounds, enjoying the sense of power. He returned the gun to Huebner, who emptied the clip into the old car.

Driving back, Elliott said, "A phrase you used: 'Strike a blow for freedom.'"

"Oh, you never heard that? I had an uncle used that expression every time he took a drink. They used to say that during Prohibition. You hoisted a few then in defiance of the law, you were striking a blow for freedom."

* * *

The gun, the first article Elliott unpacked, was the last he put away.

He couldn't think of what to do with it. Its purchase had seemed appropriate in Florida, where they seemed to have gun shops everywhere. You walked into one and walked out owning a weapon. There was even a town in central Georgia where they'd passed their own local version of gun control, an ordinance requiring the adult population to go about armed. There had never been any question of enforcing the law, he knew; it had been passed as a statement of local sentiment.

Here in New York, guns were less appropriate. They were illegal, to begin with. You could apply for a carry permit, but unless there was some genuine reason connected with your occupation, your application was virtually certain to be denied. Elliott worked in an office and never carried anything to it or from it but a briefcase filled with papers, nor did his work take him down streets any meaner than the one he lived on. As far as the law was concerned, he had no need for a gun.

Yet he owned one, legally or not. Its possession was at once unsettling and thrilling, like the occasional ounce or so of marijuana secreted in his various living quarters during his twenties. There was something exciting, something curiously estimable, about having that which was prohibited, and at the same time, there was a certain amount of danger connected with its possession.

There ought to be security as well, he thought. He'd bought the gun for his protection in a city that increasingly seemed incapable of protecting its own inhabitants. He turned the gun over, let the empty cylinder swing out, accustomed his fingers to the cool metal.

His apartment was on the twelfth floor of a prewar building. Three shifts of doormen guarded the lobby. No other building afforded access to any of his windows, and those near the fire escape were protected by locked window gates, the key to which hung out of reach on a nail. The door to the hallway had two dead-bolt locks, each with its cylinder secured by an escutcheon plate. The door had a steel core and was further reinforced by a Fox police lock.

Elliott had never felt insecure in his apartment, nor were its security measures the result of his own paranoia. They had all been in place when he moved in. And they were standard for the building and the neighborhood.

He passed the gun from hand to hand, at once glad to have it and, like an impulse shopper, wondering why he'd bought it.

Where should he keep it?

The drawer of the nightstand suggested itself. He put the gun and the box of shells in it, closed the drawer, and went to take a shower.

It was almost a week before he looked at the gun again. He didn't mention it and rarely thought about it. News items would bring it to mind. A hardware-store owner in Rego Park killed his wife and small daughter with an unregistered handgun, then turned the weapon on himself; reading about it in the paper, Elliott thought of the revolver in his nightstand drawer. An honor student was slain in his bedroom by a stray shot from a high-powered assault rifle, and Elliott, watching TV, thought again of his gun.

On the Friday after his return, some item about the shooting of a drug dealer again directed his thoughts to the gun, and it occurred to him that he ought at least to load it. Suppose someone came crashing through his door or used some advance in criminal technology to cut the gates on his windows. If he were reaching hurriedly for a gun, it should be loaded.

He loaded all six chambers. He seemed to remember that you were supposed to leave one chamber empty as a safety measure. Otherwise, the gun might discharge if dropped. Cocking the weapon would presumably rotate the cylinder and ready it for shooting. Still, it wasn't going to fire itself just sitting in his nightstand drawer, was it, now? And if he reached for it, if he needed it in a hurry, he'd want it fully loaded.

If you had to shoot at someone, you didn't want to shoot once or twice and then stop. You wanted to empty the gun.

Had Huebner told him that? Or had someone said it in a movie or on television? It didn't matter, he decided. Either way, it was sound advice.

A few days later, he saw a movie in which the hero, a renegade cop up against an entrenched drug mob, slept with a gun under his pillow. It was a much larger gun than Elliott's, something like Huebner's big automatic.

"More gun than you really need in your situation," Huebner had told him. "And it's too big and too heavy. You want something you can slip into a pocket. A cannon like this, you'd need a whole shoulder rig or it'd pull at your suit coat something awful."

Not that he'd ever carry it.

That night, he got the gun out of the drawer and put it under his pillow. He thought of the princess who couldn't sleep with a pea under her mattress. He felt a little silly, and he felt, too, some of what he had felt playing with toy guns as a child.

He got the gun from under his pillow and put it back in the drawer, where it belonged. He lay for a long time, inhaling the smell of the gun, metal and machine oil, interesting and not unpleasant.

A masculine scent, he thought. Blend in a little leather and tobacco, maybe a little horseshit, and you've got something to slap on after a shave. Win the respect of your fellows and drive the women wild.

He never put the gun under his pillow again. But the linen held the scent of the gun, and even after he'd changed the sheets and pillowcases, he could detect the smell on the pillow.

It was not until the incident with the panhandler that he ever carried the gun outside the apartment.

There were panhandlers all over the place, had been for several years now. It seemed to Elliott that there were more of them every year, but he wasn't sure if that was really the case. They were of either sex and of every age and color, some of them proclaiming well-rehearsed speeches on subway cars, some standing mute in doorways and extending paper cups, some asking generally for spare change or specifically for money for food or for shelter or for wine.

Some of them, he knew, were homeless people, ground down by the system. Some belonged in mental institutions. Some were addicted to crack. Some were layabouts, earning more this way than they could at a menial job. Elliott couldn't tell which was which and wasn't sure how he felt about them, his emotions ranging from sympathy to irritation, depending on circumstances. Sometimes he gave money, sometimes he didn't. He had given up trying to devise a consistent policy and simply followed his impulse of the moment.

One evening, walking home from the bus stop, he encountered a panhandler who demanded money. "Come on," the man said. "Gimme a dollar."

Elliott started to walk past him, but the man moved to block his path. He was taller and heavier than Elliott, wearing a dirty army jacket, his face partly hidden behind a dense black beard. His eyes, slightly exophthalmic, were fierce.

"Didn't you hear me? Gimme a fuckin' dollar!"

Elliott reached into his pocket, came out with a handful of change. The man made a face at the coins Elliott placed in his hand, then evidently decided the donation was acceptable.

"Thank you kindly," he said. "Have a nice day."

Have a nice day, indeed. Elliott walked on home, nodded to the doorman, let himself into his apartment. It wasn't until he had engaged the locks that he realized his heart was pounding and his hands trembling.

He poured himself a drink. It helped, but it didn't change anything.

Had he been mugged? There was a thin line, he realized, and he wasn't sure if the man had crossed it. He had not been asking for money, he had been demanding it, and the absence of a specific threat did not mean there was no menace in the demand. Elliott, certainly, had given him money out of fear. He'd been intimidated. Unwilling to display his wallet, he'd fished out a batch of coins, including a couple of quarters and a subway token, currently valued at $1.15.

A small enough price, but that wasn't the point. The point was that he'd been made to pay it. *Stand and deliver*, the man might as well have said. Elliott had stood and delivered.

A block from his own door, for God's sake. A good street in a good neighborhood. Broad daylight.

And you couldn't even report it. Not that anyone reported anything anymore. A friend at work had reported a burglary only because you had to in order to collect on your insurance. The police, he'd said, had taken the report over the phone. "I'll send somebody if you want," the cop had said, "but I've got to tell you, it's a waste of your time and ours." Someone else had been robbed of his watch and wallet at gunpoint and had not bothered reporting the incident. "What's the point?" he'd said.

But even if there were a point, Elliott had nothing to report. A man had asked for money and he'd given it to him. They had a right to ask for money, some judge had ruled. They were exercising their First Amendment right of free speech. Never mind that there had been an unvoiced threat, that Elliott had paid the money out of intimidation. Never mind that it damn well felt like a mugging.

First Amendment rights. Maybe he ought to exercise his own rights under the Second Amendment—the right to bear arms.

That same evening, he took the gun from the drawer and tried it in various pockets—unloaded now. He tried tucking it into his belt, first in front, then behind, in the small of his back. He practiced reaching for it, drawing it. He felt foolish, and it was uncomfortable walking around with the gun in his belt like that.

It was comfortable in his right-hand jacket pocket, but the weight of it spoiled the line of the jacket. The pants pocket on the same side was better. He had reached into that pocket to produce the handful of change that had mollified the panhandler. Suppose he had come out with a gun instead?

"Thank you kindly. Have a nice day."

Later, after he'd eaten, he went to the video store on the next block to rent a movie for the evening. He was out the door before he realized he still had the gun in his pocket. It was still unloaded, the six shells lying where he had spilled them on his bed. He had reached for the keys to lock up and there was the gun.

He got the keys, locked up, and went out with the gun in his pocket.

The sensation of being on the street with a gun in his pocket was an interesting one. He felt as though he were keeping a secret from everyone he met, and that the secret empowered him. He spent longer than usual in the video store. Two fantasies came and went. In one, he held up the clerk, brandishing his empty gun and walking out with all the money in the register. In the other, someone else attempted to rob the place and Elliott drew his weapon and foiled the holdup.

Back home, he watched the movie, but his mind insisted on replaying the second fantasy. In one version, the holdup man spun toward him, gun in hand, and Elliott had to face him with an unloaded revolver.

When the movie ended, he reloaded the gun and put it back in the drawer.

The following evening, he carried the gun, loaded this time. The night after that was a Friday, and when he got home from the office, he put the gun in his pocket almost without thinking about it. He went out for a bite of dinner, then played cards at a friend's apartment a dozen blocks away. They played, as always, for low stakes, but Elliott was the big winner. Another player joked that he had better take a cab home.

"No need," he said. "I'm armed and dangerous."

He walked home, and on the way, he stopped at a bar and had a couple of beers. Some people at a table near where he stood were talking about a recent outrage, a young advertising executive in Greenwich Village shot dead while using a pay phone around the corner from his apartment. "I'll tell you something," one of the party said. "I'm about ready to start carrying a gun."

"You can't, legally," someone said.

"Screw legally."

"So a guy tries something and you shoot him and you're the one winds up in trouble."

"I'll tell you something," the man said. "I'd rather be judged by twelve than carried by six."

He carried the gun the whole weekend. It never left his pocket. He was at home much of the time, watching a ball game on television, catching up with his bookkeeping, but he left the house several times each day and always had the gun on his person.

He never drew it, but sometimes he would put his hand in his pocket and let his fingers curl around the butt of it. He found its presence increasingly reassuring. If anything happened, he was ready.

And he didn't have to worry about an accidental discharge. The chamber under the hammer was unloaded. He had worked all that out. If he dropped the gun, it wouldn't go off. But if he cocked it and worked the trigger, it would fire.

When he took his hand from his pocket and held it to his face, he could smell the odor of the gun on his fingers. He liked that.

By Monday morning, he had grown used to the gun. It seemed perfectly natural to carry it to the office.

On the way home, not that night but the following night, the same aggressive panhandler accosted him. His routine had not changed. "Come on," he said. "Gimme a dollar."

Elliott's hand was in his pocket, his fingers touching the cold metal.

"Not tonight," he said.

Maybe something showed in his eyes.

"Hey, that's cool," the panhandler said. "You have a good day just the same." And stepped out of his path.

A week or so after that, he was riding the subway, coming home late after dinner with married friends in Forest Hills. He had a paperback with him, but he couldn't concentrate on it, and he realized that the two young men across the car from him were looking him over, sizing him up. They were wearing untied basketball sneakers and warm-up jackets, and looked street smart and dangerous. He was wearing the suit he'd worn to the office and had a briefcase beside him; he looked prosperous and vulnerable.

The car was almost empty. There was a derelict sleeping a few yards away, a woman with a small child all the way down at the other end. One of the pair nudged the other, then turned his eyes toward Elliott again.

Elliott took the gun out of his pocket. He held it on his lap and let them see it, then put it back in his pocket.

The two of them got off at the next station, leaving Elliott to ride home alone.

When he got home, he took the gun from his pocket and set it on the nightstand. (He no longer bothered tucking it in the drawer.) He went into the bathroom and looked at himself in the mirror.

"Fucking thing saved my life," he said.

* * *

One night, he took a woman friend to dinner. Afterward, they went back to her place and wound up in bed. At one point, she got up to use the bathroom, and while she was up, she hung up her own clothing and went to put his pants on a hanger.

"These weigh a ton," she said. "What have you got in here?"

"See for yourself," he said. "But be careful."

"My God. Is it loaded?"

"They're not much good if they're not."

"My God."

He told her how he'd bought it in Florida, how it had now become second nature for him to carry it. "I'd feel naked without it," he said.

"Aren't you afraid you'll get into trouble?"

"I look at it this way," he told her. "I'd rather be judged by twelve than carried by six."

One night, two men cut across the avenue toward him while he was walking home from his Friday card game. Without hesitation, he drew the gun.

"Whoa!" the nearer of the two sang out. "Hey, it's cool, man. Thought you was somebody else, is all."

They veered off, gave him a wide berth.

Thought I was somebody else, he thought. Thought I was a victim, is what you thought.

There were stores around the city that sold police equipment. Books to study for the sergeant's exam. Copies of the latest revised penal code. A T-shirt that read N.Y.P.D. HOMICIDE SQUAD. OUR DAY BEGINS WHEN YOUR DAY ENDS.

He stopped in and didn't buy anything, then returned for a kit to clean his gun. He hadn't fired it yet, except in Florida, but it seemed as though he ought to clean it from time to time anyway. He took the kit home and unloaded the gun and cleaned it, working an oiled patch of cloth through the short barrel. When he was finished, he put everything away and reloaded the gun.

He liked the way it smelled, freshly cleaned with gun oil.

A week later, he returned and bought a bulletproof vest. They had two types, one significantly more expensive than the other. Both were made of Kevlar, whatever that was.

"Your more expensive one provides you with a little more protection," the proprietor explained. "Neither one's gonna stop a shot from an assault rifle. The real high-powered rounds, concrete don't stop 'em. This here, though, it provides the most protection available, plus it provides protection against a knife thrust. Neither one's a sure thing to stop a knife, but this here's reinforced."

He bought the better vest.

One night, lonely and sad, he unloaded the gun and put the barrel to his temple. His finger was inside the trigger guard, curled around the trigger.

You weren't supposed to dry-fire the gun. It was bad for the firing pin to squeeze off a shot when there was no cartridge in the chamber.

Quit fooling around, he told himself.

He cocked the gun, then took it away from his temple. He uncocked it, put the barrel in his mouth. That was how cops did it when they couldn't take it anymore. Eating your gun, they called it.

He didn't like the taste, the metal, the gun oil. Liked the smell but not the taste.

He loaded the gun and quit fooling around.

A little later, he went out. It was late, but he didn't feel like sitting around the apartment, and he knew he wouldn't be able to sleep. He wore the Kevlar vest—he wore it all the time lately—and, of course, he had the gun in his pocket.

He walked around, with no destination in mind. He stopped for a beer but drank only a few sips of it, then headed out to the street again. The moon came into view, and he wasn't surprised to note that it was full.

He had his hand in his pocket, touching the gun. When he breathed deeply, he could feel the vest drawn tight around his chest. He liked the sensation.

When he reached the park, he hesitated. Years ago, back when the city was safe, you knew not to walk in the park at night. It was dangerous even then. It could hardly be otherwise now, when every neighborhood was a jungle.

So? If anything happened, if anybody tried anything, he was ready.

HOW WOULD YOU LIKE IT?

I suppose it really started for me when I saw the man whipping his horse. He was a hansom cabdriver, dressed up like the chimney sweep in *Mary Poppins* with a top hat and a cutaway tailcoat, and I saw him on Central Park South, where the horse-drawn rigs queue up waiting for tourists who want a ride in the park. His horse was a swaybacked old gelding with a noble face, and it did something to me to see the way that driver used the whip. He didn't have to hit the horse like that.

I found a policeman and started to tell him about it, but it was clear he didn't want to hear it. He explained to me that I would have to go to the station house and file a complaint, and he said it in such a way as to discourage me from bothering. I don't really blame the cop. With crack dealers on every block and crimes against people and property at an all-time high and climbing, I suppose crimes against animals have to receive low priority.

But I couldn't forget about it.

I had already had my consciousness raised on the subject of animal rights. There was a campaign a few years ago to stop one of the cosmetic companies from testing their products on rabbits. They were blinding thousands of innocent rabbits every year, not with the goal of curing cancer but just because it was the cheapest way to safety-test their mascara and eye-liner.

I would have liked to sit down with the head of that company. "How would you like it?" I would have asked him. "How would you like having chemicals painted on your eyes to make you blind?"

All I did was sign a petition, like millions of other Americans, and I understand that it worked, that the company has gone out of the business of blinding bunnies. Sometimes, when we all get together, we can make a difference.

Sometimes we can make a difference all by ourselves.

Which brings me back to the subject of the horse and his driver. I found myself returning to Central Park South over the next several days and keeping tabs on that fellow. I thought perhaps I had just caught him on a bad day, but it became clear that it was standard procedure for him to use the whip that way. I went up to him and said something finally, and he turned positively red with anger. I thought for a moment he was going to use the whip on me, and I frankly would have liked to see him try it, but he only turned his anger on the poor horse, whipping him more brutally than ever and looking at me as if daring me to do something about it.

I just walked away.

That afternoon I went to a shop in Greenwich Village where they sell extremely odd paraphernalia to what I can only suppose are extremely odd people. They have handcuffs and studded wrist bands and all sorts of curious leather goods. Sadie Mae's Leather Goods, they call themselves. You get the picture.

I bought a ten-foot whip of plaited bullhide, and I took it back to Central Park South with me. I waited in the shadows until that driver finished for the day, and I followed him home.

You can kill a man with a whip. Take my word for it.

Well, I have to tell you that I never expected to do anything like that again. I can't say I felt bad about what I'd done. The brute only got what he deserved. But I didn't think of myself as the champion of all the abused animals of New York. I was just someone who had seen his duty and had done it. It wasn't pleasant, flogging a man to death with a bullwhip, but I have to admit there was something almost shamefully exhilarating about it.

A week later, and just around the corner from my own apartment, I saw a man kicking his dog.

It was a sweet dog, too, a little beagle as cute as Snoopy. You couldn't imagine he might have done anything to justify such abuse. Some dogs have a mean streak, but there's never any real meanness in a hound. And this awful man was hauling off and savaging the animal with vicious kicks.

Why do something like that? Why have a dog in the first place if you don't feel kindly toward it? I said something to that effect, and the man told me to mind my own business.

Well, I tried to put it out of my mind, but it seemed as though I couldn't go for a walk without running into the fellow, and he always seemed to be walking the little beagle. He didn't kick him all the time—you'd kill a dog in short order if you did that regularly. But he was always cruel to the animal, yanking hard on the chain, cursing with genuine malice, and making it very clear that he hated it.

And then I saw him kick it again. Actually it wasn't the kick that did it for me, it was the way the poor dog cringed when the man drew back his foot. It made it so clear that he was used to this sort of treatment, that he knew what to expect.

So I went to a shoe store on Broadway in the teens where they have a good line of work shoes, and I bought a pair of steel-toed boots of the kind construction workers wear. I was wearing them the next time I saw my neighbor walking his dog, and I followed him home and rang his bell.

It would have been quicker and easier, I'm sure, if I'd had some training in karate. But even an untrained kick has a lot of authority to it when you're wearing steel-toed footwear. A couple of kicks in his legs and he fell down and couldn't get up, and a couple of kicks in the ribs took the fight out of him, and a couple of kicks in the head made it absolutely certain he would never harm another of God's helpless creatures.

It's cruelty that bothers me, cruelty and wanton indifference to another creature's pain. Some people are thoughtless, but when the inhumanity of their actions is pointed out to them they're able to understand and are willing to change. For example, a young woman in my building had a mixed-breed dog that barked all day in her absence. She didn't know this because the dog never started barking until she'd left for work. When I explained that the poor fellow couldn't bear to be alone, that it made him horribly anxious, she went to the animal shelter and adopted the cutest little part Sheltie to keep him company. You never hear a peep out of either of those dogs now, and it does me good to see them on the street when she walks them, both of them obviously happy and well cared for.

And another time I met a man carrying a litter of newborn kittens in a sack. He was on his way to the river and intended to drown them, not out of cruelty but because he thought it was the most humane way to dispose of kittens he could not provide a home for. I explained to him that it was cruel to the mother cat to take her kittens away before she'd weaned them, and that when the time came he could simply take the unwanted kittens to the animal shelter; if they failed to find homes for them, at least their deaths would be easy and painless. More to the point, I told him where he could get the mother cat spayed inexpensively, so that he would not have to deal with this sad business again.

He was grateful. You see, he wasn't a cruel man, not by any means. He just didn't know any better.

Other people just don't want to learn.

Just yesterday, for example, I was in the hardware store over on Second Avenue. A well-dressed young woman was selecting rolls of flypaper and those awful Roach Motel devices.

"Excuse me," I said, "but are you certain you want to purchase those items? They aren't even very efficient, and you wind up spending a lot of money to kill very few insects."

She was looking at me oddly, the way you look at a crank, and I should have known I was just wasting my breath. But something made me go on.

"With the Roach Motels," I said, "they don't really kill the creatures at all, you know. They just immobilize them. Their feet are stuck, and they stand in place wiggling their antennae until I suppose they starve to death. I mean, how would you like it?"

"You're kidding," she said. "Right?"

"I'm just pointing out that the product you've selected is neither efficient nor humane," I said.

"So?" she said. "I mean, they're cockroaches. If they don't like it let them stay the hell out of my apartment." She shook her head, impatient. "I can't believe I'm having this conversation. My place is swarming with roaches and I run into a nut who's worried about hurting their feelings."

I wasn't worried about any such thing. And I didn't care if she killed roaches. I understand the necessity of that sort of thing. I just don't see the need for cruelty. But I knew better than to say anything more to her. It's useful to talk to some people. With others, it's like trying to blow out a light bulb.

So I picked up a half-dozen tubes of Super Glue and followed her home.

BATMAN'S HELPERS

Reliable's offices are in the Flatiron Building, at Broadway and Twenty-third. The receptionist, an elegant black girl with high cheekbones and processed hair, gave me a nod and a smile, and I went on down the hall to Wally Witt's office.

He was at his desk, a short stocky man with a bulldog jaw and gray hair cropped close to his head. Without rising he said, "Matt, good to see you, you're right on time. You know these guys? Matt Scudder, Jimmy diSalvo, Lee Trombauer." We shook hands all around. "We're waiting on Eddie Rankin. Then we can go out there and protect the integrity of the American merchandising system."

"Can't do that without Eddie," Jimmy diSalvo said.

"No, we need him," Wally said. "He's our pit bull. He's attack-trained, Eddie is."

He came through the door a few minutes later and I saw what they meant. Without looking alike, Jimmy and Wally and Lee all looked like ex-cops, as I suppose do I. Eddie Rankin looked like the kind of guy we used to have to bring in on a bad Saturday night. He was a big man, broad in the shoulders, narrow in the waist. His hair was blond, almost white, and he wore it short at the sides but long in back. It lay on his neck like a mane. He had a broad forehead and a pug nose. His complexion was very fair and his full lips were intensely red, almost artificially so. He looked like a roughneck, and you sensed that his response to any sort of stress was likely to be physical, and abrupt.

Wally Witt introduced him to me. The others already knew him. Eddie Rankin shook my hand and his left hand fastened on my shoulder and gave a squeeze. "Hey, Matt," he said. "Pleased to meetcha. Whattaya say, guys, we ready to come to the aid of the Caped Crusader?"

Jimmy diSalvo started whistling the theme from *Batman*, the old television show. Wally said, "Okay, who's packing? Is everybody packing?"

Lee Trombauer drew back his suit jacket to show a revolver in a shoulder rig. Eddie Rankin took out a large automatic and laid it on Wally's desk. "Batman's gun," he announced.

"Batman don't carry a gun," Jimmy told him.

"Then he better stay outta New York," Eddie said. "Or he'll get his ass shot off. Those revolvers, I wouldn't carry one of them on a bet."

"This shoots as straight as what you got," Lee said. "And it won't jam."

"This baby don't jam," Eddie said. He picked up the automatic and held it out for display. "You got a revolver," he said, "a .38, whatever you got—"

"A .38."

"—and a guy takes it away from you, all he's gotta do is point it and shoot it. Even if he never saw a gun before, he knows how to do that much. This monster, though"—and he demonstrated, flicking the safety, working the slide—"all this shit you gotta go through, before he can figure it out I got the gun away from him and I'm making him eat it."

"Nobody's taking my gun away from me," Lee said.

"What everybody says, but look at all the times it happens. Cop gets shot with his own gun, nine times out of ten it's a revolver."

"That's because that's all they carry," Lee said.

"Well, there you go."

Jimmy and I weren't carrying guns. Wally offered to equip us but we both declined. "Not that anybody's likely to have to show a piece, let alone use one, God forbid," Wally said. "But it can get nasty out there and it helps to have the feeling of authority. Well, let's go get 'em, huh? The Batmobile's waiting at the curb."

We rode down in the elevator, five grown men, three of us armed with handguns. Eddie Rankin had on a plaid sport jacket and khaki trousers. The rest of us wore suits and ties. We went out the Fifth Avenue exit and followed Wally to his car, a five-year-old Fleetwood Cadillac parked next to a hydrant. There were no tickets on the windshield; a PBA courtesy card had kept the traffic cops at bay.

Wally drove and Eddie Rankin sat in front with him. The rest of us rode in back. We cruised up Sixth to Fifty-fourth Street and turned right, and Wally parked next to a hydrant a few doors from Fifth. We walked together to the corner of Fifth and turned downtown. Near the middle of the block a trip of black men had set up shop as sidewalk vendors. One had a display of women's handbags and silk scarves, all arranged neatly on top of a folding card table. The other two were offering T-shirts and cassette tapes.

In an undertone Wally said, "Here we go. These three were here yesterday. Matt, why don't you and Lee check down the block, make sure those two down at the corner don't have what we're looking for. Then double back and we'll take these dudes off. Meanwhile I'll let the man sell me a shirt."

Lee and I walked down to the corner. The two vendors in question were selling books. We established this and headed back. "Real police work," I said.

"Be grateful we don't have to fill out a report, list the titles of the books."

"The alleged books."

When we rejoined the others Wally was holding an oversize T-shirt to his chest, modeling it for us. "What do you say?" he demanded. "Is it me? Do you think it's me?"

"I think it's the Joker," Jimmy diSalvo said.

"That's what I think," Wally said. He looked at the two Africans, who were smiling uncertainly. "I think it's a violation, is what I think. I think we got to confiscate all the Batman stuff. It's unauthorized, it's an illegal violation of copyright protection, it's unlicensed, and we got to take it in."

The two vendors had stopped smiling, but they didn't

seem to have a very clear idea of what was going on. Off to the side, the third man, the fellow with the scarves and purses, was looking wary.

"You speak English?" Wally asked them.

"They speak numbers," Jimmy said. " 'Fi' dollah, ten dollah, please, thank you.' That's what they speak."

"Where you from?" Wally demanded. "Senegal, right? Dakar. You from Dakar?"

They nodded, brightening at words they recognized. "Dakar," one of them echoed. Both of them were wearing Western clothes, but they looked faintly foreign—loose-fitting long-sleeved shirts with long pointed collars and a glossy finish, baggy pleated pants. Loafers with leather mesh tops.

"What do you speak?" Wally asked. "You speak French? Parley-voo *Français*?" The one who'd spoken before replied now in a torrent of French, and Wally backed away from him and shook his head. "I don't know why the hell I asked," he said. "Parley-voo's all I know of the fucking language." To the Africans he said, "Police. You parley-voo that? Police. *Policia*. You capeesh?" He opened his wallet and showed them some sort of badge. "No sell Batman," he said, waving one of the shirts at them. "Batman no good. It's unauthorized, it's not made under a licensing agreement, and you can't sell it."

"No Batman," one of them said.

"Jesus, don't tell me I'm getting through to them. Right, no Batman. No, put your money away, I can't take a bribe, I'm not with the department no more. All I want's the Batman stuff. You can keep the rest."

All but a handful of their T-shirts were unauthorized Batman items. The rest showed Walt Disney characters, themselves almost certainly as unauthorized as the Batman merchandise, but Disney wasn't Reliable's client today so it was none of our concern. While we loaded up with Batman and the Joker, Eddie Rankin looked through the cassettes, then pawed through the silk scarves the third vendor had on display. He let the man keep the scarves, but he took a purse, snakeskin by the look of it. "No good," he told the man, who nodded, expressionless.

We trooped back to the Fleetwood and Wally popped the trunk. We deposited the confiscated T's between the spare tire and some loose fishing tackle. "Don't worry if the shit gets dirty," Wally said. "It's all gonna be destroyed anyway. Eddie, you start carrying a purse, people are gonna say things."

"Woman I know," he said, "she'll like this." He wrapped the purse in a Batman T-shirt and placed it in the trunk.

"Okay," Wally said. "That went real smooth. What we'll do now, Lee, you and Matt take the east side of Fifth and the rest of us'll stay on this side and we'll work our way down to Forty-second. I don't know if we'll get much, because even if they can't speak English they can sure get the word around fast, but we'll make sure there's no unlicensed Batcrap on the avenue before we move on. We'll maintain eye contact back and forth across the street, and if you hit anything give the high sign and we'll converge and take 'em down. Everybody got it?"

Everybody seemed to. We left the car with its trunkful of contraband and returned to Fifth Avenue. The two T-shirt vendors from Dakar had packed up and disappeared; they'd have to find something else to sell and someplace else to sell it. The man with the scarves and purses was still doing business. He froze when he caught sight of us.

"No Batman," Wally told him.

"No Batman," he echoed.

"I'll be a son of a bitch," Wally said. "The guy's learning English."

Lee and I crossed the street and worked our way downtown. There were vendors all over the place, offering clothing and tapes and small appliances and books and fast food. Most of them didn't have the peddler's license the law required, and periodically the city would sweep the streets, especially the main commercial avenues, rounding them up and fining them and confiscating their stock. Then after a week or so the cops would stop trying to enforce a basically unenforceable law, and the peddlers would be back in business again.

It was an apparently endless cycle, but the booksellers were exempt from it. The court had decided that the First Amendment embodied in its protection of freedom of the press the right of anyone to sell printed matter on the street, so if you had books for sale you never got hassled. As a result, a lot of scholarly antiquarian booksellers offered their wares on the city streets. So did any number of illiterates hawking remaindered art books and stolen best-sellers, along with homeless street people who rescued old magazines from people's garbage cans and spread them out on the pavement, living in hope that someone would want to buy them.

In front of St. Patrick's Cathedral we found a Pakistani with T-shirts and sweatshirts. I asked him if he had any Batman merchandise and he went right through the piles himself and pulled out half a dozen items. We didn't bother signaling the cavalry across the street. Lee just showed the man a badge—Special Officer, it said—and I explained that we had to confiscate Batman items.

"He is the big seller, Batman," the man said. "I get Batman, I sell him fast as I can."

"Well, you better not sell him anymore," I said, "because it's against the law."

"Excuse, please," he said. "What is law? Why is Batman against law? Is my understanding Batman is *for* law. He is good guy, is it not so?"

I explained about copyright and trademarks and licensing agreements. It was a little bit like explaining the internal-combustion engine to a field mouse. He kept nodding his head, but I don't know how much of it he got. He understood the main point—that we were walking off with his stock, and he was stuck for whatever it cost him. He didn't like that part but there wasn't much he could do about it.

Lee tucked the shirts under his arm and we kept going. At Forty-seventh Street we crossed over in response to a signal from Wally. They'd found another pair of Senegalese with a big spread of Batman items—T's and sweatshirts and gimme caps and sun visors, some a direct knockoff of the copyrighted Bat signal, others a variation on the theme, but none of it authorized and all of it subject to confiscation. The two men—they looked like brothers, and were dressed identically in baggy beige trousers and sky-blue nylon shirts—couldn't understand what was wrong with their merchandise and couldn't believe we intended to haul it all away with us. But there were five of us, and we were large intimidating white men with an authoritarian manner, and what could they do about it?

"I'll get the car," Wally said. "No way we're gonna schlepp this crap seven blocks in this heat."

* * *

With the trunk almost full, we drove to Thirty-fourth and broke for lunch at a place Wally liked. We sat at a large round table. Ornate beer steins hung from the beams overhead. We had a round of drinks, then ordered sandwiches and fries and half-liter steins of dark beer. I had a Coke to start, another Coke with the food, and coffee afterward.

"You're not drinking," Lee Trombauer said.

"Not today."

"Not on duty," Jimmy said, and everybody laughed.

"What I want to know," Eddie Rankin said, "is why everybody wants a fucking Batman shirt in the first place."

"Not just shirts," somebody said.

"Shirts, sweaters, caps, lunch boxes, if you could print it on Tampax they'd be shoving 'em up their twats. Why Batman, for Christ's sake?"

"It's hot," Wally said.

" 'It's hot.' What the fuck does that mean?"

"It means it's hot. That's what it means. It's hot means it's hot. Everybody wants it because everybody else wants it, and that means it's hot."

"I seen the movie," Eddie said. "You see it?"

Two of us had, two of us hadn't.

"It's okay," he said. "Basically I'd say it's a kid's movie, but it's okay."

"So?"

"So how many T-shirts in extra large do you sell to kids? Everybody's buying this shit, and all you can tell me is it's hot because it's hot. I don't get it."

"You don't have to," Wally said. "It's the same as the niggers. You want to try explaining to them why they can't sell Batman unless there's a little copyright notice printed under the design? While you're at it, you can explain to me why the assholes counterfeiting the crap don't counterfeit the copyright notice while they're at it. The thing is, nobody has to do any explaining because nobody has to understand. The only message they have to get on the street is Batman no good, no sell Batman. If they learn that much we're doing our job right."

Wally paid for everybody's lunch. We stopped at the Flat-iron Building long enough to empty the trunk and carry everything upstairs, then drove down to the Village and worked the sidewalk market on Sixth Avenue below Eighth Street. We made a few confiscations without incident. Then, near the subway entrance at West Third, we were taking a dozen shirts and about as many visors from a West Indian when another vendor decided to get into the act. He was wearing a dashiki and had his hair in Rastafarian dreadlocks, and he said, "You can't take the brother's wares, man. You can't do that."

"It's unlicensed merchandise produced in contravention of international copyright protection," Wally told him.

"Maybe so," the man said, "but that don't empower you to seize it. Where's your due process? Where's your authority? You aren't police." Poe-lease, he said, bearing down on the first syllable. "You can't come into a man's store, seize his wares."

"Store?" Eddie Rankin moved toward him, his hands hovering at his sides. "You see a store here? All I see's a lot of fucking shit in the middle of a fucking blanket."

"This is the man's store. This is the man's place of business."

"And what's this?" Eddie demanded. He walked over to the right, where the man with the dreadlocks had stick incense displayed for sale on a pair of upended orange crates. "This your store?"

"That's right. It's my store."

"You know what it looks like to me? It looks like you're selling drug paraphernalia. That's what it looks like."

"It's incense," the Rasta said. "For bad smells."

"Bad smells," Eddie said. One of the sticks of incense was smoldering, and Eddie picked it up and sniffed at it. "Whew," he said. "That's a bad smell, I'll give you that. Smells like the catbox caught on fire."

The Rasta snatched the incense from him. "It's a good smell," he said. "Smells like your mama."

Eddie smiled at him, his red lips parting to show stained teeth. He looked happy, and very dangerous. "Say I kick your store into the middle of the street," he said, "and you with it. How's that sound to you?"

Smoothly, easily, Wally Witt moved between them. "Eddie," he said softly, and Eddie backed off and let the smile fade on his lips. To the incense seller Wally said, "Look, you and I got no quarrel with each other. I got a job to do and you got your own business to run."

"The brother here's got a business to run, too."

"Well, he's gonna have to run it without Batman, because that's how the law reads. But if you want to *be* Batman, playing the dozens with my man here and pushing into what doesn't concern you, then I got no choice. You follow me?"

"All I'm saying, I'm saying you want to confiscate the man's merchandise, you need you a policeman and a court order, something to make it official."

"Fine," Wally said. "You're saying it and I hear you saying it, but what I'm saying is all I need to do it is to do it, official or not. Now if you want to get a cop to stop me, fine, go ahead and do it, but as soon as you do I'm going to press charges for selling drug paraphernalia and operating without a peddler's license—"

"This here ain't drug paraphernalia, man. We both know that."

"We both know you're just trying to be a hard-on, and we both know what it'll get you. That what you want?"

The incense seller stood there for a moment, then dropped his eyes. "Don't matter what I want," he said.

"Well, you got that right," Wally told him. "It don't matter what you want."

We tossed the shirts and visors into the trunk and got out of there. On the way over to Astor Place Eddie said, "You didn't have to jump in there. I wasn't about to lose it."

"Never said you were."

"That mama stuff doesn't bother me. It's just nigger talk, they all talk that shit."

"I know."

"They'd talk about their fathers, but they don't know who the fuck they are, so they're stuck with their mothers. Bad smells, I shoulda stuck that shit up his ass, get right where the bad smells are. I hate a guy sticks his nose in like that."

"Your basic sidewalk lawyer."

"Basic asshole's what he is. Maybe I'll go back, talk with him later."

"On your own time."

"On my own time is right."

Astor Place hosts a more freewheeling street market, with a lot of Bowery types offering a mix of salvaged trash and stolen goods. There was something especially curious about our role, as we passed over hot radios and typewriters and jewelry and sought only merchandise that had been legitimately purchased, albeit from illegitimate manufacturers. We didn't find much Batman ware on display, although a lot of people, buyers and sellers alike, were wearing the Caped Crusader. We weren't about to strip the shirt off anybody's person, nor did we look too hard for contraband merchandise; the place was teeming with crackheads and crazies, and it was no time to push our luck.

"Let's get out of here," Wally said. "I hate to leave the car in this neighborhood. We already gave the client his money's worth."

By four we were back in Wally's office and his desk was heaped high with the fruits of our labors. "Look at all this shit," he said. "Today's trash and tomorrow's treasures. Twenty years and they'll be auctioning this crap at Christie's. Not this particular crap, because I'll messenger it over to the client and he'll chuck it in the incinerator. Gentlemen, you did a good day's work." He took out his wallet and gave each of the four of us a hundred-dollar bill. He said, "Same time tomorrow? Except I think we'll make lunch Chinese tomorrow. Eddie, don't forget your purse."

"Don't worry."

"Thing is you don't want to carry it if you go back to see your Rastafarian friend. He might get the wrong idea."

"Fuck him," Eddie said. "I got no time for him. He wants that incense up his ass, he's gonna have to stick it there himself."

Lee and Jimmy and Eddie went out, laughing, joking, slapping backs. I started out after them, then doubled back and asked Wally if he had a minute.

"Sure," he said. "Jesus, I don't believe this. Look."

"It's a Batman shirt."

"No shit, Sherlock. And look what's printed right under the Bat signal."

"The copyright notice."

"Right, which makes it a legal shirt. We got any more of

these? No, no, no, no. Wait a minute, here's one. Here's another. Jesus, this is amazing. There any more? I don't see any
others, do you?"

We went through the pile without finding more of the
shirts with the copyright notice.

"Three," he said. "Well, that's not so bad. A mere fraction."
He balled up the three shirts, dropped them back on the pile.
"You want one of these? It's legit, you can wear it without fear
of confiscation."

"I don't think so."

"You got kids? Take something home for your kids."

"One's in college and the other's in the service. I don't
think they'd be interested."

"Probably not." He stepped out from behind his desk.
"Well, it went all right out there, don't you think? We had a
good crew, worked well together."

"I guess."

"What's the matter, Matt?"

"Nothing, really. But I don't think I can make it tomorrow."

"No? Why's that?"

"Well, for openers, I've got a dentist appointment."

"Oh, yeah? What time?"

"Nine-fifteen."

"So how long can that take? Half an hour, an hour tops?
Meet us here ten-thirty, that's good enough. The client doesn't
have to know what time we hit the street."

"It's not just the dentist appointment, Wally."

"Oh?"

"I don't think I want to do this stuff anymore."

"What stuff? Copyright and trademark protection?"

"Yeah."

"What's the matter? It's beneath you? Doesn't make full
use of your talents as a detective?"

"It's not that."

"Because it's not a bad deal for the money, seems to me.
Hundred bucks for a short day, ten to four, hour and a half
off for lunch with the lunch all paid for. You're a cheap lunch
date, you don't drink, but even so. Call it a ten-dollar lunch,
that's a hundred and ten dollars for what, four and a half
hours' work?" He punched numbers on a desktop calculator.

"That's $24.44 an hour. That's not bad wages. You want to take home better than that, you need either burglar's tools or a law degree, seems to me."

"The money's fine, Wally."

"Then what's the problem?"

I shook my head. "I just haven't got the heart for it," I said. "Hassling people who don't even speak the language, taking their goods from them because we're stronger than they are and there's nothing they can do about it."

"They can quit selling contraband, that's what they can do."

"How? They don't even know what's contraband."

"Well, that's where we come in. We're giving them an education. How they gonna learn if nobody teaches 'em?"

I'd loosened my tie earlier. Now I took it off, folded it, put it in my pocket.

He said, "Company owns a copyright, they got a right to control who uses it. Somebody else enters into a licensing agreement, pays money for the right to produce a particular item, they got a right to the exclusivity they paid for."

"I don't have a problem with that."

"So?"

"They don't even speak the language," I said.

He stood up straight. "Then who told 'em to come here?" he wanted to know. "Who fucking invited them? You can't walk a block in midtown without tripping over another super-salesman from Senegal. They swarm off that Air Afrique flight from Dakar and first thing you know they got an open-air store on world-famous Fifth Avenue. They don't pay rent, they don't pay taxes, they just spread a blanket on the concrete and rake in the dollars."

"They didn't look as though they were getting rich."

"They must do all right. Pay two bucks for a scarf and sell it for ten, they must come out okay. They stay at hotels like the Bryant, pack together like sardines, six or eight to the room. Sleep in shifts, cook their food on hot plates. Two, three months of that and it's back to fucking Dakar. They drop off the money, take a few minutes to get another baby started, then they're winging back to JFK to start all over again. You think we need that? Haven't we got enough spades of our own can't make a living, we got to fly in more of them?"

I sifted through the pile on his desk, picked up a sun visor with the Joker depicted on it. I wondered why anybody would want something like that. I said, "What do you figure it adds up to, the stuff we confiscated? A couple of hundred?"

"Jesus, I don't know. Figure ten for a T-shirt, and we got what, thirty or forty of them? Add in the sweatshirts, the rest of the shit, I bet it comes to close to a grand. Why?"

"I was just thinking. You paid us a hundred a man, plus whatever lunch came to."

"Eighty with the tip. What's the point?"

"You must have billed us to the client at what, fifty dollars an hour?"

"I haven't billed anything to anybody yet, I just walked in the door, but yes, that's the rate."

"How will you figure it, four men at eight hours a man?"

"Seven hours. We don't bill for lunchtime."

Seven hours seemed ample, considering that we'd worked four and a half. I said, "Seven times fifty times four of us is what? Fourteen hundred dollars? Plus your own time, of course, and you must bill yourself at more than regular operative's rates. A hundred an hour?"

"Seventy-five."

"For seven hours is what, five hundred?"

"Five and a quarter," he said evenly.

"Plus fourteen hundred is nineteen and a quarter. Call it two thousand dollars to the client. Is that about right?"

"What are you saying, Matt? The client pays too much or you're not getting a big enough piece of the pie?"

"Neither. But if he wants to load up on this garbage"—I waved a hand at the heap on the desk—"wouldn't he be better off buying retail? Get a lot more bang for the buck, wouldn't he?"

He just stared at me for a long moment. Then, abruptly, his hard face cracked and he started to laugh. I was laughing, too, and it took all the tension out of the air. "Jesus, you're right," he said. "Guy's paying way too much."

"I mean, if you wanted to handle it for him, you wouldn't need to hire me and the other guys."

"I could just go around and pay cash."

"Right."

"I could even pass up the street guys altogether, go straight to the wholesaler."

"Save a dollar that way."

"I love it," he said. "You know what it sounds like? Sounds like something the federal government would do, get cocaine off the streets by buying it straight from the Colombians. Wait a minute, didn't they actually do something like that once?"

"I think so, but I don't think it was cocaine."

"No, it was opium. It was some years ago, they bought the entire Turkish opium crop because it was supposed to be the cheapest way to keep it out of the country. Bought it and burned it, and that, boys and girls, that was the end of heroin addiction in America."

"Worked like a charm, didn't it?"

"Nothing works," he said. "First principle of modern law enforcement. Nothing ever works. Funny thing is, in this case the client's not getting a bad deal. You own a copyright or a trademark, you got to defend it. Otherwise you risk losing it. You got to be able to say on such-and-such a date you paid so many dollars to defend your interests, and investigators acting as your agents confiscated so many items from so many merchants. And it's worth what you budget for it. Believe me, these big companies, they wouldn't spend the money year in and year out if they didn't figure it was worth it."

"I believe it," I said. "Anyway, I wouldn't lose a whole lot of sleep over the client getting screwed a little."

"You just don't like the work."

"I'm afraid not."

He shrugged. "I don't blame you. It's chickenshit. But Jesus, Matt, most P.I. work is chickenshit. Was it that different in the department? Or on any police force? Most of what we did was chickenshit."

"And paperwork."

"And paperwork, you're absolutely right. Do some chickenshit and then write it up. And make copies."

"I can put up with a certain amount of chickenshit," I said. "But I honestly don't have the heart for what we did today. I felt like a bully."

"Listen, I'd rather be kicking in doors, taking down bad guys. That what you want?"

"Not really."

"Be Batman, tooling around Gotham City, righting

wrongs. Do the whole thing not even carrying a gun. You know what they didn't have in the movie?"

"I haven't seen it yet."

"Robin, they didn't have Robin. Robin the Boy Wonder. He's not in the comic book anymore, either. Somebody told me they took a poll, had their readers call a nine-hundred number and vote, should they keep Robin or should they kill him. Like in ancient Rome, those fights, what do you call them?"

"Gladiators."

"Right. Thumbs up or thumbs down, and Robin got thumbs down, so they killed him. Can you believe that?"

"I can believe anything."

"Yeah, you and me both. I always thought they were fags." I looked at him. "Batman and Robin, I mean. His *ward*, for Christ's sake. Playing dress-up, flying around, costumes, I figured it's gotta be some kind of fag S-and-M thing. Isn't that what you figured?"

"I never thought about it."

"Well, I never stayed up nights over it myself, but what else would it be? Anyway, he's dead now, Robin is. Died of AIDS, I suppose, but the family's denying it, like What'shis-name. You know who I mean."

I didn't, but I nodded.

"You gotta make a living, you know. Gotta turn a buck, whether it's hassling Africans or squatting out there on a blanket your own self, selling tapes and scarves. Fi' dollah, ten dollah." He looked at me. "No good, huh?"

"I don't think so, Wally."

"Don't want to be one of Batman's helpers. Well, you can't do what you can't do. What the fuck do I know about it, anyway? You don't drink. I don't have a problem with it, myself. But if I couldn't put my feet up at the end of the day, have a few pops, who knows? Maybe I couldn't do it either. Matt, you're a good man. If you change your mind—"

"I know. Thanks, Wally."

"Hey," he said. "Don't mention it. We gotta look out for each other, you know what I mean? Here in Gotham City."